Water's
Daughter

PRAISE FOR MICHELLE LOVRIC

'Wildly imaginative and action-packed, Lovric's books stand out for their authentic historical detail and inventive use of language'

Daily Mail

'Gripping, elegant and original'

Independent on Sunday

'Vivid, believable, well-written, and heart-wrenching . . . a treasure of a book'

Historical Novel Review

'An astonishing world of witches, hags, mermaids and magicians'

The Bookbag

'Sumptuous Venetian adventure . . . a great romp'

Bookseller

'Imbued with magic, mystery and a rip-roaring plot, this book is a gripping read . . . both evocative and beautiful'

Italia!

'A rollicking adventure full of history, awesome imagination and fantastic characters'

Diary of a Bookworm

'Crammed with history, fantasy and beautiful comedy, this book gets a five-star rating'

Reader's Digest

Michelle Lovric

Orion

ORION CHILDREN'S BOOKS

First published in Great Britain in 2020 by Hodder and Stoughton

1 3 5 7 9 10 8 6 4 2

All characters and events in this publication, other than those clearly in the public domain, are fictitious and any resemblance to real persons, living or dead, is purely coincidental.

In order to create a sense of setting, some names of real places have been included in the book. However, the events depicted in this book are imaginary and the real places used fictitiously.

A CIP catalogue record for this book
is available from the British Library.

ISBN 978 1 444 01035 0

Typeset in Granjon LT by Hewer Text UK Ltd, Edinburgh
Printed and bound in Great Britain by Clays Ltd, Elcograf S.p.A.

The paper and board used in this book
are made from wood from responsible sources.

Orion Children's Books
An imprint of
Hachette Children's Group
Part of Hodder and Stoughton
Carmelite House
50 Victoria Embankment
London EC4Y 0DZ

An Hachette UK Company

www.hachette.co.uk
www.hachettechildrens.co.uk

To Bruno and Susie

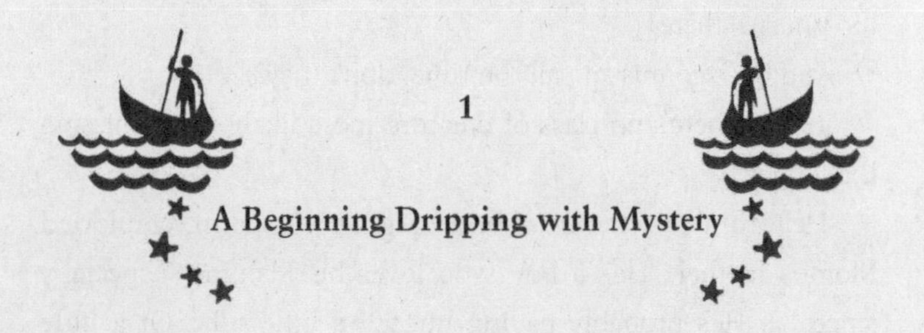

1

A Beginning Dripping with Mystery

It was a rain-pelting midnight in the spring of 1763 when Momo disappeared.

The rain, of course, was nothing unusual. On the night Momo went missing, it had already rained for *seventy* days without cease. The sky had whipped Venice with hard ropes of water, as if it hated her. Walls of rain encased the city in liquid glass, lacquering her church spires, her narrow streets and the mossy steps that marched grimly into the swollen canals.

Venetians felt like the tiny *Masaneta* crabs that scuttled around the tide's violent wash, always looking for a safe, dry place where they would not be swallowed by the water. But nowhere was safe or dry in Venice. The greedy waves carved ever-larger bites into the streets. The highest tides in living memory crumbled the bricks on the water-logged ground floors until the tallest buildings lurched and groaned on their ancient foundations. Two palaces had already collapsed, taking entire families with them. Everyone had drowned: noblemen, maids and rats. Inside every Venetian home, people now shook with fear each night as thunder raged around the city like a vengeful dragon, blowing great forked tongues of fiery lightning across the sodden sky.

So. Spring, 1763. Another rainy night in a sopping city. Nothing too unusual there.

And boys go missing all the time, don't they?

In fact, there's no class of creature more likely to go missing than a boy.

'He'll turn up,' the neighbour, Signora Gasperin, comforted Momo's mother. 'He's a boy who loves his Mamma. Especially since . . . He's probably having himself a little sulk. Or a little adventure? A great tall boy like Momo! Tall as two boys his age, one on top of the other! He'll be back for his supper.'

Signora Gasperin's eyes fell on a sumptuous chocolate cake standing tall on a chipped plate. She bent to examine it. '*Seven* layers! Apricot jam in each, if I'm not mistaken! A maraschino cherry on top! Momo's *favourite*!' Signora Gasperin sniffed and licked her lips. But Momo's mother, normally as warm and generous as the sun, did not offer her neighbour a slice. The ingredients had cost more than she could afford. She wanted to watch every crumb of that cake disappear into her son's mouth.

Supper, breakfast and lunch came and went. Momo's plate sat untouched on the table. The chocolate cake sagged, shrivelled and accommodated a small rat who ate himself a little cave in its centre before leaving through the top, taking the maraschino cherry with him. Momo's mother didn't care about the rat or the ruins of the cake. She barely noticed the water that had now risen to ankle-level in their tiny ground floor apartment, or the trembling of the walls each time another clump of bricks dissolved. She could think only about Momo. He was all she had in the world. Her tears joined the rain and never stopped falling, not even once, not even for five short minutes.

Three days later, Momo had not reappeared. It was not just the adults who shook their heads and sighed. The boys of Venice gathered on street corners, talking uneasily. For if a fine strong chap like Momo could disappear, then it could happen to any of them. As for the girls – they sighed for the handsome boy who'd always been ready with a smile and a compliment that was almost never cheeky; the boy with tender grey eyes who'd carry a heavy basket over a bridge for a small struggling person; the boy with the shock of glossy, fair hair who'd light a girl's way without charge if darkness fell early, as it so often did in those days of rain, rain, rain, when the sides of each street filled up with water leaving only a narrow hump like a crocodile's back for making your way home.

Finally, an elderly nobleman came forth with a crumb of information. It wasn't comforting. He'd hired Momo to light him back to his *palazzo* on the very night the boy disappeared. The elegant gentleman wore a face creased with worry when he came to Momo's mother with the unwelcome news that he'd last seen the boy taking a shortcut home through a graveyard in the dead of night.

'I've never liked the look of that graveyard,' the nobleman said, his hands betraying a tremor. 'I wish my home were not so close to it. Some nights, you hear an eerie noise coming from it – like some female singing, sad and sweet as a solitary nightingale. And the smell in the air . . . a bit like meat and a bit like roses? And then waves of something sweeter than honey! Drumbeats like the tribes of the Sahara. And then there's that dreadful Palazzo Bon, you know, just behind the wall on the other side of the cemetery.'

He added, in a defensive tone, 'I tipped your son well, I assure you, and I warned him to go the safe way around, even though it's longer. You don't tread on the dead, do you? It's disrespectful! Yet your boy was desperate to get home once he'd done his duty by me. But here's the strangest thing. The last glimpse I had of him – standing by the graveyard wall – he was grinning with pure delight. And, I know it sounds mad, but it was almost as if your son, madam, was *lit up*. A strange light circled his body. A *ghostlight*, that's what I'd call it.'

Momo's mother put her head in her hands and wept until tears spurted out from between her fingers. A ghostlight in a graveyard late at night. That put a whole different slant on things. An even darker one. Boys and graveyards – never a good thing. Centuries of strange happenings around the Palazzo Bon, otherwise known as 'The Palace that Eats Boys' – well, *they* gave little reason for optimism. Venetians are superstitious folk. People started to remember old tales of ghostlights and half-crazed smiles seen on the faces of other young men who had promptly disappeared forever, all within steps of the notorious Palazzo Bon.

On the darkest nights, that gaunt *palazzo* always seemed to shimmer, even though no one lived there any more. Unlike ordinary Venetian *palazzi*, whose street doors were actually on the street, the Palazzo Bon hunched up, as if secretively, behind a high-walled courtyard.

People began to believe that they'd seen the last of poor Momo.

But if his mother – and indeed every person in Venice – could have seen what had *really* happened to Momo, well, they would not have believed it.

Momo had just lit the nobleman home from the *ridotto* through the slapping rain. The gambling had gone well – Momo could read it in his customer's lilting walk and the curve of his lips. The nobleman's tricorn hat and *domino* cloak kept him dry. Poor Momo, however, was wet as a fish. He sneezed three times. The rain seemed determined to point out how poor and thin his jacket was. Momo had no change of clothes. He'd be wearing wetness for two days if he didn't get home soon enough for the embers of the fire to dry his clothes overnight.

Momo couldn't afford to languish in bed with a cold. Four years before, his father had gone to sea in a trading galley and never come back, yet another victim of the notorious Barbary pirates – also known as 'Corsairs' – who haunted the Mediterranean Sea. The Corsairs had a particular taste for Venetian slaves. Only the rich ever returned from captivity in Algiers or Tunis. The little family had no hope of raising the ransom money to bring Signor Tosi home. Now Momo was the sole breadwinner. Times were so tough that he could barely afford the pork rinds that fed the flame inside his lamp.

The nobleman gave Momo a cheery goodnight. He even waved as Momo paused to wipe his nose at the steps of the *campo dei morti*, the little graveyard near San Severo. If Momo took the path through it, he'd be home in front of the fire twenty minutes sooner.

Never take a shortcut through a graveyard at night.

How many boys have ignored that advice and ended up regretting it?

Momo was about to become one of them.

Now Momo knew as well as anyone that he should never take a shortcut through a graveyard at night. Especially not a Venetian graveyard where the plague bodies stirred under the corpses of the murder victims and the ordinary dead of the parish. Particularly, one should not take a shortcut through an unlit graveyard with miasmas curling round its tombstones. Above all, one should not do that when the graveyard is next door to an infamously haunted palace.

But the lucky nobleman's tip huddled warm in Momo's fingers inside his pocket. Momo was thinking about his mother's carrot soup, which she always began by simmering a precious pat of butter with the sweetest onions from Rialto. A generous serving surely awaited him in a pot nestling in the fireplace.

Behind him, he heard the nobleman call, 'Don't do it, boy. It's not worth it. This is Venice! Even the long way home isn't very far.'

The nobleman's voice seemed to come from a long way away. Meanwhile, ahead of Momo, something sweet and hot hung in the air, alluringly. It seemed like a sign. Nothing that smelt so good could mean him any harm, could it? He held up his lamp and tried not to notice that his hand was shaking.

Twenty steps further and Momo's head suddenly filled with remembered rumours about this particular graveyard and the lady-ghost, sad-as-a-lonely-nightingale, who was said to sing there. Behind Momo, something stirred. He dared not look round. The hair on the back of his neck prickled. He bitterly regretted the shortcut. But if he turned back now, it would be *towards* whatever was making that rustling noise a mere few yards away. Better to keep going.

Momo raised his lamp higher to spread the arc of its light. Then he was sorry. For it showed him at once that all was not well in the graveyard – if anything could *ever* be said to be well in such a place. It looked as if the tombstones had been thrown around like dice. Some had been uprooted and thrust into the wrong graves or they stood at dismal angles like the mossy teeth of an old woman who had eaten too many cakes when she was young.

Someone had been searching this graveyard, and with desperation.

A sharp tang of anguish still ruptured the air. From not far away, a drum began to beat a heart-tugging rhythm. The intense smell of honey washed over Momo, whose lantern now lit up a row of beaks grimacing at him beneath cold eyes. In shape, the birds resembled the familiar herons of the lagoon, but they were so much taller. And in the lamplight their feathers seemed a fierce shade of coral, like the embers of a fire. Their breasts rose and fell in unison. There was a warning in their exhaled breath so strong you could touch it. Except you would not want to.

What are these creatures? I've never seen such birds in Venice.

As if they heard Momo's thoughts, the great birds flapped their wings and rose up in flight, grazing his head with the sharp claws of their long toes. A rivulet of blood ran down his forehead. He opened his mouth to scream.

Something hot, smoky and silky slid down his throat, wound round his heart and burrowed swiftly to his toes. It dived down his arms and took hold of his fingertips. Momo's limbs suddenly contorted like those of a marionette whose every string had been violently yanked. He dropped his lamp and it rolled away, instantly extinguished. Momo's helpless body stretched up to the sky and then fell to the ground, hunched like a sick bat.

When Momo rose, it was slowly, as if he swam. His arms stretched out in front of him. His legs moved like a jointed doll's. As for his eyes – churning luminous grey like mercury – even Momo's adoring mother would not have recognised them. Those eyes did not blink against the raindrops that still fell, fat as little fish. Meanwhile, all over Momo's skin a halo seemed to glow. Except that it was not golden or holy: it too glimmered like silver. As the nobleman would say, it looked like a *ghostlight*. Stranger still, Momo's mouth stretched into a blissful smile. On shuffling feet, the mercury-eyed Momo began to move towards the last palace in Venice any boy ought to go.

Now, the door to the secret courtyard of 'The Palace that Eats Boys' swung open, groaning like a dying man. The silky smoke inside Momo's body marched him to the threshold.

Behind Momo, the rain still thrashed down in darkness. But beyond the threshold, a dry hot sun shone on a terracotta courtyard where palms and orange trees stood in pots. Momo's nose twitched at the smell of . . . What was it? Honey? Boiling? The drumbeats ceased and a leopardess emerged, stretching lazily, from the shadows. The great beast stopped short at the sight of the Venetian boy. She shook her head in apparent disapproval and padded away.

The silky smoke nudged Momo inside the courtyard and closed the door behind him.

Then 'The Palace that Eats Boys' itself seemed to utter a brief rich purr, like a cat that had just eaten something extremely delicious.

2

Another Very Bad Idea

Remember what everyone knows about boys taking shortcuts through graveyards in the dead of night? It's something that should *never* be done, agreed?

What about young girls meeting strangers at midnight in front of haunted houses *next* to graveyards? Even more of a no-no, yes?

An even worse case of 'asking for trouble'? Clearly.

Yet only one week after the disappearance of the lamp-boy Momo, that's exactly what was happening: a twelve-year-old girl named Aurelia Bon was trudging in soaked silk slippers through the rain towards an appointment with a man whom she'd only met once before – a man whom she had reason to believe might not be completely sane. Moreover, this same man had a hundred reasons to hate her personally and wish Aurelia Bon not just dead but disappeared from every Venetian memory, as if she'd never lived.

By now, you might well be asking '*What is it* about young people in Venice that makes them so very foolhardy and even careless of their lives?'

Yet in the case of Aurelia Bon, there really were extenuating circumstances.

They were circumstances involving cruel choices, a sneaking sister and ten most unusual fingers, which Aurelia was now flexing and holding up to the rain. Water ran down her fingertips and into her small white palms as she arrived in the little alley that opened on to 'The Palace that Eats Boys'.

Aurelia Bon was the proud – one might almost say 'smug' – owner of the most famous fingers in Venice. Ever since her eighth birthday, highborn, flamboyant Aurelia had been spilling the secrets of the city's palaces. Whenever Aurelia laid her hands on the salt-crumbled brick or the cool marble of a *palazzo* wall, images and scenes showed her what had once happened inside that ancient building. For Aurelia, it was like lifting the lid on a doll's house and – with delight – discovering all the dolls alive and busy doing the most fascinating things.

By the age of ten, Aurelia was already celebrated for unmasking historical mysteries. She'd located the very room where, in 1310, the nobleman Bajamonte Tiepolo plotted to murder the doge. She'd found the loft where the artist Tiziano hid his last portrait of his beautiful daughter, and the kitchen where the Butcher Biasio cooked his popular stew, the principal ingredient of which turned out to be children of his parish.

Aurelia Bon had a talent for telling too, recounting her discoveries with enormous gusto and many flourishes. And Venice adored her for it. Though not yet thirteen, Aurelia had a publisher: Remondini, whose great printing machines rolled day and night at Bassano del Grappa on the mainland. One book

– *Finger Histories* – had been published already. Another slim volume was on the way, with just one last chapter to be written. Sales were gratifying. Venetians loved Aurelia Bon's finger histories all the more because her special talent came packaged in a young girl of noble blood with lively brown eyes and a large, shapely nose that could best be described as 'characterful'.

As you might expect, all the attention had rather turned Aurelia's head. All Aurelia ever wanted to think about was her history-fingering. What interested her less, to be perfectly frank, was actual historical research. Everything came easily to Aurelia except detail. She was a little too grand for detail. She wasn't good at dates. She had no interest in the fusty manuscripts that thrill real historians, people whom Aurelia saw as 'dry-as-dust pernickety bores'. Consequently, when images of the past flowed into her fingers, Aurelia was never sure *exactly* how far back the events had occurred. It could be thirty minutes or three hundred years. She often had to bluff.

Never mind, though, Aurelia always told herself. The publisher Remondini had given her an assistant, a boy named Valerio Fialetti. As Aurelia was not inclined to spend her time slaving over a quill and paper – and because her spelling was, frankly, another problem – Valerio wrote out all the things Aurelia's fingers showed her. He was also tasked with tracking down the dates and facts that filled out her stories.

The pair of them could not be more different. Quite apart from the fact that Valerio didn't have a drop of noble blood, he positively loved sifting through old ledgers. He'd mastered Latin, English and even some Arabic so that no old document could evade him. He was also a talented artist, recreating in clever little sketches the scenes that Aurelia described. Many of these drawings had enlivened *Finger Histories*. Yet, Valerio's name was not printed anywhere in the book, a fact he never mentioned himself. The unfairness did occasionally occur to Aurelia, but she always flexed her fingers wide, like a pair of pink starfish, and told herself, *He's only an apprentice. He probably gets lodging and pay at Remondini, and training for his livelihood. I'm different. I'm the main attraction.*

Except at home, she had to admit. For in the noble Bon household, Aurelia's talents were far from appreciated. Her fashionable mother had tolerated Aurelia's history-fingering activities so far only because the publisher Giovanni Remondini was so utterly charming and a man much seen in the best society – and especially at the Bon dinner table. Contessa Bon, however, never tired of mentioning that Aurelia would need to 'retire' from history-fingering at the age of thirteen because that was when she must start in earnest to ready herself for a noble betrothal.

'And no bridegroom worth having,' Contessa Bon had told her daughter yet again at breakfast that morning, 'wants a bride more famous than himself.'

The fact that Aurelia found the notion of marriage intolerable meant nothing at all to her ambitious mother.

Unfortunately, Contessa Bon had also taken against Valerio. She followed up the usual bridegroom comment with her regular lament: 'I despair of you, always running around with that guttersnipe apprentice! A boy in trade and shabbier than a footman! No wig. No powder. An orphan! And who were his family anyway? *No ones!* You should be spending more time with young Marco Spatafora. *There's* a proper friend for you.'

'A *proper* friend,' echoed Aurelia's younger sister Catarina. When they were little girls, Catarina and Aurelia had played together as amicably as any pair of sisters separated by only a year in age. Catarina was so witty that it was actually rather delicious to argue with her. It was only when Aurelia had discovered her history fingers that they had grown apart, with Catarina taking a passionate interest (exaggerated, Aurelia sometimes thought) in all matters of fashion. Catarina had also taken to telling tales on her older sister whenever she could.

'Marco Spatafora.' Catarina took the opportunity to linger on his name. 'Marco Spatafora is the crème de la crème. He won't even *look* at his manservant when he's being dressed. He takes *pride* in not knowing the servants' names. He doesn't even *see* people from the lower classes. *You* don't even *care* about what's fashionable. When did you last go to see the *Poupée de France*?'

The fashions worn by Venetian women were ruled by this stiff-legged doll who was propped up in a shop window in the Mercerie. She was known as the *Poupée de France* because she was always dressed in a miniature version of the latest fashion from Paris. Every seamstress in the city copied the doll's clothes for their wealthy clients.

'I never go to see the *Poupée de France*,' Aurelia retorted. 'I avoid her at all costs. I think she looks constipated.'

'How do you actually dare say that?' There was, however, something that sounded almost like awe in Catarina's voice.

Contessa Bon pretended not to know what 'constipated' was. She said, 'Marco Spatafora always takes care to be perfectly *à la mode*. He gets his wigs done at the best studio in the Calle del Parrucchiere . . .'

Catarina sighed, 'Of course his future *wife* will have all the same privileges.'

'Aurelia!' her mother said suddenly. 'You're not listening, are you?'

Aurelia was not. She was thinking about one of Valerio's superb sketches.

And later that same morning, Valerio himself came to her, his serious eyes dancing with excitement about something he'd found in the archives, something about the notorious old Palazzo Bon itself, the site of her very next history-fingering. Nothing, normally, could have been more interesting to Aurelia. Valerio had a knack of bringing her titbits that made her stories shine.

That morning, however, Aurelia needed to vent her frustration more than she needed to listen.

'Don't talk at me about the archives,' she snapped. 'I'm going to find out everything we need the moment I lay a finger on the gate to Palazzo Bon.'

Valerio's mood had not been dampened. 'I *know* you think the archives are boring. But it's *amazing* to touch papers written by people hundreds of years ago.'

'Are you comparing *that* to my history fingers? Fingers that *no one* else has? Or ever had?'

'You see pictures. Easy as that. But I go on adventures. I hunt down the things that were important enough to *write down*.'

Despite Aurelia's scoffing, Valerio continued, 'An archive is like a campfire. It warms up facts. Everyone can sit and feel that warmth. Even a boy like me, with nothing – no money, no family.'

Valerio could not have known how sore a subject this was for Aurelia. But he soon suffered the consequences of mentioning it.

'Oh,' she retorted, 'are you a boy? I hadn't noticed. I thought you were a pile of books with legs and a mouth. A *dusty* pile of books. Yes, dusty. You're so shabby that I can't even pretend that you're my *footman* when we're out in public. Did you *never* think how much easier it would be for me if you could just *look like* my footman? But no, you have to be the hero . . . of indexes! You hang around waiting for me to make a mistake so you can have your puny moment of glory by correcting me. What have you ever done but clutter up my amazing stories with boring facts?'

'You need me,' Valerio responded with dignity, 'to give those stories roots and branches in real history, which actually adds to the wonder.'

'I need you like I need an extra ribbon in my hat. You're like a street sweeper. No one wants to see you and they'd notice you only if you hadn't done your job properly. Yet you're far too perfect to ever make a mistake. So no one *ever* notices you.'

Aurelia saw the hurt in Valerio's green eyes. But the hurt behind her own was too strong. She could not stop being strong, and being strong meant being angry.

It was only something from the archives he wanted to talk about, she told herself.

So it was bound to be boring.

So. Another argument with her mother about Marco Spatafora. The usual irritating behaviour from a little sister. The *Poupée de France* thrust in Aurelia's face once more. A little rupture between friends.

But none of this can truly account for what had driven Aurelia Bon to open her bedroom window and shimmy down the wisteria vine outside it without the merest whisper of a sound, apart from the faint swishy thud when she had landed on the wet flagstones below.

None of this quite explains why Aurelia would leave her safe, comfortable home to trudge through the angry rain to an abandoned palace beside a graveyard – a palace that had only recently demonstrated its danger so vividly and tragically yet again.

The reasons for such reckless behaviour are still not really obvious, are they?

It's time to tell exactly what had brought Aurelia to this desperate pass.

It was her worst nightmare: a dinner party.

3

Few Things More Delightful

You might think that there could be few things more delightful than a Venetian dinner party, with two dozen beautifully dressed people seated around an elegant table, picking at pretty morsels served on fine porcelain.

But you'd be thinking that way because you are not Aurelia Bon, for whom that night's dinner placements were an actual punishment designed by her mother to demonstrate the painful fact that the road of Aurelia's short life had *already* arrived at a crossroads. Choices needed to be made. The trouble was, the only two choices on offer to Aurelia were both utterly hateful to her.

On Aurelia's left, Contessa Bon had seated Marco Spatafora, a boy whose face was chiselled out of pure smugness. Aurelia could hardly bear to look at him. That didn't matter to Marco: he was entirely occupied with admiring himself in a gilded mirror conveniently placed on the wall opposite.

But when Aurelia's eyes skittered away from Marco, they fell on Padre Pino, seated immediately opposite her. He was a strutting turkeycock of a man; the ugliest, most corpulent and most ruthless priest in Venice, overseer of the convent at San Zaccaria. Threats had been made by her parents, more than once, that Aurelia would be despatched there at the age of fifteen – if she was still refusing to marry Marco.

Aurelia felt the priest's cold eyes on her. She knew just what he was thinking. If she became one of God's little brides – as nuns were called in Venice – then the Bon family would pay Padre Pino's convent a thousand ducats by way of a dowry. Given Aurelia's reputation for being somewhat headstrong and something of a show-off, Padre Pino might even be able to extract more from her parents to take a troublesome girl off their hands.

'Isn't it dreadful?' Aurelia's mother was saying, a little further down the table.

The disappearance of a *codega*, a young lamp-boy, was the main subject around the dinner table during the first few courses. Equally interesting was the disappearance of a much admired society surgeon who specialised in hands and feet. He'd treated the delicate ankles of many of the ladies in attendance. Sprains were the frequent result of the tall shoes that fashion obliged them to wear out in the slippery streets.

'How,' asked Padre Pino, 'could a grown man simply vanish? Especially when business was so good for him?'

'Perhaps he slipped, fell in the water and drowned?' suggested Marco Spatafora in his usual contemptuous drawl.

Yet no bodies had been found floating in the canals, not even by the Company of Christ and the Good Death, who'd been kept busy rescuing the corpses of unfortunate Venetians swept away by the rain that had made every bridge and *fondamenta* so treacherous. The Company gave decent burials to those whose families could not be found.

Marco's mother, Contessa Spatafora, offered, 'And now some mad apothecary apprentice claims that he saw a mermaid in the Canal di Noale.'

'Isn't it dreadful?' said Contessa Bon. 'Mermaids will eat all the good fish.'

If there was a point – unless it was about a wedding – Aurelia's mother would always miss it. The guests, as ever, did not know what to do with Contessa Bon's silliness. The mermaid was swiftly dismissed by Padre Pino: 'Must have been a monk seal taking refuge from the storms.' Then the guests hastily returned to the other ever-present and unhappy subject in Venice – the incessant-driving rain.

Some of the guests around the Bons' table that night had reason to be pleased with the rain, for they were growing rich on it. Just weeks after the wet weather started, a brand new society suddenly appeared, with its own freshly painted boats nosing like sharks through the canals. The motto on the side of each boat: *I Fedeli – una missione a salvare la nostra Venezia* – The Faithful Ones – a mission to save our Venice. Well-dressed men from a small circle of aristocratic families were seen aboard, looking important and holding rolls of diagrams under their cloaks to shield the paper from the water that rolled thickly out of the sky.

Soon enough it came out that *I Fedeli* had persuaded the Venetian state to hand over thousands of ducats to build three great gates to stop the rainwater from flooding the lagoon and swallowing the city. They were also raising vast walls, which they called *murazzi*, to protect Venice from any enemy, be it in the form of water or Barbary pirates. Not only that, *I Fedeli* boasted, but they would also clean out the mud in sluggish canals. They would restore all the water-logged *palazzi* that were quaking and threatening to collapse. In fact, there was almost nothing that *I Fedeli* did not promise to do. In the meantime, they'd been giving the biggest and best fireworks displays the city had ever seen. *I Fedeli* knew their way into people's hearts – Venetians were addicted to firework displays, even in the rain. Night after night, the men of *I Fedeli* tempted Venetians out into the Piazzetta to watch the barges in the lagoon shoot off fountains of light that painted the water in a beautiful blur of drenched colour.

At tonight's dinner party, half a dozen *Fedeli* kept their heads turned towards Daniele Spatafora, the highest officer in *I Fedeli*, and the father of the odious Marco. No one was more deferential, not to say fawning, towards Daniele Spatafora than Aurelia's own father. If Aurelia and Marco were to be betrothed, then Conte Bon was sure to be invited into the secretive, exclusive ranks of *I Fedeli*, where he longed to be. It did not seem to matter to her father that Aurelia would thereby be delivered into the household of a man who was, like Padre Pino, renowned for ruthlessness, a man known to terrorise his own family and terrify his servants.

Fortunately, Daniele Spatafora was tonight seated as far as possible from Padre Pino, which also meant as far as possible from Aurelia. Although the two men were remarkably similar in character, the nobleman and the priest had been mortal enemies since *I Fedeli* had snatched one of Padre Pino's most profitable businesses: harvesting money to pay the ransoms of hundreds of

Venetian slaves held by the Barbary pirates in Algiers. *I Fedeli* now collected ransom donations door to door. And each week *I Fedeli* now also emptied the alms boxes 'for redeeming of the slaves' that were to be found in every Venetian church.

Contessa Bon and the other wives did their best to steer the conversation clear of difficult matters like the Barbary pirates and who should get their hands on the ransom money. Anyway, the ladies had much more consuming problems, for the unrelenting rain was very hard on women of fashion like themselves. There is a poor person's rain, the kind that had Momo's mother wading to her sleepless bed every night – and there is a rich person's rain. That's the kind that laughs down umbrellas and sneers through the brims of expensive hats. It's the kind of rain that inserts droplets inside even the tightest corset and slicks the heels of every pair of silk slippers, turning them into skates.

Contessa Bon lamented, 'This rain! It jumps up your legs like a thousand tickly grasshoppers.'

'And important hairstyles – that take five hours to create – are destroyed in five minutes by this ghastly humidity!' lamented Contessa Spatafora, casting a quick nervous look at her husband.

Aurelia would almost have felt sorry for Contessa Spatafora. The woman needed more hours than most to try to look 'important' enough to match her husband's ambitions. Unlike their son, both Spatafora parents were notably short and scrawny. The downtrodden Contessa Spatafora tried to increase her height with extravagant wigs. Daniele Spatafora, in contrast, made his small stature invisible with emperor-sized aggression. His temper took up a lot of space in any room.

The other ladies generously agreed with Contessa Spatafora that this new kind of rain was ruinous to their looks. 'Isn't it dreadful?' asked Aurelia's mother.

For the next three hours, Aurelia was obliged to sit up straight with her neck at an achingly graceful angle, to smile without teeth, and to never ever mention her opinions, her feelings or, most of all, her history fingers and their discoveries.

Her eyes modestly downcast, Aurelia's mind was able to retreat into the sweet spot where she kept her dreams and plans. As the ladies delved ever deeper into hats and hairstyles, Aurelia's mind's eye was watching a slightly older version of herself hurrying down dim corridors at the great University of Padova to deliver an important historical lecture to a hundred amazed and admiring professors. She saw herself aboard a wide-berthed trading cog, like the one sailed by her great-great-great-great-great grandfather, the merchant Aurelio Bon – with whom Aurelia shared the large and characterful family nose, if the portraits were anything to go by. Aurelio Bon, when not much more than a boy, went as far as Arabia and even Zanzibar, trading Venetian mirrors for wonderful items like frankincense, myrrh, copper and cinnamon. Best of all were the swan-necked, lily-lipped bottles in which Arabian brides collected the tears that gave the measure of their love for husbands away fighting wars. A few of those tear-catchers had survived the centuries. Aurelia's mother used them to store hat feathers.

Aurelia's imagination embroidered on the journey south, ruffling her hair with hot breezes as she sailed through the waters of Morea, the harbours of Crete, past the towers of Alexandria and all the way to the Straits of Ormuz. She strode about in divided skirts, giving orders to obedient sailors, tickling her nose with deep sniffs from sacks of spices lined up on the deck. Merchant vessels from every nation passed by, saluting Aurelia and her crew. Making landfall, Aurelia applied her magical fingers to pyramids, the sphinx and minarets, revealing all their secrets. And, almost best of all, she saw the great outcome of her fantastical travels – a vision of herself scribbling '*The End*' to a marvellous book about her adventures and flourishing her quill in triumph.

'Daughter!' her mother's urgent whisper broke Aurelia's reverie. 'Close your mouth! Smile, don't grin!'

Back in the real world, in the stuffy over-decorated dining room, things were taking a turn for the worse. The conversation had swerved from rain-ruined bonnets towards the subject of marriage. Aurelia's mother, smiling so hard that her skin stretched over her cheekbones, said to Contessa Spatafora, 'See how my little flower Aurelia is budding into a proper young lady.'

Aurelia shot her mother a look of undiluted venom. Every word Contessa Bon had just uttered, including the 'my' and the 'a', was coated with insinuation. The dinner party was suddenly transformed into a marketplace, and the merchandise on sale was Aurelia herself.

How does Mamma even dare, thought Aurelia. Then she felt the familiar constriction in her chest. Contessa Bon dared because she could, because there was pathetically little that a nearly thirteen-year-old Venetian girl could do to defend herself against this ghastly game of matches and marriages.

'And my boy,' purred Contessa Spatafora, 'is turning out prodigiously well.'

Well, if you like empty in the head, thought Aurelia.

Marco had not the barest interest in history. Like Aurelia's sister Catarina, though far less clever, he was obsessed with clothes and fancy dance steps. And if he wasn't loving himself in a mirror, he was out shooting innocent, warm-blooded creatures on his country estate, which adjoined that of Aurelia's own family. Contessa Spatafora was said to have a bottomless jewel box and needed a daughter-in-law to whom she could hand down the treasure. Aurelia had a distrust of emeralds and rubies. She thought they looked like solid droplets of poison. The thought of being next in line to wear the celebrated Spatafora jewels made Aurelia shiver.

Mid-shudder, she caught Catarina looking at her sharply. As the eldest, Aurelia would have to marry first, or Catarina herself would remain forever unwed.

Just what the little tell-tale deserves, thought Aurelia. *Never to wear a wedding dress!*

Meanwhile, her mother was assuring Contessa Spatafora, 'Yes, it's absolutely true. The unfortunate episode with the fingers is very nearly over.'

Catching Aurelia's eye, she added emphatically, 'Forever.'

4

On Her Other Side

All this time you've doubtless been wondering who was sitting at Aurelia's *other* side during the interminable dinner party and why none of the noble guests had addressed a look or a remark in that person's direction.

That's because the seat on Aurelia's right was occupied by an ageing historian. Simoneto Ghezzo was also published by the charming Giovanni Remondini, who was of course seated beside Aurelia's mother herself. Ghezzo had appeared on the guest list in a 'pity place', as Contessa Bon described it. But how had he ended up beside the daughter of the noble house?

Aurelia knew what her mother did not: earlier that evening her hairdresser, Nanetta, told her that Simoneto Ghezzo had bribed the butler for a place beside her.

'Can't have much money, from the dulled shine on his frock coat and the moth-eaten state of his wig,' Nanetta had said, putting the finishing touches to Aurelia's hair. 'Must want to know you very badly.'

Aurelia had nodded, a tiny bit flattered to hear it, if surprised. It wasn't only Ghezzo's coat that was faded, she knew. His reputation had grown threadbare too, and this was at least partly thanks to Aurelia herself. The theories in Simoneto Ghezzo's books were constantly disproved by Aurelia's history fingers. People had noticed. There had been some jeering in the Venetian news-sheets known as '*avvisi*'. The historian had every reason to hate her. But to Aurelia, in her forlorn state, Ghezzo at least offered the hope of a more entertaining conversation than Marco Spatafora did.

Marco was busy lisping about the Honiton lace on his sleeve ruffles to Catarina, seated opposite. Catarina, whose wit was in fact sharp enough to slice raw meat, nevertheless hung on Marco's every empty word. Aurelia's only escape from this inanity was to talk to the historian. *Poor old man*, she thought, slightly turning her head to avoid the mouldy smell of Ghezzo's collar and the dust that fell in little clumps from his wig. His voice was smooth but uncomfortable, like a too-tight hat. It squeezed her ears unpleasantly. Unlike the noble guests, Simoneto Ghezzo did not complain about the food, which was as usual overdressed with many reductions of honey and rose petals and too much brandy sauce. The historian ate wolfishly, as if he were actually hungry, a state that a girl like Aurelia had never had reason to know.

Contessa Bon continued to shoot Aurelia nothing but reproachful looks. Aurelia's unenviable choice of destinies – Marco or Padre Pino – sat within inches of her. The old historian's lined face and large grey eyes seemed gentle by comparison. He was eager to hear about her history fingers and spoke admiringly and in detail of several of her discoveries. Touched by this generosity, Aurelia even let him take her hand for a moment, under the table, to examine her famous fingers. She tried not to flinch at his eager touch and the papery feel of his fingertips. No one had held her hand since she and Catarina were affectionate little girls, in the time before Aurelia's history fingers had made themselves apparent and a distance had grown between the sisters.

Ghezzo stared at her fingers, mumbling, 'My little lady, I see *nothing in particular . . .*'

She agreed. 'Mamma says they won't even be pretty with an engagement ring on one of them.'

'Unkind, most unkind.' At the sympathy in his voice, Aurelia felt a twitch at the edge of her eyelids. *But I never cry*, she thought. Even at Catarina's worst jibes, she made a point of not crying. Because then Catarina would win.

A gust of jasmine cologne announced Marco Spatafora rising to leave his seat. His mother was waving at him from the other end of the table. Catarina's face grew instantly both bored and resentful. 'Who's this?' she asked Aurelia, pointing at Simoneto Ghezzo. It looked as though she was pointing not at the man but at his worn-out frock coat. Catarina's mouth curved into something closer to a sneer than a smile when Aurelia said, 'Simoneto Ghezzo, the historian.'

Catarina showed not the remotest polite interest in Simoneto Ghezzo or his profession. Instead, she asked him, 'Do you know that boy seated beside Aurelia? She should be so lucky! A Spatafora. With a father in *I Fedeli*. The Spatafora are the most golden of Golden Book families . . .'

Simoneto Ghezzo cleared his throat. 'In fact, my dears, my research in the archives has revealed that the Spatafora family are not actually native Venetians. Indeed,' he said, smiling at Aurelia, 'they might be regarded as *upstarts*, since they came here from Sicily only in 1409—'

Aurelia couldn't resist, 'Even though they act more Venetian than the Venetians.'

Catarina meanwhile was yawning ostentatiously. 'There's nothing so boring,' she said, 'as a know-it-all who knows all about things no one cares about.'

It was unclear whether she was referring to her sister or the historian, or both. She added, 'It's interesting how no one is more snobbish than a non-noble. Especially one who has to *grovel* to get his boring books published by Remondini.'

'You abominable horror,' snarled Aurelia. 'Apologise to Signor Ghezzo.'

'*You're* the one who should be apologising to him. *You're* the one who's ruined him with your history fingers. *You're* the reason why his frock coat is such a disgrace.'

Aurelia flinched and stole a look at Simoneto Ghezzo. An impenetrable expression crossed his face.

Catarina too turned to the historian. Her eyes sparkled with malice. 'And who knows if my sister Aurelia truly loves history or if she actually just adores being famous for it?'

Not for the first time, Aurelia thought, *It would be easier to deal with Catarina if she were stupid. The pity is, she's not. The* danger is, *she's not.*

A waft of jasmine announced the return of Marco Spatafora. Catarina's face pinked with pleasure. Aurelia, in contrast, felt her the skin between her shoulders prickle: Marco Spatafora's reappearance made the vision of a convent seem terrifyingly real.

Simoneto Ghezzo's features rearranged themselves into a sorrowing kind of smile. He whispered gently, 'My poor child, what a burden you bear. What a choice you have to make. I don't envy you. One with your exceptional talents and free spirit . . . should never be buried alive in a convent or in a marriage to a bird-brained popinjay.'

Aurelia shot him a grateful look, which seemed to lend him heart. He sat up straighter in his chair. 'I wonder . . . I scarcely dare ask . . . but would you,' he murmured, dipping his head, dropping his voice, 'do me the honour of a *private* demonstration of the great power of those clever fingers of yours?'

Aurelia's first and very happy thought was, *How much would Mamma hate me to do that?*

Her second thought was, *What a thing to ask! Is he mad?*

Then she caught her mother's eye, narrowed with disapproval.

'Where shall we meet then?' Aurelia asked Simoneto Ghezzo in the quietest of voices, barely audible above the roar of *I Fedeli* laughing rather too hard at a joke made by Daniele Spatafora.

'I'd suggest "The Palace that Eats Boys",' said Ghezzo. 'The Palazzo Bon, I mean. This very night.'

'Why there?' Aurelia asked. 'Because it's where I'm doing my History-Fingering on Palm Sunday? But why go there at night? What about—?'

Of course Aurelia knew all the rumours about the haunted palace. Palazzo Bon was, after all, the ancestral home of her own family. Generations ago, the Bons had forsaken the blighted old building for the newer palace in another part of town where Aurelia herself had grown up. But the glamour of mystery and death that surrounded the original Palazzo Bon was the main reason Remondini had chosen it for the Palm Sunday event.

'Because,' Simoneto Ghezzo floundered, 'because—'

Before she could stop herself, she'd said dismissively, 'I suppose you want to publish something exciting about it.'

She did not add, 'For once.'

Yet, because of her tone, those two cruel words were in the air, slapping Simoneto Ghezzo's thin face. Indeed that face crumpled for a second, as if it had been punched. Aurelia felt a little bit sorry. Yet the words could not be taken back.

It's not my fault, Aurelia told herself. *He keeps writing new books, even though I've shown his ideas are utterly wrong. He simply doesn't learn. It's his own fault his career's gone crooked. He can't possibly blame me for it.*

Anyway, she thought, *I'll make it up to him with this private demonstration he wants so badly. Then he will think that I'm marvellous, and he'll forget the insult.*

Everyone at the dinner party suddenly paled and fell silent as the building shifted uneasily on its rain-sodden foundations and the chandelier swung, its glass droplets twittering like frightened birds. A single pink glass flower dropped from the chandelier straight into Daniele Spatafora's wine glass. It exploded, painting his face with blood-red liquid.

Aurelia cried out gleefully, 'Wait till Signor Rioba hears about this!' and then clapped her hand over her mouth.

Two dozen shocked faces swivelled towards her; two dozen mouths opened in horror. Signor Rioba was *not* a name to mention at a dinner attended by *I Fedeli* – because Signor Rioba was the solitary source of complaints about Daniele Spatafora and his men. No one else in Venice dared say a word against them.

Signor Antonio Rioba did not actually complain aloud because he was made of stone, being a statue of a Moorish man who stood stalwart as a pillar by the edge of a northern canal, glowering. Close by were his brothers Sandi and Afani, equally severe in their expressions. Since *I Fedeli* had come into power, notices had begun to appear on Signor Rioba's broad marble chest, as they always did in times of murky doings in Venice. Even the rain could not wash away the ferocious words.

On a scale of pigs to sharks, I Fedeli *be the very Gods of Greed, stripping Venice down to her skin and bleeding her dry.*

I Fedeli? *Fiddling the books, more like! Account books with double columns – one for the seedy truth and the other for the gullible public. That's yesselves, I be naming, Venetians!*

I *faking* Fedeli *swear they'll stop the Barbary pirates from picking off Venetian galleys in the Mediterranean Sea. Yet not one single* Fedeli *boat's been launched against them Corsairs. What if the pirates learn what's* not *going on in Venice? Steaming vats of horror all round! It would take too long to curse* I Fedeli *– they need storing!*

With each passing week of rain, Signor Rioba's rants had grown angrier, shorter and ruder.

Wot do ye keep under your hair, Venetians? Sausages? It certainly ain't brains. Nothing but stupid as far as the eye can see. An anchor *would understand that there be something wrong here.*

Finally, even Aurelia herself had received a mention in Signor Rioba's rants.

People say that Aurelia Bon's fingers be the famousest in Venice. My oath! Methinks Aurelia Bon's history fingers are nothing *to the digits of* I Fedeli, *most of all the stubby little ones that belong to Daniele Spatafora, the mightiest miniature bully this town's ever seen. Look at those fingers of his dipping into every coffer!* Those *be the busiest fingers in Venice, and they be busy a-stealing. So what are ye going to do about it, Venice?*

I thought so. Nothing. Be it on your own heads then.

So it was hardly surprising that *I Fedeli* and their wives were now looking at Aurelia with horror. Daniele Spatafora had jumped up – not that it made much difference to his height – with his fist raised. 'How dare she, insolent chit of a girl?' he shouted. Contessa Bon danced about, dabbing at his stained frock coat with a napkin.

The *palazzo* itself now made another lurch and uttered one more long groan from deep inside its foundations, as if it also found Aurelia's indiscretion just too much to bear. The ladies shrieked and clung to the table.

'My daughter isn't herself tonight, dear Daniele,' said Contessa Bon. 'She's been feeling faint. So delicate, she is, and so terrified of her home collapsing.'

'I'm struggling to care,' rasped Daniele Spatafora.

Contessa Bon whimpered, '*Everyone* is trembling for their houses! And is it not terribly *close* in here tonight? I feel somewhat faint myself. Don't we all?' She appealed to the other ladies, flapping the stained napkin in front of her face. 'Aurelia, my dear, would you like to go upstairs to rest a little?'

Aurelia could think of nothing she'd like to do more.

But as she rose, crimson-faced, to leave the room, Simoneto Ghezzo whispered, 'I'm sure a girl as clever as you can contrive to escape this house, where no one seems to care about your happiness. I shall meet you at Palazzo Bon in one hour's time.'

5

At 'The Palace that Eats Boys'

Aurelia's breath tore through her narrow chest. After sliding down the wisteria vine, she'd run away as fast as her legs would carry her and without a backwards glance (an omission that would prove unfortunate). But Simoneto Ghezzo was not waiting for her as promised when she arrived at the Palazzo Bon. The great walls that surrounded the palace were shrouded in vines that rustled alarmingly, even though there was no wind that night. And there was the graveyard, all too close, the tombstones slicked black with rain.

Once upon a time the Palazzo Bon had been the home of Aurelia's own great-great-great-great-great grandfather, Aurelio Bon, youthful merchant of mirrors. The scents of the goods he traded for those mirrors – mouth-watering spices, tooth-tingling sweetmeats, nose-twitching frankincense, achingly sweet myrrh – still hung alluringly around his palace three centuries on.

There was something unusual not just in the air around the Palazzo Bon but also in its architecture. No one remembered when the courtyard wall of Aurelio Bon's old home had acquired a dainty frill of ornamental brickwork atop its plain Venetian stone – but it was frequently remarked that this wall would have looked more at home in Arabia than in Italy.

Meanwhile, over the years, the palace had also acquired a reputation for ghostly goings-on.

Now, ghosts were like noses in Venice – everyone had one, and some were as characterful and interesting as the Bon family nose. Moaning nuns and headless butlers bearing silver trays stalked the dim halls and cobwebbed attics of all the noble houses. But most Venetian ghosts were forlorn rather than frightening. Venetians were sorry for them, shared their homes with them, came to regard them as family.

Unfortunately, any ghost attached to the Bon family was bound to be a problem. '*Bon*' means 'good'. Yet too many of the Bons had been bad. For centuries, the Bons were so bad that it seemed as if hardly a single member of the family had ever been good. There was one Bon who wanted to be a priest, but his bad blood overcame his good intentions. He burned down the church, having stolen the priceless silver candlesticks first. Another had drowned his mother in the Grand Canal. A century before, a Bon had been executed for something too evil to be talked about. The reek and murk of the bad Bons' spirits clung to their old palace, stronger than the perfumes of Aurelio Bon's traded wares.

Even the famous merchant of mirrors had a dark side. Stories of his adventures in Arabia always trailed away to whispers, raised eyebrows and, eventually, silence. The talented, brave Aurelio Bon had suddenly given up his travels at a young age, with no reason ever given. No one quite knew exactly what became of him in the end.

It was near the vast *portone* in the Palazzo Bon's courtyard wall that each of five young men had last been seen. Every fifty years or so since the early 1520s, another Venetian youth had disappeared there. Each one had been smiling with an almost unearthly joy, a silvery ghostlight playing around his body.

Of course the Palazzo Bon had been abandoned for a long time now. Meanwhile, over centuries, with much effort, many charitable donations made and slave ransoms paid, the Bons had slowly become respectable again – to the point where a match could be contemplated between a Bon daughter and a Spatafora son.

Yet the old Palazzo Bon continued to throw a dark shadow, looming over its canal like a bad dream. Without the voices of children and servants, the Palazzo Bon was now a ghost of a palace, empty and silent, except for that lonely female voice sometimes heard keening its impossibly sweet and tragic song.

This was absolutely not a place to be alone on a dark night.

Valerio's earnest face came into Aurelia's mind. Thinking about Valerio and what he'd say about this midnight meeting, Aurelia flushed and tossed her head at the same time, which made her a little dizzy. Then, in the space between her dripping shoulders, Aurelia suddenly felt an alarming sense that someone was watching her. She turned to flee. At that moment, Simoneto Ghezzo lunged out from behind a thick swag of vines. He greeted her with a dozen compliments, bowing too low for his comfort or hers.

I can almost hear his back creak, thought Aurelia.

'Shall we start, my little lady?' he asked, a greedy expression on his face. 'We could begin with this great door in the wall?'

'Of course.' Aurelia placed the second and middle fingers of her right hand against the carved wooden door. Her palm was already tingling with an expectation of pleasure. Her body flushed with warmth. This, her history-fingering, was what Aurelia lived for. This was the one special thing about her, the talent that put her on top of the world; also, the very thing that she'd soon be forced to give up. She must make the most of every second. She smiled at Simoneto Ghezzo, suddenly grateful that he'd given her this unexpected opportunity.

But when her fingers touched the gate, she exclaimed in surprise, 'This is not Venetian wood!'

Her voice grew dreamy and she put her nose against the door. 'This smells of . . . frankincense! A door made of frankincense wood?'

Simoneto Ghezzo's ingratiating grin wobbled at the corners. 'Is there even an infinitesimal possibility that you could be wrong, dearest miss? That wood grows only in Arabia. It's too knotty to be suitable for carpentry.'

Aurelia thought, *He thinks I'm making fun of him!*

Aloud, she said, 'I suppose you've heard of my ancestor Aurelio Bon . . . you know he travelled there, trading in mirrors?'

'There's nothing I don't know about young Aurelio Bon,' purred Simoneto Ghezzo. 'From the mirrors to myrrh to the swan-necked tear-catcher bottles—'

'Oh – why—?' But Aurelia was interrupted by a young voice screaming from beyond the wood: 'Help me!' The plea seemed to tear the owner's throat in two. The words were uttered in a low Venetian dialect in the voice of a very young woman or possibly even a boy. 'Help me! I don't want to die in here.'

Aurelia cried, 'There's someone trapped behind this wall! Somewhere in this palace. In trouble! We need to help her! Or him?'

History-fingering was never a precise art, particularly because Aurelia was so very hazy about dates and historical settings. And this was something new. In the past, of course, her history fingers had revealed scenes in which the protagonists talked among themselves. No one had ever seemed aware of Aurelia herself or called out to her. Now she could see no one, but she could hear a voice.

So perhaps, thought Aurelia, *this isn't history. Is she a girl from now? From the past? Would that mean – beyond my help? But—*

She wished very hard that Valerio was there. He would have been able to make sense of this. He'd find some clue that connected this girl – if it was a girl – to a particular date in the historical past. Valerio, calm and serious, would clear up the confusion and panic.

Her actual companion, meanwhile, seemed to be rather enjoying Aurelia's confusion. 'Some *young person* in the wall?' he asked with a mocking smile. '*Really*, miss?'

The historian inclined his ear towards the wood. 'I hear nothing, I fear. But I know this is an imaginative kind of girl,' he added, as if Aurelia were not there. 'How does one tell truth from her childish stories?'

'There's nothing childish about me!' she said. 'I thought you admired me! You were so complimentary at dinner. Otherwise I'd never have risked sneaking out here to meet you.'

He mused, 'No doubt the fingertips would work better on another . . . one with more knowledge, experience . . .'

'How could *that* happen? I thought you wanted to see what *I* can do with these fingers,' Aurelia frowned. 'And now there's this poor person—'

'Of course,' Simoneto Ghezzo said smoothly. 'May I, dearest miss, put my hand over yours to feel, as it were, *through* you? Perhaps then I too might hear this . . . *creature* . . . you speak of.'

Before Aurelia had a chance to recoil, the historian covered her hand with his. It was quite tiny for a man's, clammy and wrinkled. He tightened his grip, his fingers slipping between hers so that the back of her own hand was entirely enclosed.

His face suffused with surprise. 'Frankincense!' he muttered. 'And something else . . . like burning blood and roses? Honey? . . . And what the deuce?'

'The voice?' she cried. 'Do you hear the voice?'

The girl still called pitifully, the words thick with tears. 'Help me! I have to lick the rain off the walls. Sometimes someone throws me a few dates. Otherwise I'd be dead. I want my mother!'

A change rippled over Simoneto Ghezzo's face. It became cold and crafty. 'Sorry, my dear, no, no *human* voice here. Perhaps you hear the wind whistling in the empty corridors of the palace? I can perhaps hear something like that. But a boy or girl? No, absolutely, not at all.'

Aurelia pulled her hand out from under his. How could he

smell the frankincense yet not hear the voice? This new face of Simoneto Ghezzo's was frightening. 'I must go home immediately,' she insisted. 'I shouldn't be here at all.'

'Of course, dearest miss. You've already humoured me too much. Do take care of your precious self! Don't slip – the rain has varnished every flagstone. Shall I accompany you—'

'Absolutely not!'

Simoneto Ghezzo said, 'Now, my dear, no one needs to know about this meeting, do they? It would only get you into even more trouble, and that's the last thing we want. And the screaming, no doubt the wind . . . and the frankincense . . . they shall be our little secrets too. Yes? What an honour it is to share secrets with you!'

He was still grovelling as she ran away.

6

Utter Disgrace

It was harder climbing up the wisteria vine that it had been to slip down it. And when Aurelia arrived, panting, at the windowsill, she found Catarina waiting for her.

In her haste to leave the Palazzo Bon, Aurelia hadn't noticed Catarina's face at the window, watching her leave. You might think that Catarina would have called out then to her wayward sister and urged her not to run out into the dark, wet night. But instead Catarina had settled down to wait.

Now, she greeted her sister with a cat-like smile.

Please, Aurelia begged silently. *Just please for once leave me alone.*

She should have known better. Catarina always knew far too much about things Aurelia had never discussed with her. Aurelia suspected Catarina of spying on her diary. Once she'd found a long red hair inside it, even though she always hid it under her mattress. Aurelia's own hair was dark and curly – Catarina's, tellingly, was straight and the colour of an autumn leaf.

Now, Catarina had painted her spiteful tale-telling face on like a mask and had opened her mouth to scream.

'Why didn't you do that before?' Aurelia asked. 'If you knew I was gone?'

'Because it's going to be more amusing this way,' replied Catarina.

'If you keep quiet, I'll give you my silver bracelet,' Aurelia begged, starting to slide it off her wrist. 'I know you've always wanted it.'

'This way I'll get my *own* silver bracelet, a prettier one,' said Catarina, opening her mouth once more.

Two minutes later both parents and half of the servants were standing in front of Aurelia.

The rain had sopped her clothes against her body. Her panniered petticoat, heavy with water, sagged under her skirt. The damp had done its betraying work on her hair, which, for the dinner party, had been styled into little bread-roll curls and powdered till it crunched. Now dark wet rivulets straggled down her back. There was absolutely no possibility of pretending that Aurelia had *not* been out in the rain in the middle of the night.

'Where have you been?' demanded her father. 'Not only do you insult our most honoured guest but then you disappear. How dare you? What were you up to? With whom? How did you become so arrogant and so wild? If it were not for Catarina's good sense and sharp eyes, we'd never have known how far you've gone down this terrible road. You are an utter disgrace to this family.'

'What . . . what are you going to do . . . to me?' Aurelia asked. It was hard to imagine the punishment she'd face now, because she had never seen her father so angry.

'The first thing I'm going to do is send a messenger to the *Signori di Notte*. I'll have them guard this house tonight and every night.'

Conte Bon snapped his fingers at the butler, who bustled out of the room.

'The rest of you may return to your beds,' Aurelia's father told the servants. 'And not a word of this is to be breathed outside this palace. Do you understand? Or there will be consequences.'

He turned to Aurelia. 'We have indulged you too long. And look where it's led. The nonsense with the fingers – it's over. Now.'

'What about Palm Sunday at the Palazzo Bon? The book! It's all arranged.'

'My dear,' said Contessa Bon to her husband, 'it is true that we have promised this one last event to dear Giovanni Remondini—'

'Giovanni Remondini!' said Conte Bon. 'That's a name I won't be sorry to stop hearing.'

Contessa Bon flushed as she protested, 'My dear, you know we're *as one* about the end of the history fingers. But the Bons must be seen to honour their promises. This is such a *sensitive* time for us. *I Fedeli* . . . But once Palm Sunday is out of the way—'

'I *won't* stop!' cried Aurelia. 'If you make Remondini give me up, then I'll just do my history-fingering whenever I'm out on the street! The crowds will come!'

At the look on her father's face, Aurelia's defiance suddenly drained away. Her hands trembled as she pleaded, 'Please, Papa. You must let me have just a little more time. I'm too young to be betrothed. It's not even legal to marry at my age.'

She lowered her head humbly.

'As you well know, certain *understandings* can be formed years in advance of any important marriage,' said her father pompously. 'Families can agree in principle to future alliances. You can be *earmarked*. And you're not too young to be out in society, showing yourself as a girl who can secure the right kind of husband for the good of her whole house.' His voice was cold and even.

Rage surged back into Aurelia's heart. 'The right kind of husband being one who suits *you*, not me. You don't care about me,' she shouted. 'All you dream about is getting in with *I Fedeli*. I'm a girl, not a chess piece. That's how you see me – or as a cut of meat in a horrible flesh market. Well, yes – I *am* like a lamb or calf. You'll have to *kill* me first if you want to sell me!'

Aurelia's own images suddenly struck her as pathetic. But she stiffened her back and lifted her chin defiantly.

'Listen to her!' lamented Contessa Bon. 'This evening, after the *incident*, Contessa Spatafora asked me if there was madness in our family!'

Conte Bon snapped, 'Tantrums and melodrama won't change your destiny, daughter. That is your answer then? You'd rather *die* than do what your family wants? Well, Aurelia, you may now prepare yourself to renounce the world.'

'What do you mean?'

'After you ruined our dinner, I had a very interesting conversation with Padre Pino. He was most sympathetic. I'll have to pay more, but Padre Pino indicated that he'd be prepared, as a special favour, to take you into the convent early. He'd make it his business to break your bad habits, cure your showing off. Silence is the rule of the day, the year, of life at San Zaccaria. You don't want to spend nights in your own bed, daughter? Well so be it. The day after Palm Sunday, San Zaccaria will be your new home.'

Surprisingly, it was not Aurelia but Catarina who burst into tears. Contessa Bon put an awkward arm round her younger child's shoulders. 'Hush, hush. At least we still have one respectable daughter . . . the Spatafora might yet forgive us for last night's offence.'

Aurelia turned to Catarina. 'Why are you whimpering? Wasn't this your plan all along? *That*'s why you betrayed me this way. Not just because it was "amusing".'

'No!' gulped Catarina. 'At least . . . I thought this was what you *wanted* – to be free of Marco! I didn't know about Padre Pino. I swear I didn't.'

'You'd have done it anyway,' said Aurelia flatly. 'I'll never forgive you. You are not my sister any more.'

Catarina's face paled, then reddened as if it bore the imprint of a slap.

Aurelia's father loomed over her. 'This malice shows me that I'm doing the right thing. If poor Catarina ever consents to visit you at San Zaccaria, you'll be safely behind an iron grille like all the other nuns.'

Aurelia felt as if the breath had been snatched out of her lungs. She was gulping and trying to swallow, but there seemed to be some kind of obstruction in her throat.

She tried to tell herself, *Papa's lost his temper. He never does that. He's temporarily insane with it. He'll be calmer in the morning. He will forgive me. Everything can go on as before. At least it can for a while longer.*

Exhaustion flooded through her. So much had happened in such a short time, none of it good.

And too much of it is entirely my own fault, she thought. *Why ever did I mention Signor Rioba? Why didn't I say, 'Of course not!' to Simoneto Ghezzo? Why did I not check if Catarina was spying on me when I left? Why did I shout at Papa? I should have kept quiet and apologised humbly.*

She sank into a chair and put her head in her hands.

'I did not give you permission to sit,' thundered her father. 'From now on, you'll be asking permission for *everything*. The answer will usually be, "Absolutely not!" And from now, until Palm Sunday, you're confined to this room.'

'No!'

'What makes you think you have the right to say "no" to anything, daughter? Think of this week,' her father told Aurelia, 'as a rehearsal for the convent.'

Aurelia lay on her bed, too shocked to take off her sodden clothes, too shocked to cry, even now that she was alone. It had been terrible to face a choice between Marco Spatafora and the convent. But it was absolutely unspeakable to have no choice at all.

In her mind, images of San Zaccaria's grey walls alternated with those of Padre Pino's greasy face and his fat fingers pointing at her.

She was just drifting into a wretched sleep when suddenly it came back to her – the sound of the voice in the wall at the Palazzo Bon.

'Help me,' it had moaned.

I forgot all about it! What kind of human being am I? That poor person is trapped; I'm trapped. I should have felt for her more than anyone. That little person might be dying.

Or is she a ghost, already dead, from long in the past? What should I do? Even if she's from history, I owe it to her to find out, if it's the last thing I do.

Aurelia began pulling on clothes. She'd go back to the Palazzo Bon and batter down the door and save that poor person – if they existed in the present and were in a state to be saved. But as she eased the window open, she saw an officer of the *Signori di Notte* raising his lantern up to stare at her.

Aurelia walked sadly to her bed.

I promise you, she told the voice, *that I shall come back for you. I promise you, on . . . my history fingers! When there are lots of people there to help me, on Palm Sunday. I've hundreds of admirers! They will all help. And even Simoneto Ghezzo. Creepy as he is, he's a human being and a Venetian. He felt the strangeness of the palace through my fingers. He will explain that we need to save you. I know he'll help. Of course he will. Whoever you are, just two more days.*

If you're still alive to be saved . . . hold on till then.

7

Condescension

Aurelia's last insult to Valerio was still burning in his memory the morning after the fateful dinner party.

It was so easy, he reflected, for a noble girl like Aurelia to make use of a person while thinking so little of him. Valerio couldn't even blame her for taking him for granted.

I'm simply supplied, he thought, *like everything in Aurelia's privileged life. She never has to think about where her next pair of silk slippers comes from. It doesn't occur to her that others are not so fortunate. She never asks how I manage to live. Which is – just about scraping by on my small stipend, only because Giovanni Remondini houses and feeds me in the apprentices' dormitory.*

Yes, Aurelia condescended to talk to Valerio, even to smile at him sometimes. But, as he'd just seen, she was also happy to use him as her whipping boy when her own frustrations boiled over. Did she even *think* about Valerio as a fellow human being with feelings and worries of his own?

Meanwhile, only Valerio himself knew how much of Aurelia's history-fingering would be half in the realm of fairy tale were it not for his own long unthanked – no, *mocked* – hours in the archives, rounding out her flavoursome but wispy stories until they meshed with actual history, even drawing the pictures that brought her visions to life on the page. And yet Valerio received no credit for his work. The almost-quite-pretty noble girl was good for selling books to Venetians, Giovanni Remondini insisted. 'It would dilute the publicity if we had to admit she needs help. And what if the public were to learn that the helper is a penniless ink-stained boy from the mainland!'

Venetians were known for looking down on land-dwellers. In fact, there was no class of person they looked down on more than people from the mainland.

It's not personal, Valerio told himself, swallowing Remondini's insult the way he'd swallowed Aurelia's.

In fact, despite everything, he couldn't help feeling anxious about Aurelia. She'd been so pale and distressed when he last saw her – possibly feverish, he'd worried. And Valerio had just now acquired some information that would upset her even more. What Valerio had just discovered was that Aurelia had an enemy. He meant to do Aurelia some kind of harm, and he was possibly quite dangerously mad. The enemy's name was Simoneto Ghezzo.

Sent to collect some corrected page proofs from the historian's home, Valerio had found his collar seized by Ghezzo. He was dragged into the dark hallway and subjected to a rant. Like everyone in Venice, Simoneto Ghezzo knew nothing about Valerio's work with Aurelia Bon. To Ghezzo, as to the rest of Venice, Valerio was just a boy-shaped piece of nothing. To Ghezzo, Valerio was also a piece of nothing against which he could vent his anger.

An incoherent torrent of words had poured out of Simoneto Ghezzo, shaking his narrow frame. But gradually Valerio – his research skills a definite help here – began to make out the arc of a story. It was this: until Aurelia Bon first pressed a hand against a *palazzo*, Simoneto Ghezzo had apparently considered himself the greatest historian in Venice. Remondini had printed everything he wrote. 'My ideas,' Ghezzo declared, 'were always perfectly good enough for my fellow Venetians! Then Aurelia Bon and her history fingers pushed into the scene and that was the end of everything good in my life.'

Valerio knew that Simoneto Ghezzo had never married, had no children. His cadaverous looks must have always counted against him where romance was concerned. There'd never been anything for Ghezzo but his work, and that was exactly where Aurelia Bon had beaten him down, destroyed him. These days, Remondini slipped Ghezzo's books out into the market as if faintly ashamed of them.

'That little drama queen,' Ghezzo had raved, 'doesn't even *care* about facts or dates or actual accounts.'

Although he'd remained silent, Valerio could not but agree that 'drama queen' was a title that quite suited Aurelia.

Ghezzo had snarled, 'Everyone says, "how charming, how picturesque." They don't see that this impudent chit of a girl is making our history *stupid,* like a game of chance, not skill. They don't see the contempt in what she does.'

Valerio thought, *Yes, there's contempt in Aurelia Bon.*

'Yet, by the time her tales are printed, there's substance on the bones of her little tales. No doubt there's some anonymous minion actually researching and writing her books for a pittance, while she gets all the glory.'

Ghezzo had worked himself deeper into his rage. 'She cannot imagine it, so poverty itself is nothing to her. She's never heard her own stomach rumble with hunger. I, Simoneto Ghezzo, am nothing to her, and my fall is nothing to her. She's crushed me as she might step on a cockroach, not even aware of the suffering beneath her foot.

'All these years, I've been keeping an eye on her, totting up her triumphs, every one of them made at my personal expense. But now everything's changed. Finally I've met her for myself. I'd always heard that she was a dainty kind of girl. Yet what I saw was an angry little thing dressed up in expensive silk. There's nothing special about the famous fingers. I was enraged with how ordinary they are, like those of any child. And I'm not a man who likes children.'

Valerio's shoulders had tensed at the coldness of Ghezzo's tone. 'Sir—'

Then Valerio was distracted by a noise coming from somewhere upstairs in Ghezzo's narrow house. It sounded like the clanking of a chain. And were those *prayers* he could faintly hear? Or was it begging? In a man's voice? Valerio, craning his neck to see where the stairs led, didn't hear Ghezzo's next words, which were, 'And I know from my own experience now that the girl doesn't scruple to take risks and disappear in the dead of night if it suits her.'

The clanking stopped. Valerio turned back to Ghezzo, who was saying, 'I've only to wait until Palm Sunday. It could not be better for me. The fates are smiling on my plans.'

'Your plans?'

Ghezzo pulled a fat pile of scribbled sheets out of a drawer and waved them triumphantly under Valerio's nose. 'Look, boy! Forget about those old proofs! *Here* is the book that Venice has been waiting for. My own masterpiece, *The Palace that Eats Boys*, will knock everything else out of the water. My life will turn around. Aurelia Bon will sink into oblivion. For she and I, I've long since known, are like the figures of moon and sun on one of those newfangled Swiss clocks. We can never appear in public at the same time. I've been the moon for too long, living by the grey light of poverty. Now it's *my* turn to be the sun. And with Aurelia Bon . . . gone . . . Simoneto Ghezzo shall never have to go indoors again.'

Talking about himself in the third person, thought Valerio. *Isn't that a sign of a disordered mind?*

The historian was saying, 'Simoneto Ghezzo isn't someone you can trifle with. *Some* people are about to learn that the hard way.'

I must go to Aurelia, Valerio had thought, *and warn her. I've got to make her stop talking about herself long enough to listen.*

But first Valerio had to take this new manuscript back to Bassano del Grappa. He couldn't imagine that Giovanni Remondini would be delighted to see it. Then he'd return to Venice and let Aurelia know that she must be careful with her new so-called friend.

Time enough after Palm Sunday, thought Valerio. *Nothing bad could possibly happen in front of the huge crowd Aurelia always draws.*

Ghezzo's a madman, but all he can do is rave.

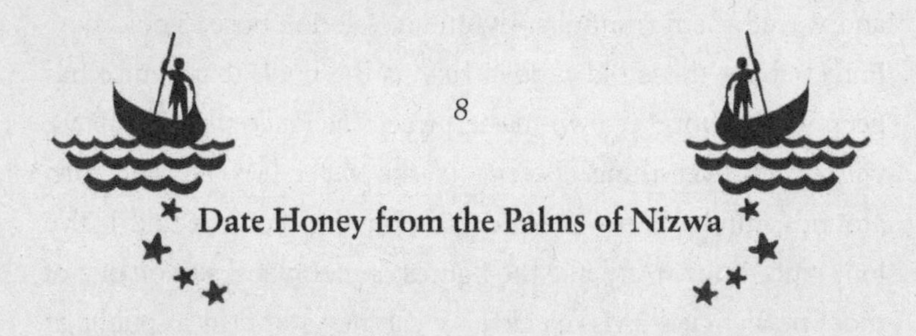

8

Date Honey from the Palms of Nizwa

The usual Palm Sunday Procession had taken place, even though the merest straggle of Venetians had braved the rain to see it. The usual silk standards had been carried by the usual trumpeters, who were followed by the chamberlains of the doge in their vestments, the equerries bearing the golden crown and then the doge himself in his *corno* hat and ermine cape. Behind him trotted the usual ambassadors of the usual nations, and finally the Venetian senators in their long black robes.

Every single one of them was drenched. The standards clung limply to their poles; the trumpets gurgled on rain. The chamberlains slithered on the mud; the equerries tried in vain to keep the precious items dry; the doge looked as if he was wearing a nest of drowned white rats on his shoulder. The ambassadors were grumbling and sneezing, while the senators' hems dragged in the water, tripping them up.

The French ambassador was heard muttering to his Portuguese counterpart, 'The Venetians live like fish – permanently wet.'

The Portuguese ambassador nodded grimly. 'Anyway, Venice is a backwater now. With the emphasis on "*water*". That was a joke, you know.'

The French ambassador grimaced. *The Portuguese*, his expression said clearly, *should really refrain from joking.*

While most Venetians had stayed away from the damp pageantry in Saint Mark's Square, their curiosity had sent them in droves to the tall wall outside 'The Palace that Eats Boys' for the new – and absolutely the last – history-fingering by the famous Aurelia Bon. Standing under battered hats, the huge and enthusiastic crowd greeted her with a rapture. Contessa Bon, chaperoning, was locked in conversation with Giovanni Remondini. Because his employer was here to soak up the glory, Valerio was reluctantly absent – checking proofs on the press, back up at the Remondini printworks in Bassano del Grappa. The French and Portuguese ambassadors, however, were in attendance, eager to see the history-fingering they had heard so much about.

Aurelia's mother broke free from her fascinating chat long enough to deliver a reproach to Aurelia. 'Listen to those peasants! A proper noble girl never does anything to attract the mob's attention. The more people buy your little book, the *commoner* it gets. And *why* did you wear that old black dress?'

'I'm in mourning for my life, which is about to end,' said Aurelia so quietly that her mother, already turning back to Remondini, failed to hear her.

It felt strange to be out in the open air after the long days confined in her room. Meanwhile, in Aurelia's mind three thoughts jostled: *Will the weeping voice still be there? Still alive? This is my last chance to help.*

For the occasion, the carved wooden gates were decked with ribbons and flowers, both straggling under the onslaught of rain.

A canopy protected Aurelia, her mother and her publisher. Aurelia curled and uncurled her fingers and wiped them on her dress. Slow, wet minutes passed and still Giovanni Remondini stood with his back to her, chattering with Contessa Bon. Impatience crackled in the air. Then a slow clap started. 'What's keeping you?' yelled a man.

Remondini glanced back. He told Aurelia, 'You might as well start.'

This time, Aurelia decided, *I won't touch the door. I'll try the wall. The door might have been brought from far off on a ship . . . but the wall must be Venetian stone. It will tell me where the poor girl is.*

The crowd fell into a rapt silence as Aurelia lifted her hands. No one in the crowd, of course, could have guessed why she was so pale, or why, for the first time, Aurelia Bon looked nervous.

When Aurelia put her fingers on the *palazzo* wall, each crumb of stone vibrated underneath them. A shock of pain and revulsion shot from her hands to her heart. Quickly, she pulled her fingers away from the wall. They came away sticky with something of a dark red colour. It trickled between her fingers and thumbs.

'This is not from Venice,' she said slowly, holding up her stained fingers. 'This is honey and human blood from the Castle of Jabrin.'

Aurelia thought, *How do I know that? I cannot know that. What is the Castle of Jabrin? I don't even know how those words came out of my mouth.*

The crowd stared, jaws slack and eyes wide.

'The honey is not from Venetian bees,' said Aurelia's voice. 'It's date honey from the palms of Nizwa.'

'Nizzzzwah?' The crowd tasted this word in its many mouths. 'Nizwa? Where's Nizwa? What's she talking about?'

The Portuguese ambassador cleared his throat. He said importantly, 'Nizwa was, er, *is* the name of a great town situated in my nation's former Arabian colonies. For thirteen decades, the Portuguese flag waved over this noble city on the edge of the Arabian Empty Quarter.'

Aurelia said, in a tone devoid of emotion, 'That explains why some of this blood is Portuguese, and some Arabian.'

The ambassador stepped back, his face drained of colour.

'So that *your* flag could wave here . . . many deaths took place,' Aurelia told him, in a slow, sleepwalking voice she barely recognised as her own. She continued, 'Inside the courtyard, I see a fresco of a lion.'

'There's nothing unusual about a lion in Venice!' remarked a smooth tight voice in the crowd. For a moment, Aurelia thought it sounded like Simoneto Ghezzo's, except much sneerier. The voice said, 'Being the symbol of our patron Saint Mark, there are lions painted on half the important walls in Venice and at least nine in the Doge's Palace. Any *educated* person would know that.'

'This lion is different,' Aurelia said. 'The style . . . well, it looks as if a Venetian artist *might* have painted it and . . . yes, there's the Doge's Palace in the background, and our Venetian boats . . . but . . . on the shore . . . there are palm trees! And tall pink birds with long necks, like egrets. Yet, their beaks are more like those of parrots.'

The same smooth voice said, 'It seems the girl is speaking of Arabian flamingos. She must be *confused*.'

'And inside the palace itself, the walls,' Aurelia continued, her eyes screwed close with concentration, 'are lined with terracotta. Oh! I see so many wonderful things. Gracious halls with soaring walls *bathed* in light. *Two* courtyards with wells, orange trees and flowers.'

In wonder, Aurelia described to her audience the exquisite carpets draped from tall arches; the windows shaded with delicate fretwork; the ceilings painted in elaborate designs; the walls carved with lettering that seemed to dance like flowers in the wind. The colours of the carpets, walls and ceilings were rich, infused with the sun. Everything sparkled, clean and orderly.

'In fact,' Aurelia murmured, 'it's more beautiful in here than my own home. Certainly a lot less gloomy.'

Contessa Bon glared at her daughter, shaking her head.

Aurelia's fingers took her through reception chambers, a library and a room set with a dozen low desks.

'A classroom, perhaps? There's a table spread with drawings – of the stars! – and a magnificent telescope stationed at a deep-silled window.'

Aurelia carried on, entranced by her vision, thrilled to be sharing it. 'And there are graceful men in turbans and gowns writing beautiful scripts on wooden panels! Now one is looking through the telescope, while another, with a long beard, is making diagrams with such a skilful hand,' she marvelled. 'Oh! I've noticed something else. In this great palace, there are cushions on the floors. Not one single chair! There's a man – so dignified and so suave! – seated on one of the cushions. It looks as if he's receiving an important guest. The guest approaches, bowing, and is welcomed.'

Aurelia's fingers took her up a flight of steps to a vast open roof terrace.

Leaning over the wall, Aurelia told the crowd, she saw thick clusters of palm trees, a network of swift, silvery streams. 'Such beautiful birds too, flitting through the trees – there's a see-see partridge, a redleg chukar and a muscat bee-eater sitting together on one palm tree! Oh, and I can see a tall slender tower in the distance. A man with a deep voice is calling out from a room at the top.'

'How could you see any of that? Or hear it?' hissed someone. 'How could you know those bird names?'

Yes, thought Aurelia. *How can I know? These are things that have never existed in Venice, not even in history, not at any time.*

The smooth voice inquired, 'So what *year* are you seeing then? Let's have a bit of detail! Those are supposed to be *history* fingers on your hands, aren't they?'

If only Valerio was here, Aurelia thought. *He'd have been able to help.*

Even without the archives at his disposal, Valerio's head was always full of useful facts, and he had an extraordinary knack for tying loose ends together and working things out.

I never give him enough credit for that, she thought. Then the sensations under her fingertips drew Aurelia's attention back to the castle.

'And all around, in the distance,' Aurelia continued, 'there are rolling dunes of beautiful golden sand. For miles.'

'Sand?' sputtered people in the crowd. It was hard to speak clearly with the raindrops swilling into their mouths. 'What's she on about?'

Aurelia's fingers were taking her down many flights of steps to a large room, open to the blue sky. 'Ah, now I'm in a kitchen . . . there's a kettle as big as . . . a small child kneeling . . . with a serpent of a spout. It's sticky . . . with date honey. That's what it's used for.

'I can smell fresh dates . . . getting closer, stronger. Ah, now I see room after little room, so strangely constructed. In the ground are thick runnels of stone like a ploughed field. Piled up on them are sacks of dates. And the weight of each sack is crushing the sack below and so a clear liquid is running out through the runnels, and in the end, it trickles into a . . . oh, I see a terracotta pot collecting the honey. It's juice, as thick as honey, and so . . . delicious.'

Aurelia's mouth was watering.

'*Asil*,' she said with satisfaction, 'that's what date honey is called, "*asil*".'

'Correct,' pronounced the Portuguese ambassador. 'That is indeed what they call it in Nizwa.'

'Now I've found some stairs . . . to a different part of the building. And there are prayers written along the staircase, prayers to keep safe all who live here. Going-to-bed verses! In Arabic. They will insure a healthy and a holy sleep. What a charming idea.'

'How can you read prayers in Arabic, miss?' someone called from the back.

'I don't know,' said Aurelia. 'Normally I can't.'

'Nothing normal here,' observed that smooth tight voice. Aurelia wanted to see whose it was. But her fingers were insistent, and so was the need to keep sharing what they were showing her, even though they were starting to reveal details that were harder to describe and less joyful to share.

'There are hinged lids covering holes in the stairs. Oh! Someone's creeping up in the dark. And look, the lid has dropped and his leg has plunged down to his knee. Something is hissing inside the hollow space beneath the step. A cobra! And . . . there are grates hidden above the thresholds.'

'Ah, she speaks of "trip-steps" and "murder holes". In the old days,' explained the Portuguese ambassador, 'boiling date honey was poured through those grates on to the heads of any unwelcome visitor.'

Aurelia said, 'Yes! I smell the honey on the boil. I can feel the heat of it!'

The crowd raised its many noses to sniff. People at the front pressed their faces against the wall, making loud snuffling and snorting noises. Their faces creased with disappointment. Contessa Bon pulled her skirts away from them, disgust on her face.

Aurelia said, 'Oh, I've just seen a passageway where men are walking, bent over double because the ceiling is so low.'

The Portuguese ambassador said, 'I've seen this myself. Convicted criminals must pass a "Walk of Shame" as they depart the sheik's court for a life of disgrace.'

Aurelia continued, 'Now here's a room without windows. There's a piece of iron nailed to the wall, with two loops.

They're tying a woman to it. And there's hole in the roof of the cell. Oh, I see, a spear or an arrow or a bullet, aimed through the hole, would kill the woman immediately. No need to even touch her.'

'You can't know these things!' cried the man at the back, less smooth now.

'But exactly how is this worse,' the Portuguese ambassador remarked, 'than certain rooms I've heard about in the Doge's Palace, where prisoners of the Venetian Republic are treated to a cruel kind of hospitality?'

This observation went down badly with the crowd. The mood was darkening. Her Venetian admirers had always believed in Aurelia, rejoiced in her, even. Yet now she could feel doubt rippling through their mutters.

Giovanni Remondini regarded Aurelia with displeasure. She could see what he was thinking: *This little performance isn't going to sell books.*

Contessa Bon seized Giovanni Remondini's arm and gabbled, 'Isn't it dreadful? All those stories about her great-great-great-great-great grandfather Aurelio Bon and his travels to Arabia – they must have turned my daughter's silly head!'

Aurelia shot her mother a look. That look was fierce but the truth was that Aurelia felt herself shrinking inside her own skin. Had her fingers betrayed her? *Is this*, she wondered, *what self-doubt feels like?* It was so strange a feeling that she didn't understand it at first. Anger, she'd felt – with Catarina and her mother. Frustration, yes. Fear of a life walled up inside a convent – certainly, without cease lately. But – self-doubt, no. This was a first.

The Venetians were exchanging glances, shaking their heads. For them, the girl had gone too far. They could see for themselves that *outside* the walls of this palace were the usual canals, bridges and plumes of rain. No date palm trees. No honey. Not a single grain of golden sand.

Suddenly, at the very back of the crowd, Aurelia noticed Simoneto Ghezzo, the historian, rubbing his hands. Why didn't he support her? He *knew* that she was genuine. When he'd laid his hand on hers, he'd smelt the frankincense. He'd heard the noise of something wailing, even if he thought it was the wind, not a person.

The girl! Where to find her? In this Castle of Jabrin? Or in the Palazzo Bon? And how can one building hold two palaces at the same time? It's as if 'The Palace that Eats Boys' got so greedy that it swallowed an entire Arabian castle, as well as all the young men and now, it seems, a young girl too.

The muttering grew nastier. The Venetians were united against Aurelia. They were whistling, catcalling, shouting to one another, 'Appalling! Does she think we're *stupid*? She's doing this just to attract attention. Or she's gone mad! Typical Bon! A Bon gone bad like they all did in the past!'

Giovanni Remondini discreetly made himself scarce. Aurelia's mother followed his retreating figure with regretful eyes.

Aurelia leant against the wall, her whole body trembling. The crowd was enjoying itself. Gossip and jokes jostled the air like playful summer thunder. And all the jokes were against Aurelia Bon. And all the gossip was about the bad Bons of history. Everyone had a story about the bad Bons and their dishonourable deeds.

Again, Aurelia caught sight of Simoneto Ghezzo. He had somehow shed his look of a pathetic old man. He seemed taller, stronger. She saw him pass a purse into the hands of the man who was shouting the loudest. Was Ghezzo paying these people to insult her?

It flashed across Aurelia's mind that her history fingers had subjected Simoneto Ghezzo to a quite similar humiliation many times before.

'But I was right, and he was always wrong!' she whispered to herself. 'Wrong, wrong, wrong.'

A small voice inside answered back. *Really, Aurelia? Are you* always *right*?

Aurelia didn't wish to notice that small voice. And something else had caught her attention. Once more, she could hear the sobbing breath and agonised whimpering of the person panting inside the Palazzo Bon.

'Help me! I've been trapped in here for *days*.'

'Who are you?' she breathed. 'Are you from now? Or are you from the past?'

'I am Momo . . .' the voice trailed away to a gasp.

Momo, thought Aurelia, *is the name of the lamp-boy! The* codega *who disappeared after taking a shortcut through the graveyard near this very* palazzo. *Why didn't I think of him before? Because I wanted to think he was a girl, trapped like me! I've been too wrapped up in my own misery to think clearly.*

'What's going on now?' yelled a woman in the crowd.

There are at least two things going on, Aurelia thought. *I can barely keep them both in my head. There's Momo, who is from Venice, and from now, and there's this Arabian castle with all its strangeness, from another time.*

'Tell us!' shouted the crowd.

Aurelia held up her hand, begging for silence. 'It's the missing lamp-boy,' she told them. 'He's trapped in there. Just be quiet so I can listen, please!'

Instead of silence, there was a stone. It was well-aimed and it struck Aurelia's forehead, scraping off the skin so that a line of blood rolled down her cheek.

'Leave young Momo out of it, why don't you?' a man cried. 'A girl like you. Rich. Spoiled. Looking down that big nose at us, as if we were a stink under it! What do *you* know of poor lost boys?'

A younger man screamed, 'Momo's not from history. He's from *today*. He's my friend!'

Under Aurelia's fingers, the pleas of the lost boy were easing out, weakly yet passionately. For a moment, she actually felt his agony, his tight belly, his dry mouth.

She whispered, 'We have to get inside this place to save the lamp-boy!'

The crowd was sick of standing in the rain outside a wall, listening to a girl talk nonsense. Someone yelled, 'Why don't those fancy fingers do something useful for once! Press them on a wall that'll tell us who cursed Venice with this evil weather and why?'

As the man spoke, there came the distant screech, thud and splash of yet another building collapsing in the water. Anxious faces followed the sound, each person calculating whether their own home was still safe.

'Let's force this gate and see the truth for ourselves!' called someone. Angry shoulders were set against the vast *portone*. Someone splintered the keyhole with a knife, allowing a tantalising glimpse of a beautiful courtyard and a vaulted hall beyond it. A few charges by a tribe of burly gondoliers and the fragile damp wood gave way completely, leaving a jagged mouth through which the crowd rushed like a storm tide, shaking the rain out of their sodden hair in arcs of spray.

'Like dogs,' said Contessa Bon. 'Has it come to this? Our ancestral home invaded by dogs?'

For a moment, the dripping Venetians stood still and silent in the overgrown courtyard, taking in eyefuls of a place inside which no one had been for years, and which everyone in Venice had grown up fearing.

Then they surged in.

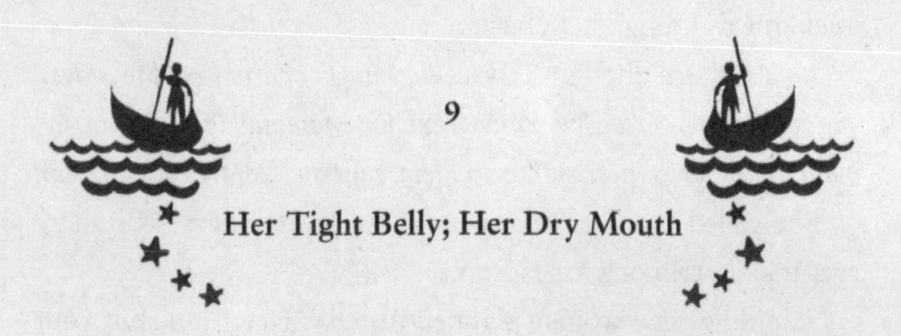

9

Her Tight Belly; Her Dry Mouth

That little show-off Aurelia Bon was clearly wrong, mad or bad. That's what the crowd was shouting now, along with a number of things that were rather less polite than that, as they pushed from the courtyard and into 'The Palace that Eats Boys'.

It was immediately obvious to everyone that all was exactly as it should be inside an ancient Venetian palace: the usual array of painted beams, cavernous fireplaces, Gothic windows, tired tapestries and damask curtains sighing in rags as the rush of eager bodies disturbed the stale air. This was *exactly* how any abandoned Venetian *palazzo* looked, whether now or five hundred years ago.

Not one of the wonders that Aurelia had described was to be seen: no terracotta walls, Arabic calligraphy or date stores, nor a prospect of palm trees from any window. Not one sign of anything that was in any way out of the ordinary.

'Not a single chair, *she* said?' yelled a man, pointing to a corridor lined with gilded sofas with decayed velvet seats. 'Chairs everywhere! Enough for every bad Bon bottom!'

Aurelia stole in behind the crowd, her mother following reluctantly. Aurelia gasped. Here, in front of her own eyes, was living proof that her history fingers were not invincible. A sharp grief knifed through her chest.

It's a sign, she thought. *The history fingers part of my life is over. I've lost my powers. How convenient for Mamma! But that doesn't matter right now. There's a boy in there, suffering. I have to get to him.*

She called out, 'Yes, everyone! Look everywhere! The more eyes the better! Look for Momo.'

A middle-aged woman slapped Aurelia's face. 'You shut your posh little mouth about Momo. What do you think this game of yours will do to his mother? She's my neighbour. He isn't some history trick to *her*. To her, he's real and it's tragic.'

The imprint of the woman's hand was burning on her cheek as Simoneto Ghezzo came to stand by Aurelia. Their eyes met – his glittering with triumph, hers tight with tears she was struggling not to shed. On her other side, her mother now seized her arm. The historian listened intently as Contessa Bon said spitefully, 'Satisfied now? You've upset everyone. And you have achieved nothing. That's the inglorious end of your history fingers. Now you can bury your shame in the convent.'

Aurelia broke away from her mother's hard fingers and ran though the grand entrance hall of the Palazzo Bon.

'Momo! Momo!' she called. 'Where are you?'

Aurelia was the only one looking for him. The crowd was still tumbling through the deserted palace, yelping with joy. Their numbers gave them courage against all the old rumours of bad deeds and ghosts. Of course, all Venetians were partial to a novelty. Here was a place that no one had seen for hundreds of years. Its very cobwebs and dust were glamorous! Women were throwing open shutters to let the rainy light stream in, dazzling the hundreds of black-spotted mirrors so that they seemed to boil like cauldrons. Men and boys swarmed all over the place, some helping themselves to silver candlesticks.

In the mêlée, no one noticed Aurelia shouting at them, 'We must find Momo! He's trapped here, somewhere, *suffering*.'

No one was interested in Aurelia Bon or what she had to say any more.

Except one person.

Aurelia ran through chambers tumbling with faded frescos of cherubs. She paused momentarily in each to listen for the weeping boy. She plunged back down the stairs, wrenching open cupboard doors, calling out for him, lifting the lids of all the many carved coffers that were large enough to hold a person of her own dimensions. A stitch clanged sickly in her left side. But she still had the luxury of breath; if she stopped looking, the boy Momo soon might not. She was bent over another coffer, discovering her own pale face in a surprise of tarnished mirror under the lid. Her dark hair and eyelashes were painted silver with cobwebs; her nose, hands and tongue wore grey gloves of dust.

She was deep in the sight of her own frightened eyes when a blow between the shoulder blades sent her skimming across the flagstones. She lay on her belly, gasping, unable to move. Light footsteps pattered behind her, dragging something.

A dark weight slithered over her, the light suddenly filtered through a tracery of stitched flowers.

A tapestry. But why did it smell – how could it? – of frankincense and honey?

Then the kicking started. Struggling to crawl away, Aurelia was instead rolled around inside the tapestry until she was completely enveloped by the canvas. Then she felt herself lifted up – hard hands seeming almost greedy on her bruising. She heard the grunt of the man who had to bear her slight weight and that of the tapestry's freight of thread and dust.

A few lurches later, Aurelia was airborne. She landed painfully, grazing her elbows on ridges of wood that rocked on the seethe and suck of water.

I'm in a boat! Whose boat?

A heavy snake of rope thumped down beside her and then came a shove, cleaving the boat from the *fondamenta.*

The only person who knows where I am is the one who's doing this to me.

That's him stepping into the boat now.

Then came a sudden loud splashing and some coarse girlish voices shouting, 'Avast ye! Dat ain't in no way right. Yoiks! Dat man be worser 'n' a Barbary pirate.'

The man did not react. It was as if he did not even hear them.

Instead he began to heap something on top of her – wet sacks, Aurelia guessed, from the weight of them. She felt the air being crushed from her lungs. It was *her* tight belly, *her* dry mouth now. Someone not too spry, began to row, groaning quietly with the effort.

Aurelia opened her mouth to scream. But as she did so, something hard and heavy thumped down on the tapestry just where her head was.

10

Graveyards, Sewers & Places Where Waters Meet

'Someone's touching my castle!' I cry, pressing my pretty nose against a window for a better look at this outrage. 'How dare she? Some Venetian bint! She must be a *sehura*, a sorceress. Telling the secrets of my beautiful castle to the Venetians – who are fortunately too foolish to understand them!'

Then I hear someone call the bint by her name: 'Aurelia Bon'.

That name tolls in my heart like a bell. To mask my unravelling, I try to joke. 'If she's even twelve years old, I'd be surprised. A tiny bonbon of a thing! See what I did there?'

My cat, Musipul, strokes her moon-white *vibrissae*. They're not mere whiskers. I should mention that Musipul is a leopardess. Like most cats, she lacks a sense of humour, and all my marvellous wit's wasted upon her. She's also an Afreet, one of the most atrocious kinds of spirit (though may she never hear me so say, as even I am a little afraid of her).

Musipul remarks, 'Yet the Venetian girl is attractive. By which I mean, she looks quite like a cat.'

If Musipul is an Afreet, what am I? Obviously, you're craving to know.

I'm everyone's beautiful dream; sometimes also everyone's worst nightmare – an Arabian Djinniya. (That's a single female of my race. A male is called a 'Djinni'. If you're speaking of a number of us, we're called 'Djinn')

And there are thirty-one kinds of Djinn. Special as I am, I've a bit of all of them in me. For example, I dance as sinuously as a Si'lat; I'm as unruly as a Marid; I have donkey feet like Gul; like a Nasnas, I've a superb talent for enthralling humans.

The Divine Being, may He live forever, created Djinnkind just as He made you humans. It would be a bad mistake to treat me as if I were just a metaphor! You humans were fashioned from dirt, the Angels from light and we Djinn from smokeless fire. Like you dirt-persons, we Djinn have thoughts and passions and free will. So we can choose to be bad or good. Like you, we are judged at the end of our lives. If we don't go to Heaven, we are firewood in Hell.

I myself have become one of those Djinn who believe that Djinnkind were invented to make Humanfolk tremble. And we Djinn have special ways of doing that.

How do we do it? We haunt you dirt-persons *from the inside.* We can slip into your mouths like a breath. Then there's no limit to our power over you. That's why people say of a victim, 'He's *wearing* a Djinni.' We become part of you, like a second clutch of heart-and-brain. We light up something behind your eyes and set a silver glow about your skin – yet it's subtle, not so bright that your loved ones notice something is wrong or different, except sometimes at night. But rarely even then. (I find dirt-persons wonderfully and usefully unobservant.)

You may believe you're happy, think you're in Heaven, and then a Djinni or a Djinniya can enter your happiness and kick it down to Hell. We will scare the hairs off your arms. We can make you kill the person you love most; even your own child. Dirt-persons therefore rightfully fear Djinn. They should be even more afraid of a female like myself. As we say in my country, we ladies are smoother than a breeze and faster than fate, especially when we want to get inside someone.

Places of filth are our favourite lairs for hunting humans. We haunt chamber pots and unscrubbed bathtubs. We're partial to sewers, wells, caves and places where waters meet. If you want to avoid the attention of a Djinniya, you must say '*bismillah*' – 'please' – and say it *nicely* before you eat or go to the necessary room. If you're so disrespectful as to take a Holy book into that room with you, we're practically authorised to jump inside you. We like graveyards too – anyone who steps carelessly on a tomb had better watch out. And if you go walking in the night on your own when you really should not . . . that's when Djinn are quite likely to rise from the earth and slip into your body.

Djinn can also fall in love with humans, dirt-persons though you be. This is a danger for women who look too beautiful or for men who are too handsome for their own good. Djinnkind may fall in love faster than your Romeo and Juliet and feel jealousy more fiery than Othello's.

Once I've been inside someone, I can, if I choose, *always* be inside them. Annoyingly, other Djinn can get into the same dirt-person's body. I once occupied a boy with thirty-two Djinn already crowded inside. The bickering was terrible. I quickly got out. Like my Djinn brethren, I usually leave through the fingertips or the toes.

Some humans try to expel Djinn by having a holy and learned sheik say the Ninety-Nine Most Beautiful Names of God to the dirt-person who's possessed. Or by having the sheik read the Verse of the Throne from the Qur'an. Once I too was a pious and good Djinniya who always respected those sacred words. Hearing them, I departed obediently from whatever dirt-person was wearing me.

I'm no longer that kind of Djinniya. Musipul says that these days my only religion is the worship of my own face. Only this morning, the pompous cat sighed dramatically, saying, 'Our Arabian lands have produced the most sophisticated science, mathematics, poetry, art and music. We invented geometry, astronomy, windmills, all manner of marvels! Yet, you make it seem as if our female creatures were born only to gaze in the mirror and eat sweets. You betray our magnificent ancient culture. Badly done, Ghazalah. Badly done.'

So there you have it now – my name. 'Ghazalah' means 'female gazelle'. And yes, you must have guessed it. When I take human form, I'm as beautiful as a gazelle. The expression in my green eyes is as melting as honey. You never saw eyelashes as long or lush. I'm so beautiful that if I allow any mortal boy to see me, he's generally struck dumb and starts to drool and drop things. I've heard myself described (notably by my Uncle Nusrat the Gul – may his knees knock forever) as a greedy, ignorant little Djinniya. (Might I ask, *whose fault* is it that I was trapped in an amethyst flask when I could have been getting an education?)

But irregardless of Uncle Nusrat's carping, I'm always *gameela*, beautiful.

My attention is drawn back to the outrage outside my courtyard. I stare at the girl's face – the lively brown eyes, the mess of dark hair in extravagant curls, the large and shapely nose.

The bint doesn't just bear his name. In those eyes, that hair and most of all that nose, she exactly resembles the creature – may his liver be continually torn by vultures – who was my weakness, my downfall, my reason for being trapped in this rotten, misbegotten city.

Several sad centuries ago, it was my misfortune to lose my heart. The person who stole it was Aurelio Bon – may curses rattle his bones – a young merchant of Venetian mirrors.

Although but seventeen, he'd already won fame both for his gift for languages and for his daring magnificent trades. He was visiting the Castle of Jabrin – my home – to parley with the imam for permission to sell his shimmering wares to the folk of Nizwa. This was not long after the Portuguese had invaded my land in 1507, massacring Arabian people and cutting off noses. *This*, the Portuguese did while pretending that they were a cultured nation coming to 'civilise' the people of my country and my faith. A few dirt-persons fought back, even nailing one Portuguese soldier to our castle wall – because no country actually *owns* behaving horribly, does it?

We Djinn didn't like being colonised any more than the dirt-persons did. But we had little power against the Portuguese, who did not believe in us. So we avoided them.

Venetians, however, ah, that was another matter. When they came to my country, it was not to invade or to change our religion, but to trade. That's what they're like – great merchants and travellers. Who doesn't know what they say of themselves? 'First Venetians, then Christians.' Meanwhile, it's common knowledge Venetians are easily tempted by something beautiful.

So, it turned out, was I.

It started when Aurelio Bon released me from the jewelled perfume flask where I'd been bound a hundred years for a *tiny* misdemeanour, a petulant and too-careless spell gone wrong, surely not bad enough to justify locking up a lively young Djinniya who was just starting to taste life.

While other young Djinn were learning who they were, how to be and how to live with other beings, I was trapped and alone. While the other youngsters were playing, studying and honing their spell skills, I sat solitary, waiting. While they were exploring all the exciting worlds at their disposal, I had nothing to think about but myself. While my fellow junior Djinn were discovering the subtle arts of flirting, I had no one to look at – and there was no one to look at me.

In those long years inside the flask, my feelings and frustrations welled up, so there was bound to be trouble when I was finally set free. I had too much to give and too much to take from these worlds, because I'd been prevented from giving and taking for far too long.

I threw all of it into the first being I saw.

I picture him now: Aurelio Bon, his life about to be changed by the curiosity and impatience of youth. Left to wait for the imam in an antechamber, he spied my amethyst prison on a high shelf. Being a merchant and the son and grandson of merchants, he immediately lifted the lid for an appraising sniff. I sprang out, shaking the dust and boredom of centuries out of my hair, ready for anything. I took one look at Aurelio Bon and decided to appear to him in human form. I had absolutely no desire to protect that boy from my beauty.

Aurelio Bon! Those dark eyes! Those cheekbones! And most of all, his large shapely *masterpiece* of a nose! That nose made me remember that I had a heart in my breast. Not only did I have a heart, but it was a vast ferocious organ, beating like the sun on the Sahara. That heart had gone hungry for decades. Now it was starving for attention, for life, for sunlight, for the scent of roses, and for the taste of Turkish delight, *halva* and cardamom pudding with camel butter. Above everything else, I needed someone to look at me, to admire me and to tell me that they did.

The young fellow himself was mightily surprised to see me. Of course, he already spoke beautiful Arabic, for negotiating with our peoples was a tool of his trade. And he knew exactly what manner of being I was, addressing me with respect and an adorably formal vocabulary. He was obviously turning over in his pretty head that infidel idea, a twisting of some old tale, that we Djinn must grant three wishes to anyone who liberates us from confinement. This is, of course, a far too literal and crass interpretation of the mystical powers of Djinnkind, even though highly convenient for those foreigners who believe that those of our faith are savage and backward and therefore somehow *improved* by obeying them and even privileged to do so. However, the fact is that we Djinn were not put in this world to serve dirt-persons.

Sometimes, Djinn *do* appear to grant a human a wish or two. But that's just us being tricksome, as usual. In fact, we often just facilitate things that the dirt-persons themselves can make happen. Sometimes, Djinn *prefer* to let the dirt-persons persist in their delusion about the three wishes, because it makes them weak and foolish with greed. And that's a state we can take advantage of. The Djinn Djoke is on the dirt-persons. (Did you see what I did there?)

Dirt-persons often make ridiculous demands: immortality and everlasting love. Only the Divine Being, bless His name, can grant you those things. To use a Djinn to supply them is simply not godly work. Anyone of true faith knows that only evil humans would *want* to use supernatural powers or sorcery to achieve their desires. So most Djinn are experts at frustrating greedy dirt-persons with bewildering wordery. This not only punishes them for wanting what they don't deserve, but it makes them feel bad about themselves, for they generally believe it's their own fault that their wishes are never granted.

Handsome Aurelio Bon was only human. So of course he believed he could profit from the surprising situation in which he'd found himself. But he *was* cleverer than most dirt-persons. Instead of demanding the usual wishes, he now asked in his beautiful voice if I would allow him to think about what he might request. As his eyes met mine again, I almost fainted with delight. Just to be looked at again – it was almost more thrilling than I could bear.

Soon he began with the wishes. Clever as he was, Aurelio Bon was no match for me. Despite being a century out of practice, it was easy for me to twist his wish-words, and trip up his tongue. He was left with an apple, a toy sword and a small bag of rice – I don't even remember what he actually wished for! The main thing was that he was then at my mercy, sick with self-disgust at what he believed to be his own stupidity.

Yet even then I did not leap inside him – because what I wanted was for *him* to keep looking at me, talking to me. Even now, more than two hundred years later, I remember him standing in a shaft of sunlight, with the sun making gold threads of the fine dark hairs on his arms, his eyes fixed on me in astonishment – on *me*, who'd been looked at for centuries by precisely no one. My skin still rusts with the memory of that moment.

Then I danced for him, my skin thrumming with the joy of its release from the amethyst flask. I treated him to the *Raqs Sharqi*, the loveliest of our dances, all the while singing the most melodious songs of our peerless poet Imru' al-Qais. While I danced, the walls grew starry with pinpoints of light from my hip-belt's crystal drops, beads, sequins and gold coins. I performed all the many shimmies I could remember. I clicked my fingers. I turned my limbs into fluttering leaves. With my fiery hot hands, I tickled unseen kittens, patted invisible butterflies, released imaginary doves.

It didn't work.

Aurelio Bon turned his warm brown eyes away from me, which felt to me like the sun being extinguished over the whole world. His face reddened with shame. In the tender tone of a prayer, he uttered a name: 'Silvia'. I helped myself to the image inside his head. It was of a dark-haired Venetian girl with an eager, lively – perhaps even slightly wilful – face and a golden ring on her finger. I saw her wink naughtily at Aurelio Bon. Behind that bint – far too evidently his betrothed – lay his miserable hometown all a-glimmer, a clutch of towers and palaces lying on a silky shawl of sparkling water. Aurelio Bon made to leave the room. I blocked his path. We Djinn are far faster and stronger than dirt-persons. I had that advantage over him, but I could not stop his mind's eye from abandoning me. Even as I put my burning hands to his face, forcing him to gaze into my own incomparable green eyes, he was still thinking only of *her*, and of Venice.

I let my hands drop to my sides. Aurelio Bon left me abruptly. The next day I saw his camels ready for departure, their saddlebags bulging with goods exchanged for his mirrors. I'll always regret that I did not rifle those saddlebags when I had a chance. Meanwhile, almost the entire household of dirt-persons – the sheik, scholars, ambassadors and servants – had taken themselves out into the courtyard to bid farewell to the famous young Venetian.

The only creatures still indoors were my Uncle Nusrat, the astronomer, at work on a scientific tract, and a dozen servants preparing some trays of *baklava*. And there was Musipul, the leopardess, curled up on her cushion after delivering a searing lecture that ended with, 'It's only a *crush*. Nothing but a crazy girlish crush. You're just desperate for attention from the first creature you laid eyes on when you escaped the flask. You've tried your first little *flirt*. You've had your first rejection. You're not in love. You're in love with the idea of being in love! *Real* love is when you want the best for someone. If you really loved him, you'd just let the Venetian go, Ghazalah.'

It was not in me to let him go. As a smiling Aurelio Bon mounted his camel, I made to leap inside his body through those shapely lips of his. But it was lamentably too late. Something had changed in me. My spirit of fire, which should be free to take any form, had suddenly solidified in the shape of a human girl. This was possible because I had an upset stomach from too much rose petal Turkish delight and too much *halva* . . . After all those centuries of deprivation, it's easy to understand that I was in need of sweet consolations, is it not? And to be *painfully* honest, it was also because my magic was always a little . . . oopsical, even before the flask. That's not to say my magic isn't wonderful. It's like a diamond with a little flaw that makes it even more scintillating in certain lights.

Scintillating as it is, because of that beautiful, terrible boy Aurelio Bon – and my too sudden, too desperate need for his attention – everything now went horribly and tragically wrong. Anyone who knows anything about Djinnkind knows that it's one of our powers to cover enormous distances in an eyeblink. In my disordered state, that worked against me.

So instead of *me* jumping into Aurelio Bon, my Castle of Jabrin somehow leapt inside Aurelio Bon's palace, thousands of miles away in Venice.

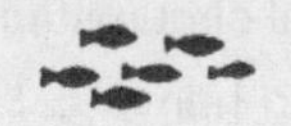

So here I am, and this is how it works. On the outside, the gaunt old Palazzo Bon still looms over the graveyard and canal as it always did. And indeed, any ordinary Venetian dirt-person or rat who enters will see nothing out of order in the *palazzo*. It's as grand and gloomy as it ever was, filled with tapestries and dust and Aurelio Bon's mirrors, now tarnished and unreliable.

But in a different dimension of time and possibility – the one that I inhabit – the interior of the Palazzo Bon now imprisons the magnificent Castle of Jabrin's soaring terracotta walls, date stores, carpets and living beings . . . including myself.

Unwillingly transported along with my castle, I was forced to watch Aurelio Bon arrive back in Venice some two months later by the slow, human means of his ship. By that time, I was fluent in his own native tongue, ready to dance for him all over again. Alas, I saw the joy on his face as he greeted his bride-to-be, Silvia.

Then he presented her with a swan-necked Arabian tear-catcher. 'But *you*, dearest,' he told her, 'shall not need to measure your tears at my absences. That was my last trip to Arabia. My brothers shall undertake those journeys from now on. I've done everything in my life too young. Now I wish to slow down and let the world catch up with me.'

I was forced to endure Aurelio Bon's happy life with his Venetian wife and children.

The loneliness was lamentable, all too much like living in the amethyst flask. And I never had a second chance to dance for Aurelio Bon. Under normal circumstances, I can choose whether to be visible or invisible to humans. I like being visible because then I can see my effect on dirt-persons. Yet somehow, in Venice – may this city sink and splutter to death in her own mud – I was invisible, un-hearable and unfeel-able to Aurelio Bon.

Like many too handsome people, Aurelio Bon did not make old bones. Even while I mourned him, I was obscurely happy that he did not live long enough to see his grandchildren. It would have made me feel old, whereas usually I just feel eternal.

With Aurelio Bon dead, I was flooded with desire to return to the beautiful land where I was made, to live again in a place where the sun sparkles through a whole town, where airy terracotta halls are hung with exquisite rugs, where scholars quietly bend over great works, and where dignified ambassadors come to parley with wise sheiks. I missed the sophistication, the civility of life in my old home. I craved the sight of date palms and graceful minarets scribbling their shadows on clean white sand. I longed for the solemn music of the call to prayer sailing through a high sapphire sky.

Time to leave, I told myself. I went to look on certain high shelves in the antechamber where I myself had once languished in an amethyst flask.

The shelves were empty.

It was then that I realized that the Venetian merchant, while still in Nizwa, had stolen not only my heart but also seven young Djinn who'd been maturing in terracotta urns on the same shelf as my amethyst flask. Before he left Nizwa, the Venetian must have gone back to the room where he'd found me. He must have guessed what those urns contained. So he'd seized them and hidden them in his camels' saddlebags, no doubt thinking that he'd be more skilful with the Djinn inside those urns than he'd been with me.

You may ask why this pirate act of Aurelio Bon's was so heinous and so hurtful to me. I'll tell you before Musipul does. The dreadful truth is that, my own magic being just a little lacking, I knew I'd need the help of those young Djinn to scoop the Castle of Jabrin out of this miserable *palazzo* and transport it back to the glorious desert of Nizwa.

So where did Aurelio Bon hide my little Djinn? I've turned this building upside down hunting for them. I've spent days, nights and years looking for them in coffers, cupboards, drains. I've scorched fireplaces and chimneys with my hot breath, hoping to dislodge jars tucked away. I never find them. The frustration is enough to tear my heart in half and make me weep. Sometimes I sing my sadness, just to let it out.

Meanwhile, I don't lack entirely for company here. There's Musipul, if you can call her company, moody as she is. She has taught herself to play the drums and makes up mocking songs about me. She wraps her back legs round the antelope skin drum, cradling it between her front paws. She plays with little lilts of her great golden head and archings of her furry elbows, patting out the mighty heartbeats of homesickness. Other times, the drum chuckles softly as she skitters her paws over it, as if she were walking on water.

Then there are my servants – a dozen graceful tall men with black beards and elegant eyebrows. When they're offering their customary greeting to me, 'Madam, I live and breathe to serve your tiniest whim', they arch those eyebrows into delicate half-moons.

They are so subtle and so suave, my men, that I almost suspect them of *irony*. Musipul has noticed this too and has been unkind enough to observe, 'You see, *no one* takes you seriously!'

And finally there's also my difficult uncle. His name, 'Nusrat', means 'help', but he isn't much. Nusrat was once a respectable Djinni, a great scientist known for his marvellous astronomy, a discoverer and namer of the furthest stars. It was by accident that he became a Gul, the most unpopular kind of Djinn with dirt-persons, because Gul are creatures of the night.

All I'd wanted was for Uncle Nusrat to go down on his knees to serve me a rose jelly. This, to apologise for uttering the outrageous lie that I was . . . fat! Instead he told me, 'You eat more than a fire and you're heavier than a mountain.' I'd lost my temper, cast a childish, crooked spell and the lamentable consequence was that he became a Gul with a purple beard. And the even more lamentable consequence had of course been that Uncle Nusrat punished me by binding me in that amethyst flask.

Uncle Nusrat's still a marvellous astronomer, of course, but a Gul. A Gul who knows it's my fault that he is one. A Gul who isn't at all certain that I should be allowed to live outside my amethyst flask even now. A Gul who has his suspicions about exactly why we're all trapped here, frowning every time I assure him it was a Shaitan, one of the evil kinds of Djinn, who sent us to the Hell of Venice. A Gul who bears a grudge as sticky as date honey. A Gul who might take it into his head to bind me back into a flask at any moment. Hence the difficulty with Uncle Nusrat.

As an older male Gul with a long (now purple) beard, he takes it upon himself to scold me as if I were a schoolgirl, even though

I'm a great grown-up Djinniya of about three centuries – the same as approximately seventeen dirt-person years. Uncle Nusrat the Gul has tried to order me to stay indoors. 'I will not have you wreaking havoc in this city!' he says.

And indeed at first, I was helplessly confined in this place. I simply could not find a way between the walls of the Arabian and the Venetian palaces, not to mention the fact that I was constantly under Uncle Nusrat's mistrustful eye. But gradually he became lost in his great new work of mapping the stars in the Venetian heavens. He spends so much time between telescope and parchment that his vision is sometimes blurred. 'I must be getting old,' he says, rubbing his face.

It took some time and dozens of failed experiments before I found a grated round window loose in its stone frame in a storeroom. Through the holes and cracks, the damp smells of Venice were seeping in, which, I realised, meant that the smells of the Castle of Jabrin could get out. *If smells can get out, then so could I!* I worked hard to enchant, confuse and dazzle that window till it spun and floated out of its wall. I let my invisible spirit squeeze through the aperture from the Castle of Jabrin into the Palazzo Bon, and then out into this strange city.

Ever since then I've roamed Venice looking for my lost Djinn. Over the centuries, I've become methodical, taking one square after another. I rip up graveyards in case they are buried there. I look in forgotten niches and boat sheds, under bridges and inside mould-stinking attics.

All the while, I long for the spacious quiet of the desert! It disgusts me, this city of water flowing underfoot and now – for the last two months – beating down from the sky. The cursed rain! Even though I float just above the ground, my silk pantaloons are bedraggled. I cannot afford to sink into a puddle. I'm made of fire so my delicate hooves would sizzle and melt. I'd be left with mere stumps at the end of my beautifully hairy legs. I must carry a parasol and dodge between gables to make sure I don't dissolve. The persistent dripping drives me as deep into hate with this city as I was once in love with a Venetian. I loathe its every narrow street, its every looming palace, the dizzy loops of its endless canals, its pride!

My Djinn are nowhere to be found. I return home empty-handed each time. Then I roam around my castle, shaking my fist at the curtains if they so much dare to twitch in the wind. I am furious. Every so often the fire in me burns too hot I can no longer bear to live within my own skin. That's when I know that I need something, and that Venice is going to have to give it to me.

What's a Djinniya to do? What I need, more than *halva* or rose milk, is *attention*. I need to recreate that extraordinary moment when Aurelio Bon first released me from the amethyst flask; that moment when I was first free. And yes, that first moment of seeing the wonder in a boy's eyes. No wonder I've helped myself to a Venetian boy every five decades or so. It was as easy as knocking bottles off a wall. Young men the world over are careless and they're partial to creepsome places like ruins and graveyards. For dares, they will walk over the dead, climb forbidden walls, throw their little sisters' dolls down wells. Then they're mine. I've a right to them.

At first I hunted for young men who looked like my Aurelio Bon. I saw Venetians with the alluring jut of *his* jawline. I saw

Venetians with *his* dark curls pillowed on *his* cheekbones. I saw Venetians with my love's lively brown eyes, and his large and shapely nose.

But they were not him. They are never him. So I hate them all.

Which doesn't stop me taking them.

Musipul claims I don't even see my captures as living beings created by God, may he be exalted. 'They're merely "supply" to your ridiculous craving for attention,' she growls.

My conscience rests unpricked. It's true that, since I escaped from the amethyst flask, admiration and attention are like food. Every fifty or so years, I need another meal. It's also true that, since Aurelio Bon, all dirt-person boys are the same to me and once I have them in my grasp, I find they're not what I want at all.

Musipul snorts in her muzzle. Well, she can talk – she, a leopardess, and Afreet leopardess at that, is all excited about meeting a real *lion!* A Venetian lion. Painted on the wall of this palace.

'Why the frankincense can't I be friends with a lion?' argues Musipul. 'Just because he's a bit different from me. Does that mean that he's bad?'

'Enough about you,' I tell her.

Thanks to my habit of collecting young men, this *palazzo* has acquired an amusing nickname: 'The Palace that Eats Boys'. Once I even heard it described by a frightened dirt-person as 'The Palace where Boys Go to Die'.

'Died of joy!' I said proudly.

Yet Musipul, who specialises in saying inconvenient things, reminded me that in fact the fellows have not actually died.

'*Al'abalah!* Idiot! They're not dead! You have consigned them to the dead because you're not interested in them any more. In fact, you were never interested in them, not once you'd actually caught them.'

'We can hardly let them back out into the streets to tell tales on us. That could be dangerous for us all.'

'We? Us?' She flicked her tail with unmistakable sarcasm.

So presently five young men are living in different rooms of my castle. They're frozen at the age of seventeen or eighteen or however old they were when they arrived. They don't need to eat as they're under one of my more effective enchantments. Uncle Nusrat the Gul takes care of them like a father. He's taught them to play chess and instructed them in the names of all the stars in the one universe that dirt-persons know about.

Musipul grins, 'And what about the boy you lured in this last time? Are you going to stand there on your hooves and tell me that's not another fine example of exceptionally amateurish Djinnery?'

Her tail is twitching and her eyes are fixed on me, enjoying my discomfort. Nothing escapes that cat, may her Egyptian ancestors' mummies be ground up for medicine.

I hate to admit it but I've made a mistake. In the pouring rain that night, I didn't get a proper look at him. He was tall and gangly. In the dark, wet graveyard I mistook him for a young man. Lamentably, he's only a boy. His whimpering gets on my nerves (or what Musipul prefers to call my 'conscience'). He's not going to give me the rapt attention that I want, not when he's busy whining for his mother. He makes me feel like a cat playing with a rat it doesn't actually want to eat.

So I've locked him in an empty chamber on the first floor and have tried to forget about him. Why should I care? Uncle Nusrat probably gives him dates to eat.

For when he found out about the lamp-boy, Uncle Nusrat shouted, 'No more!' He lifted a skein of long hairs from his purple beard and tied a knot in it. My belly shrank in fear – because one knot is the beginning of a binding spell. A few more knots, and my fate will literally be sealed.

'I warned you!' he growled. Because there's also the small matter that I did slightly quite promise Uncle Nusrat fifty years ago, out of the goodness of my fiery heart, that there'd be no more wretched fellows for him to look after.

Now Musipul puts her head on one side and asks, 'So did you also take that surgeon all the Venetians are looking for? Have you secreted him in some cellar?'

'No!' I scream. 'That's a dirty slander.'

'Why the frankincense should I believe you? I'll find him soon. And then I'll tell your Uncle Nusrat. And there will be a scene that'll compare with the day you made an atrocious mess of jumping into Aurelio Bon which ended with us here. Your uncle will tie *all* the knots in his beard for a new binding spell, and that'll be the end of your mischiefs and sideshows.'

'Mischiefs and sideshows' reminds me of the Venetian bint – may she roast in a thousand infernos – who can somehow see the Castle of Jabrin inside Palazzo Bon, unlike any other dirt-person I've ever come across.

Again, I feel the Venetian girl's fingers on my walls. What's happening now? Stirred up by the Bon bint – may her skin dry up and fall off like a snake's – the crowd has broken down my gate and crashed into my courtyard. Look at those Venetians pouring in!

Of course they shall not find my castle. The ignorant rabble – apart from Aurelia Bon – simply does not have the eyes to see it. All they'll see is the ruined palace of Aurelio Bon, my cursed liberator, my handsome twisted bough of frankincense, my destiny and my enemy, my evergreen wound, the twisted pain of the story of my life.

But the little dark-haired bint – that's another matter.

She must have been delivered to me for a reason.

By his blood in her dirt-person's veins, *she* is marked out for my revenge.

11

Pain There Will Be

As far as she could make out in the dim light, Aurelia was lying on a table. Her arms, legs and neck were bound by leather straps. There was even one stretching between her lips, reeking of old meat and tasting horribly salty.

As her eyes became accustomed to the near dark, the next thing she saw was – books. Piles of books, everywhere. The table was in fact a plank resting on four columns of books. The bookshelves themselves were made of books. She tried to make out the titles on their spines. They all seemed to have something to do with history.

The rain beat down somewhere not far above her head. *I must be in an attic*, she thought, *to be so close to the sky. But whose attic?*

Over the rain came the sound of chains clanking. A man of middle years with a shackle on one leg approached, a forlorn expression on his face and a beaker in his hand. He tipped some sweet-tasting liquid round the edges of the leather strap and into Aurelia's mouth.

'*Malvasia* wine, watered,' he said. 'It will help.'

With his face so close to hers, Aurelia realised that she'd seen it before – printed on handbills around the town. *This* was the fashionable surgeon whose disappearance was the subject of so much speculation in the salons of Venice.

'What are you doing *here*?' she asked indistinctly, through the leather strap. 'Your family is so worried.'

Then, just behind the man's shoulder, the face of Simoneto Ghezzo swam into view.

At first Aurelia's heart lifted. The pathetic old man had been so nice to her at that dinner. *He must be here to rescue me!* she thought. Then her stomach clenched as she remembered how he'd betrayed her when things went wrong during the disastrous history-fingering at the Palazzo Bon. He'd watched her humiliation with pleasure in his grey eyes.

Aurelia's mind flickered back to the last things she could remember.

Her ancestral palace had been overrun by Venetians who mocked her description of an Arabian castle within its walls. They had insulted her, thrown a stone at her and then ignored her. She remembered trying to find the lamp-boy, Momo, starving to death in some hidden part of the *palazzo*.

I never found him, mourned Aurelia. *I failed him. I couldn't make the Venetians believe me. What's happened to him?*

Why and how had she come to be lying on this table, though? Was it Simoneto Ghezzo who'd thrown the tapestry on her and carried her into the boat? He was certainly at the scene and had shown himself her enemy.

How dare he?

Simoneto Ghezzo was a man who'd been *honoured* to sit next to her at dinner. He was lowborn, not to mention a failure as a historian.

In fact, he's low of stature in every way. He's barely half a man. A History Half-Man! With absolutely no right to lay a finger on me!

'Kindly untie me,' she mumbled through the leather strap in as lordly a tone as she could conjure.

But Simoneto Ghezzo was no longer humble and deferential, as he'd been at dinner. No, now he was swelled up with something – was it power? He seemed twice as substantial as before, towering over her. The surgeon was afraid of him – she could see that.

Should I be afraid too?

'Now,' Ghezzo said, 'let me tell you what I'm going to do to you, my little lady. First, may I introduce you to Dottor Fantin, who is here to enact my wishes? When I summoned him a few days ago, he thought he was coming to deal with my gout. He's known for his excellent work with hands and feet. He never expected to be my guest for so long. For a surgeon, he was easily tricked with drugged wine.'

'His absence hasn't gone unnoticed,' Aurelia struggled to speak clearly through the harness in her mouth. 'He has a desperate wife and frightened children. This is not—'

'The idiots who write the *avvisi* have linked his disappearance to the mystery of the lamp-boy. So they'll never suspect the truth. I'm the only man in Venice who knows that the two kidnappings have absolutely nothing to do with one another.'

Aurelia's eyes strayed over the piles of books once more. In a hot rush of indignation, she suddenly knew why Simoneto Ghezzo had betrayed her at the Palazzo Bon. All these volumes – *he* was the author of every single one. 'You bought your own books, didn't you?' she whispered. 'To make Remondini think that they were still selling well. But they weren't. And now you're angry with *me*, just because I am a success? It's not *my* fault that *you* are a failure.'

Aurelia was thinking like a child, the kind of child who insists everything must be fair. She was so intent on being right that she forgot the danger she was in. It was only when she felt Ghezzo's breath on her own face that her rage subsided into fear. As she watched his spiteful little mouth moving just a hand's span away from her own, her whole body clenched in horror.

When Ghezzo had finished describing what the surgeon would do to Aurelia, he stopped for a moment with his hand on his chest, as if the joyful beating of his heart couldn't be contained. His eyelids fluttered.

He's mad, thought Aurelia. *Completely mad. Dangerously mad.*

There was a glitter of triumph in those grey eyes.

The best thing, she told herself, *is to play along and act as if I believe he would really do the appalling thing he's describing.*

'Will there be pain, sir?' she asked humbly.

'How can the surgeon amputate without it?' asked the historian. 'Pain there shall be, little lady.'

For the first time in her life, Aurelia did not feel ashamed of the tears that pooled at the corners of her eyes. They spilled out, dripping on the floor.

Perhaps, thought Aurelia, *he'll think the better of this . . . savage . . . revenge, now he sees me terrified and humbled. Perhaps he'll pity me.*

He must have a heart.

Mustn't he?

12

A Sliver of Skin

'Stop snivelling,' ordered Simoneto Ghezzo. 'We're not going to cut your actual fingers off! Didn't you ever fall and scrape the skin off your hand? Did you carry on as if you were dying then? I want just a sliver of skin from each fingertip. So thin it'll be almost transparent, won't it?' He looked to the surgeon for confirmation, which was offered in the form of a melancholy bow. 'That's all. Is that too much to ask?'

Yes, thought Aurelia. *No decent person would ask that. But we're a long way from decency and sanity here. If I provoke him, he's capable of forcing the surgeon to amputate my hands entirely.*

Pins and needles stabbed her fingers. Suddenly, to Aurelia, they were not just famous but also precious. *I touch with them and I feel with them. They're connected to my heart and my mind. What will happen to me if he does this? Will my fingers become blind? Will I lose my sense of touch?*

'You don't have to do this, sir,' Aurelia pleaded. 'We could work together. I could tell you what my fingers show me, secretly, and then you could write it all up with *your name* on it. You're such a good writer. And of course, you're a *real* historian. You'd do it so much better than me. And you *know* my family have been trying to stop me publishing my work. They wanted me betrothed to—'

Even a future that included Marco Spatafora now seemed a better option than having her fingertips amputated.

Ghezzo stared at her in considering silence. Then hatred clawed control of his features once more. Aurelia said quickly, 'Of course, you don't need to decide this minute. And before anything, we *must* return to the Palazzo Bon. I fear the boy, Momo, hasn't much longer to live. You don't want his death on your conscience, surely?'

Ghezzo laughed bitterly. 'You don't care about the boy,' he said. 'You think that if you find him, you'll be some kind of heroine. You'll prove that you still have powers. Well, of course I know you do. But the whole of Venice stopped believing in you today.'

'Drink the wine, child,' said the surgeon, holding a cup to her lips. 'It will dull the pain. You cannot escape this any more than I can.'

She saw in his eyes both a kindness and a kind of cunning. He began to talk quietly to Simoneto Ghezzo. Like Aurelia, he adopted a respectful tone. 'No one has ever undertaken this kind of surgery before, sir. I cannot be sure about the grafting process, so I need to try one finger at a time. Also, I've heard that fame has turned this silly girl's head and that she has an unfortunate tendency to turn hysterical. That would make her blood flow too fast. If I attempt a whole set of fingers simultaneously, she might bleed to death before I've finished. In this damp weather, things . . . rot . . . at an exaggerated rate. So the vitality of the fingertips might be lost before I could graft them on your own. And of course I need time to prepare your *own* fingertips to receive the delicate new flesh.'

Simoneto Ghezzo grimaced at the mention of his own fingertips. It was a tiny consolation for Aurelia to know that to receive her stolen skin, he'd have to suffer his own being scraped off. 'Just one finger to start with,' he agreed grudgingly. 'But I can change my mind at any time, remember?'

He strapped Aurelia's hand to the table with an old leather belt. As he pushed her silver bracelet up her wrist, a new and unwelcome thought gripped Aurelia. She was too terrified to hold it in. 'What will happen to me . . . after? Will you let me go home?'

'Well that would hardly be safe, would it? You'll go whimpering to your parents and they'll fetch the *Signori di Notte*. Being a *proper* historian, I'm familiar with their work – things would doubtless get very tedious, and then quite painful for me.'

Aurelia pleaded, 'There are hardly any *Signori di Notte* now since *I Fedeli* soaked up their wages. And the few who are left are much too busy to be bothered . . .'

'. . . with one bleating girl, already proved a liar. True.'

'Will you . . . kill me when you're done . . . Is that what you're going to do?'

'I haven't decided what I'm going to do. A lot will depend on how much of my time you insist on wasting.' Ghezzo turned to the surgeon. 'Is there any reason why you can't start immediately, *Dottore*?'

'Forgive me, girl,' whispered the surgeon, bending over Aurelia with the beaker. 'Take a nice deep swallow. It'll help.'

Aurelia screamed as the knife approached her skin.

The rain outside seemed to beat down with special fervour just then, like a drum roll.

She felt the blade enter the tip of the middle finger of her left hand and fainted.

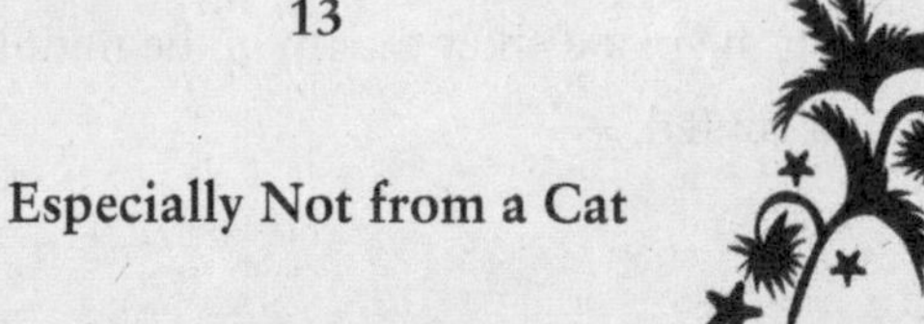

13

Especially Not from a Cat

After a battle of screams (mine) and snarls (hers) with Musipul, I've been obliged to storm out of the palace through my secret portal.

Not content with accusing me of stealing the Venetian surgeon, that cat – may mud clot the gloss of her fur – has blamed me for making the rain in Venice.

'Al'abalah!' she told me. 'You fool!'

The trouble is – Musipul's right. Somehow, she's guessed that yet another spell of mine went wrong. I was trying once more to extract the Castle of Jabrin from the clutches of Palazzo Bon, imagining into very life the wonderful scene of my sun-drenched home wrenching itself from the grey Venetian stones, floating into the air and riding a splendidly fluffy cloud south towards Arabia. But suddenly a nasty Venetian *scolopendra* – a scuttling insect with far too many legs – ran up my arm. The cloud in my vision broke in two. The castle plummeted back to earth. One busy moment later, it had embedded itself comfortably back inside the Palazzo Bon with a smug kind of clunk. Meanwhile, the cloud was fatally ruptured. And through this fissure in the heavens came rain, *matar*. *Matar matar matar* for months. A flouncing, foot-stamping, tantrum-spinning, headache-strumming kind of wet, wet, wet.

'*You* made that hole in the sky!' Musipul sneered. 'You made the *matar* fall through it. Your Uncle Nusrat—'

Uncle Nusrat the Gul is the last person I'd want to know about this little mistake. So far he's *almost* swallowed my story about the Shaitan bringing us to Venice. I've kept very quiet about Aurelio Bon and the theft of the seven Djinn in their terracotta urns. I've always told Uncle Nusrat that I *accidentally* charmed the young Venetians. Each time, I've pouted, saying, 'Oops! I'm a bit accident-prone when it comes to boys.'

'Bad choices,' he always growls, shaking his head. 'Bad choices and too much attention-seeking. A terrible combination.'

'Speaking of wanting too much, you could also eat less *baklava*,' Musipul put in. 'And fewer rice puddings. You eat so much *halva* you're giving *me* pimples. One day that ruby is going to pop right out of your navel.'

'You have to understand, all those centuries without a single sweet to eat . . .' I reminded her. 'Please keep it to yourself about the rain,' I begged, hating to lower myself to it. 'Remember the words of the wise – "A secret is like a dove; when it leaves your hand it takes wing".'

Then – may her moist nose dry up like the Sahara – Musipul told me that Uncle Nusrat cannot distract the lamp-boy from his longing for his mother. Games of chess won't do it. The boy does not want to look at the stars or learn the names of the planets. He's fading away. Musipul poked my belly with a paw, saying,

'Unlike you!' and returned to her taunts about the rain. It was all too much. I am a sensitive being with a broken heart. Musipul never takes that into account. Well, of course, she's an Afreet, and so devoid of softness or compassion.

'Where's this going, Musipul?' I yawned. 'I don't enjoy preaching, especially not from a cat, who has no business to teach me morals.'

Musipul, busy with her paintbrush, ignored me with that maddening superiority she shares with all felines. Having executed a fine portrait, I admit, of her friend the lion, she's now attracted the attention of a great horde of Venetian cats, all as vain as they can be – which is *very*. They want their portraits done. So a great line of them stretches outside the palace, all sitting on their haunches, preening.

Musipul claims that many of them are distant relatives. 'They're *Syrian* cats, originally imported to Venice during the Middle Ages to eat the rats aboard the trading galleys. The soft-as-butter Venetians took to cats, just as they take to every luxury. Now cats rule thousands of Venetian homes with thorny little fists in velvety gloves.'

I scolded Musipul, happy to have an opportunity for once. 'That queue of cats – it could draw attention to this castle, which is the last thing we want.'

'After all those boys!' Musipul retorted. 'How the frankincense can you complain about a few cats?'

It was at that point I stormed away, angry as ten Afreets.

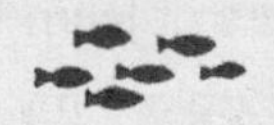

The slanty rain whips the canal water into serpent trails. The argument with Musipul is still stinging my brain. I don't want to go home. So I roam around Venice again, listening to the Venetians, looking for my Djinn in their terracotta urns. I jump into the bodies of several men, in the hope of hearing some conversation in a coffee house or a merchant's office that will reveal where those urns are.

I've checked every church, every bank, every place where Venetians keep the things they love or treasure. I've come up with nothing. The argument with Musipul has set my brain on fire. Out of the flames is smelted a shiny new idea. It occurs to me suddenly what the problem is: I'm thinking like a proud Arabian Djinniya. Instead, I should be thinking like a sneaksome Venetian merchant of tricky mirrors.

I say out loud, 'Maybe it will take a *Venetian* to work out where a Venetian has hidden something.'

I consider the young men Uncle Nusrat tends and teaches about the stars. Perhaps one of them might be persuaded to help? But astronomy isn't what I need. And those boys were foolish enough to fall into my hands. I want an ingenious Venetian slave to serve me and lead me to my Djinn, who are surely matured enough by now to be help me get my castle back to Nizwa.

Suddenly, it comes to me. I know exactly who'd serve my purpose and gratify my hatred of the Bon family all at the same time – the bint with the interesting fingers! The dark-haired bint with the large shapely nose; the bint who looks so much like the man whose attention I once craved! Perhaps his descendant can be of use, before I exact my revenge.

Those fingers of hers could surely find my stolen Djinn! Aurelia Bon might know something she doesn't even know she knows, deep in her core, flowing in the family blood in her veins. That blood could be spilled, a little, if necessary. All in all, this Aurelia Bon seems like a useful creature. I'll go and find her.

Yet now I remember that the pesky chit has disappeared. I myself saw the girl's capture during that lamentable hour when all kinds of unscrubbed Venetians surged into my castle. I saw her captor too, though I didn't hear his voice. An unpleasant-looking creature. I would know the man if I saw him again. And I would know how to handle him.

I begin to roam Venice with a new purpose instead of the usual hopeless misery. Looking for information about Aurelia Bon makes a welcome change. I jump in and out of bodies – senators, fishermen, gondoliers. Tedious stuff. Then I have a bit of luck. In a silk emporium in the Mercerie, I find a red-haired Venetian bint who's dreaming of a wedding dress to make every girl in Venice die of jealousy. I like her style! But she's also guilty of vainglorious thoughts, so I'm entitled to jump inside her. I slide in through her mouth, only to discover that this girl, Catarina, is the very sister of my quarry. She fingers the fabrics the way Aurelia Bon touches walls – with pleasure and desire. I hope Catarina's thoughts will lead me to her sister. But when Aurelia crosses Catarina's mind, she brushes the image away as if it were a stinging insect. Interesting. I never had a sister, yet I believe a disappeared one might make me wonder *just a little*.

Catarina thinks for a moment about a lowborn, ink-stained boy called Valerio Fialetti. This makes her toss her head. Apparently the urchin is a publisher's apprentice. And then I discover that he too is desperately looking for Aurelia Bon! Catarina's mind tells me that he sometimes works nearby, in a big bookshop known as 'Remondini's'. In my country, we say, '*If the wind blows, ride it.*' It's but a minute's work to find the shop, and the boy.

He's tall and slim, with brown hair and eyes as green as my own. He's not actually doing anything he shouldn't – nothing worse than burying his nose in a fat book. So it's slightly quite wrong of me to jump in anyway and make myself at home inside his body. I tell myself that he's *sure* to have done something wicked in the past. He's a boy, isn't he? *And anyway*, I chuckle to myself, *he's bound to be up to no good any minute now, with me inside him.*

Soon I'm learning everything that Valerio Fialetti knows and worries about. That's quick work as there's almost nothing in his head except thoughts of Aurelia Bon. It's as if the girl has done a Djinni on him!

Can't have any other dirt-persons noticing what's going on, so I don't turn the boy's eyes to boiling mercury or permit much of a glow to surround his body. Valerio Fialetti doesn't know he's wearing me, of course, so he lets his thoughts run freely. Dismal, they are. He's sombre to his core. He's remembering how he went to the door of Aurelia's home to ask for the bint, having heard of her painful disgrace at the Palazzo Bon. He wanted to console her. But the mother shook him off like a spider crawling up her arm. She said, 'She's taken advantage of the riot she provoked to run away. She can't be far. Hunger will soon drag her back. My daughter's not equipped to live away from luxury.'

Then the father appeared, looking at the boy with suspicion. Jabbing his finger in Valerio's chest, he snarled, 'We don't want the *Signori di Notte* embarrassing this family! Perhaps you're on her side, boy. Come to spy on us? You're mixing yourself with big trouble here.'

The boy's memory travels further back, and I see the angry face of Aurelia Bon herself in his mind's eye. She's speaking harshly to him. The insults are terrible! Yet what miracle of sweetness is this? He doesn't hate her! When he thinks of the bint, his heart softens and then tightens, beating faster, like I wish Aurelio Bon's heart had beaten for me.

The boy's thinking now. *Yes, she was cruel. But she lashed out because she was desperate. It was all coming to an end for her. A convent or a five year betrothal to an empty-headed noble boy. No one could envy her. And now she's gone. I can see why she would run away, but where would she go?*

These are the thoughts in Valerio's mind as he's hurrying through the rain towards an unpleasant task. It appears that he's going to see a man he dislikes to deliver bad news, an errand he dislikes too.

Ah, here we are. With reluctance clenching his belly, the boy batters at the door of a house that is more falling down than standing up.

A window is flung open upstairs. A petulant male voice floats down to us. 'What is it? I'm busy with important work!'

Ah, I think. *The boy, Valerio, has come to dun this buffoon for money. No wonder he's unhappy about it.*

The boy flinches. I see – he's afflicted by guilt, one of those useless emotions felt by some dirt-persons. This Valerio is no one, an errand boy, yet he presumes to be sorry for the pompous fellow upstairs? As is the habit of Djinn, I decide right then and there to put a bit of fire in the boy's belly and a zesty prod of fork in his tongue.

'Well?' the petulant voice upstairs urges. 'Out with it. My time is valuable. If it's the butcher's boy, then your account will be settled next week. If it's the wine merchant's boy, then it will be the week after. I'm due an enormous payment for the great success of my latest masterpiece!'

I laugh to myself. *Who's he fooling? And the shame of it; to leave the butcher and the wine merchant unpaid so that boys must batter at the door! He has no dignity left. Not a scrap of it. As we say in my country, you cannot fall out of a ditch.*

The boy and I crane his neck to see the face from which these commands came. But the pestiferous man does not oblige, keeping well back from the window.

The boy calls out, 'Sir, in fact it's Valerio Fialetti, from your publisher. So come down this instant!'

Good, I think, pleased to be the author of this little bit of impatience. *No more polite little gentleman!*

The old man's tone changes to a wheedling sort of politeness. 'Of course! I'll be right down.'

We hear muffled instructions, a slammed door, something clanking and then steps crackling down the stairs for a minute or two. Many groaning latches are pulled back.

Interesting, I think. *Why does the penniless old man need so many locks? What can a writer have to hide except a lot of dusty books?*

Valerio's shoulders tighten. I feel something uncomfortable there. He's a little afraid of this old crock. He fears the man may be mad and even dangerous. Irregardless, that shouldn't be enough to knock the courtesy out of this boy. So I push a wave of anger though his body till he shouts, 'Hurry up!'

'Coming! Coming!' says the man. 'As fast as history!' he jokes, pathetically.

He's a historian? I think. *History's about what's already happened – where's the interest in that? Anyway, dirt-person history is so dry and boring. This errand cannot be anything to do with me or the bint Aurelia.*

My lovely round belly suddenly utters a little groan. I realise that I'm positively weak with hunger. It has been *minutes* since I last had any *baklava*. I remember one of my servants was buttering a fresh tray of it when I left . . . My spirit leaps out of the boy's body and into that of a passing seagull. Whoosh! It's a ride I adore! And I don't have to teach a seagull bad manners! Seagulls are always fair game for Djinn. Thousands of them wear us, as you can see by their bold behaviour all over the world.

Hovering above, I watch as the boy Valerio, finally empty of me, wakes up as if from a dream, as my victims usually do. He rubs his face, stupefied, amazed and clearly not quite himself at all. He won't know himself for quite a while now. From this day forward, he will always have a bit of Djinniya inside him.

I ride the seagull back to my castle, only to find the *baklava* is burnt. I'm so unhappy that I eat it anyway. All the while Musipul stands there grim-faced. My irascible Uncle Nusrat is rampaging too. He's tied another knot in his purple beard! All this fuss because the lamp-boy, Momo, has fallen into a fever and might die. According to Musipul, it's my fault. And she's still demanding to know where the accursed surgeon is.

'You've got him stashed somewhere, haven't you?' she growls.

'Never been within spitting distance of that surgeon!' I protest. 'Not fair!'

I make faces behind her back as she pads off.

14

More Falling Down Than Standing Up

Valerio didn't want to be shut up alone with Simoneto Ghezzo. Nor, however, did he wish to deliver the blow outside on the doorstep, in earshot of the neighbours, shaming the old man even more. So he asked, 'May I come in, sir?' in a tone of respect. Inside his belly, however, Valerio felt a fierce desire to stand up to the pompous historian. Standing up for himself was not something he usually did, not even when Aurelia was being as arrogant as possible.

Little as he liked Simoneto Ghezzo, Valerio also hated today's mission. The publisher had sent him to inform the falling-down historian that, due to falling-down sales and mocking reviews, there would be no more Simoneto Ghezzo books coming out at Remondini. No writer could hear such news without deep pain and bitter humiliation. And to hear it from a mere apprentice? That was cruel of Giovanni Remondini, and Valerio knew it. Cowardly, too. Speaking of which, hadn't the publisher abandoned Aurelia and her mother to the mob when it turned ugly?

Aurelia! The mystery of her disappearance tormented Valerio afresh every time he thought of her – his thoughts barely left her.

He resented this unpleasant errand all the more because it tore him away from the search for her.

Grunting, Ghezzo allowed Valerio into a dusty hall where strips of faded wallpaper hung down in dishevelled curls. Before he shut the door, the historian shouted loud enough for the neighbours to hear, 'I suppose you've come to hurry me along with my latest great work? To tell me that Remondini has cleared his presses, waiting for the final pages of my manuscript?'

As the door closed, Valerio said bluntly, 'Sir, I've come to tell you that there's no hurry at all on your new book.'

From a satchel hanging over his shoulder, Valerio took out a thick pile of densely-written paper and laid it in the dust of the hall table. 'Here is your last manuscript. Remondini won't be printing it. Nor any more books of yours.'

Ghezzo was incredulous. 'What idiocy is this? No one knows Venice as well as I do. Every nook and cranny. Every hidden secret. This book reveals everything that could ever be known about the sinister Palazzo Bon.' His eyes narrowed. 'Is this because of that little drama queen, Aurelia Bon? Has she bankrupted Remondini? Am I paying for *her* disgrace here? Well, that's ironic.'

'Ironic?' The contempt in Ghezzo's voice fanned the flames of Valerio's own strange anger. He picked up the rejected manuscript and hurled it at the historian so hard that the old man staggered and fell headlong.

From the floor, Ghezzo moaned. 'How dare you? Have you gone mad, boy? Get out of my house.'

Perhaps Valerio *was* a little mad today. He could hardly contain the ferocity tingling under his skin or the confusion that blurred his thoughts. He hated this dank old house and now he had every excuse to leave it for ever. Yet somehow he did not want to go. His feet seemed to have aggressive ideas of their own. He jumped over the historian and ran down the hall, deeper into the building. Progress was impeded by piles of dusty books everywhere. They lurched from side to side in crooked columns. They were all Remondini editions of Ghezzo's work.

He's been buying his own books, Valerio realised, *to make his sales look better than they are. But he's too poor to buy enough of them to make a difference. The truth is that his sales must have dwindled only to the books he pays for himself. How pathetic is that?*

'Where do you think you're going?' demanded the old man, cradling his head. He struggled and failed to raise himself from the floor.

'I don't *know* where I'm going!' answered the boy. But even as he said the words, it came to Valerio that this dirty house was just about the only place in Venice that he had not yet scoured for Aurelia. Ghezzo was a pathetic specimen, but he loathed Aurelia. Had the failed historian gone mad with hatred? Would he dare to imprison a young noble girl? Would he do her harm?

I have to make sure he hasn't, Valerio told himself, opening a door.

He noted with distaste the remains of humble meals in the pit that served as a kitchen. He opened the door to the privy and then closed it again hurriedly. He checked cobwebbed cupboards and the void under the stairs where the mould feasted pungently on the walls.

He searched the first and second floors. He found nothing alive, except cockroaches. Finally he ascended to the third rickety floor, with the footsteps of the historian now spattering weakly behind him.

Simoneto Ghezzo, whining and panting, reached the third floor landing just as Valerio did. He pushed himself in front of Valerio and stood with his arms crossed. 'Oi! What the devil are you doing? Leave my house!' he ordered the boy. 'I shall send for the *Signori di Notte* to clap you in irons. This is trespassing. Perhaps even thieving. Maybe kidnap.'

All at once, Valerio knew. With that one word 'kidnap', Ghezzo had given himself away.

Valerio's green eyes shone like polished jade. He hissed, 'You *do* have her!'

Next thing, there was a cry and the sound of a body tumbling down the stairs.

15

Not an Unknown Boy

Aurelia had come out of her faint, still trembling, though not with pain. To be really honest, the pain was not even as a bad as the last time she grazed her hand shimmying down the wisteria vine outside her window.

The middle finger of her left hand was bandaged, with the linen looped and knotted around the silver bracelet on her wrist.

The surgeon was bending over her anxiously. 'I'm so sorry,' he kept saying. 'I had no choice.'

'I'll tell you about choices! You *chose* to be bossed around by a weasel like Simoneto Ghezzo.' Aurelia screamed at him. 'A pathetic old man like that? A maniac? You, an educated family man, would mutilate a *girl* because you're so afraid of *him*?'

In answer, the surgeon showed her his shackle. He pointed to a large key hanging from a hook on the door, just out of his reach. 'Could be to the door. Or it could be to my chains.'

'You know, if you undo these leather straps, I could get the key. Then I could also undo *your* shackles.'

The surgeon hesitated. 'What if Ghezzo comes in and catches us in the act? I fear that he doesn't quite believe me when I tell him that you need to be *alive* for the fingertip transplant to work.'

He pointed to a glass dish where a tiny filament of transparent skin was visible. 'I've preserved your fingertip – for the moment – in a salt solution purified with flakes of gold.'

Her stomach turned to see it. Aurelia cast her eyes around the room until they fell on one of Ghezzo's largest and heaviest books. It was as long as Aurelia's forearm and twice as thick. The surgeon's eyes followed her glance.

'Oh, I couldn't,' he said. 'I'm a doctor. I cannot hurt people. It goes against the oath all physicians take to never hurt anyone.'

'Then what did you do to me?'

'The madman told me that he'd starve me to death and then hurt my own children if I didn't do as he demanded.'

But the surgeon began to unbuckle Aurelia's straps. As soon as she was free, Aurelia leapt up and seized both the key and the heavy book, wincing as it came into contact with her damaged fingertip: fresh blood welled up through the bandage. The surgeon shot her a stricken look. He dabbed at the blood with a rag. Aurelia shrugged him off and tried to force the key into the padlock of the surgeon's shackle. It was far too big.

'Ghezzo must keep the key to your shackle in his pocket,' she told the surgeon.

The door's keyhole yielded. The door itself, however, proved to be firmly bolted from the outside. A glance out of the window showed Aurelia a five-storey drop from the attic room – not into the gentle water of a canal but on to the hard stones of an empty square. No one could survive such a jump.

So Aurelia and the surgeon settled down to wait, each holding a heavy volume of Simoneto Ghezzo's unwanted words.

Hours passed. Their bellies gurgled. They were both nodding with famished sleep when they heard light footsteps on the stairs, not Ghezzo's usual bumbling, heavy tread.

Simoneto Ghezzo thinks he's getting a new fingertip today! He's so happy that he's dancing, Aurelia thought.

Someone tried the door handle, but it spun uselessly. The door was still bolted.

Has he forgotten about his own bolt? Aurelia wondered. *Is he so far gone?*

Then she heard Ghezzo's steps, his voice shouting, 'Oi! What the—?' and an exchange of threats or insults – she could not make out which. The second voice seemed younger. Through the thick door, Aurelia could not make out if it belonged to a child or an older woman. Then came a scuffle, a shout and a tumbling noise.

The bolt groaned open. Positioning herself behind the door, Aurelia raised her book. As the door swung inwards, she struck blindly. The intruder dropped heavily to the floor on his belly.

Aurelia approached her victim.

It was not Simoneto Ghezzo. That much was clear from his height and his brown hair. Her stomach panged, and she dropped the book.

'Who is it? Have you killed him?' asked the surgeon.

'I think that's for *you* to tell *me*, *Dottore*,' Aurelia said.

'It's a young boy,' he said, kneeling and beginning to turn him over. 'A poor unknown boy. What have you done, girl?'

'Not an unknown boy!' Aurelia cried. She'd just recognised his shoes and the cut of his worn jacket.

Valerio's face had no colour at all, except for a streak of blood running out of his parted lips.

My friend's lifeblood, running away, thought Aurelia. *I'd rather it were my own. Valerio does not deserve this.*

'I've just killed the one person I could trust,' she said wildly. 'The one person who has always believed in me and helped me. The fact that he's here shows that. He was obviously coming to rescue me.'

The surgeon said, 'Wait, child, you are noble, are you not? The consequences need not . . . it *could* be seen as an unfortunate mistake.'

'Because I'm noble, it's acceptable to kill a poor boy?' In a storm of grief, Aurelia pushed past the surgeon and ran through the open door. 'You don't understand,' she shouted over her shoulder. 'This boy is – was – far more noble than I'll ever be.'

'Stop!' the doctor shouted. 'I think—'

Aurelia sobbed, 'Nothing can make this better, ever again!' and ran down the stairs.

At the last landing, she stopped short. Below her the historian lay on his back, looking up at her, kicking his legs feebly. 'You've got me down, little lady, I'll give you that,' he wheezed. 'But I'll get you yet.'

Why had she killed Valerio and left Simoneto Ghezzo breathing? It was all wrong. Guilt tumbled through Aurelia's head, now enriched with memories of the too many times she'd interrupted Valerio and never let him make his point, never appreciated his truly fine sketches, never acknowledged how much he had contributed to her success.

Aurelia lifted her skirts and ran down the last flight of stairs, pausing at the third to last step to leap over the historian. His hands raked at her hem. She kicked them aside. The door was open, and she hurtled through it.

It was raining so hard that Aurelia allowed herself a few tears on the grounds that they were invisible and swept from her eyes as fast as they ventured out. She kept pounding the soaked streets until she got to the Misericordia, the northernmost tip of Venice, to the wall of the building known as the House of the Spirits, which jutted on a limb of green land into the lagoon. She'd literally run out of places to run.

What now? She could not go home. Her parents would march her straight to San Zaccaria.

I should really go to the Signori di Notte *myself,* she thought, *and report that I've murdered . . . a boy. And tell them what Simoneto Ghezzo tried to do to me.*

Aurelia leant against the wall of the House of the Spirits, just by the edge of the water. Absentmindedly, out of force of habit, she pressed her fingers against the bricks. As ever, a vision appeared promptly in her mind. This one was fully as strange as the Arabian castle inside 'The Palace that Eats Boys'.

Aurelia's fingers showed her an underground cavern half filled with water. The ceiling was gilded and vaulted like the Basilica di San Marco. The swooping walls were lit by sconces in the shapes of scallop shells that lifted a thousand winking candle flames into the darkness. Down in the water, graceful figures swam languidly. Female figures with long tousled hair, blue tails and lovely faces. From their rosy mouths, however, came unlikely swear words and rough curses. Someone shouted, 'Blood for breakfast!' Aurelia coughed; her nose had just filled with the fragrance of powerfully spiced food.

She told herself, *My fingers aren't working properly. It's the pain, the shock about . . .* she still could not allow herself to utter Valerio's name, even silently, inside her head.

I must go to the Signori di Notte, she told herself, turning to leave. *There's nothing else left do to. He . . . Valerio will not be an unknown boy in death, at least.*

But the rain had made the flagstones treacherous. Aurelia skidded helplessly. Before she could save herself, she was in the water, and something had taken hold of both her legs and was pulling her down into the dark blue depths.

16

Premature Coffin

Valerio woke to an excruciating pain in the back of his head.

'Who are you?' he asked the man who'd placed a cool wet rag on his forehead. 'Don't I know your face? Oh, my head aches! My eyes are blurry! What's happened to me?'

Valerio thought he could make out a shackle and the chain attached to the man's leg. What? He must be dreaming. And where was he? What was this room with dusty beams low overhead?

The man opened his mouth to answer. But at that moment an uneven dragging step on the stairs widened his eyes with fear. Valerio's vision misted over completely and he fell back into a half-faint. He thought he saw the historian, Simoneto Ghezzo, walking unsteadily through the door. The last thing he heard was Ghezzo asking, 'Is he still alive?'

'Y-e-e-es,' stammered the doctor. 'Severely concussed, however. He will be confused and have problems with both vision and memory for a while.'

'Excellent news. No one will take this boy seriously if he runs and blabs about what happened here. Now tend my leg. I think the boy broke it when he kicked it out from under me.'

Ghezzo sat heavily on a pile of books. The surgeon examined him carefully. 'No, not broken. A sprain to the ankle, which is of course as painful as a break. I'll bind it.'

'Did the boy see her?' Ghezzo asked.

'He never had a chance.'

'Even better. Can he walk?'

'Yes probably, but I wouldn't advise—'

'Good,' muttered Ghezzo. 'He'll lead me to her.'

Valerio felt himself pulled off the plank where he lay. Simoneto Ghezzo, limping, hustled him down the stairs and out into the street.

'Be off with you!' he said roughly.

What just happened in there? wondered Valerio. He stumbled through the slippery streets. They were familiar, yet in a distant way, as if they belonged to a parallel Venice, like the real one but not quite the same because it shimmered so. He felt strangely angry, dizzy and frightened.

He was also faintly aware of someone following him.

Who would care enough about me to do that? Valerio wondered.

Yet that question was simply too complicated for his throbbing head.

An hour later, Valerio still could not remember what he was supposed to be doing.

The sky was already darkening. Perhaps he should go back to the bookshop? Giovanni Remondini had asked him to do something, hadn't he? Had he done it? Then Valerio's mind returned to Aurelia, as it always did. When he thought of Aurelia, his mind was painfully pin-sharp. Poor girl, forced to spend the night alone out in the rainy streets. Was she hungry? Was she frightened? Where would she hide?

Of course she's not only hiding from her parents and that vixen of a sister, poor thing. She's also hiding from her shame about what happened at the Palazzo Bon.

He'd been in Bassano del Grappa that day, but the other apprentices had gossiped endlessly about the details of what went wrong with Aurelia's last history-fingering.

'So,' Valerio said aloud. 'The Palazzo Bon is the last place Aurelia was definitely seen. Perhaps she's holed up in there still! Why didn't I think of that before? Well, I suppose thinking isn't my best thing just now.'

He turned his steps towards San Severo, stopping every few yards to close his eyes in a vain effort to lessen the dizziness. Every time he paused, the footsteps behind him stopped also. But there was a wave of pain and sickness when he even thought of trying to turn his head quickly enough to catch sight of whomever was following.

The gate to the Palazzo Bon was still broken. Valerio hesitated in the street. This was after all the infamous 'Palace that Eats Boys'.

Perhaps, he thought, *this palace has also eaten a girl now?*

There was only one way to find out.

He paused inside the gate, listening for the sound of a girl sobbing. Of course he'd never seen Aurelia cry. He'd seen her distressed. Yet she was much too haughty to shed a tear in front of him. The apprentices had spoken with grudging admiration of how she'd stuck to her story at the history-fingering event and hadn't broken down even when someone in the crowd threw a stone at her.

A sound like ragged breathing, very close by, reminded Valerio that he was not alone. He tucked himself behind a swag of vines and waited to see if he was right.

Simoneto Ghezzo limped into view. At the sight of the historian, Valerio remembered his unpleasant mission. *I was at his house, wasn't I? When?*

Valerio blinked. Even that tiny movement of his features hurt his head horribly. 'What are you damned well doing here, Ghezzo?' he asked, surprised at the roughness of his own voice.

'The actual question is, what are *you* doing here? Why are you staring, boy?' said Ghezzo. 'I merely want to look around the Palazzo Bon, without the crowd, so I can add some more details to my masterpiece.'

Turning his back on Valerio, the historian whispered to himself. 'Would she come back here? Unlikely. The boy knows nothing. Unfortunate. Never fear, Simoneto Ghezzo has a plan. It will probably work out as I do have *one* safely extracted. And I *will* get more.'

'I don't know what you're talking about,' said Valerio. 'Why are you speaking of "Simoneto Ghezzo"? You *are* Simoneto Ghezzo.'

'None other.' Ghezzo smiled. Then his expression changed to one of wonder as he sniffed the air and stared over Valerio's head into the courtyard. 'The girl was right about this place; I'll give her that. I don't know why, on Palm Sunday, this place made it appear as if she were wrong about it. She's right again now and I suspect that on the whole she is always right, damn her. For yes, this time I see the painted date palms in the foreground of that painting of a lion. I smell the sweet decay of dates.'

Suddenly Valerio smelt them too. He pushed the gate wide open and slipped past Ghezzo. The courtyard was abloom with hibiscus flowers. Orange trees were heavy with fruit. Strangest of all – outside the gate, the rain continued to lash the street. But inside, not a drop fell from the sky and a hot sun beat down.

'Yet, dearsweetgod,' whispered Ghezzo, 'there's something amiss here.'

Something was creaking under the flagstones, which slowly shuddered apart to allow a large wooden box to rise up into the courtyard.

'A coffin!' said Valerio. It was closed, with a small brass plaque glinting on the top. He leant over it to read aloud,

'Simoneto Ghezzo
1710 – 1763'

The historian whispered, 'That is my birth year, 1710. And 1763 is this very year.'

As he spoke, the coffin lid began to raise itself very slowly. Ghezzo was breathing like a toad – his panic visible from his mouth to chest, pumping in and out. His pipe-thin legs trembled. The historian's hands were clenching, as if they were round the neck of a creature he wanted to kill.

He wants to see what's inside that coffin, thought Valerio. *And yet it's also the last thing he wants to see.*

The historian limped over to the coffin and thrust both hands into the narrow space that had opened under the lid. The lid promptly thumped down, trapping Ghezzo's fingers. He howled – a high hideous note of pure pain.

At first Valerio felt triumphant, as if someone had clapped him heartily between the shoulder blades. A moment later, pity swept through him, as it ould through the old kind Valerio. Little as he liked Simoneto Ghezzo, Valerio could not enjoy this horrible trick played on the old man. He put his hands round Ghezzo's wrists, tugging with all his might until the historian's fingers slipped free. The coffin snapped shut.

A change of mood came over Ghezzo. Tucking his reddened hands under his armpits, he drew himself up to his full height. Proudly, he told Valerio, 'People don't make coffin plaques for *forgotten* men. Nor fine brass plates like this one, inscribed in perfect letters by a consummate craftsman. This coffin proves my immortality.'

Valerio said, 'Immortals don't have coffins, I think you'll find. Only mortal men. Who have *died*.'

I could have said that more kindly, thought Valerio. *Why didn't I?*

Ghezzo scoffed. 'Death does not worry me, for my fame shall never perish. If I am to die this year, it will be after my greatest glory. This *proves* that Remondini *will* publish my book about this palace. So long as I have my greatest glory, I shall not miss this life. Or anyone in this world. And they have spelled my name correctly, as few do. I'll give them that.'

'There's no exact date of death, sir,' Valerio pointed out, but gently now. 'Just the year.'

'Surely my death date isn't today, when I've so much business to transact in order to *get* to my greatest glory?'

The flagstones were groaning again and something else was nudging up from below, that place where nothing should be. A great grey thing. A great slab of a thing.

It looked like . . . it was . . . a tombstone. And Ghezzo's name was on it, again, and those dates.

This time there was an inscription underneath.

Missed by no one, it said.

In smaller letters, it continued, *Except by the chocolatier in the Ruga Giuffa. And all the many others to whom he owed money.*

Valerio turned to the historian. Only the paleness of Ghezzo's face betrayed any reaction to the coffin and its words.

He just can't take it in, thought Valerio. *Nor could I, if it were me.*

Instead, the historian was wrinkling his nose. 'I smell a cat here! I loathe, despise and excoriate cats! They are parasites, every one, especially the Venetian cats, spoiled like noble children. Those striped Syrian cats are the worst. Smug beasts! I feel even the smallest Syrian kitten looks at me as if to say, "When you lie down I shall feast on your body. I won't wait till you're dead." Of course even a so-called "affectionate cat" loves its owner falling sick, so it can lie on his stricken body in bed and enjoy the warmth of the fever.'

From somewhere nearby came the sound not of a miaow but a growl.

Valerio pointed a shaking finger towards the shadows under

the arch of the great hallway. A vast, spotted cat stretched lazily, displaying its full length. Then it gathered its elegant limbs and began to lope towards them.

Ghezzo whispered, 'This is no kitten, I'll give it that. It's bigger than I am.'

And it was getting closer.

A female voice laughed, a musical trill of growls. The laugh – impossibly – seemed to come out of the leopard's mouth.

Then it said to Valerio, 'Get out! There are more dangerous predators than me here.' The leopard turned to the historian. 'As for you—'

'*Nice* kitty,' crooned Ghezzo, with his head on one side.

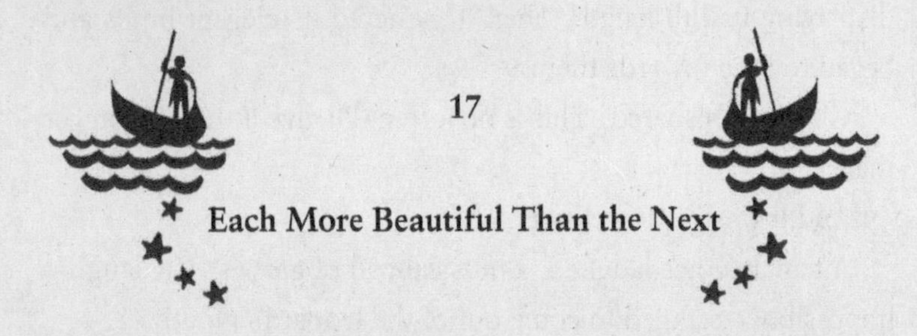

17

Each More Beautiful Than the Next

Amid the swirl of her own petticoats and the froth of the water, Aurelia thought she saw long hair trailing and opal blue tails coiling.

For a heartbeat, she was jerked back up to the surface of the water. 'Take yerself a deep breath!' commanded a girl's rough voice. 'Yoiks! A long slow one or ye'll choke.'

I know that voice, thought Aurelia. *I've heard it before.*

She remembered where and when: it was the moment that Simoneto Ghezzo had thrown her, wrapped in a tapestry, into a boat outside the Palazzo Bon. That voice had protested against her kidnap in no uncertain terms.

So it must belong to someone who's on my side.

Aurelia stopped struggling against the strong hands that held her.

'Dat's roight,' said the voice, 'breathe again. Deep as ye loik.'

But then she was dragged under water again, swiftly propelled along a dark passageway and finally pushed to the surface inside a vaulted cavern a-glitter with gold mosaics softly illuminated by candles – the very place she'd seen with her history fingers as she rested against the wall of the House of the Spirits.

Shivering, Aurelia spat out a mouthful of water and rubbed her eyes clear of salt. Then she saw them – ranks of tousle-haired mermaids with coral lips and eyes smooth-lidded like pale cowrie shells. Some were blonde; others were as dark-haired as Aurelia herself. One had a head of curls in a fierce and fiery red that suddenly reminded Aurelia of Catarina. Each sported a single gold hoop in one ear, and each was more beautiful than the next. None appeared more than sixteen years old.

Mermaids, of course, were part of Venetian legend, and sometimes even rumoured to exist. *How wonderful that they do!* thought Aurelia. Even in her fear and confusion, Aurelia was glad that Padre Pino, at the frightful dinner party, had been absolutely wrong to say that the apothecary – or was it an apprentice? – had mistaken a monk seal for a mermaid.

These ladies certainly were *not* monk seals, but were they a vision of some long ago past? Aurelia's next question was, *Have I been dragged through the water into another time? Will I ever be able to return to the present?*

Fear grabbed her shoulders and made them shake.

'Pore drowned rat of a maid she be!' the red-haired mermaid called, knitting strong brows. 'Look at dem gnashers on her, chattering loik a pirate's parrot. Let's be getting 'er dry!'

Gentle hands guided Aurelia to the edge of a pool and hoisted her on to a walkway beside it. A large cobwebby towel was thrust over the edge of the pool to the place where she sat shivering.

'Be wrapping yourself in that dried seaweed, maid,' suggested a voice that was more serious and more elegant than that of the red-haired mermaid. The blanket dried Aurelia's skin and clothes instantly, enveloping her in as much warmth as if she lay inside a delicate pocket of warm bread.

'Now,' said the serious mermaid, 'my name is Lussa, and I lead these taily ladies. Why be ye missing a sliver of fingertip?'

Aurelia looked down. Sure enough, the small pink wound on her left hand was visible because the bandage had slipped off her finger during the tumultuous journey to this cavern.

Why indeed? What have I to lose? she thought. The faces around her were kind and concerned. *And don't I need new friends? Because I've . . . lost . . . the only one I had.*

'It's quite a long story,' she said.

'Then let it begin at once.'

Aurelia told them everything – avoiding only the parts where she killed Valerio and failed to save Momo, both being simply too painful to share. Her account of her history fingers met with cries of 'Roight smart!' and 'Put dem cunning dooks up so we can see 'em with our own peepers!'

There were satisfying insults for Simoneto Ghezzo. 'Slicin' fingertips off little maids? Blood for breakfast!'; 'Only a *Half*-Man would be such a belly-crawlin' coward!'

For the first time, Aurelia had a respectful audience when she talked about the Castle of Jabrin somehow existing – sometimes – within the Palazzo Bon. The mermaids did not see anything impossible about it, once she'd explained her two history-fingerings there, and their very different results.

'The only question,' said Lussa, 'be *how* the multiplication of this palace did come to pass.'

'So you agree? I really was right all along!' Aurelia said. 'My history fingers did not fail. It was *everyone else* who was wrong on Palm Sunday!'

'Perhaps,' said Lussa mildly, 'there be in fact more than one way of being right.'

'Yes. I was right *both* times – when it was the Palazzo Bon and when it was . . . the other place, the Castle of Jabrin, it's called.'

But Aurelia's voice was hollow. Stronger than smugness was the pain of loss. What was the point of being right about something that was still mostly a mystery? And with whom was she going to share the triumph? *Valerio* would have known how to find out how two ancient buildings could – sometimes – be in the same place at different times. Valerio would not have rested till he'd uncovered the Castle of Jabrin's history. Somewhere, in the archives, Valerio might even have been able to find some old documents to show exactly how the Arabian castle came to be inside the Venetian palace.

'Why so sad and silent, maid?' Lussa asked.

Still Aurelia could not bear to tell the mermaids about Valerio. But this seemed the right moment to explain about the suffering lamp-boy trapped inside Palazzo Bon. There were cries of horror and alarm.

'Shame to leave a little Venetian stripling starvin' in a cell!'

The mermaids began to muse on the many delicious things that a boy like Momo would enjoy eating, all of them highly spiced.

Aurelia interrupted. 'Remember we have to get him out of there first.'

'Jest give us a "please", miss!' said the mermaid with violently red hair. 'Ye may be a noble, and decked out in silver bracelets, but ye ain't above manners! Plus, we don't be knowin' whether da stripling be in the Castle of Jabrin or Palazzo Bon at dis time.'

'Or both,' said Aurelia.

'Zackly! How can dis have come to pass? Did ye, wiv dem magical fingers, *summon* dat Arabian castle to Venice?'

'No! I just *saw* it.' Yet a disagreeable sense of guilt dragged at the space between her shoulders even as Aurelia protested. Perhaps her arrogance, her desire to show off the secrets of palaces, did in fact have something to do with the situation?

'Be charitable, Chissa,' Lussa urged the red-haired mermaid. 'And save your ire for our true enemies. I apologise for our language, my child. We learnt to speak Humantongue by eavesdropping on pirates. Our studies have tainted our vocabulary with a rude kind of poetry even while painting it more colourful.'

Pirates, thought Aurelia. *Why is everyone talking about pirates?*

As she spoke, Lussa took Aurelia's hand, first stroking on a red ointment that made the skin crackle and fizz but in a pleasant way, and then rebinding the finger with a webbing of dried seaweed that was even softer than the blanket.

'Fermented Chili Jelly,' explained Lussa. 'The skin will grow back over the wound and your hand shall be plenty pretty once more. This particular digit, however,' she said, pointing to the damaged finger, 'will no longer possess the handsome powers ye have just described.'

Well, thought Aurelia, *I was going to lose the use of my powers anyway – thanks to Padre Pino and the convent. Also, in the end that power has brought me only trouble and pain.* Then Aurelia's conscience jolted her out of self-pity. A flush heated her face. *Trouble and pain to me*, she thought, *but Valerio has lost so much more, and at my own hands.*

Lussa was gazing at her thoughtfully.

Mermaids, Aurelia thought, *are magical creatures. Much more magical than I ever was! Perhaps their magic can undo the harm I did?*

'Could . . . could you ladies,' Aurelia's voice vibrated tensely in her throat, 'bring back a boy from the dead? A boy murdered . . . by a book?'

Chissa said sharply, 'And wot boy be this? Dere be no such thing as a murdering book. Da person wot deploys da book be da *actual* murderer.'

Aurelia flinched. 'I mean a boy whose murder was carried out, *using* a book. Could you bring him back to life?'

'Yoiks, no, maid. Not if he be proper dead. We be magic. But not *that* magic.'

More gently, Lussa said, 'Even if we might wish to do so with all our hearts.'

A dark pain took hold of Aurelia's chest and pinched it with hard fingers. Chissa said, 'Only da one wot killed him might be able to bring back a dead boy. Sometimes it be done by da murderer saving another life.'

'Another life?' Aurelia thought of the lamp-boy starving in the Palazzo Bon. *Could I save Momo to get Valerio back?* Then she thought, *Not without help, I can't.*

'I'm afraid I've something else to explain,' she said. 'About . . . an . . . accident . . . and a boy—'

'Well stop drivelswiggin' and get on wiv it,' growled Chissa. 'Doan gabble, mind. Slow 'n' clear loik cucumber wine, even on the dingy doings. No matter how hard it be for a codswalloping commodity loik yerself.'

'No one,' whispered Aurelia after a short silence, 'has ever spoken to me quite like that before.'

''Bout time somebody did,' said Chissa.

18

The Water's Daughter

The mermaids listened with unreadable faces to Aurelia's faltering account of Valerio's demise. Then, without comment, they drew away and made a circle, their backs hunched against her. They began to talk rapidly in a language she could not understand.

After five minutes, the huddle broke up and the mermaids swam back to the ledge where Aurelia sat, swaddled in her towel and feeling as vulnerable as a baby. She braced herself for their anger.

'We have calkillated who ye really be,' said Chissa. There was something especially intent in her fiery gaze.

But I know who I am, thought Aurelia. *And I told them freely*.

'"The Water's Daughter",' said Lussa. 'That's who ye be. The Water's Daughter of our ancient prophecy. Which goes like this:

When falls hard rain that swells the water
that drowns the town that must be fought for,
then we shall need the Water's Daughter –'

The nape of Aurelia's neck had commenced to tingle at the word 'prophecy'. *Prophecies,* she thought, *usually involve threat and mayhem, don't they? And dreadful consequences for the whole world?*

She said aloud, 'I suppose *any* Venetian girl may be described as "The Water's Daughter".'

'Belay,' said Lussa, 'there be more . . .

With knowledge that her fingers taught her,
this haughty Daughter of the Water –'

It was Chissa's turn to interrupt. 'And ye be plenty haughty, girlie.'

'I'm not!'

'So wot else would ye call dat little grandeur situation ye've got going on there? Now did ye by chance have an ancestor in the looking glass bizness?'

Aurelia could only nod. Lussa put on her prophecy-telling voice again:

'This girl with gifts as well as hauteur,
the mirror merchant's daughters' daughter,
shall see the threat that's hid as naught
by folk who claw coins from the paupers –'

Chissa interrupted again. 'Be ye apprised, young Water's Daughter, of dem scoundrels wot claw the coins?'

'*I Fedeli,* I'm guessing. The taxes. The slave-ransom money.'

Nodding, Lussa continued,

'While Djinn and Duchess haunt these waters,
to steal our sons and steal our daughters,
some sell their souls and sell their city
without scruples, without pity –'

'What's a Djinn?' asked Aurelia.

'A Djinni – that be a single one – be a spirit made of smokeless fire,' said Lussa. 'The Djinn – that be the plural, confusinglike – come from Arabia, just like the castle ye beheld within the Palazzo Bon. So 'twould be no great astonishment were a Djinni to be mixed up in the present mysteries.'

'What's an Arabian Djinni doing in Venice? Stealing sons?' said Aurelia. 'That must mean Momo! And the other young men who disappeared near the Palazzo Bon!'

Lussa said, 'Allow me to finish.

A looking glass, the Water's Daughter,
who took her one friend to the slaughter –'

That's Valerio, thought Aurelia, in agony. *I slaughtered him.*

Lussa gave her a penetrating look, concluding,

'– this looking glass, the Water's Daughter,
must not quail, must not falter,
must parley with the blue-eyed marauder
and mend the past that stains these waters.'

'What blue-eyed marauder?' asked Aurelia. 'The Djinni? Or what was that before about a *Duchess* haunting these waters?'

Lussa said, 'About the Duchess, we must consult the turtle shell.'

A large empty turtle shell descended on a silvery rope from the ceiling. As it settled at mermaid eye level, its belly parts grew smooth and watery at the same time, like a mirror having a dizzy spell.

'Tell us,' Lussa commanded the turtle shell, 'of this Duchess.'

Words formed in the middle of the shell, red and staccato as if written in crackling flames: *The Irish Duchess is the most fearsome lady in Christendom. 'Twas Venice that made her so.*

'Quite the title,' said Aurelia. 'So *she's* the "blue-eyed marauder"? How could Venice make her *fearsome*? She's Irish and in Christendom, but is she in Venice?'

The turtle shell answered, though not exactly: '*If not now, soon. Be afraid, for she hates Venetians.*'

Aurelia shivered. 'We have to warn people. About *I Fedeli*. About the Djinni. And this blue-eyed Duchess too.'

'About *I Fedeli*, we have tried our best. But this pretty city remains stubbornly deaf to the warnings of the Seldom Seen Press,' said Lussa pointing to a little island – not much more than a rock – in the middle of their pool. Perched on the rock was an ornate jewel box of a machine constructed of oyster shells and fishbones and decorated with pearls. Bending over the machine was a mermaid in a black-stained smock. She cranked a bone handle and a sheet of paper slid out, dense with ink. The mermaid swam over to the walkway, holding the page aloft, and handed it to Aurelia.

Aurelia read aloud, '*Have a care, Venetians! Stop swallowing those gullet-gagging lies* I Fedeli *tell you. Don't believe that bunch of scuts! On a scale of whiffy to stinky,* I Fedeli *are a sewer.*

'*Put it in your mouth and taste the truth, if ye can't see it. Rancid as last week's fish. Pardon me while I spit. Meanwhile, there's a danger that ye rain-sodden citizens be too brain-drenched to see. Danger – I feel it in the lard of me belly and the hairs of me nose!*'

Aurelia said, 'I know this lettering! *You* print the words for Signor Rioba!'

'We do dat thing,' said Chissa proudly. 'Ruder than dirt he be, but he knows wot he be about when givin' it large 'bout *I Fedeli*.'

Staring hard at Aurelia, she added, 'Da Seldom Seen Press be a deadly secret, as be our very existence. Do ye promise not to blab our bizness to anyone? Do ye?'

'Of course! I would never tell.'

Silently, Aurelia wondered, *And who would I tell? What friend do I have in this world now, with Valerio gone? And who'd believe me anyway?*

'Good. Because ye have work to do now at the Castle of Jabrin. Or the Palazzo Bon. Ye must creep up on da Djinni wot is evidently in residence—'

'Why do I need to—?'

'Because,' said Lussa, 'we need some of his hair. With that, we can contrive a spell to bind him into a pot or a vase. Then, on a promise of freedom, we can mayhap persuade him to help us against whatever danger – the blue-eyed Duchess, for example – has brought our old prophecy into play just now.'

'And this time I'll find Momo too,' said Aurelia. 'And free him.'

Chissa scoffed. 'So full o' herself, dis girlie!'

But Lussa said, 'That would be to your credit, maid, as be the thought. However, I fear the stripling, Momo, be the Djinni's prisoner. The Djinni may not take kindly to ye carrying off the boy. Ye must take the utmost care, for Djinn can make themselves transparent and float above the ground to catch ye all unawares.'

'So what if the Djinni . . . detects me . . . before I can creep up on *him*?'

'Djinn be 'fraid of iron. Ye should shout "*hadeed*" – dere word for iron – when ye see 'im,' advised Chissa. 'Should scupper 'im prompt-like.'

'Why are Djinn afraid—?'

'Da tribe of Djinn has not blood but fire in dere veins. Iron can pierce skin. If it do, da Djinni's own flames will gush out and burn 'im to death.'

'*Hameed*,' Aurelia tried out the word. 'But how did *this* Djinni come to Venice? Why?'

'Not *hameed! Hadeed*, it be. Be ye so bilge at detail? We know not wot brought da Djinni here. Yet 'tis said that Djinnkind like wells, ruined houses and the junctures of streets, seas, rivers—'

'So this Djinni must *adore* Venice!' said Aurelia.

'So we must hope,' said Lussa. 'Especially if there be some Venice-hating Irish Duchess on her way here to harm us.'

Aurelia had a strong feeling that she'd not yet heard everything she needed to know about the Djinni at Palazzo Bon. And she was right. Chissa warned, 'Even if he loves Venice wiv all his fiery heart, ye must keep yer wits about ye with da Djinni. Monstrous cunning, Djinnkind can be, loik ten sharks pooling all dere cunningness together.'

Lussa said, 'Yet Djinnkind in general be creatures of good faith, living invisible and peaceful in a world parallel to this one. But just as in Humankind, there be some wicked Djinn who love mischief more than peace. Or who take it upon themselves to punish Humanfolk for their failings. Sometimes Djinn encourage Humanfolk to believe an old tale of three wishes granted to whoever lets them out of confinement. Then they trick the Humanfolk – whom they like to call "dirt-persons" – into wasting the wishes they *think* they have, which just gets the poor mortals into deeper trouble, at the same time revealing their deepest secret desires to the bad Djinn, who can then make use of them.'

Humanfolk like me, thought Aurelia. *How do I have the wits to deal with a Djinni? The cleverest person I've had to deal with until now is Catarina.*

'And when you return from your mission,' said Lussa, 'we shall contrive our Djinn-trap.'

'How does that work?' asked Aurelia. 'Haven't you just said they're tremendously cunning?'

Lussa said, 'We need a portrait of this Djinni, tied and bound, done with a brush made of the hair you shall bring back. That picture must be painted at the bottom of a bowl. By whom, I know not yet. Then we fill the bowl with water. Someone must drink the water and turn the bowl over . . . and then the power of the spirit shall be overturned and the Djinni must do our will.'

Valerio, of course, was wonderful at drawing, Aurelia thought. *But there is no more Valerio.*

'Finally, be warned, maid, that Djinn often keep dangerous pets,' said Lussa.

At this, the younger mermaids sighed deeply and clasped their pretty hands together as if in pleading prayer. Aurelia looked at them, mystified.

'Ah,' said Lussa. 'My sentimental ladies be always longing for a pet. It be a constant campaign with them. "Please let us have a canary! Why can't we have a canary? Or a newt? Ple-e-e-e-a-se." Wearying, it be. Now, one last thing.'

One more *last thing*, thought Aurelia. *It is already too much.*

Lussa's voice was tight with warning. 'At all costs, *do not let that Djinni get inside your body,* maid. Agree anything rather than permit that.'

'Get inside me?' Aurelia shuddered.

'Dat be wot da conniving ones do,' said Chissa. 'Dey jumps in through yer mouth or yer nose. From dat instant, ye becomes dere creature intirely. Dey whispers in yer brains to operate yer limbs and mouth.'

'No! How will I even know if that's happening?'

'Ye might feel something hot 'n' silky slippin' in. But then it's too late to stop 'im.'

'And then what?' cried Aurelia.

'Once da Djinni be installed, yer skin will shine wiv ghostlight and yer eyes will look like boiling balls o' mercury. Later, ye might succumb to sleepwalking or sleepless nights. Ye might start cryin' out in your sleep wiv nightmares about dogs, graveyards or blood. Ye may feel quivery as water, have headaches, lazy-hazy feelin's and fits. If ye was a nice person heretofore, ye'll suddenly become begrumpled, cold, rough, blamin' and cursin'. Even a small girlie like ye might become stronger 'n' fiercer than a lion. Ye'd probably develop a hate on soap and start to gravitate towards dirty wet places. Ye may start to hate da person ye once liked more 'n' anyone. Ye may see da head of an animal or a bird on dere shoulders.'

Finding herself on the edge of whimpering *Why me*?, Aurelia set her lips in a line and crossed her arms in front of her chest.

'Doan give me dat face!' growled Chissa. 'Ain't no line in the prophecy sayin' everything's s'posed to be easy as pea-pie for da Water's Daughter. Stand on dem lubbersome legs and go! Have ye no desire to save yer own city? Be ye built of milk-broth, girlie?'

'No!' Aurelia flushed.

Lussa held out a pair of green spectacles with dark lenses. 'I be no scholar in their great faith, but once I overheard a pirate swear that black glass works as *taweez* – an amulet – against the Djinn. Anyway, it surely cannot hurt to wear these inside the palace. Or the castle.'

Aurelia hooked the spectacles round her ears.

Through them, the world suddenly looked eerie, dark and dangerous.

And that, thought Aurelia, *is because it absolutely is.*

19

To the Palace of Her Ancestor

On her way east towards the Palazzo Bon, Aurelia helped herself to a news-sheet lying damply on the wet flagstones. Djinn-possession momentarily forgotten, she scanned the *avviso* anxiously for news of a dead apprentice from the House of Remondini. There was nothing.

Had Ghezzo disposed of Valerio's body in secret?

That's exactly what he would *do. Then he could also pretend that I was lying about being kidnapped.*

Of course Valerio had no family of his own to investigate his disappearance. Would Giovanni Remondini stir himself to look into a missing employee? Even one as talented as Valerio? Apprentices ran away all the time. They were known for it.

No one cares about Valerio, except me, Aurelia thought. *And how have I shown my caring? By piling a heap of insults on his head the last time I saw him, and then killing him with a blow to his head.*

There were, however, more mentions of the missing surgeon. His family was in despair, wondering if they should hold a funeral for him.

Poor man, she thought. *Poor family.*

She paused by a small shop that sold paper and ink. *There's one thing I can do, at least. I'll write a letter to the* Signori di Notte *and tell them where the surgeon is. Then they'll take care of Ghezzo too. And if they find Valerio's body, he can be buried properly. The surgeon will tell them what happened to me. He will explain it was all a horrible mistake. But I shall absolutely take the consequences . . . the punishment. I shall offer . . .*

Aurelia was not accustomed to carrying money; there was always a maid or a manservant with a purse for purchases. Now the man behind the counter gave her short shrift when she asked to 'borrow' some paper.

'Are you going to give it back when you've finished scribbling on it? Can you even write? A snivelling ragamuffin like you? Why the dark spectacles, anyway? Are you blind?'

Aurelia tore off the spectacles. Tucking them in her bodice, she glimpsed her reflection in the window. Her face was blotched with clenched-in tears. Her clothes, though dry now, had been reduced to a ragged state when she was dragged through the tunnel to the mermaid's cavern. Her hair hung in dark straggles. She did not any longer look like a pampered rich girl.

I've been too accustomed to being treated well because of being born noble. Valerio's probably had to deal with rough words like this every day of his life. Yet he never complained.

'Where did you get that silver bracelet?' the man asked now, peering at her wrist. 'Did you steal it? You *look* like a thief.'

Her ears smarting with the man's insults, she retreated to the street, where she remembered the *avviso* still in her hand. Her eyes fell on a small paragraph containing her own name. *Rumours abound*, said the piece, *that Aurelia Bon is missing after her disgrace at the Palazzo Bon on Palm Sunday. Her parents have declined to comment.*

Despite her fury with her father and mother, this squeezed Aurelia's heart. Surely they should be urging everyone to look for her, expressing distress at her absence. Were they really so nail-hearted?

A sadly ironic thought struck her: *Perhaps Giovanni Remondini and Mamma are thinking Valerio and I ran away together? That would be a scandal that they'd be extra anxious to keep quiet.*

The Palazzo Bon loomed up in front of her before Aurelia was quite ready to confront it.

Will it be, she wondered, *the Castle of Jabrin or the Palazzo Bon today?*

Then she thought, *If that Djinni can steal boys from nowadays, that means he can move between the different buildings and different times like . . .*

The image that came into her mind was not a comforting one.

Like a shark through water.

She heard Chissa's voice saying, 'Monstrous loik ten sharks.'

20

A Boy with a Bad Headache

Valerio ran as fast as he could. Unsteady on his feet, he lurched from side to side, several times just a slither from falling into a canal. He had no plan except *away from the leopardess!* and *away from the mad historian!* He was dimly aware, from the way the light sent the shadows down the path, that he was heading north.

He felt vaguely guilty about leaving the historian to the tender mercies of the leopardess.

But did I really see a leopardess? Did she speak? Was it a hallucination? Did I dream that coffin, that tombstone?

Valerio clutched his belly, which was churning with self-doubt. The bones of his nose seemed to be pressing deep into his face, while a tribe of rats with long sharp toenails scurried across his forehead. He tried to run again, but that made his teeth and cheekbones rattle as if they were coming loose. The top of his head felt as if it had a hole in it like a chimney.

Is that where my mind's gone? he thought. *Because it's not where it should be.*

He put his hand to the back of his head, where pain tolled like church bells. His fingers came away sticky and red; the cut there must have reopened. The sight of his own blood made Valerio retch. Even when his stomach was empty, he stood over the canal, swaying. The rain-pocked water seemed to be coming closer.

'Am I having a fit?' he asked aloud. 'I feel so weak!'

He closed his eyes and let the rain batter his lids.

For a moment, he thought he heard Aurelia's voice down in the water, and then he saw her, dressed in an old black gown, swimming away from him.

'Aurelia!' he called. She turned her head to look at him. But it wasn't Aurelia's head. It was an enormous chicken's head, with tiny shrivelled eyes and a crest of red at the top.

Yet somehow it was Aurelia too and the monstrous half-chicken began to swim towards him, her beak open.

'No!' he screamed, and everything faded.

21

Once the Walls Have Been Breached . . .

There he goes, down into the green water. Quite a small splash. I wait, but the boy Valerio does not resurface. He'll probably drown.

Why should I care? I'll contrive another way to find the bint Aurelia irregardless.

It's exactly the wrong moment, though, for everything to go wrong. Because my magic is really breaking down now. Hundreds of years of the same old, same old – feeble spells not quite working, wandering around Venice in a rage, occasionally helping myself to an unsuspecting Venetian.

Now I can't even keep the secret of my castle tucked inside the palace. Ordinary Venetians like the boy and the ridiculous historian are starting to see things that they should not. I punished the Ghezzo creature with my coffin-and-tombstone trick. Not the first time I've deployed that one on a mortal who annoyed me. But somehow it wasn't truly satisfying this time.

How can an ordinary dirt-person like Ghezzo see the Castle of Jabrin? Of course the lamentable Bon-Bon started it – may her tongue become a flap of lead. I wonder again – is she a Venetian sorceress? Who knew this city had them too?

More than ever, I need those Djinn in jars to help me. I fear that now the walls have been breached, anyone can get into my desert home. If news of the Arabian castle gets out, the Venetian mob will come back, gawping, looting . . . and if *Ghezzo* can see the castle, then perhaps everyone will soon be able to see me too?

Then they'll find my . . . mistakes . . . and I will be in trouble. They'll work out what I am . . . All those lost boys will be blamed on me. It won't occur to the Venetians that I was able to take those young men precisely because they were being disrespectful. Walking over the dead in a graveyard! Those comely louts were practically *asking* for a Djinniya to take them!

The Venetians will want me ripped out of this place. They'll find some shamming dirt-person sorcerer to come with beating drums and trumpets to make a *ruqyah*, an exorcism, on me! This charlatan will sacrifice a sheep. The Divine Being, may He be ever-blessed, loves all His animals – He doesn't want them killed. Yet the trickster exorcist will throw blood and milk in every corner of the Palazzo Bon. Given the lamentable state of my own magic, and knowing my luck, the fake exorcist will blunder into destroying my safe haven of the Castle of Jabrin, leaving me vulnerable and exposed to Venetian vengeance.

And then I will never get back to my incomparable Arabia. It will all be over with me.

The breach between the worlds is now visible in these very walls. My poor castle is a mass of leaks. Venetian rain is my enemy, finding tiny cracks and turning them into gaping fissures. Water trickles down the walls and turns them green.

It makes scabs on the painted wood and pustules in the skirting boards.

I must find the bint Aurelia Bon and have her do my will. How can I get her back to my castle? It's my only hope.

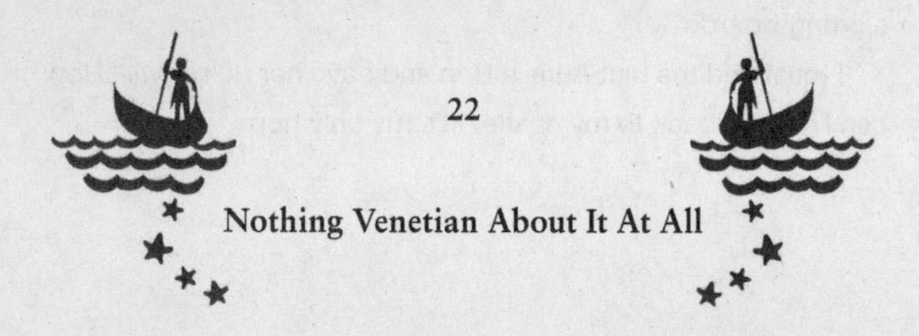

22

Nothing Venetian About It At All

When Aurelia walked through the gates of the Palazzo Bon, the sweet tang of date honey hung in the air once more. Beyond the broken gate, she found herself not in a Venetian courtyard but in the garden of an Arabian castle.

To check, she walked back through the gate. And yes, there was Venice again, ordinary, gloriously beautiful Venice, just wetter than it had ever been. And yes, it was still true: *outside* the wall, the rain beat down, while *inside*, a fierce white sun gilded the leaves of the trees and wafted the perfume of the orange trees into her nose.

Warily, a careful eye out for the fearsome Djinni – or even the rustle of a leaf to show a transparent Djinni creeping up – she entered the hallway and climbed the stairs. She explored the interior of the terracotta castle, noting the trip-steps, the Arabic calligraphy on the walls, the murder holes, the date stores, the view of white sand dunes and palms from every window. This could *only* ever have been an Arabian castle in a sun-scalded southern desert. There was nothing Venetian about it at all.

'Momo!' she whispered at every locked door she found. 'Momo!' But there was not a breath of a response.

The castle meandered like a city, full of blind alleys. When Aurelia saw her own footprints in the dust ahead of her, she realised that she must have been wandering in circles.

I need to be organised, to search every inch. I'll start from the beginning again.

She scurried back down the stairs to the entrance hall. The painting of the lion took Aurelia by surprise, for her sun-dazed eyes had not noticed it lurking in the darkness when she first entered. Now she saw the tawny fur. So real did the beast seem, its flesh almost pulsing in the light, that she screamed and took a step backwards. Then she clapped her hand over her mouth: what if the Djinni had heard? The sound of her own whimpering reminded her of the last time she'd seen Catarina, when she'd said, 'I'll never forgive you. You are not my sister any more.'

The thought crossed her mind: *these things never happen to Catarina.*

Would I want to be Catarina? No, decidedly not.

Well, Aurelia told herself, *I'm here for a reason. I'll find that Djinni and I'll have a piece of his hair, whether he wants it or not. And* I shall *find Momo. Chissa will see I'm as good as my word.*

She pulled the green spectacles out of her bodice and placed them firmly on her nose.

'Momo!' she tried once more. 'Momo!'

'Ah!' the voice that answered her was full of triumph. 'There you are!'

It was not the voice of the lamp-boy.

It belonged to historian, Simoneto Ghezzo.

23

Face to Face

Aurelia flattened herself into the corner where she was trapped. Simoneto Ghezzo advanced on her, limping.

How did he get inside the Arabian castle? Did he enter it by using my fingertip grafted to his own?

Her eyes flew to his hands, which were swollen, angry and red. Yet there was no bandage or wound on his fingertips.

Not yet, then.

The historian placed his two arms either side of Aurelia's head and leant into her face, so she was cocooned in his musty breath. He removed the green glasses and tucked them in her bodice.

'How dare you even think of laying a hand on me, sir?' she demanded, thinking, *I need those glasses on in case the Djinni appears.*

'So,' Ghezzo said, 'have you been keeping the rest of my history fingers safe? You're good at self-preservation. I'll give you that. Good and cunning. But the fingers are mine. By right.'

Aurelia hid her hands behind her back. 'What did you do with Valerio?' she snarled.

'Me? Nothing! Aren't *you* the one who should feel guilty about his fate?'

'He wouldn't have been in your house if he wasn't looking for me.'

'And here we see the full selfishness and self-admiration of the little drama queen. You forget, in your arrogance, that I too am a Remondini author. He came to talk to me about *my* book. It wasn't *me* who smashed his head.'

A gush of sweet smelling air flowed into the courtyard. It was followed by the powerful but not-so-sweet tang of an animal. Simoneto Ghezzo began to shake with fear, mumbling something about a coffin and a leopard.

'Leopards in Venice? You're a lunatic,' Aurelia told him.

'Quite the opposite, little lady. I'm quite excruciatingly sane—'

Aurelia made a sudden bolt for freedom, whipping out the glasses and smashing them against his face. A black glass fragment embedded in his left cheekbone. Blood spurted from the wound. Ghezzo uttered a howl of rage and pain. Then Aurelia was being chased around the castle, both of them trying to avoid all the trip-steps.

Over the sound of her own panting, Aurelia could hear Ghezzo stumbling after her, grunting threats. His leg was evidently troubling him greatly – and was the only reason why she was still at liberty.

If he catches up with me, this time he will actually kill me, she thought, clutching the remains of the spectacles.

I might still need them for the Djinni, she thought, tucking the black glass into her sleeve and pushing her silver bracelet over her cuff to keep it in place.

Finally, Ghezzo's footsteps behind her faded. Aurelia found herself alone, trembling and struggling for breath, in the great entrance hall. In front of her loomed the painted lion. Now she noticed that arranged around it on easels and pinned to the wall were smaller portraits of what were unmistakably Venetian cats, mostly the Syrian type with striped fur.

'I see you've met my magnificent friend the lion,' purred a deep female voice. 'He's only a painting . . . at this moment. Don't be afraid, Aurelia Bon. At least not of the lion.'

'How do you know my—?'

When Aurelia looked behind her to see who owned that fascinating voice, she discovered that it belonged to a leopardess who was most certainly not a painting.

'The lion inspires my best work,' said the creature. 'Unlike these beasts!' She pointed to a picture of four black cats with eye patches and peg legs. 'Just two days ago they appeared from nowhere. They shouldered the local cats out of the way – even deploying their wooden legs for swift kicks to the posteriors of their Venetian counterparts – and insisted on this group portrait. Hideous gurning all round! "Corsair cats", they call themselves. "Rude and rough", I call them. And it was in that character that I painted them. Now, take care, Aurelia Bon. There's at least one creature in this castle that means to make use of you.'

Tossing her tawny head, the leopardess walked through a doorway to some steps, where candles lit up her spotted pelt like a dark galaxy as she disappeared into the upper regions of the building.

The mermaids were right about a dangerous pet, thought Aurelia. *But they could never have guessed it would be a leopardess who talks.*

And then Simoneto Ghezzo limped into the *androne*.

Aurelia's heart seemed to beat louder than an orchestra.

The chase was on again.

Many long hectic minutes later, Aurelia found herself on a wooden staircase in a part of the castle she'd never seen, not even in her mind's eye when she'd pressed her fingers against the wall. She'd finally lost her pursuer again. If she hadn't been so utterly drained, she could have danced with relief. She gave a tired little hop. And then Aurelia succumbed to one of the trip-steps and fell flat on her face.

She looked up to find her nose level with a pair of silk slippers with unusual curled-up toes, floating just above the ground. Above the slippers were the cuffs of voluminous and diaphanous pantaloons, through which luxuriant tawny hairs could be seen. And above a jewelled belt was a plump and shapely young belly, bare except for an enormous red stone glittering at its centre. Aurelia did not dare look any higher. Even during *Carnevale*, she'd never seen anyone dressed quite like this.

Could this be the Irish Duchess? wondered Aurelia. Then she noticed one even more extraordinary thing about this female: Aurelia could see through her skin to the walls behind.

Lussa's words came back to her: 'Djinnkind can make themselves transparent and float above the ground.'

Is this the Djinni? Yet the mermaids had referred to the creature as a 'he'.

Aurelia pulled out of her sleeve the few fragments of black glass that remained from the smashed spectacles. She held them up in front of her. Finally raising her head, Aurelia saw a pair of green eyes and a heart-shaped face framed by flowing honey-coloured hair.

The beautiful girl was laughing at her. 'My dear little dirt-person, you've been getting the wrong advice. This black glass is supposed to be *taweez*? "Amulets" you call them here, I believe. The Divine Being, bless His name, does not believe in amulets! In fact, it's blasphemy to wear one! It won't protect you.'

The girl's Venetian was excellent. Aurelia crawled backwards away from that purring voice. *What was that word the mermaids had told her to use to defend herself? The Arabic for 'iron'? Chissa was right: she* was *bilge at details. Was it 'handmaid'?*

'Handmaid?' She faltered.

The girl in pantaloons leant down to put her finger under Aurelia's chin, tipping up her face. Her fingertip was burning hot. '*You* want to serve *me*? No, you're pretending, for I know that you're noble, Aurelia Bon.'

'You know my name?'

The girl laughed. 'Don't you think I've seen you touching my castle? Letting in the filthy mob? Also, I've been inside your friend Valerio. I know not only who you are but the blood you're bred from. I've centuries of reasons to hate you and all of your family. I've hardly any reason at all *not* to boil you in date honey.'

The thought of poor Valerio, allied to the strong fragrance of hot dates, finally brought the necessary word, or something more like it, into Aurelia's head. '*Hadeed*', she whispered.

'What? You fling that word against me? You wretch! The threat of iron might frighten a puny male Djinni. But I am no male, in case you hadn't noticed! I am a lady and I laugh at iron! I am a Djinniya!' Her voice rang with triumph. 'I'm the very model of a terrible Djinniya too.

'You'd have been *so* much safer, bint, with a mere male Djinni.'

24

You Were Born to Pay for His Treachery

Aurelia was surprised to find herself still alive. She'd listened to the Djinniya's story of her encounter with her ancestor, Aurelio Bon, famous merchant of mirrors and originator of the characterful family nose Aurelia herself bore. She learnt about the surprising nature of Djinn-wishes and about the wrecked plans of the Djinniya herself. It was a relief of sorts to know exactly how the Arabian castle had come to exist inside the Venetian palace – 'in certain dimensions of possibility', as the Djinniya had explained.

Less good was the rising anger in the Djinniya's voice as she said, 'And now you have delivered yourself to me, neatly packaged in one little dirt-person, I have everything I need to finally enact my revenge.'

Talking about revenge is one step from enacting it, Aurelia thought desperately. *I need to change the subject.* She gabbled, 'Can you explain again about how . . . the wishing thing . . . works? Are Djinn not magical creat—'

'Bristling with the most superb magic! *Not* exotic grovellers whose only wish is your command! Some storyteller slandered Djinnkind that way, and the slander has stuck in the minds of the ignorant. And how can dirt-persons be trusted with magic?

Anyway, that's beside the point. In my opinion, bint, you were born to pay for the hurt your great-great-great-great-great grandfather did me. You will make right what your ancestor rendered so wrong! You! No one but you! You and that nose of yours! *His* nose! You owe me for his treachery!'

'Yet was it really treachery?' asked Aurelia. 'He just didn't choose you. He chose my great-great-great-great-great grandmother, Silvia. He kept his promise to her because he loved her. Is that a crime?'

The Djinniya's eyes flashed.

'Anyway, *I* can't give you the kind of . . . attention you wanted from him.'

'Obviously not. Here's the thing. Aurelio Bon didn't only steal my happiness. He also stole seven Djinn I had claim to, maturing in terracotta pots. I need their help now.'

'But you said you're fiercer than any Djinni. You're not even scared of the word "*hadeed*". Why would you need other Djinn?'

'Well sometimes even a Djinniya slightly quite needs a little help,' confessed the girl. 'Here's all you have to do. It's simple enough for even a dirt-person to understand. You use your history fingers to discover where your ancestor – may his bones boil in Hell – hid my pots. I offer you considerable boons, bint, if you'll use your enchanted fingers to find what I want.'

Could her fingers find things to order? So far, everything they'd shown Aurelia had been a surprise to her. She'd no idea what her fingers were capable of doing. After all, those fingers had killed Valerio. She suddenly missed him, vividly and painfully. A series of memories played out in her mind: Valerio handing her a copy of a document from the archives with a smile; Valerio making an excellent suggestion about a turn of phrase for her book . . . Then she thought of Momo. Her fingers had found *him*.

'Pay attention!' barked the Djinniya.

'I *could* try to find your pots,' said Aurelia. 'But here's what I want as my "considerable boon". The boy Momo is here, isn't he? I'll help you if you let him go back to his poor mother.'

'Absolutely not.'

Beneath the anger, Aurelia was aware that other emotions were troubling the Djinniya. From her red cheeks and her eyes, which looked everywhere but directly at Aurelia, the Djinniya's chief feeling seemed to be *embarrassment*.

'Has Momo died then?' Aurelia asked, her heart full and pounding. 'If he's dead, perhaps he doesn't have to stay that way?'

Aurelia's eyes began to shine. Not only Momo but also Valerio might be saved if she just helped the Djinniya out with her history fingers. She flushed with something that felt almost like hope. 'You said Djinn can use magic even if humans can't be trusted with it. So can you bring a dead boy back to life?'

The grim answer was: 'Only as a graveyard-haunting Gul. And a Gul is what you'll become, bint, if you don't help me. Enough of this. If you won't do it voluntarily, I've ways of making you.'

The Djinniya suddenly disappeared from sight. Aurelia felt something hot and silky hovering around her lips. Her hands lit up with a ghostly light. She dropped to her knees as her limbs fell slack and her brain throbbed with confusion.

Lussa had warned, 'At all costs don't let the Djinni get inside your body. Agree anything rather than permit that.'

Aurelia whispered, 'I'll do it! I'll look for your urns! Just keep out of me!'

Aurelia spent the next hour history-fingering all over the palace of her ancestor under the Djinniya's petulant supervision. She felt all the walls from the dusty storerooms by the watergate to the dim fragrant attic. While she hunted for urns, Aurelia also hoped with every scene to conjure up Momo. Yet there was no more sign of the lamp-boy than of the lost Djinn in jars.

The only place the Djinniya did not take her was a wing on the first floor. She declared, 'This section's been thoroughly combed already, wall to wall, century to century.'

It's where Momo is, thought Aurelia. *The Djinniya knows what I'm up to.*

But she dared not say anything. It comforted her that the Djinniya did not want her entering that space, because it seemed to prove that the lamp-boy was alive.

Something's different today, Aurelia was realizing. Sometimes when she put her fingers on the walls, she saw scenes of imams, ambassadors and scholars from the castle's past. At other times however, she saw her own ancestors playing out various scenes in their Venetian home. It seemed that there was a melting of the barriers between the two realms of possibility. It was messy. It was confusing and frightening. Nonetheless, it was also absolutely fascinating.

Valerio, she thought, *would have been thinking ten-to-the-dozen, working everything out.*

But inside no wall, no door, no carved panel did Aurelia see her ancestor Aurelio Bon, and she never saw any transaction including terracotta urns.

'So this proves it. Your sneaksome ancestor hid them somewhere *else* in Venice,' said the Djinniya.

'I swear I've not seen Djinn in jars in any of the other *palazzi* where I history-fingered. Not in the Priuli, not in the Barbaro, not in the Pisani, not in the Contarini . . .' Aurelia ticked them off, thinking wistfully of the scenes of her former triumphs, when life was so much less complicated. And so much less dangerous.

'You're no use to me. I need to find someone who is,' said the Djinniya. Even Aurelia was moved by the desperation in the girl's voice.

She said, 'Palazzo Bon *is* one of the oldest buildings in Venice. But there are older palaces and even more ancient places in this city. We need to go back further into the past perhaps. What about Signor Rioba and his brothers? They've been in Venice longer than almost anyone. They may know something.'

'Who?'

'A family of Moorish men in turbans on the Fondamenta della Sensa.'

The Djinniya's eyes began to dance. Aurelia did not want to spoil the moment by mentioning that the Riobas were statues.

'Leave the fellows alone, Ghazalah!' growled Musipul. 'There are more important things afoot. I've come to tell you—'

'You're called "Ghazalah"?' asked Aurelia.

'Yes, because of my gazelle-like beauty and the ineffable grace with which I move.'

Musipul yawned. 'All the grace of a lame hyena.'

Ghazalah pretended not to have heard, saying, 'And this overgrown cat is "Musipul". Take no notice of her impudence. Now, bint, escort me to your Rioba fellows.'

'The Fondamenta della Sensa's not far,' said Aurelia. 'Don't you need to go back into your lamp now? So I can carry you there?' She tried not to look cunning as she cast her eyes around the room for something that looked like an oil lamp with a stopper.

'Oh, you too with the lamps and the rubbing and the puffs of smoke! With the right spell, any creature, not just Djinnkind, can be bound into *any* vessel. I suppose you also think *proper* Djinn are fierce, fat, bald old men wearing pantaloons in tasteless colours under round bellies and slippers with curled-up toes? I keep telling you, Djinn were *not* put in this world – or any world – to serve dirt-persons like you.'

'There's more than one world?'

'*So many* worlds you humans know nothing of! In front of you is one proud free Djinniya—'

The leopardess muttered, 'Free? Really? *You*'re trapped in Venice.'

The Djinniya scowled. Aurelia stammered, 'But you have the pantaloons. And the slippers. And the—' She stopped herself short of 'round belly', sensing danger.

'Pantaloons are the most comfortable thing you'll ever wear. No getting tangled up in a skirt! And the slippers are useful. Not having toes as such –' she lifted a glossy brown hoof from the slipper – 'I can tuck a tiny scimitar into the front part. Such a blade can divide a man in two from his throat to his belly.'

'*Very* pretty,' said Musipul. 'Off you go and give the chaps the old squidge-eye then. Perhaps you'll come back in a better mood with a silly little flirt under your belt.'

Signor Antonio Rioba had the strongest face and the sternest eyes of the three brothers, especially now, at dusk when the whiteness of their stone lent the men a ghostly appearance.

In front of Signor Rioba, Aurelia performed a curtsy her mother would have been proud of, saying 'Good evening, kind sir,' in a tone of the utmost respect.

Ghazalah's fury heated the air. '*Statues*, bint? You think *statues* can help?'

'Now curtsy, you,' Aurelia told her.

'Oh, really, bint,' Ghazalah sneered. 'I'm not going to make a fool of myself for this great galumph of a statue – may itches and insanity befall him, if they didn't already. The face on him! And he looks as grumpy as six dromedaries with bellyaches.'

Aurelia caught the slight whiff of ancient moss on stone. She looked over Ghazalah's shoulder and clapped her hand over her mouth. 'Oh no,' she said. 'Now you've done it!'

Behind the Djinniya, the stone had begun to grumble: a noise like sandpaper being scratched by a cat.

'Girlie mine,' growled a deep voice. 'I'll show yer grumpy! Boof!'

'"Girlie"!' said Ghazalah, turning to face Signor Rioba. 'You dare talk to me like that? More of that and someone will tickle your discourteous tongue with a scimitar. And that someone isn't far away.'

The jutting jaws of Signor Rioba kept moving: 'Ye blitherin—'

But then a remarkable thing happened. As Signor Rioba's gaze fell on her, Ghazalah swayed a little. Aurelia saw in wonder how the Djinniya somehow softened and elongated her eyes, fluttered her lashes like fans at Signor Rioba, who spluttered to a stop. 'Well, if ye put it *that* way. What can I do for ye, dearest lady? Just name it . . .'

'My dear man,' trilled Ghazalah, 'you're clearly someone in the know. I need your talent! I'm looking for certain merchandise, *stolen* merchandise actually, brought to Venice back in 1508 or so. It would be extra adorable of you to . . .'

But Signor Rioba knew nothing at all of 'Djinn in jam jars'.

'Ask me bottom about it!' he barked. 'All I can say is, don't let *I* filching *Fedeli* get their hands on 'em. Dance a minuet with those gentlemen and ye'd go home without your pearls.'

'Certainly,' smiled Ghazalah, 'These *Fedeli* sound like a bunch of Afreets to me.'

'Frightful as!' Signor Rioba wanted to talk more about the 'parlous state' of the Venetians: 'Blind as day-old bats to the real dangers facing 'em! Where be the brave spirit and the muscles Venice used to hide beneath her lacy petticoats? Boof!'

Ghazalah murmured, 'But at least Venice has a handsome hero in *you*, sir!'

She smiled, elongating her eyes again.

'Put me down for some o' that,' said Signor Rioba. It was only then that he dragged his own marble eyes away from Ghazalah long enough to notice Aurelia standing behind her.

'What's this girlie for? Methinks I knows that face?'

Aurelia longed to tell him that she knew all about the Seldom Seen Press in the cavern under the House of the Spirits. Yet she knew she must not reveal the existence of the mermaids to Ghazalah. She'd promised not to 'blab' their 'bizness' to anyone.

'The bint's not important,' said Ghazalah, firing another dazzling smile at Signor Rioba. 'Well, my dear sir, I'm sure that you'll set that fine mind of yours to finding my Djinn.'

'I'll be doing naught else till I see ye again! Which will be soon, I pray?' Signor Rioba creaked into a bow, muttering under his breath, 'Love me a well-haired leg on a lady.'

'However could I keep away? Till ever so soon!'

With a hot iron grip on Aurelia's shoulder, Ghazalah turned back to the Palazzo Bon.

'I'm guessing,' said Aurelia miserably, 'that this was not enough help?'

'To spare you my revenge? Ha! *That* was not what I would call a debt paid,' the Djinniya said. 'I would call it insult added to injury. Rude statues. Promises needing to be flirted out of statues with mouths like chamber pots. Gross grumbling about some dirt-persons being dirtier than others? How is that *my* problem? You have done *nothing* for me yet, bint. If you can't do better, you're going to be even sorrier than I thought. And sorrier than you could ever imagine.'

25

A Choice of Choices

Ghazalah reclined on a cushion on the floor in front of a silver tray mounted on a wooden stool inlaid with mother-of-pearl. 'Sit,' she ordered Aurelia, pointing to a cushion.

Aurelia's mouth watered at the sight of round flat cakes of bread slick with date honey. With the mannerlessness of the hungry, she reached out but Ghazalah slapped her wrist. 'The mistress of the house always eats first to allay suspicions of murder by poison.'

'Why would you poison me?' asked Aurelia.

'Why wouldn't I?'

'Because you haven't given up on the idea that I can help you,' said Aurelia, thinking, *This is rather like arguing with Catarina, only a bit more dangerous.*

Ghazalah snapped her fingers. An elegant servant appeared with a basin, a tall ewer and a fine linen napkin hanging over his slender arm.

'Wash your hands!' the Djinniya commanded. The servant showed Aurelia that she should hold out her fingers. Arching his delicate eyebrows, he poured rose-scented water over them and then dried them briskly with the napkin.

By now the smell of warm bread was stronger than good manners. Aurelia reached for it with both hands.

'Right hand only!' shouted Ghazalah. 'Infidel!'

'Who are you calling "infidel"?' demanded Aurelia. 'Aren't you a kind of devil?'

She regretted it instantly. Not only did she know better than that – for hadn't Lussa explained that Djinn were spirits made of fire – but insulting her hostess was both stupid and dangerous.

'Forgive me, I beg you,' she asked humbly. 'Hunger has stolen my manners.'

'This once, I shall,' said Ghazalah. 'For I'm feeling more than a little peckish myself.'

The servants carried in silver platters of fragrant lamb stewed with apricots and stuffed aubergine. There was also a sharp sweet drink, which one of the men announced as '*hebeedh*'.

'Fermented date honey,' said the Djinniya, burying her nose in a deep chalice of it. 'Consider yourself lucky to be allowed a taste of anything so good, bint.'

Is it safe to eat Djinn food? Aurelia wondered. But it turned out she was too hungry to care.

The leopardess Musipul had meanwhile entered the room and sat purring on a Persian rug.

'Here are my new terms,' said Ghazalah. 'If your fingers can locate the Djinn jars – clearly somewhere outside this palace – I shall condescend to refrain from killing you myself. I shall also have my Uncle Nusrat the Gul give some extra food to the boy Tomo.'

'Momo,' sighed Musipul.

'My leopardess,' said Ghazalah, 'is an Afreet, another kind of Djinn. In her case, a very *pedantic* and *carping* kind. As you can see, she's a restless spirit who takes beastly form – extremely beastly – and she's no scruples about using those claws.'

Over the Djinniya's voice, Aurelia could hear dragging footsteps. The sick twist in her stomach told her they were Simoneto Ghezzo's. Quickly, she explained who he was and the historian's plans for her fingertips. Ghazalah nodded. 'Yes, I know there's an unpleasant creature wandering around my domain. All afternoon, I've felt as if there was a cockroach scuttling under my skin. He's already had a taste of my temper. Yet he must be bad as Musipul has apparently refused to eat him so far. Meanwhile, you can stop the trembling, bint. I've spun a dazzle-circle around this room. Unless I want him to do so, this Ghezzo won't find us.'

Musipul said, 'It's the *one* spell she's infallible at.'

'If and when he's allowed to find us,' said Ghazalah, 'he'll wish he hadn't. Now, to the honey kitchen!'

A few moments later, Aurelia was standing red-faced in front of a cauldron in a curious hinged metal basket suspended over a fire. The cauldron had a wide spout. Ghazalah was shouting, 'Stir!' and Aurelia pushed a wooden spoon nearly as tall as herself through the bubbling syrup.

'Do we really need all this honey?' she asked. 'Is it for the servants' suppers?'

'No, you fool! It's for pouring on your enemy, Simoneto Ghezzo. I need you alive to serve me. And he seems to wish you dead.'

'Boiling honey? No!'

Just one floor below them, Aurelia could hear the historian groaning with frustration, his footsteps faltering to the stumble of absolute exhaustion.

'Come here, bint. I need to see if it's hot enough to burn skin.'

Ghazalah took the spoon out of Aurelia's hand. Then, smiling, she tipped two drops of sizzling honey on Aurelia's own wrist. Pure agony pushed a scream out of Aurelia's mouth.

Musipul said, 'She doesn't feel anyone else's pain. She literally wasn't around when the sensitivity was being handed out. When others were learning about pain endured and pain inflicted, she was locked in a flask.'

'Sssh!' said Ghazalah, inspecting Aurelia's wrist. 'Is a blister forming? Excellent. Then it's hot enough to kill if we pour the whole pot over him. Death will take a while, of course. There'll be a lot of howling first.'

'No! Wait!' Aurelia said. 'I don't want to be part of a killing. Ghezzo never actually spelled out that he'd murder me. He only wanted what I have – history fingers.'

'By Satan's elbows! Look, there he is, just waiting for death.' Ghazalah pointed down through a grate in the floor. Simoneto Ghezzo stood below them, panting against a wall.

He looks so old, so hopeless, so desperate, thought Aurelia. *And it's partly my showing off that has got him that way.*

'Let him go,' she pleaded, surprising herself.

'Are you so sentimental? The honey's boiled now. Someone has to die. Tell you what. You make the choice: the lamp-boy's life or the historian's. How generous am I? Giving you a *choice* of choices!'

'But there shouldn't be *any* choices like that!' cried Aurelia. 'Why can't they *both* live?'

Ghazalah said tranquilly, 'Well, you could always offer yourself as a sacrifice in their places. Dirt-persons are always talking about sacrificing themselves, as if it's a *good* thing. So what about it, bint?'

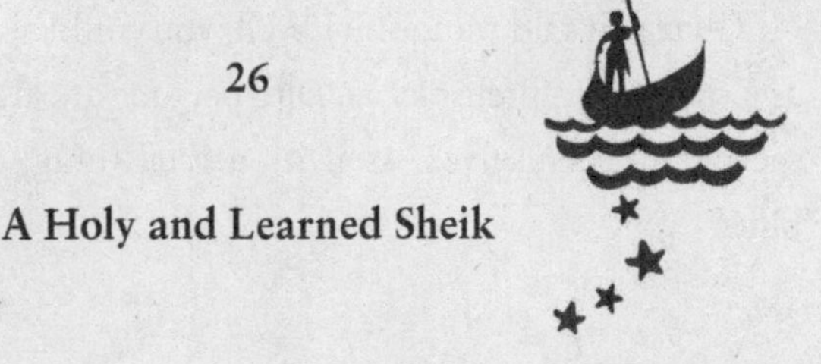

26

A Holy and Learned Sheik

'No answer? Well, I'll choose then,' said Ghazalah. 'I choose the old fool.'

'Signor Ghezzo!' screamed Aurelia, falling on her knees so she could lower her mouth to the grate. 'Move!'

Ghazalah kicked her aside and lowered the vat on its hinged cradle.

'What the—?' The historian leapt out of the way just as the seething stream of date honey coursed down through the grate towards his head.

He leant against a wall, only one arm lightly spattered with the boiling honey. That, however, was more than enough to make him shriek and sob. He was evidently too shocked and in too much pain to run away.

'How dare you, bint? His destiny was death! He's your enemy and I offered you his demise as a *gift*!' Actual heat flowed from Ghazalah, searing Aurelia's face.

Of course, she's made of pure fire, thought Aurelia.

'I'll make you sorry, you lamentable Bon-Bon!' the Djinniya raged. 'I'll hurt you. I'll make you hurt yourself. I'll make you strangle yourself with your own hands. I'll hurt everyone you care about. Including the boy Gomo.'

'*Momo*! No!'

Then everything became as blurred as if she saw it through mullioned milk glass. The last thing Aurelia heard was Musipul asking Ghazalah, 'Why the frankincense did you do that? It was a risk. You're *ridiculously* bad at Stun Spells. You *so* need a learned and holy sheik to put you in order . . .'

When Aurelia woke up, she was lying on an old carved chest in a small room with a single window high up in the wall. The door was open, but it might as well have been locked and bolted.

For nailed in the wall was a brass plate with two loops. A rope tied round Aurelia's middle was tethered to those loops. She knew where she'd seen that mechanism before – when her history fingers had guided her around the Castle of Jabrin on Palm Sunday. This was a murder room!

She searched for the murder hole. Its dark eye stared out of the white ceiling just above her. She jerked upright, only to discover that the ropes allowed her just a small envelope of space in which to move. That meant Aurelia was tied to the exact place where a spear or an arrow or a bullet, aimed through the hole, could kill her in an instant. She dropped back on the chest, panting.

It was painfully uncomfortable on the ridged surface of the chest. Aurelia shuffled her thighs along it. Her finger caught on a lever and the lock sprang open.

'Ouch!' she screamed, holding up a thumb dripping with blood. The lever's razor sharp edge had gashed her. The ropes were just long enough to allow her to roll off the chest and settle into a kneeling position – always in the line of fire if the Djinniya decided to use the murder hole.

Perhaps, she thought, *I could get inside the chest. The lid would block the spear or the arrow. So long as I can breathe in there . . .*

Putting her thumb in her mouth, Aurelia lifted the lid of the chest with her other hand.

Ghazalah was suddenly beside her, smiling her lazy, terrifying smile.

The Djinniya demanded, 'So, have you come up with a way to find my Djinn yet?' She looked meaningfully up at the murder hole in the roof and back to Aurelia.

'Not yet. I'm trying . . .'

Ghazalah muttered to herself, 'The trouble is that if I jump inside the bint, then she loses her free will. She cannot take me anywhere but where I want to go. She cannot lead me somewhere new.'

She uttered a shriek of fury. Then she was gone.

I have to get out of here now, thought Aurelia. *Ghazalah's in such a state she could do anything. She might even give up on me, and then my worth to her would be nothing. And then . . .*

The throbbing in her injured thumb reminded Aurelia of the razor edge of the chest's lever. Lifting up the ropes that bound her to the wall, Aurelia won enough length to allow her to turn her back to the murder hole. Keeping her back absolutely still, she scraped the ropes back and forth against the chest's metal lever until they began to fray. Fifteen minutes later the first rope was severed. But Aurelia kept her back motionless, certain that Ghazalah's eyes were on her, or could be at any moment.

It was then that Aurelia remembered the last thing Musipul had said – that a learned and holy sheik was needed to put her mistress in order. Surely Ghazalah was the most out of order Djinniya imaginable.

I urgently need to find a holy and learned sheik.

Aurelia thought about the Fondaco of the Persiani, near the Rialto Bridge. This was where many of the Arabian merchants stayed.

That's where the sheiks must be!

It occurred to Aurelia that she should go back to the mermaids to report on all she'd discovered. She knew she really should seek their counsel before taking another step. Yet her plan was flowering elaborately and attractively in her mind as she worked away at the second piece of rope.

I'll go there and ask for an audience with a holy and learned sheik. If he's learned enough, of course he'll be able to speak my language. I'll tell him that there's a dangerous Djinniya wreaking havoc in this city . . .

A properly devout sheik would see straightaway that Ghazalah needed dealing with. Aurelia was confident that she could persuade him to go immediately to Palazzo Bon. Then Aurelia would *definitely* go to the mermaids and tell them all about what had happened and how cleverly she had solved the Djinniya problem.

The second rope gave way. Aurelia leapt up, rushed out of the open door and ran down the stairs. Mercifully there was no sign of the Djinniya or the leopardess.

There's more to me than Ghazalah thinks! She rejoiced, reaching the courtyard.

But as soon as she stepped out to the *fondamenta*, a hand reached out of the canal and grabbed her ankle, dragging her into the water.

'Not so fast, girlie. Where d'ye think ye're goin'?'

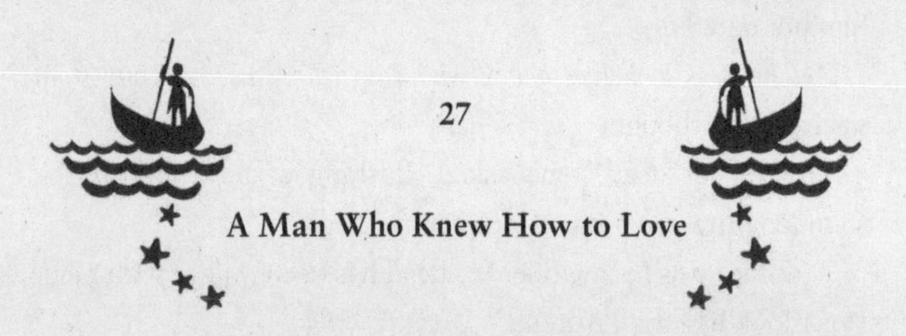

27

A Man Who Knew How to Love

'Staggerin' seahorses! Did ye think ye could do finely wivout our help?' asked Chissa. 'For why did we have to *drag* ye down here to the cavern? Why did ye not come to us wiv yer news and yer troubles? A mutineer ye be! Lackaday!'

Aurelia flushed. *I was supposed to bring Djinn hair. I forgot! No Momo. No hair. I've failed entirely.*

'Look how da pore maid hangs her head,' called a younger mermaid whose black curls were similar to Aurelia's. 'Mayhap she needs a coddlin', not a cursin', Chissa?'

'Why be ye so glum, maid?' asked another young mermaid whose face was lightly scribbled with pretty freckles. 'Ye looks like one who lost a pearl necklace and found a small white pebble instead.'

Lussa said quietly, 'Or one who lacks a friend in this world.'

'I used to have one. But I . . . killed him.'

Aurelia's shoulders sagged and her blood seemed to stop beating, as if drained by the words.

'No, you did not kill him,' said a familiar voice. Valerio emerged from behind a rock, staring at her with terror in his eyes, as if he feared she might *yet* murder him. He mumbled, 'But your face is your face. It's not a chicken's face any more.'

Aurelia's heart beat fast and joyously. She wanted to embrace him but dared not.

Yet he does look like a boy who desperately needs a hug from someone, she thought.

'You're not dead?' she asked, flushing at how foolish she sounded. 'Are you a bit . . . mad in the head?'

'I think I was for a while. My head has been on fire with pain. Don't look like that, Aurelia.'

'Aren't you furious with me for hitting you?'

Among other things, Aurelia thought, remembering those cruel words she'd thrown at Valerio, back before everything turned so dangerous.

Is now, she wondered, *the time to tell Valerio that Ghazalah's been inside him? And that's why he feels so strange and sees people with chicken heads? No,* she decided, *it would be too embarrassing.*

Valerio smiled, 'Should I be angry with you because secretly you've *always* wanted to hit me on the head? I know you never liked the way I improved your manuscripts! Yes, that was quite a blow you dealt me. But you thought I was Simoneto Ghezzo coming back to the attic, didn't you?'

Aurelia nodded.

'I was out cold for just a minute, the surgeon told me.'

'Did he tell you why Ghezzo had kidnapped me? How he wanted to graft my fingertips on to his own?'

'What? No! When I came to, Ghezzo hustled me out straightaway. But the poor doctor's still shackled up there.'

I've barely given the surgeon a thought, Aurelia realised. *How am I better than Ghazalah?*

Chissa said, 'And then our friends da good gulls reported a stripling blue about da gills, capsized in 'is wits and raving about girls wiv chicken heads. As it happened, he fell in da water so we tugged him by da leg and brought him down here. We soothed da fever wiv Fermented Chili Jelly, healthful chanting and a good feed of Curried Sea-Cucumber and Coriander Pea Cakes.'

Seeing Aurelia's nose twitch at the delightfully spicy aroma lingering in the air, Chissa added, 'Help yerself, girlie. There's plenty.'

When did I last eat? wondered Aurelia. *With Ghazalah, too long ago!*

A mermaid in a tall white hat swam over with a platter of small golden dishes. Aurelia took it eagerly. Each spoonful warmed her mouth with delicious new flavours.

Lussa said, 'And we've kept him here as it seemed a safer place for him than streets where the History Half-Man is raging around with murder in his soul.'

'How do you know about that?' asked Aurelia, putting down her spoon.

Lussa turned the turtle shell towards Aurelia. When Aurelia peered deep into it, she began to make out moving pictures, rather like the ones she herself saw when she pressed her history fingers on a wall. She flinched when she saw Simoneto Ghezzo limping through the streets, moaning to himself and cradling his burnt arm with a swollen red hand. The skin around the cut on his cheek had puffed up alarmingly.

'Now childer, shake hands and make up,' said Lussa. 'There be bigger perils afoot than a pair of striplings with shaky feelings. Maid, did ye find the Djinni? Did ye get his hairs?'

Aurelia said quickly, 'Better than hairs! Information! I've so much to tell you! There *is* a Djinni, except it's a Djinniya! A girl Djinn! She acts very sophisticated yet she doesn't really seem to be much older than I am. She's the one who has taken the boy Momo. I was looking for her, but all the while she was hunting for *me*. She thinks I owe her something because she . . . sort of . . . fell in love with my ancestor, the merchant of mirrors, Aurelio Bon. Unfortunately, he didn't feel the same. Her name is Ghazalah.'

Chissa replied, 'Gorblimey! I'm wagering that dis scurvy Djinniya answers to da crimes agin all dem other striplings wot disappeared from Palazzo Bon. "Ghazalah" ye say she be called? I do think she be better named "da Man-Guzzler from Arabia".'

'The thing is, she doesn't actually *devour* men,' said Aurelia, thinking about the encounter with Signor Rioba. 'She just *really* needs them to pay a bit of attention to her. Anyway, Ghazalah has an artist in her house. A . . . leopard. Who *might* help us.' Aurelia was making this part up as she went along, but it sounded quite good to her. Musipul had not seemed overly enamoured of her mistress.

'Cats be mixed up in trouble wherever dey can be, da beasts. Sink me! A leopard in Venice, wot next?'

'A leopardess, actually, and she paints portraits!' Aurelia said. 'We need an artist, don't we? She's been making likenesses of many Venetian cats.'

'Conceited beasts themselves!'

'They queue up for their pictures. So I was thinking that I . . . we . . . could persuade Musipul to paint a picture of her mistress at the bottom of a bowl? There might be a tiny problem in that she's not merely a leopardess but also an Afreet –'

'It do get worse,' said Lussa. 'An Afreet be highly unlikely to cooperate just out of niceness.'

'Call Apothecaress Anna!' the call echoed through the cavern. The word 'Anna' bounced off the walls so many times that it sounded like 'Annananannananna'.

Valerio's face showed the echoes swimming inside his head. He staggered back to the rock and leant against it.

A serious-looking mermaid with straight brown hair approached the walkway, pushing in front of her a little skiff of driftwood on which rested a large book.

'Wot have ye, Anna,' asked Chissa, 'for puttin' an uppity leopardess in her place?'

There was a minute's silence while Anna donned spectacles, opened the book and leafed through the pages. Then she held up one finger.

'Leopard's Bane,' she announced. '*Doronicum orientale*. If you dangle some from a ribbon, she'll come to chase it. Any cat would. One long sniff and she'll become suggestiblish as a kitten.'

'Suggestiblish?' asked Aurelia

'She'll do whatever you suggest. The effect may not last long, however. Once she's not suggestiblish any more, she might also be somewhat peeved. At you.'

The thought of Musipul, peeved, was all too vivid in Aurelia's imagination.

'Where in the world am I going to find Leopard's Bane?'

'That's the easy part. *Doronicum orientale* is that little yellow daisy that pokes out of every crevice in Venice around Easter time. Ye'll pick some up on your way, and here's a ribbon.'

'But the rain . . .' Aurelia didn't want to disparage Anna's idea. The mermaid was so confident.

'Now, girlie,' said Chissa, 'be there more to your fancy plan?'

Aurelia explained her elaborate plan about the Fondaco and the sheik to a circle of beautiful, unimpressed faces. Valerio, seeing how things lay, looked to the gilded roof of the cavern, the water – anywhere but at Aurelia.

That's kind, she thought. *He doesn't want to see me floundering. Would I be so kind?*

When Aurelia ground to a halt, Lussa said, 'While ye've been fancying yesself a great Djinn-tamer, it's come to us that there be another prophecy. The turtle shell has told us that ye're not the only one with a special destiny to protect this city. This stripling—'

'Valerio has his own prophecy?' It was strange to see him the centre of attention. To be honest, it was not all good. Aurelia felt a little singe of jealousy between her shoulders. 'So what's this prophecy about Valerio?' she asked, trying not to sound cynical but not quite succeeding.

This time Lussa sang, her soft voice twining around notes in a mournful minor key.

'How to solve troubles that history begat?
seagull, rat, cormorant, cat
It's not a man who'll help us with that.
seagull, rat, cormorant, cat

Who will find out what needs to be known?
sailboat, fish, gondola, moon
It's not a woman who'll face down our doom.
sailboat, fish, gondola, moon

Who has the patience, who takes the time?
regrets, blame, sobbing and shame
Who sees what others don't care to name?
regrets, blame, sobbing and shame

A land-prince forced out on the sea
foam, waves, storms and swells
destined there always to lose his belly—'

'Is that true?' Aurelia asked, 'That you get seasick?'

'Really,' said Valerio tersely. 'You can't imagine.'

'Even the gondola from Mestre or Fusina to Venice—?'

'It's a nightmare. I have to avoid food and drink for a day before I come into town. On the boat, I just take deep breaths while a thorny snake courses through my intestines. I feel as if someone is shaking me till I get dizzy. I've never seen the skyline of Venice because I need to keep my eyes closed. If I open them—'

'Belay this organ recital,' said Chissa impatiently. 'Dere be something more important here than da rumpusing of da stripling's chitterlins!'

The latter part of the prophecy was less lyrical and more urgent. Lussa's voice uttering it was quieter too:

'But set him a-sail in a chart or a book
this soldier of archives
knows just where to look

By delving deep in dusty shelves
full-graceful he'll fathom
our ancient selves

In our letters and contracts, our scripts and our texts
he'll find in the past what we need next
and so lead us to safety, doing what he does best.'

'Ye see!' said Chissa. 'And 'tis true dis stripling's been busy in da archives. He's found a letter from your great-great-great-great-great grandfather, Aurelio Bon.'

Valerio looked at Aurelia. 'I was trying to tell you about that, when—'

'I was appallingly, unforgivably and unjustifiably rude to you. A letter to whom?'

'To an apothecary.'

'But he was a merchant of *mirrors*. Why an apothecary?'

'Not just mirrors. Aurelio Bon must have known many apothecaries because he brought back the ingredients they needed . . . *mummia*, pepper, hippopotamus teeth and all the spices from Arabia and beyond that made medicine seem magical in those days. And smell delicious too. And when Aurelio Bon himself stopped travelling, his family – *your* family – continued to supply a little empire of apothecary customers.'

'You know more about my family's history than I do,' said Aurelia. Valerio bowed his head modestly. 'But why is a letter to an apothecary so important?'

'Indeed,' said Chissa. 'Think harder, girlie.'

'Ghazalah the Djinniya is from Arabia—'

'The mermaids have been telling me about this Djinn-creature. I'm beginning to suspect she was inside my body!' said Valerio. 'Using me like a puppet!'

'You're right. When she was hunting for me, she jumped inside you and listened to your thoughts. The symptoms of Djinn possession are hallucinations, headaches, weakness. And acting out of character; being aggressive if you were gentle before, for example.'

Valerio blushed. 'I was all those. So it's not just because you hit me on the head?'

'That's what you thought? Ghazalah also told me that she could get inside you any time now. So it's best you keep away from her. And please don't take it personally. She uses *everyone* like a puppet. Except my great-great-great-great-great grandfather, who seems to have been the one human being able to withstand her powers. He was also the person who caused her to lose her head. So much so that she made a terrible mistake with her magic – with which she wasn't very brilliant, in fact, in the first place. She *meant* to bind Aurelio Bon fast to her but instead she accidently slipped her own Castle of Jabrin inside the Palazzo Bon. One moment it was in Nizwa, and the next in Venice.'

'It be true that Djinnkind can travel long distances in a short time,' said Lussa. 'One hopes that they may also travel *back* that way.'

'One definitely hopes. What was so special about Aurelio Bon,' asked Valerio, 'that he could stir up so such trouble?'

'He was handsome. But the real problem, as far as Ghazalah was concerned, was that he loved both Silvia, his betrothed, and his hometown.'

'It be seeming that this loving man also cared very deeply for his friends.' Lussa waved the letter. 'Being a man in general who knew how to love.'

Aurelia took the faded page from Lussa's hand. She read aloud:

'*My dear friend, I ask you a great favour. I shall shortly be returning from an eventful trip to Arabia. With me, I bring something both wonderful and perilous. What do I ask of you, my soul-brother? I cannot keep these items in my own home. They might draw danger to me because . . . someone will be looking for them. Someone who might put my family at risk. I need you to hide them –*

'This must be the very thing Ghazalah seeks!' said Aurelia. 'I was about to tell you. She's desperate to get her hands on seven terracotta pots with young Djinn inside! She's sure Aurelio Bon took them from the Castle of Jabrin.'

Aurelia turned back to the letter. 'It's dated 1508. That's more than two hundred and fifty years ago. In all this time, surely someone would have been curious enough to look inside a pot marked "Djinn"?'

Valerio said, 'They might have been keen on getting some wishes granted too.'

'Ah, but the wish story isn't quite what you think. What if they were not actually marked "Djinn" but something else to put people off the scent?'

'It would have to be something there was not much call for, I guess,' said Valerio.

'And remember, Aurelio Bon warned the apothecary to *hide* the things he was bringing. Maybe they're *still* hidden. This letter,' said Aurelia, turning over the page, 'is addressed to the Redeemer apothecary in San Marco. We should go there and have a look—'

The turtle shell suddenly filled with a ghostly light. Lussa bent towards it, flinched and then turned the shell away so that Aurelia and Valerio could not see the image it held. She exchanged worried glances with Chissa.

'Indeed, to the apothecary with ye, post-haste,' urged Lussa. 'Be ye utmostly and utterly careful. There be something dark afoot out there. And to spare ye another ducking in cold water – yon staircase leads to a trapdoor in the floor of a chapel in the garden of the House of the Spirits and out to the apple orchard and then the Misericordia. Ye may return the same way.'

'If dey does return,' muttered Chissa grimly, gazing deeply into the turtle shell.

She did not mean us to hear that, thought Aurelia.

Valerio's pale face told her that he rather wished they hadn't.

28

A Cleaving of the Bowels?

'Can I help you?' asked the elderly apothecary, peering over the counter at Aurelia and Valerio. 'Is it a tickly sore throat? A dubious sensation in the belly parts? An embarrassing rumble?'

'Um,' mumbled Aurelia, shaking the raindrops from her hair. 'No. Nothing like that.'

Her eyes flickered around the shop. So many shelves, rising to the ceiling and lining every wall! And on each shelf – so many ancient dusty pots! How could they possibly find the ones with Djinn in them? Aurelia's anxiety was compounded by the memory of the sombre look on Chissa's face when she'd looked into the turtle shell.

'A cleaving of the bowels?' persisted the apothecary.

'No.'

'A weakness of the limbs and a general debilitation?'

'No.'

'Twitching of inappropriate muscles?'

'No.'

'Foul-smelling stool?

'Doesn't every—'

'Dark urine?'

'No'

'Pale urine?'

'No.'

The apothecary of the Redeemer pushed his sleeves up, grinning. He was clearly the kind of gentleman who enjoyed a challenge.

'A tingling in the smallest toe?'

'No.'

'A curious swaying of the legs when leaving a gondola?'

'No.'

The apothecary bowed. 'I conclude that you two young people are blessed with perfect health and are a credit to your mothers' kitchens. So why are you really here? Aldo!' he called, causing a boy – evidently an apprentice – to hurry over from a desk where he'd been weighing herbs and wrapping them in paper packets.

At the sight of Aurelia, Aldo whistled, 'Just a second, don't I know who you are? The girl with the fingers! I want to ask you something. About mermaids. I thought I saw one, you see – in the Canal di Noale, near the House of the Spirits.'

But Aurelia wasn't listening. With her back against the wall, she was pressing her fingers against a bare patch of plaster. Images arrived swiftly in her head. A young man strode into the apothecary. She knew it was Aurelio Bon because he looked so much like herself – the brown eyes, the dark, curly hair, the slant of the cheekbones and above all the large, shapely nose. Her ancestor threw himself into a warm embrace with the apothecary of nearly three centuries back. Aurelia noticed that the apothecary, too, bore a strong resemblance to his modern descendant, though he was decades younger. Aurelio Bon was accompanied by two servants carrying a barrel-shaped trunk by an iron pole threaded through four thick handles. With grateful groans, the servants let their burden sink to the floor.

'So you'll keep these articles safe for me, my friend?' Aurelio Bon asked the apothecary. The timbre of his voice was familiar, a little like Aurelia's father's. 'Will you hide them and never give them up to no one but me or someone who is part of me? What I ask you is no small thing. It could be dangerous.'

The apothecary frowned. Yet he clasped Aurelio Bon's hand. 'For you, for the love between us, for my love for your whole family, yes.'

The eyes of both men flew to the trunk.

At that very same instant, Aurelia's vision faded.

No! she thought. *Too soon! I need to see what was inside that trunk.*

'Valerio,' she whispered. 'Yes, I think he brought the jars here! I saw it!'

Then she felt the hand of the present day apothecary on her shoulder. 'Dear girl,' he smiled, 'my apprentice is sometimes quicker witted than myself. I've just realised who you are, Aurelia Bon. Of course you are – look at that nose. And you're not actually unwell, are you?'

There was something about the twitch at the corners of his mouth – and the clear intimacy between her ancestor and his – that made Aurelia want to trust the man. 'Indeed,' she said, 'our main symptom is curiosity. My friend Valerio and I have a great desire to see some old terracotta pots from Arabia, and we've reason to think they are here.'

'Why didn't you say so in the first place? Come with me. Aldo, lock the door to the street and stand guard.'

In a small room at the back of the shop, the apothecary led them to a panelled wall. Aurelia and Valerio looked at it blankly. The apothecary said, 'For hundreds of years, each generation of my family has guarded the secret of this wall. We were told that this secret might be revealed only to one with Aurelio Bon's blood in their veins and his nose on their face. And here you are: the right person with the right name and the right nose, asking the right question. Behold!'

He tugged a thick tasselled rope.

It looks like a bell to summon servants, thought Aurelia.

Yet no servants came. Instead, a part of the panelling drew aside, revealing a shelf. Seven terracotta urns stood dustily upon it. Their labels were wrapped in cobwebs; their tops were stoppered.

Valerio blew the cobwebs off one of the yellowing labels, revealing the words *Hippopotamus dung* in ancient writing.

'Not much call for that!' said the apothecary as Aurelia reached a trembling hand out towards the jar.

It felt cold and dusty in her fingers, which revealed nothing of the contents.

The stopper was of cork, twisted into a thick neck of terracotta. Aurelia began to work it open, her belly clenching with each small turn. From the look on Valerio's face, he felt as she did: desperate to see inside but terrified too.

Finally the stopper ran out of tread. The lid was loose and ready to be lifted.

Aurelia held out the jar to Valerio.

'You want me to open it?'

She confessed, 'My hands are shaking too much.'

Valerio laid the jar on a counter and lifted the lid. At first there was nothing but a dry rustling inside, like autumn leaves at the bottom of an abandoned boat. Then violet-coloured smoke swirled out of the jar's neck, closely followed by a miniature woman dressed in pantaloons, a plain corset and not much else, except an earring. The apothecary took a step backwards, clearing his throat.

Unlike Ghazalah, however, there was no pout or flirt to this girl. Her hair was pulled back in an uncompromising knot. Where Ghazalah bloomed, this Djinniya was bony. Indeed, she looked rather severe. Disapprovingly, she blew the dust off her shoulders, crossed her arms in front of her meagre chest and made the barest bow to Aurelia.

'You know the way this works?' she asked wearily in an Italian that was filtered through a strong accent.

'Yes, three wishes. That is, I think—'

'Then let's get on with it,' the Djinniya said impatiently.

Aurelia turned to Valerio. 'We didn't really think this part through. What we need to wish for is quite complicated. The whole wish thing isn't quite as it's been told in *The Arabian Nights*. We don't *deserve* wishes just because we opened a pot. And humans *using* Djinn to serve our own desires is against their Muslim faith. Djinn are tricky. They can twist our desires into—'

'Excuse me,' said the Djinniya. 'I'm here, listening. Waiting, by the way.'

'I wish this wasn't so hard,' sighed Aurelia, and then clapped her hand over her mouth. For the jar in her hand had turned into a cloud of soft cotton. The Djinniya stretched out on it with a comfortable sigh. 'Lovely!' she said, with a tight mocking smile.

'That's not fair!' shouted Valerio. 'When my friend said "this", she meant our situation, Venice's situation, not that pot. You *deliberately* wasted that wish.'

'And now it's gone. And your second wish?' asked the Djinniya, looking crafty.

'Can we wish for extra wishes?'

'What do *you* think?' asked the Djinniya sarcastically. 'You can't wish to kill anyone either. And you can't make someone fall in love with you.'

'We don't want to do that,' said Aurelia quickly.

'Can we discuss this privately?' asked Valerio, pulling Aurelia out into the main part of the shop. Glancing behind him, he whispered, 'You mustn't grab the first idea that comes to you and think that it's good enough. As *you* were telling me.'

'This isn't really about Djinn, is it? You're talking about history fingers, aren't you? You think it all comes too easily to me, don't you?'

'No, Aurelia, it's just that the most interesting things are not on the surface but under the surface, *shaping* the surface.'

'You're saying I'm *shallow*?'

Aldo the apprentice coughed, apparently smothering a laugh.

'Eavesdropper!' accused Valerio. He turned back to Aurelia.

'No! I'm saying that you'd have more pleasure from what you see with your fingers if you . . . joined me in the archives sometimes.'

'Then I shall.'

Valerio asked, 'Simple as that? No bad feelings?'

'None. Archives it is.' There was resignation in her voice, followed by sorrow. 'If this nightmare ever ends.'

And if it does, thought Aurelia, *there's still the convent to deal with. But I won't burden him with that.*

Valerio sighed, 'It was all so simple before, wasn't it? Do you remember, before the rain, before *I Fedeli*, when Venice was a happy place? It was all about dancing and joy. I wish it was like that again.'

'Ahah!' said the Djinniya from the other room.

'Oh noooo!' said Aurelia.

Suddenly Aurelia and Valerio were no longer inside the apothecary. They found themselves outside in the great square of San Marco, where everyone was dancing in the rain, all the men and boys seizing the hands of women and girls to whirl them around. The dance was not a minuet, or a gavotte not even the *furlana*. It was something much wilder, as if blood from a far earlier century stirred in everyone's veins, reminding the Venetians of hunting and bonfires on lagoon islands and the deep deep darkness of a world without lamplight.

Valerio seized Aurelia's hands and danced her up and down the length of the whole Piazza. She, who hated her dancing lessons, suddenly loved this dance and found inside her bones a quickening grace she'd never known.

Suddenly each person had a lighted candle in their hands! The rain fell on their little flames without quenching a single one. Where those candles had come from, no one knew, but the square was instantly perfumed with beeswax and lilac, saintly and earthly all at once, and all the wonderful scents intensified by the damp air. People began to throw the candles to one another with such perfect skill that not one was dropped and no one was burnt. The candles flew and danced like burning butterflies.

Then the rain grew heavier. It made everyone wetter and the wetness made them more wild. People danced themselves into grinning blurs. Youngsters threw themselves across the wide puddles, skidding through the water like human gondolas. The candles continued to defy the rain. All the boys in San Marco were lost in the joy of the dance. All the men, too.

The girls and women, however, were beginning to pull free and stand apart, with frowns on their faces.

'It's the Djinniya!' Aurelia said out loud. 'She doesn't look like a flirt, but she knows what to do. She must have jumped into the men, one after another.'

Valerio looked at her uncomprehendingly, a beatific smile on his face.

'Oh no! You too! Valerio! Wake up! One Djinniya was more than enough!'

He stared past her. Aurelia turned to see what he was looking at. The rain had changed. Now each raindrop was as big as a handful of water patted into a teardrop. Inside each was a little sardine. People were overcome with pity for the sardines, and so gathered handfuls from the stone floor of San Marco and threw them back into the water of the lagoon, to save the little fishes' lives.

The rain became still more serious. It pelted down on the Venetians like enemy fire. People took refuge under awnings but it sought them out even there.

'This kind of rain does not mean us any good,' Aurelia told Valerio.

'But it means us joy. And we have never seen any of these raindrops before,' he told her. 'Imagine, each raindrop is a completely new thing, a fascinating novelty.'

'Oh, you're Djinniya-struck!' she shouted. She grabbed Valerio's hand and pulled him back into the apothecary, where the Djinniya stood back on the counter, her arms folded. 'Yes, sires?' she said. 'Ready for your next and last wish?'

Aurelia was the first to catch her breath. 'I wish the rain would stop,' she said.

And, just like that, it did.

29

Taking Refuge in a Rat

I feel it in my burning bones. New Djinn magic has been released in Venice. This can mean only one thing. Someone has found the terracotta pots.

Suddenly a constellation of little lights washes across the ceiling. Those starry reflections – they can only happen when the sun comes out. The rain I accidentally caused has ceased. That confirms it. Unless a Djinni or Djinniya made it stop, it would have rained for the rest of time.

So now I'm as lost as the moon in the mist, as we say in my country.

After maturing inside all these centuries, the Djinn inside the jars must be potent, fierce and more than a little bit angry. And they will be looking for me. They will want to punish me, because they could have been released only by my enemy, the bint, Aurelia Bon, descendant of the thief who took them. I trusted her to look for those Djinn on my behalf! Instead, she's betrayed me, and will use my very own Djinn to enact her own desires. Or she'll waste their powers with foolish requests. And I shall never get back to Arabia.

A new thought distracts me – a great craving to see the sun lighting up the rich tones of my skin. I hasten to the nearest mirror. My lovely complexion is blooming in a shy ray of sunshine!

Musipul the leopardess trots up. She too has noticed that the rain has stopped.

'Even your bad spells are weak,' she tells me, 'because you love yourself so much. If you could stop investing all your love in that vision in the mirror, your magic would be stronger. These Venetian mirrors are bad for you. They wear you, the way your victims are worn by you.'

'You're wrong,' I tell her.

Is she, though? She watches a ray of sunshine stretching starrily over the wall. 'You know what this means?' Musipul continues. 'The great-great-great-great-great grandchild of Aurelio Bon has more power than you now. She'll tell the Venetians everything they need to know. You're in real danger. The two buildings, Palazzo Bon and the Castle of Jabrin, are melting into one. Humans will find their way into our castle. They will find the young men you took. They'll want revenge for what you did.'

'This is the first place they will look for me!'

She nods. 'Goodbye,' she says, uncaring and uncurious.

I hurry out of the door and into the nearest square. For the first time, Venetian women see me. They poke one another in the shoulder and point at my bare belly and its enormous ruby. I command my body to be invisible to them, but it remains stubbornly and triumphantly on show. Just when I need them most, my powers are weakening by the second.

I absolutely must leave this visible body and inhabit something else. That won't fool the newly released Djinn, of course. But it will fool the foolish dirt-persons who think they are owed wishes. What's this? A piece of paper wrapped round my slipper?

La Serenissima, the most serene one, this city likes to call herself. There's serene and there's supine – lying down waiting to be taken, like some prone soprano all gone bung and heaving her dying bosoms at the end of an opera tragica. *Wake up, Venice! Get off yer freckle and defend yesself! Oh, what's that? There's no gunpowder at Arsenale because it's all been used for fireworks? Boof!*

I believe I detect the tone of my new friend Signor Rioba here. What *is* he going on about? A rant is not attractive in a man. Did he conspire with the Bon bint to find the Djinn? Human men! Human boys! You cannot trust them, even if they're made of stone.

Something scuttles in the corner of this square. Ugh. A rat. The biggest rat I've ever seen. The biggest rat in Venice!

But then I think, *Rats can get everywhere and no one wants to get too close to them.*

I squeeze my eyes shut and take a last breath of clean air. Then I slip out of my exquisite human-like body and inside the body of the rat who's now nibbling a scavenged crab right by the side of the *fondamenta*. Inside the rat, I taste the sour sweetness of the disintegrating crab flesh. But the rat – and I – keep swallowing it.

That is bad enough. Yet there's worse. Ah! Something is watching. Something has witnessed me jumping inside the rat.

It's something adorably plump with huge, lovely brown eyes, long, lush lashes and a flirtatious look. With what skill this creature has applied her kohl! Obviously, a female. These bewitching dark eyes remind me of Aurelio Bon's. Those lashes too! So luxuriant, shading the cheeks like palm fronds. As his did. Then again, does not everything attractive remind me of the first being I saw when I was released?

The creature is half in the water. All I can see is her head, which is covered all over with a silky kind of hair. I'm not a fool, even though I missed out on so much education when I languished inside the amethyst flask. Fur, I know, means that she's not a crocodile. Nor a reptile, or a fish. She has warm blood. And yet she's a sea-dweller? I never saw a creature like this before. So she must be magical! A mermaid, perhaps? No, there are no scales on her tail, which is tiny.

I must lay a spell on this creature not to tell a soul what she's just seen – a Djinniya slipping into a rat. Not only for secrecy and my safety but because of the shame of it! She's closed her eyes now as she basks in the sun. Stealthily, I approach her, using rat teeth to nip off a tiny sprig of fur. The creature doesn't even notice.

Now I must go back to the Palazzo Bon, where I've the makings of some possible curses. I'm disgusted to feel myself scampering and scuttling. Still worse, at one point, I stop to nibble a mouldy cake thrown on the ground.

An hour later, I'm home. In the safety of my castle, I'm longing to be my beautiful self again. I throw a few quick spells at my rat body. Perhaps my rat eyes grow a little more lustrous. Perhaps my fur is a little glossier. But I am still a rat. I thank all the stars of the desert night that Musipul isn't here to see me mismanaging the magic again.

Later, I will return to my beautiful self, I tell myself. *When I've had time to replenish my energy with* halva *and* baklava. *The more urgent matter at hand is to silence that exquisite creature with the eyelashes.*

Using three of my little claws, I lay three lumps of incense under the threshold. At least rat paws are dextrous and in this form I've the advantage of the sharp teeth too. Using them, I pull three long threads of silk from a curtain. I knot them round tiny bunches of the creature's fur. Then I heat a bullet of lead in a tiny cauldron that I normally use for warming the black kohl that lines my own eyes. I bind the threads together with a line of molten lead, having first put seven black beans in my rat mouth. With the beans in my mouth, I mumble the necessary words over the lead-bound knotted threads and send puffs of my breath swirling around them.

'Now,' I say, 'I hereby bind up the mouths of all warm-blooded, magical female creatures . . . with lustrous hairs . . . and luxuriant lashes. That covers it, yes? I bind up all their mouths.'

There's a shiver in my spine because I know what Musipul would say. She'd snarl that this curse is lazy and inaccurate. Because I don't know how to name that she-creature who witnessed my transformation, I'm hereby cursing all females of this description to silence. But it's a detailed description, isn't it? And sometimes there just *is* collateral damage. Anyway, this is urgent.

So I pronounce the final words of the curse. 'Such she-creatures, hold your tongues from this moment forth!'

It is done. *I am invincible*, I think. I open my mouth to celebrate with a little whoop. Not a sound comes out.

It is in that second that I realise that I too am a magical, female creature with lustrous hairs and luxuriant lashes. I'm made of smokeless fire, so my blood is warm to boiling.

I want to scream. But I'm bound to silence by my own curse! I run – no, *scamper* – out into the courtyard towards the street. Somewhere in this dreadful town of stone, I must find a garden with the herbs for an unbinding spell. I think I can remember about half of the ingredients. I know lemon is involved, white camphor and rue. I need sea salt. On the way to the garden, I must contrive to snatch a silver chain from the neck or wrist of some Venetian woman, or rifle a jewellery box in someone's bedroom, because I need a broken one to complete the spell.

It occurs to me that it's just as well I have – temporarily – remained as a rat. It will be easier to sneak through the streets on my mission.

Suddenly a shadow rears up on the wall in front of me. Its rear quivers in that way all felines' bottoms do just before they pounce. I cannot believe it. There's a cat brave enough to take on the biggest rat in Venice?

This is how it ends?

30

Mouthless Mermaids

'I'm off then,' said the little Djinniya in the apothecary shop. 'Thanks and all.'

She disappeared in more violet-coloured smoke.

The apothecary hastily pulled the rope that looked like a servants bell, closing the remaining six jars behind the panel.

'Horse. Bolted,' said the apprentice, Aldo, unnecessarily. 'What now?'

'We need to consult with some . . . friends,' said Aurelia, pulling Valerio to the door. 'You'll keep the remaining jars secret and safe, won't you?'

'Safe as life,' promised the apothecary, his hand over his heart.

'Since when was life safe?' asked Aldo.

Outside, the sun was already drying the paving stones. 'Look,' said Aurelia. In the crevices between the grey slabs, thousands of the small yellow daisies were quickly raising their battered little heads to warmth and light. 'Leopard's Bane! The mermaids said these flowers could subdue Musipul.'

'Tiny, aren't they?' said Valerio doubtfully. But he helped her pick handfuls of daisies, which Aurelia tied together in the ribbon that the mermaids had provided.

'But before we make the leopardess "suggestiblish", we need to tell the mermaids about finding the Djinn jars,' said Valerio. His pale face showed what Aurelia felt – a sense of having managed the thing badly.

The gate to the House of the Spirits opened for them as promised. The garden was sunning itself in the wonderful new warmth. Birds sang a cheerful welcome. It felt as if the apple trees parted to let them pass through the garden as swiftly as possible.

But down in the mermaid cavern, a strange silence reigned.

Ignoring the posies of Leopard's Bane that Aurelia flourished in front of them, the mermaids were literally holding their tongues, examining them for damage in coral framed mirrors. Finally noticing Valerio and Aurelia, the mermaids made frantic signs with their hands round their necks, miming what looked horribly like strangling.

Aurelia struggled to guess what they were trying to say. 'You have sealed up sore throats? We should go back to the apothecary for something?'

Frantic shakings of heads.

'No?' said Valerio. 'Is this something that *happened* to you quite suddenly?'

Frantic nodding.

'Have you been *cursed* by someone?' Aurelia guessed.

The mermaids clapped their hands. But relief was short-lived on their faces. They began to mime other things with their hands. From the expression the mermaids wore, those things were huge and fearsome.

'They're trying to warn us of something,' said Valerio.

Aurelia guessed, 'Great big somethings?'

The mermaids redoubled their efforts, pointing and making grotesque shapes with their arms. Under any other circumstances their charades would have been hilarious. From their worried faces, however, Aurelia could see that this was no game.

'Great, big somethings with big chests?' Valerio blushed as he said it.

Ghazalah's chest is . . . quite luxuriant, thought Aurelia. *Could it be her?*

'Can you write it down for us?' asked Valerio.

Dozens of mermaids shook their heads dolefully. Lussa held up a piece of paper with child-like scrawls on it.

'You can't even write properly now?' said Aurelia.

Vigorous nodding.

'Ghazalah has done this!' said Aurelia. 'Who else would?'

Chissa squared her shoulders, made her expression even fiercer than usual, raked up her hair with her hands and lumbered around the pool.

'Something messy?' guessed Aurelia. 'So not Ghazalah then.'

On a sheet of paper from the Seldom Seen Press, Valerio tried to draw what they were describing. A bear. A dragon. Sharks attacking. Each time, the mermaids almost turned themselves inside out with frustration. Finally, Lussa threw both hands in the air, her lovely face grim.

'They've given up on us,' said Aurelia, ashamed. 'They couldn't make us understand.'

Lussa nodded, now pointing to the Seldom Seen Press and a pile of printed sheets on the walkway.

Valerio said, 'This must be what they were working on when

they were struck dumb – something for Signor Rioba!' He snatched up a sheet and read aloud,

'Those proud sea walls, the murazzi, *were supposed to be the height of four men standing one on top of one another, and the width of nine men lying end to end.*

'But look inside the murazzi! *They're nought but shimmering shadows of what they should be. A fizzling swizzle! How can walls of paper save this city from fire and water? Look inside the Arsenale! What happened to the arms to save the city from the* real *threat? Boof!*

'Methinks you're nought but walking shadows, gazing with dead eyes at what's about to be done to you—'

Aurelia searched for the next sheet. There was none. 'You were silenced before you could prepare it?' she asked the mermaids.

Nodding, Lussa pointed to the stairs.

'She's telling us to go out into Venice and see for ourselves,' guessed Aurelia. The mermaids put up their fingers to their heads and made triangles.

'Musipul?' asked Aurelia. 'You still want us to use the Leopard's Bane on Musipul and make her paint a portrait of her mistress in a bowl?'

The mermaids shook their heads.

'Too late? Something worse has happened?'

The mermaids nodded and hugged themselves with worried expressions.

Valerio said, 'I think they're warning us to take care of ourselves.'

Aurelia and Valerio ran up the steps of the cavern and into the apple orchard of the House of the Spirits – and towards whatever huge, fierce and dangerous thing was waiting for them out there in Venice.

31

Death by Cat

The death of a rat is not very interesting. Who could mourn the passing of a creature that looks nasty, eats what rots, kills even those of its own kind, inhabits dank and unsavoury places, steals eggs from nests and lies in wait to murder chicks who fail in their first attempt at flying?

I'd thought the size of the quivering shadow was exaggerated by the sudden sun. But now I realise that the predator about to eat me is my very own leopardess.

'Musipul!' I scream. Of course, nothing comes out of my mouth except air. I've bound myself to silence along with all magical, female creatures with luxuriant hair. Even if I could speak, would a hungry leopardess listen to me?

Musipul's fur is sleek and glossy. Must she be silent too? A blessing, at least. But wait, I can hear her panting for my blood. And there's a purr in anticipation of her meal. Of course, my spell specified creatures with long lashes. Musipul has none. So I won't be spared a commentary on how delicious I taste.

There was I splendouring myself for being so clever as to silence that long lashed sea creature with a spell. And now I've condemned myself to an ugly, messy death.

Musipul will kill me as well as the rat I inhabit, whose low habits I've been forced to adopt.

As a rat, I shall die. I imagine my rat bones picked clean as a harp. A woeful end to a wondrous Djinniya. The pathos of it breaks my spirit, leads my thoughts into darkness. I begin to wonder, *Why should I fear death?* Everything is hopeless. I'll never find my Djinn. I'll never leave this dreadful city. What is my life here but a living death? As we say in my country, I'm already drowning so why should I fear getting wet?

Musipul picks me up in her jaws. Suddenly I understand that it's not merely her words that can be sharp.

These are real teeth I feel, as yet gentle, on my rat skin.

As a rat, I shall die. I don't suppose anyone who knows me will be sorry that I die anyway. So much for all my self-splendouring. If only Musipul knew, she too would rejoice, to know that I'm dying as a result of my own incompetence.

Musipul's teeth are chattering. She's rehearsing the moment when she shall crunch on my throat and sever my spinal cord.

But she'll play with me first.

32

One Less Rat in Venice

Valerio and Aurelia hurried back towards the Palazzo Bon. Aurelia kept her hand in her pocket, curled round a bunch of yellow daisies.

She stopped short. 'Something is different. I can't work out what it is.'

'We're just on edge because the mermaids are upset. And because what they were miming's a bit . . . frightening,' said Valerio. 'But I don't see anything wrong out here.'

'Of course you wouldn't see, you land-prince! It's the boats! While we've been down in the cavern, every single boat in Venice has disappeared. Every canal is empty.'

'Who'd take the boats?'

'And why?'

They were already outside the Palazzo Bon. This time, there was no sign of the Castle of Jabrin inside the broken down *portone*. No airy terracotta halls. No exquisite rugs. No orange trees in the courtyard, no astronomical drawings, no cushions on spotless floors. Nor was Ghazalah to be found inside. Aurelia and Valerio combed every inch of the palace in vain. Finally, out in the courtyard, they found the leopardess standing by a patch of earth, with a large rat in her jaws.

Ugh! One less rat could only be a good thing, thought Aurelia.

Then Valerio whispered, 'Something tells me that Musipul's not a dainty feeder. A leopard devouring a rat – that's one grisly spectacle I really don't want to see.'

Aurelia pulled the bunch of daisies out of her pocket and dangled it in front of the leopardess.

'What the frankincense?' cried Musipul. Then she lay on the ground and put her legs in the air, the rat still in her mouth. From deep in her chest came purring as loud as carriage wheels on gravel. Her eyes glazed with distant pleasure. Aurelia dared to run her fingers through Musipul's luxuriant spotted belly fur. 'Oh, I always wanted to do that. So soft! Even more than I could have guessed. It's not lions but *leopards* who are the queens of beasts. A noble creature like you should feed on *noble* meats. Let the rat go,' she cajoled. 'You'll only catch something if you eat it.'

The rat took advantage of Musipul's distraction to struggle out of the leopardess's jaws and make an attempt to scuttle away. But Musipul rolled over and slammed one huge paw on its tail, pinning it down.

'Don't interrupt me when I'm killing,' hissed Musipul, fully restored to her normal hauteur and ferocity. 'Leopard's Bane? You're using that on me? Whoever told you about it forgot to mention that its effects don't last very long.'

Valerio said, 'There's something strange about that rat. Its eyes . . . are very large and—'

The rat scratched something in the earth with a shaking paw.

'It looks *almost* like words! What does it say?' asked Aurelia.

'Or is it a drawing? You're the one who's always squinting at ancient manuscripts, Valerio. Can you make it out?'

Valerio knelt near the rat, who bared its teeth.

'Actually, I think it's trying to smile at you,' said Aurelia. 'Hideous!'

Valerio squinted at the squiggles in the earth. 'If these *are* words, they could say, "Man-Guzzler"? This rat eats *men*? Why would it tell us that?'

'Let me see,' said Musipul, nosing Valerio out of the way. 'Oh. It says, or rather it's *trying* to say, "*I am Ghazalah*".' Musipul drew back her lips and hissed at the rat. 'Really, it's come to this, that you take refuge in a rat? How low . . .?'

'Why didn't she tell you who she is? Or us?' asked Aurelia. 'She can't talk?'

Musipul laughed bitterly. 'I would guess that . . . she tried to put an enchantment on someone and as usual it all went wrong and she ended up putting it on herself as well.'

The rat nodded humbly.

'What kind of an enchantment?' asked Valerio.

'By the stars, a mouth-binding curse! To stop someone speaking!' Musipul exclaimed, poking the rat with her muzzle. 'You know you *never* get that one right. And *you* of all people should know how grievous it is to be bound!'

The rat looked down, shamefaced.

'So you tried to bind the mouth of some kind of creature – let me guess, female? Beautiful? The way you see yourself?'

With eloquent paws the rat mimed a large, shapely creature with enormous, soulful eyes. Then it pointed to the water and made swimming movements with its paws.

'A monk seal!' said Aurelia. 'But they don't even talk anyway!'

The words 'you idiot!' hung unspoken in the air.

'And that spell must be why the mermaids can't speak now,' said Valerio. Aurelia kicked him. The mermaids had said not to 'blab' their 'bizness' to the Djinniya.

Musipul looked up sharply. 'You have Fishwomen in this town? I've seen a few by our Arabian coasts. Wild. Fierce. Are yours good or bad mermaids? Because they can go either way. Like Djinn.'

'Definitely good,' said Valerio. 'Yet now silenced, so we can no longer benefit from their ancient wisdom. It's a disaster.'

Aurelia shook her head at him. She wished she could bind Valerio's mouth with a spell now.

'One of many disasters,' said Musipul, glaring at her mistress. 'Will it never end?'

The rat stood with one paw over its heart, miming piteously. It was somehow obvious to all of them that Ghazalah was saying, 'So kill me now. I cannot be disgraced further. I might as well die.'

Aurelia said, 'Don't be so melodramatic, Ghazalah! And shoo, Musipul! I don't believe you'd eat your mistress.'

'I'd be doing the world a favour,' grumbled Musipul.

'Ghazalah,' said Aurelia, 'There's work for you to do. Get out of that rat, you!'

Musipul sighed. 'She's probably already depleted her remarkably feeble stock of magic trying to wish herself back into Djinniya form. We'll need to go back inside the castle, feed her up with *halva* and then find the ingredients for an unbinding curse for *all* her victims.'

Musipul looked at the silver bracelet on Aurelia's wrist. 'Hand that over, for a start.'

Then she picked up the rat in her mouth, as if it was a kitten . . . though perhaps rather less gently than a mother cat might do that thing.

33

The Irish Duchess

Even before Aurelia had finished berating him for talking about the mermaids, Valerio started shaking his head and wrinkling his nose.

'Can you smell something?' he asked.

Aurelia sniffed. 'Yes! Something not very nice.'

A dozen black cats suddenly ran past the courtyard entrance, close together, as if in formation. There was an unusual tilt to their whiskers and to the slant of their eyes. Such fierceness, such fire was never seen in the eyes of Venetian cats, even in those of the Syrian tabbies who'd arrived centuries before on merchant ships. Several of the black cats were wearing black eye patches, and two boasted one wooden leg apiece. The wooden legs clicked lightly on the paving stones as they scampered off in the direction of Arsenale. The skin on the back of Aurelia's neck prickled as they passed. She whispered, 'Did you see—?'

Valerio clutched her arm and dragged her back from the doorway, his face white and his lips pinched. 'Shhhh,' he hissed.

Peeping out from behind the gate, Aurelia saw a tall, narrow-hipped young woman, with reddish hair cropped short, large blue eyes and a face that was none too clean. Plentiful freckles, however, were visible – even at twenty paces away – on her thin cheeks. Her purple mantle and blue skirt were fine but tattered. It was not just the scimitar glinting on her belt that put a tang of danger in the air around this girl, it was also the evident fear of the bearded man standing next to her. He kept bowing and touching the back of his neck.

He was dressed – more like Ghazalah than a Venetian – in a long waistcoat over wide pantaloons and a broad sash round his waist. A spotless muslin turban framed an intelligent, anxious face. The two were talking urgently. Aurelia could make out only scraps of the conversation.

'If that's Italian,' she murmured, 'then it's some kind of odd dialect.'

Valerio whispered, 'I think it's the *lingua franca* that sailors and slave traders use all over the world – some Greek, some French, some Arabic, but mostly Italian.'

'How can you know that?'

Valerio shrugged. The word 'archives' hung in the air unsaid. After listening for a few more seconds, he said, 'They're talking about the *badestan* and *bagno* in Algiers. The slave market and the slave dormitories. They're *pirates*! This must be what the mermaids were trying to warn us about when they were miming something dangerous.'

'Pirates on the streets of Venice?'

'Not just pirates, but *Barbary* pirates!'

'Can girls be pirates?' asked Aurelia. She realised she should know more about Barbary pirates but she also knew from the look on his face that Valerio was about to deliver a little lecture on them.

'Barbary pirates come from the northwest coast of Africa, the Maghreb. For centuries, they've preyed on the ships and the coastlines of the Mediterranean, searching for plunder and most of all slaves – because Muslim masters will enslave only Christians and not people of their own faith. Christians, I regret to say, are not always so . . . particular, when it comes to taking slaves.'

Aurelia was swiftly becoming accustomed to the language that the two strangers were using. It was a matter of listening to groups of words rather than one at a time. From the man's respectful manner, it was clear that they were eavesdropping on an *important* female pirate. That was confirmed a heartbeat later when the man bowed, stammering, 'Yes, Duchess. But is it really necessary to—'

Aurelia whispered, 'That blue-eyed Duchess in the mermaids' turtle shell – she's a *Pirate* Duchess! Is this girl Irish? I suppose the red hair . . . but do Duchesses have freckles?'

'Rather more importantly, the turtle shell said that she *hates* Venice.'

'But she looks extremely young,' said Aurelia hopefully. 'She can't really be very dangerous, can she?'

With her very next words, the Pirate Duchess dashed any such hope.

'Ye don't have to tell me that the men are frustrated,' she told her companion. 'I've seen the sour pusses on 'em so. But I've not passed all these years in the company of Barbary pirates not to know in my noggin what they're like. The sniff of an ingot of gold will distract those guzz-eyed gowls from any order to hang back *strategically*, the better to pounce. I'm sharing my plans with ye now *on the condition* ye tell the men only what's necessary, *when* I say it's necessary, one order at a time. Or ye'll suffer for it.'

'Yes, Duchess.' The man lowered his head humbly, which meant he did not see her whip the little scimitar from her belt. She grabbed his beard, lifted it and held the scimitar against his bare, pulsing neck.

'Ye're not understanding me, me old flower,' she hissed. 'Ye're to swear secrecy *on your life* or I'll cut the throat out of ye, no word of a lie. Yours would not be the first babbling mouth I've silenced.'

'Please, please, spare me,' pleaded the man, his eyes bulging with terror. 'Whatever you want, my lady, is my humblest and dearest desire—'

'That's better now,' said the Duchess, releasing his beard and returning the scimitar to her belt. 'Here's the plan. Once we've taken all the womenfolk, we'll sail out a few miles to just beyond the horizon. We'll let the Venetian men have a day's dose of missing their daughters and wives and maidservants and cooks. Then we'll hoist a white flag – peace – ha! – and heave back within sight of the shore. We'll let it be known that the men can come and negotiate ransoms for their womenfolk. If the Venetians offer a tadeen more than we'd get for the females at the *badestan* in Algiers – we'll let the ladies go. If not, we'll help ourselves to the men who were too mean to pay properly. Isn't my nose a-telling me that we'll bag a fair few that way?'

'You will really let the women go?' the man asked. There was unmistakable relief in his voice.

Aurelia looked at Valerio questioningly. 'I suppose not all pirates are the same,' he whispered.

She replied, 'Not all Venetians are the same. Look at Ghezzo. At Padre Pino. *I Fedeli*.'

The Duchess waggled her finger in her companion's face. 'Will ye come on now? Putting sentiment on me, when I've none in my stony heart so. Cash in hand is always good. Make a blazing profit immediately. Lovely altogether. Also – given conditions belowdecks, there's always wastage on the way back to Algiers.'

Wastage, thought Aurelia, reading the sombre look on the man's face. *That means people dying! Girls dying!*

'Of course, I must keep all the famous musical girls from the orphanages at Mendicanti, the Ospedaletto, the Incurabili, the Pietà . . . both the orphans and their instruments. I've a hankering for some musical handmaidens. As for the Venetian men, I've got to balance the biteen of pleasure it would give me to run a sword through the lot of 'em – against the coin they'll fetch in Algiers. Or the ransoms I'll get for 'em from their noble cousins in their villas on dry land. I'm thinking three hundred and fifty ducats a man so I am.'

The man said, 'A fortune! But your Duchess-ship, what if the people simply can't pay? Not all Venetians are rich.'

'Don't I know that? But our friends *I Fedeli* are *rotten* with money, as ye know, through certain bargains made. At a signal from me, they'll be ready to lend money to desperate families at *mutilating* rates of interest.'

The man flinched at the word 'mutilating'. He said, 'So strange to behold how these so-called *Fedeli* prey on their own citizens. *I Fedeli* are slave traders with a difference! Barbary pirates would never betray and sell their *own* people. Yet these Venetians will sell their souls and their city, so long as the money's good.'

'Sell their souls', thought Aurelia. *The exact words from the mermaids' prophecy.*

The Duchess grinned. 'Sure they weren't behind the door when the greed was being given out! Thanks to those cadging fellows, *our* people will soon rejoice to see our boats arriving back in Algiers low in the water, weighed down with Venetian slaves.'

'Indeed, your *adopted* people love you very much,' acknowledged the man, with a slight edge. 'They'd be afraid not to.'

''Tis so long since I was Irish that I've forgotten how to be so,' she replied. 'I've a belly on me to enjoy seeing the Venetians set to hard labour, building walls in Algeria! Those delicate white hands will grow a few calluses so they will. Those soft Venetians will learn what it is to live on manky black bread made of barleycorn the horses turn their noses up at. As for clothes, won't they be grateful for the one time a year they're allowed some new ones? The tough treatment will encourage 'em to write pure heartrending letters to their relatives, which'll help us raise bigger ransoms.'

'Indeed,' said her companion, looking uncomfortable.

'At least harvesting these slaves won't cost me any money, or men. *I Fedeli* happened to blather that any gunpowder they haven't sold to us has been used up in fireworks. Buttering me up like an oatcake so they are.'

'*I Fedeli*'s plots are bottomless!'

'Sure I know. So how can I be trusting men like that? That's why my cats are on their way to Arsenale to confirm this with an inspection. The beasts are trained to sniff for gunpowder. If they find any, they'll deploy their ample bladders to render it too damp to use.'

'I *knew* those cats were up to no good!' whispered Aurelia.

'Now we've taken all their boats,' the Duchess was saying, 'the Venetians have no way to escape from us.'

The man asked, 'How have you been able to take the Venetians so thoroughly by surprise?'

'Well for one thing, the cats have been on the prowl for a week now and have reported how the land lies. Then, this morning, I sent in a special advance group of my most agile men. Armed with maps—'

'– doubtless furnished by *I Fedeli* –'

'—my men have climbed up every church tower in the city and removed the bells.'

The Duchess's eyes glinted like sapphires by starlight. 'No one will be ringing any warning bells today. My men were all the more eager because melted-down bronze fetches such a good price in Algiers. Plus, of course, they hate the sound of those noisy bells. Meanwhile, the Venetian girlfolk are keeping mum as we take 'em – because we stuff their mouths with cork.'

So the churches and the girls have been silenced. Like the mermaids! thought Aurelia. *Ghazalah's timing could not have been worse!*

The Duchess continued, 'There's only one Venetian I'd give a figgy pudding for and *I Fedeli* have seen to him. Angelo Emo – a true thorn in their sides. I captured some of Emo's men. They told me how the Emo lad tried to make the Venetians listen to the warnings of their mouthy Mister Rioba. Angelo Emo is a true friend of sailors and of his home city. For him – respect. Aye, Angelo Emo almost gives the Venetians a bit of a good name. Almost.'

'How's the lad been "seen to"?' asked the man.

'By demotion to menial duties. But more by skilful ridicule and humiliation,' she replied. 'Speaking of which, I gave my men the added pleasure of permission to use the wooden saints in the churches for target practice with their bows and arrows so!'

Valerio and Aurelia listened in horror as the Pirate Duchess revealed that, while her cats did their spying, her fleet had been concealed behind the teeming columns of water when the rain was upon Venice. They'd had plenty of time to mass their hundred-oar galleys there.

The Duchess laughed. 'I've amused myself sending messages to colleagues in their secret roosts in Salé, Rabat, Algiers, Tunis and Tripoli, where they hide from officers of the law from every country, including their own! And in they've swarmed in-very-deed – more mad-eyed Barbary pirates than I've ever seen in one place.'

'True. There are some who've been waiting centuries to get their hands on Venice.'

'And now the ending of the soft weather's forced our own hands, so it has,' said the Pirate Duchess. 'We're after having to show ourselves. But the end of the rain means one very useful thing. Once we've taken everything . . . and everyone . . . we want out of Venice, we can put the city to the torch. Those men of mine who cut the bell ropes – they didn't go in empty-handed. Didn't they leave oil-soaked rags in every church tower in Venice?

I reckon we can strip the city of girls and gold by the end of this day, add another two for the ransoming, and then on the fourth evening, from the comfort of their own lagoon, I'll be able to watch a splendid bonfire and listen to Venetians a-weeping and a-screaming for mercy.'

The Duchess and her companion began to walk away, she chuckling and his intelligent face pale and tense.

Valerio stared at Aurelia in horror.

'You stopped the rain at exactly the right moment to allow the pirates to burn down Venice,' he said.

34

Shouldn't Be Alone in This

'We shouldn't be alone, should we?' said Valerio. 'All Venice should be fighting this.'

'What exactly were *I Fedeli* doing in their important boats then?' asked Aurelia. 'Obviously *not* patrolling for pirates. And where are those boats now?'

'Perhaps the pirates took *their* boats too?'

'More likely the *Fedeli* are holed up somewhere safe. Giving the pirates a free hand in this city. Oh no!'

A pirate boat had appeared from round a corner. Manned by two pirates, it was loaded with girls and women, tied together and covered with nets. They struggled and moaned quietly, but they could not cry out; their mouths, bound with rags, were bulging with large pieces of cork.

A hank of dark red hair drew Aurelia's attention to one of the girls.

Catarina.

Aurelia's feelings were torn painfully down the middle. She told herself, *Papa will pay her ransom. She'll soon be home safe. Anyway, she betrayed me. She's no longer my sister. And if I call out to her, I'll only draw attention to our hiding place.* But inside Aurelia's heart, a painful feeling drowned out all those very rational thoughts: she could not bear for anyone to hurt Catarina.

Valerio said, 'Aurelia, you're a girl.'

'And? That isn't the most profound observation you've ever made.'

'If you're wearing a dress, the pirates will take you.'

A boy ran past, his face distorted with terror. Aurelia recognised him as Aldo, the apothecary's apprentice. 'You!' he panted. 'San Marco's been looted. And the Doge's Palace. And now they're breaking into the apothecaries and stealing all the precious spices. If you protest . . . they . . . hurt you. When we heard what they did at the Crowned Wolf, my master and I decided to run. But somehow, in all the confusion and panic, I lost him.'

'Did you take the Djinn?'

'You know how heavy those jars are! My master said they'd be safer behind the secret panel than if we tried to run with them. There's not a man on the streets now, so we'd only arouse suspicion.'

'Where are all the men?'

'Hiding! Because they know what happens to Christian slaves in Algiers. They think the pirates really want *them* because men fetch higher ransoms. But the women! You should hear the women! They're *telling* the men to hide. They're telling them *where* to hide, because of course it's the women who know all the secret places in the city, all the niches hidden behind linen-presses and wardrobes. They're magnificent, the women. The pirates should be afraid of *them*.'

'Which reminds me,' said Aurelia. 'I need your clothes.'

'Get lost!' said Aldo, some of his former spirit returning.

Aurelia was already undoing the buttons of her skirt. 'I have work to do that would be dangerous in a dress. A true gentleman would do anything to keep a lady, or even another gentleman, out of danger. Are you saying you're not one?'

'Of course not.'

'So turn your back and take off your trousers. I won't look if you won't look. That includes you, Valerio. Here, take this skirt. Give me your cap. Aldo, do you know how to get "between the linings"?'

'I'm Venetian,' scoffed Aldo. 'Of course I know the secret back streets.'

'Then you need to run to the Incurabili, the Pietà, the Mendicanti and the Ospedaletto, and get the orphans. The pirates have a shopping list and musical girls are on it.'

'You know this how? Never mind. Where do I take the girls? Is anywhere safe?'

'Can you lead them – always through the linings – to the House of the Spirits? Inside the walls there's an apple orchard and a chapel . . .'

When Aurelia finished telling Aldo about the mermaids and their cavern, he nodded. 'I knew it,' he said. 'The Canal di Noale – it's right by the House of the Spirits. I *did* see a mermaid. Not a monk seal.'

'And you're definitely not mad,' smiled Aurelia. 'Remember to stay between the linings while you're dressed like a girl!'

'You don't have to tell me again! And once I've delivered the girls – and changed back into a decent pair of trousers! – I'm going to organise the apprentices. The apprentices of the shoemakers, blacksmiths, candlemakers, oarlock fashioners . . . all of us. The *men* may be hiding, but we young ones can make a stand,' said Aldo very proudly for a boy who was currently wearing a skirt that was several inches too short for him.

'What are *we* going to do?' Valerio asked Aurelia, who was tucking her hair up under Aldo's cap.

'We need to get those Djinn from the Redeemer apothecary. We're going to need their help.'

35

An Empty Apothecary; An Empty Arsenal

By circuitous loops, via the courtyards and gardens that made up Venice's secret linings, Aurelia and Valerio found their way to the Redeemer apothecary in San Marco without encountering a single pirate. But the door was hanging off its hook. Just inside the shop, Aurelia tripped and fell headlong over something long and thin lying on the floor. As he helped her up, Aurelia held it out to Valerio, gasping, 'It's the rope for the secret panel!'

And in the inner room, the panel gaped open. The shelf that once held the Djinn jars bore only the dusty impressions of their long presence there.

Valerio said, 'Of course – the pirates were looking for girls to take away. All over Venice they must have been ringing servants bells. Girls came running – and fell straight into their hands. This time, when they pulled that rope, the pirates got something much more unusual.'

The pirates had left a pile of kindling and some oily rags on the shop counter.

'Not just in the church towers then,' said Aurelia. '*Everywhere*, ready to burn the city down. If they went into Palazzo Bon with those rags – all the vats of date honey would burn like an inferno. The place would go up in a second!'

'And we can't even wish for the rain to come back, because the Djinn are with the Barbary pirates. The Pirate Duchess can wish for anything she wants, including the destruction of this whole city.'

'Will she, though?' asked Aurelia. 'Look – all the jars of precious herbs and spices have been looted. The pirates *might* not have realised that the Djinn jars are any different. Remember, the labels say, "Hippopotamus dung". Let's hope the pirates aren't partial to it in their stew! If we get the Djinn back quickly, we might still have a chance.'

'How do we take them off a pirate ship? How do we get out there with all the boats gone from Venice? Shall we . . . shall we get ourselves captured?'

'No, we need to go to Arsenale. There must be some old rotten vessel there that the pirates couldn't be bothered with! Just seaworthy enough to get us out to the ship and get Ghazalah's Djinn back.'

'*Which* ship? The Duchess said there are masses of them there now!'

'We'll have to check them all. Once we've got the Djinn, we can tell the sailors to shoot cannons at the pirates – What's the matter, Valerio?'

'You're forgetting how many Venetian girls are already aboard those ships.'

'A human shield,' said Aurelia, aghast. 'Including my sister.'

'The Pirate Duchess has thought of everything,' said Valerio. 'She must have been making plans for years.'

'And now we have hours, or even just minutes, to undo them.'

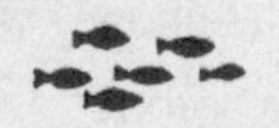

At Arsenale, where all the guns, the boats and the canons to protect Venice should be stored, the halls were empty apart from a strong smell of cat urine.

Aurelia stooped to pick up a piece of paper that was lying on the floor. It was an elegant receipt.

'*One cog complete with canons and rowers – 100 ducats, sold to the Duchess Emer Fionnuala O'Dowdy and her esteemed company of Corsairs.*'

'Emer Fionnuala O'Dowdy!' said Aurelia, stretching out the strange syllables. 'What a name!'

Valerio pointed to the crest of *I Fedeli* at the top of the page: three golden coins. 'That's what the Pirate Duchess meant when she said that *I Fedeli* are "rotten with money", ready to lend at high interest for ransoms! So while they said they were collecting funds to save Venice and redeem the slaves, they've actually been selling off our assets to the enemy!'

A shadow fell over the paper. A young officer with a fresh round face told them, 'Indeed. Everything *I Fedeli* said was pure perfidy. In the last hours, their vileness has been unveiled!'

'And you are, sir?' asked Valerio politely.

'Angelo Emo. I warned *I Fedeli* that our oared naval galleys were out of date and no match for Barbary pirates' clever rigging, quick sails and cannons. Our round-bellied merchant ships, slow and barely defended, are like fat floating piglets for the pirates to pick off. I *told* them!'

And the Pirate Duchess somehow knew you told them, thought Aurelia.

'But *I Fedeli*,' continued Emo, 'put all the experienced officers out to pension and informed *me* there was no need for a modern fleet – "Venice hasn't been at war with anyone for decades. Why waste the money?" they said.

'"*Pirates! That's why,*" I warned them,' Emo scowled. 'And *I Fedeli* boasted of protection treaties signed by the doge, no less. And I explained that pirates are no great abiders by treaties . . . But every time I protested about something, they scoffed at me, and told me that I should be best friends with crazy Signor Rioba.'

'Who isn't crazy at all,' said Aurelia. 'In fact, I think you should come to meet him.'

'How does one meet a statue?'

'In certain circumstances he's more than . . . stone. But to see his . . . best . . . side, you also need to believe in magic.'

Looking around the deserted halls, Angelo Emo growled, 'I believe in pure evil, corruption and greed because I've seen them with my own eyes. So I must believe in magic too, I suppose. Now what about the *murazzi*?'

Aurelia said, 'Signor Rioba was just about to tell Venice that those walls are made of paper.'

'Paper! Before you introduce me to that gentleman, I propose that we go see what he means. I've always kept a *sandolo* hidden in the bushes at Quintavalle in case of emergencies.'

'You can stay here, Valerio,' said Aurelia kindly. 'He gets abominably seasick in little boats,' she explained to Angelo Emo.

'No,' said Valerio, 'this is something I have to see. *Paper* walls?'

'Paper walls and *solid* treachery,' said Angelo Emo.

At the great walls, all appeared to be as it should – at first. From the shore, the walls *seemed* to be as thick as nine men lying down. The stone structures towered over the lagoon, casting long shadows. But as they clambered ashore, Aurelia spied a small door hanging open. When they entered, all three of them shouted out loud. For the walls were just one thin stone thick. Inside was simply thick, dank air. Walls like this would not withstand pirates or floods.

They could, Aurelia thought, *be pushed over with one hand.*

The three of them climbed back into Angelo Emo's secret *sandolo*. In silent misery, apart from Valerio's retching, they rowed back to the shoreline at Quintavalle. Aurelia and the officer withdrew discreetly behind a bush so Valerio could scrub his stained shirt with grass.

Aurelia finally broke the silence. '*I Fedeli* made the city pay heavily for those walls. Where's the money gone if it didn't go into these walls?'

'Where indeed?' said Angelo Emo gloomily.

'Into the pockets of the high officers of *I Fedeli*! Men like Daniele Spatafora,' said Aurelia. 'Signor Rioba should hear about this right now! He's only a few bridges away. Let's go to him. He'll enjoy being right. And after he's enjoyed it, perhaps . . . he . . . can help us tell the Venetians that it's really true.'

'The Venetians haven't listened to him so far,' said Valerio, joining them.

Angelo Emo said, 'Venetians didn't have pirates stealing their wives and daughters before. Perhaps that will open their ears and their eyes. Oh no! Why didn't we hide the *sandolo* straightaway?'

Even as they watched, three pirates appeared in a small Venetian boat. Spotting the *sandolo,* they shouted excitedly. In two minutes, they had hitched the little craft to their own vessel and were off.

'The last boat in Venice,' said Aurelia. 'Gone and not coming back.'

After the necessary introductions and explanations, Signor Rioba said, 'I thought I'd snort me head off when I heard *I Fedeli* had promised to help those hungry families robbed of their breadwinners by the Barbaries.'

Aurelia thought, *He enjoys being right as much as I do . . . did.*

'So ye're tellin' me,' roared Signor Rioba, 'that instead of helping pay the ransoms of Venetian slaves – *I Fedeli* are handing Venetians *over*! Yet it makes a sordid sort of sense. Why couldn't they see the cracks here, those befooled Venetians?'

With a creaking motion, Signor Rioba waved the receipt for the cog that they had brought him. 'I got me a noseful of them pirates here today. And one o' them rowdy Corsair cats sat on my head licking its unmentionable yesterday – after poking its wooden leg in my eye on the way up there.'

'Ugh and ouch,' said Aurelia.

'Speaking of cats, Venice is now weak as a day-old kitten against them Barbaries, precisely because of *I* filthy *Fedeli*. And with our mermaids deprived o' words, all I could do was write this sign mesself!' He pointed to a clumsily scrawled sign on his stone chest. It said, simply, *PIRATES! HIDE!*

Angelo Emo's face was a picture. 'Mermaids?' he asked.

'We thought we'd tell you about the mermaids *after* you got used to Signor Rioba,' said Aurelia.

'Despite the present scuttish situation, 'tis a great pleasure,' said Rioba, 'to meet the one man in Venice who also saw through *I* flapdoodling *Fedeli*. Even if he didn't have the wherewithal to fillet the lot of 'em with his sword.'

Angelo Emo blushed.

'Ah, spare me yer shame, sir!' railed Rioba. 'Ye can be no better, no braver, no wiser than ye are. Ye're but a boy. Methinks ye shall grow into yer virtue soon enough. Meantime, yer instincts have done ye credit.'

He turned, creaking, to Aurelia, 'Methinks that fox-sleeky miss ye brought here might be the one to help . . . though sadly all the rackings of me many brains have not yet found her Djinn in jam jars.'

'Ghazalah the Djinniya? She's not quite up to—'

'A Djinniya!' exclaimed Angelo Emo. 'With hairy legs and donkey feet?'

'And what be wrong with a well-haired leg?' thundered Rioba. 'On a lady?'

Aurelia told Signor Rioba, 'I know you think Ghazalah's gorgeous. I'm sorry to tell you this, but the reason she needs her Djinn back is because her magic's pathetic without their help. I'm afraid she was too vain to tell you the truth about that.'

Signor Rioba's face fell. 'Nobody's perfect,' he rumbled.

'And the Djinn jars are currently aboard a pirate ship in the lagoon. And *we* have no boats to get to them. Should we try to swim?' said Aurelia.

Valerio turned a little green. 'I can't.'

'What a wibbling waterlily of a boy!' complained Signor Rioba. 'There's a swift solution for ye, though. Fancy a swim on the backs of those finny ladies? I reckon 'twould be one of life's finest experiences. Wot, boy? Ye look as if ye'd rather shave a warthog than—'

'Don't insult him, you great granite bully!' said Aurelia. 'He's been through enough. Being hit on the head. Being treated badly by everyone just because he's not noble. Stop it!'

'Yes, girlie, ye get angry,' Signor Rioba said to Aurelia. 'Yer belly corrodes if ye leave yer anger unshouted. Ye hold it in too long, it makes ye sick.'

'I'm sure the Pirate Duchess and the Djinniya are not ashamed to have fifty fits whenever they feel like it,' said Aurelia, 'but that's not the view in Venetian society. If I get angry with my family, I'm generally humiliated and threatened. At home, I'm less influential than the *Poupée de France*.'

'Some French mongrel favoured over ye? I hate me a pretentious puppy. Boof! Never ye mind that. Anger's how ye protect yesself. From wrong or danger. Why should girls or ladies be deprived o' protection?'

'What's your position on crying?' asked Aurelia.

'If it needs to be did, it needs to be did. But anger's wot's needed now, and urgentish,' said Signor Rioba. 'It's time to stir this stale cesspool of infamy with the stiff finger of righteousness. But wait! It's just dawned in me stone head who ye two are. Not the history-fingering girl and her seasick friend, but who ye *really* are: the little folk from the prophecy! The Water's Daughter and the Landsman Prince with the belly of a princess! This is your actual task. This is wot ye was borned for.'

Aurelia's first instinct was to frown. *In this prophecy, I'm only a Daughter. Valerio gets to be a* Prince.

Then she smiled. *Yes, Valerio* is *a prince. Well, he deserves to be one.*

And as if to prove it so, Valerio now said bravely, 'Let's go to the mermaids and ask them for that ride.'

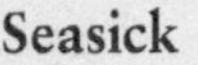

36

Seasick

Down in the cavern, Aurelia and Valerio found a hundred Venetian girls practising their violins, flutes and cellos in a grand cacophony. Aldo was conducting with great enthusiasm but little talent.

Chissa pointed to her mouth. Her expression said it all: *Better a little noise than this unbearable silence.*

The orphans stopped playing and listened intently as Aurelia and Valerio explained what they had learnt. Some girls snuffled back tears. Others clutched their instruments to their chests. The mermaids made grimaces and gestures of desperation.

'And here's what we propose to do,' said Aurelia. 'Now all the pirates are swarming through the city searching for these musical orphans, we need you ladies to swim me and Valerio out to their ships so we can save the Venetian girls already taken and recover the Djinn jars.'

The mermaids rose up, slapping the water with their tails.

'That's applause?' asked Aurelia.

Grins appeared on the faces of the mermaids. Yet when it was time to leave for the lagoon, Valerio's smile soon vanished. If you think riding a small boat through a lagoon might make a land-dwelling boy seasick, you should imagine that poor pale person on the back of a mermaid, undulating and dipping through the waves. Valerio began vomiting the instant they left the cavern and didn't stop until his belly was empty.

'I wish you'd stayed behind!' said Aurelia, embarrassed for him and upset for Lussa, who was carrying Valerio and getting the worst of the vomit.

'Be careful what you wish for,' gasped Valerio. 'If I were you, I wouldn't want to board the ship of a Barbary pirate alone.' Between dry retches, he added, 'And you *really* do need to be careful what you wish for when we find the Djinn! Don't just blurt out the first thing that comes into your mind. Again.'

'Same applies to you. Hard as it might be to believe, it's equally possible that the too utterly brilliant Valerio Fialetti might actually make a mistake.'

Aurelia was sorry as soon as she said it, and sorrier still when she saw Lussa's pursed lips. She was concocting an apology in her head when the pirate ships revealed themselves in the distance, a shabby grand huddle of vessels on which weathered gilding jostled against painted figureheads.

And here was something strange: the tall, gaunt vessels looked as if they were perched on wooden islands. Closer in, the islands were revealed as rings of stolen Venetian boats tied to every pirate ship.

There was not a guard in sight.

So confident are they, thought Aurelia, *that they've caught Venice entirely on the back foot! They despise us and imagine us weak, ignorant and without help.*

Aurelia used her history fingers to feel the ships' timber. After the first vessel, she did so gingerly. Terrible scenes were revealed on each of them: images of prisoners beaten and starved, of outbreaks of the plague killing all aboard, of floating becalmed for weeks while people died of thirst. But nowhere did she find a scene of Djinn jars being loaded aboard.

After the tenth fruitless ship, Valerio said, 'You have *history* fingers. Perhaps the stealing of the Djinn jars is so recent that it isn't history yet.'

'Where does history start anyway?' asked Aurelia. 'And the centuries are all mixed inside the Palazzo Bon. History isn't as simple as I used to think.'

'Let's concentrate on finding the ship of the Pirate Duchess,' said Valerio. 'Because that's where the Djinn jars will probably be. And if we can find out more about her past, as well – that would be useful too.'

Aurelia said slowly, 'Because her past is the clue to her present hatred of Venetians. Remember the turtle shell said *Venice* made her the way she is. It's the *archive* of her motives. If we understand her, we'll know better how to deal with her.'

Lussa smiled. And Valerio's amazement was enough to pause him mid-retch.

If he wasn't clinging to Lussa with both hands, Aurelia thought, *he might even have clapped.*

Finally, on one of the oldest, shabbiest boats, Aurelia – through her fingers – caught a glimpse of a girl who resembled the Pirate Duchess, though somewhat younger and considerably less fierce.

'This is it,' Aurelia said, climbing off Chissa's back and on to the rope ladder that hung off the boat. The vessel was named, she noticed, the *Nancy Bridget*.

Strange name for a Barbary pirate to choose, Aurelia thought.

Valerio clambered off Lussa's back to join Aurelia a few rungs below.

Questions they couldn't ask lifted Chissa's and Lussa's eyebrows.

'You want me to tell you what I can see?'

They nodded. Aurelia's fingers pressed down on the planks behind the rope ladder. A new image arrived immediately. It took only a couple of minutes for Aurelia to understand exactly why the Duchess hated Venice with such venom and ferocity.

And I can't really blame her, Aurelia thought.

Treading on the Dreams of Dead Girls

Aurelia's history fingers showed the ferocious Duchess as nothing more than a young Irish girl on the deck of this very ship, arriving in the Venetian lagoon from the south, on a day of gilded sun and pillowy clouds. Looking barely twelve years old, the girl gazed at the towers and palaces of Venice, her face rosy with awed pleasure. She whispered to herself in heavily accented Italian.

''Tis a very heaven here, just as Signor Tosi said it was. No word of a lie, the tales I told the little sisters! 'Twas well worth my working so hard on the language they parley here, with many thanks to Signor Tosi too for his kind teaching. I see why he longs so for home, when home looks like this! That I might stay here a while, so I might! 'Twould be the murdered dreams of the little sisters made true.'

Her expression had suddenly turned to the wistful side of woebegone.

Where are those murdered little sisters? wondered Aurelia, her shoulders prickling with the knowledge that her own little sister was now in peril. *Who is Signor Tosi?*

The next scene showed a black-robed Venetian senator boarding this very boat with a delegation of craven secretaries.

With a shock, Aurelia recognised Marco Spatafora's father, also just a few years younger than he was now. He had his son's love of elegant attire but there'd always been a cruel turn to Daniele Spatafora's mouth. As ever, he showed all the barely repressed aggression of a man too short for his vanity. He carried his silver-tipped cane like a weapon. The sight of him brought home one more reason why betrothal to Marco was so repugnant to Aurelia: it would put her entirely in the power of Daniele Spatafora, head of the family and head of *I Fedeli*.

Aurelia quickly recounted all she saw to the mermaids and Valerio. 'Now I see Daniele Spatafora,' she whispered, 'talking to the little Duchess herself.'

'The captain of this ship has been befuddled by your pretended innocence,' Spatafora told the girl. 'It's done you no good, however. My suspicions were *aroused* when our spies intercepted a letter your captain sent to the British consul, Mr Smith. How I laughed when I read those claims that you're a Christian, kidnapped from Ireland, bereaved of two little sisters also taken by pirates but drowned. How *touching*! The captain apparently believes your story; that you have slaved in the Beyliç *bagno* in Algiers for two years, that you learnt your surprisingly good command of our tongue from some Venetian slave there, and that you escaped. *No one* escapes from the Algerian slave masters. That's the first obvious mistake in your inventions.'

'How so, my lord?' the girl protested. 'I'm everything I say. Sure I am. Why would I give you or Mr Smith a lie? How else would I learn to speak your tongue except with Signor Tosi teaching me?'

'Tosi?' said Daniele Spatafora. 'Common enough Venetian name for you to latch on to. You'll have to do better than that.'

The girl continued earnestly. 'But most of all, I would not take the deaths of the little sisters in vain, not for anything in this world or the next. I *promised* to bring them here – three years past when their pure souls were still breathing on this earth – and that is why I've come myself. Venice, not any other city in Christendom but this one, is sacred to the memory of the little sisters. I give you my hand and word.'

She held out her small hand. Daniele Spatafora dashed it away with his stick. The glint in his eyes reminded Aurelia of a butcher's knife. He sneered at the girl. 'I see through you. There are no little sisters. There never were. Wherever you were whelped, you're a pirate now. You merely *pretend* to be a Christian. We shall tolerate no spies here!' Stroking his long black beard, he drawled, 'Request for clemency denied! A thing like you will *not* be a drain on the Venetian state. Or a danger to it.'

The captain stepped up. 'This girl's suffered so much. She has no one and nowhere—'

'I'm struggling to give a damn,' yawned Daniele Spatafora, turning away.

Another voice piped up behind him. 'Should not Mr Smith the consul at least hear of this case? He could perhaps arrange for the girl to go back to Ireland.' The young man who asked this was round and fresh-faced, and dressed in the costume of a middle-ranking sailor. Aurelia knew his frowning face immediately. She told Valerio and the mermaids, 'Angelo Emo, the officer we met at Arsenale!' Then she turned back to the scene.

'Emo!' barked Daniele Spatafora. 'Stop interfering! Mr Smith shall never hear this farrago of lies. Dismissed.'

The girl said quietly, 'I care nothing for what happens to me, but you are treading on the dreams of dead girls. What is your name, sir?'

It was the young officer who told her, 'That's Senator Daniele Spatafora.'

'I shall not forget it.'

Aurelia saw the girl kneel and curl up on the deck, her arms cradling her head. His work done, Daniele Spatafora simply walked over her and descended – with a great appearance of disdain – the rope ladder to his gondola. Meanwhile, the crew looked down at the girl, shaking their heads. There was affection as well as pity in their eyes. She stayed curled up on the deck for a long time. Eventually, she sat up, her cheeks smeared with tears. Angrily, she wiped them away, rose and went to the captain. 'I'll work my passage back,' she said, 'as crew, if you please.'

'Back to Algiers?' he asked, surprise in his voice. She nodded abruptly. 'Haven't I been shown more decency by Algerians than by Venetians? Including yourself, sir. I thank you.'

Just as Venice shimmered on the edge of the horizon, the girl asked the captain to back the mainsail. She drew herself to her full height and shook her fist at the city, now a mere silhouette of pale church towers and tawny palaces. She threw her voice across the sea.

'There will be murder about what happened here. I'll be back,' she said, 'when I'm in a position to get my revenge. Don't forget about me, Venice. Aye, that would be bad for your safety.'

After repeating the girl's final words, Aurelia told Valerio and the mermaids, 'And now the ship's disappearing over the lagoon's horizon, and the scene is fading.'

She looked up to see wetness in Valerio's eyes, fury and grief on the faces of the mermaids. Chissa held up the fingers of one hand with a questioning expression in her eyes.

'When? From Angelo Emo's face and the lack of grey in Daniele Spatafora's beard, I'd guess three or four years ago.'

'So what happened next?' wondered Valerio.

'Perhaps,' said Aurelia, 'we'll find the answer aboard this ship.'

Chissa nodded, turned on her tail and started to swim away, followed by Lussa.

'You're not going to wait for us? Was it the vomiting?' called Valerio.

'I'm sure it didn't help,' Aurelia said. 'At least we have all the boats we need here to get back.' She began to climb the rope ladder.

'Should I go first?' asked Valerio. 'The Duchess is ashore but we may need to take care of a guard or two on board.'

'Take care with what?' asked Aurelia.

'With you. With what we know now. And with whatever it is we have inside us that put us in the mermaids' prophecy.'

Lussa turned back to them and smiled grimly. Then she disappeared beneath the waves.

38

Catarina in a Cage

Climbing over the rim of the deck, the first thing Aurelia saw was a cage full of Venetian girls. Tugging at the lock, Aurelia asked them, 'Did you see the pirates bringing some terracotta urns aboard this ship?'

'No, but that doesn't mean they didn't,' said a voice from inside the cage. 'They threw a sail over us so we couldn't see any of the plunder they were lugging aboard. We heard lots of heavy things being dropped and a great deal of what sounded like swearing.'

Aurelia's hands dropped to her sides. That voice was Catarina's, and it was calm and strong.

Catarina made her way to the front of the cage, saying, 'I almost didn't recognise you in boy's clothes. Ladies,' she said to her companions, 'this is my sister, Aurelia Bon.'

'The famous one, with the fingers?' asked a small girl.

The next words that came out of Catarina's mouth were the last ones Aurelia expected: 'Yes. And thank God she's here!'

Catarina's eyes met Aurelia's. It felt like the first time Aurelia had really looked at her sister in years. What she saw was not what she'd imagined. In Catarina's face there was tenderness and sorrow as well as fear.

'I've been so worried about you,' Catarina said. 'Can you ever forgive me, Aurelia? Please – oh, look behind you!'

The keys to the cage were dangling on the belt of a pirate boy who was now approaching. He did not, however, look very fierce. His face was pale as the moon.

He's probably younger than me, thought Aurelia as he drew his scimitar and held it in a shaking hand, his lip wobbling too.

Aurelia said in a gentle voice, 'Are you actually some kind of slave?'

He nodded. 'I'm . . . Saul'.

'How did they take you?' asked Valerio.

'In a raid. They boarded our boat just off Gibraltar. They already sold my parents who were travelling with me.'

'Will they kill you if you let these girls go?'

'Obviously.'

'Then you must leave this ship with them. And quickly. The pirates could be back any moment.'

Tears softened the boy's features. From under his cap, long hair was starting to straggle out. Aurelia said suddenly, 'You're not even a boy are you? You're a girl.'

Saul looked directly at Aurelia. 'It takes one to know one.'

'I'm sure there's a good reason?' Aurelia asked gently.

'Yes, the pirates would have sold me as a farm slave if they thought I was a girl. Boys fetch higher ransoms. So they tend to stay alive longer.'

'Can you row . . . Saul?'

'Sally.' She nodded. Aurelia pointed in the direction of the island of Poveglia.

Catarina said, 'Yes! A secret channel runs through the middle, and there's a freshwater stream too.'

'How do you know that?' asked Aurelia.

'I've rowed there many times,' replied Catarina.

Aurelia stared. That did not in any way make sense.

'There are many things you don't know about me,' Catarina said. 'Including the fact that Mamma allowed me to have rowing lessons if I would consent to keep an eye on you. It was easy to do that because of your complete lack of curiosity about *me*. You didn't even spy on *my* diary. But that's hardly the point right now. We can take the girls to Poveglia in one of the boats tied up below and hide on the island until . . . you have made Venice safe for us again. Because that's what you're going to do, Aurelia.'

Aurelia had no words to frame her astonishment.

'We'll need more than one boat,' said Sally, unlocking the cage. 'We'll collect the women from the other pirate ships too.'

Catarina spoke up. 'I can show some of the stronger girls how to row. Now, we may be some time in Poveglia. Sally, where are the provisions kept? You two,' she pointed to a pair of taller girls, 'go with her to the galley and bring as much food as you can. Not the pirate stew,' she said, wrinkling her nose.

The other girls scrambled to follow her orders, their fears clearly soothed by having something sensible to do. Aurelia said, 'I've misjudged you.'

'Yes,' said Catarina. 'As I read, repeatedly, in your diary. I pretended it didn't hurt. I tried to be defiant about it. I even exaggerated my interest in clothes – though I do also *really* love them – because I knew it irritated you. A girl can love clothes and still have a brain in her head, still learn to row, still have little adventures that no one knows about. Books. Covers. Judging, you know?'

Aurelia reached out to give Catarina what would have been their first real hug since they were very little girls. But her fingers touched only empty air. Catarina had just turned to Valerio, offering him her hand to shake. 'I also owe you a dozen apologies. Now do what you need to do aboard this ship. You were speaking of terracotta jars? I hope you find them, whatever they are. By the time you're done, we'll be safely at Poveglia. And the Pirate Duchess will have no hostages to ransom. That should make your work easier, no?'

Aurelia said, 'I look forward to getting to know you . . . when this is all over.'

'*If* this is all over! Hurry!' Catarina urged. 'But me too . . . about the getting to know.'

Aurelia and Valerio found the Duchess's parlour by following the smell of cinnamon, saffron and leather.

'She doesn't spare herself any luxury, does she?' noted Aurelia, staring at the elegant chamber.

After searching caskets of wine, crates of figs and a basket of tear-catcher bottles, Valerio spied a torn label saying *Hippopotamus dung* sticking out of the corner of a straw-lined box. The remaining six urns were far heavier than Aurelia could have imagined. One by one, they lifted them from the box and lined them up on the massive desk that dominated the room.

Valerio was still staggering across the floorboards with the last one in his arms when a fearsome voice behind them screeched something that sounded like, 'Stand away from them jars. Now! Hawwww! Don't you turn round. If I sees your ugly faces, I'll cut 'em in quarters. Hawwww!'

39

Be Really Careful What You Wish For

The voice was rough and loud. The accent was coarse. It was impossible not to visualise a particularly large pirate, armed with a rusting scimitar.

Why didn't Sally mention him? thought Aurelia. *Is she a traitor? Are our girls safe with her?*

Aurelia allowed her panicking eyes to swivel towards Valerio. He still held the jar. She saw his hand make tiny movements. He was trying to open the stopper without the pirate behind them noticing it.

My task, thought Aurelia, *is to distract the brute so Valerio can let the Djinni out.*

Without turning her back, she said to the pirate, 'How do you do?'

'How do you *do*? Hawwww!' screeched the pirate in scandalised tones, as if she'd just asked him to undress and dance a hornpipe over hot coals.

'I do beg your pardon!' Aurelia told the pirate humbly.

'Pardon? *Pardon?* PARDON? Hawwww!' shouted the pirate. 'I'll lop off your lily white legs and slice your scabby eyelids! You'll get two bumfuls o' me boots and then I'll knot yer nose hairs! Hawwww!'

Aurelia's head was pounding, both with the grating noise of the pirate's voice and the images it described. From what Valerio had told her, Barbary pirates were capable of absolutely anything.

The pirate clacked, 'Helping yourselves to me hippopotamus dung what I'd been so looking forward to! There be good chewing in that! Drop that jar or I'll have your livers in me stew! Hawwww!'

But at that moment, Valerio finally eased the stopper from the jar and a skein of blue smoke coiled out. This time, however, it was not followed by a cunning person in pantaloons. It wasn't even a person.

The pirate bawled, 'A cat! I hates me a cat! Hawwww! Hawwww! They steals yer tailfeathers. One ate me cousin. Nasty black-biled creatures with black souls too! That's me getting out me trusty blade and cutting a few fingers off them children what's let a cat in here to torment me.'

The cat, now unfolding itself out of the jar, was the size of a small kitten. It had the proportions – and proud demeanour – of a fully grown leopard, though it was black as coal all over.

'Are you a hairy-legged cat Djinni?' whispered Aurelia, thinking, *I must not use the word 'wish'. I must not use it till we're ready.* She stared at Valerio, willing him to show the same caution.

'A cat *Djinniya*, you'll find,' replied the cat, licking her paw and wiping it behind her ear in a gesture that was unmistakably flirtatious. She inspected the *Hippopotamus dung* label with manifest disapproval and then stared coolly over their shoulders while the pirate let loose a stream of words in what was presumably the sweariest, screechiest lexicon of the *lingua franca*. Although the sentences were unintelligible, the content was clearly both outraged and insulting.

The cat spoke coolly to the pirate, 'Oh do stop that ridiculous noise, bird brain!' Turning to Valerio, she asked, 'So, *master-who-released-me* –' her tone deeply ironic – 'what do you wish for?' she sighed with exaggerated boredom.

'Be careful, Valerio!' cried Aurelia over the continued angry babble of the pirate behind them.

The pirate was saying, 'And that's me trussing up them blatherskiting children what brought narrrsty cats on me, tying them weasels to the heaviest anchor, and throwing them vermin spawn overboard . . . Don't turn around! Hawwww!'

'I've been thinking about it for the last five minutes,' whispered Valerio. He turned to the cat. 'I wish every pirate on this ship was tied up, with his scimitar fallen away to ashes on the floor.'

'Are you quite sure you wish that?' asked the cat lazily.

'Why?' Aurelia felt a clutch of anxiety in her belly. Was this a double-crossing trick? Pretending to be helpful? Djinnkind were capable of that. *Djinniya* cats were almost certainly more than capable of it.

Valerio said tersely, 'I'm sure. It would seem to solve our immediate peril.'

'Because, much as I'd adore to disoblige you, I cannot grant you an impossible wish. There's no pirate presently on this ship.'

'Then who—?' Valerio and Aurelia spun round.

In the direction from which all the noise had come, stood something that looked like a lantern on a tall pole draped with a fringed square of scarlet velvet. Even as they stared, a curved triangle of yellow poked out and wrenched the fabric away, revealing an enormous, green parrot perched on an ornate wooden stand. A stalagmite of solidified droppings rose from the floor below it.

'Whaaaaaaat?' the bird complained. 'Hawwww! What are you about, you shower of savages? Breakin' 'n' enterin' into me private parlour! I nearly had a canary there!'

'How can you have a canary?' sniffed the cat Djinniya. 'You are a parrot.'

''Tis but a figure of speech in the parley of me mistress,' admitted the parrot, 'what taught me to speak.'

'What's your name, anyway?' Aurelia asked.

A fervent porridge of syllables gurgled in the parrot's vivid, feathered throat.

'That sounds like "Suleyman",' said Valerio. 'The great king who was the downfall of the Djinn.'

Aurelia didn't know whether to laugh or cry with relief. Valerio seemed to be doing a bit of both. But the cat Djinniya was staring with great seriousness at the parrot.

'I don't believe your problems are over,' she observed.

The parrot was lifting its large wings, preparing to fly at them. Its beak was shaped like a scimitar and looked as if it could inflict similar damage. The flapping of its wings made a sound like a sail being torn end to end. It screeched, 'That's me preparing to take a few eyes out now.'

Valerio said, 'I wish—'

'No!' screamed Aurelia. 'Don't waste a wish on one bird!'

'Waste?' squawked the parrot. 'Hawwww! May your mouth become a dog's latrine!'

Thinking rapidly, Aurelia held up a pair of pleading hands to the parrot. 'It can't be very nice living in a *cabin*,' she said. 'And those nasty black cats who wouldn't begin to appreciate a *hero* among birds. Cheeky, I'll bet? I expect that you have to eat weevilly biscuits? When did you last crunch into a lovely fresh apple? Or . . . or . . . some nicely matured hippopotamus dung? I expect that the pirates teach you only terrible words and no poetry? What *wouldn't* I give to hear you reciting Dante or Shakespeare! Never happened, has it? I call that a shame. A fine bird like you. Such a beauty!'

The parrot put its head on one side, listening intently.

Suddenly Aurelia remembered what Lussa had said about the younger mermaids: 'My sentimental ladies be always longing for a pet.'

Aurelia continued, 'And you're a land bird, not a seagull! You must be sick of voyaging! Surely you'd like to stay put in one place? Sit in a tree? And isn't it lonely? Wouldn't you like to settle down and maybe meet another parrot? Get, um, married? Have some chicks?'

The parrot put its head on the other side. It made a noise that sounded a lot like someone gargling. The cat Djinniya put her front paws together to make a noise that sounded like slow sarcastic clapping.

'Not bad, bint,' she said. 'Not entirely lamentable, anyway.'

Aurelia told the parrot, 'I know some mermaids, who serve excellent curries and have access to all kinds of substances from other times and places, probably including the dung of many rare and even mythical animals.'

'Mermaids? Hawwww!' But this time the 'hawwww!' was cautiously enthusiastic. 'That's me likin' what I've heard about mermaids. Nice women. And never known to keep a cat, bein' as how cats be partial to fish flesh.'

'There's not a single cat in the mermaids' cavern,' said Aurelia truthfully. 'So, in exchange for your not tearing us apart, we shall take you to the mermaids and you can become their cherished pet. Upstairs, at the House of the Spirits, is a lush garden and an orchard full of apple trees, more than any one parrot can eat. So we shall fetch the parrots from the other boats, and you can all be together.'

The parrot started lifting and lowering his head, as if nodding happily.

'So that's sorted,' said the cat Djinniya. 'Now back to me.'

She really is like Ghazalah, thought Aurelia.

Valerio said, 'You still owe us three wishes for releasing you.'

'Duh,' said the cat rudely.

'We need to *discuss* this first. So we don't waste our wishes.'

'Good luck with that,' said the cat, commencing to wash her smug face.

'Should we wish for all the pirates to leave Venice?' asked Aurelia.

'If we did, we'd run the risk of their prisoners disappearing with them. They're still rounding up girls,' said Valerio.

Aurelia sighed. 'If only time could wind back . . . to the day before the pirates arrived in Venice. Before it was too late to stop them?'

'Sounds like a wish to me,' said the Djinniya.

'I don't mean it as a wish. How can I? I don't even know exactly when they arrived or what I was doing when they arrived. But if I myself went back to those circumstances, before it was too late, then I *could* perhaps—'

'*I I I!* It's all about *you*, isn't it? And there's no *way* that's not a wish, miss,' said the cat Djinniya.

And with that, Aurelia was back in Ghezzo's attic, tied to the table made of books.

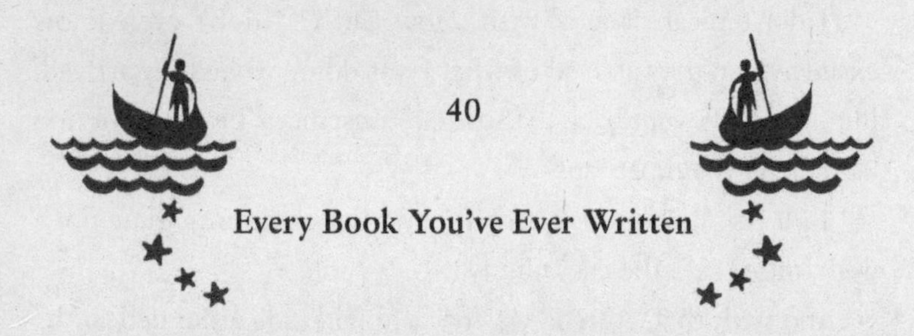

40

Every Book You've Ever Written

Simoneto Ghezzo could scarcely believe his luck.

There was Aurelia and her nine still usable fingertips suddenly strapped down to the improvised table as if the last few disastrous days hadn't happened, as if his face, his leg, his arm and his hands were not afire with pain, as if everything were finally going his way.

Aurelia too was struggling to believe her luck, but in a different way. Selfishly, she had claimed the wish just for herself. From Simoneto Ghezzo's new injuries, it was clear that only Aurelia herself had been transported back to the time and place where she'd been before her escape, which must have been the same moment the pirates arrived in Venice.

And looking at the surgeon, still shackled to the floor, she also knew that her own carelessness and selfishness had hurt more people than just herself. When she had first escaped, she should have told someone about the surgeon locked in the attic. She'd planned to write a letter for the *Signori di Notte*. But then she'd seen a mention of her own name in an *avviso*, and so many things had happened in such a short time. The surgeon's fate had slipped her mind. The man looked years and not days older than when she'd last seen him.

Ghezzo barked at him, 'Where is your scalpel, man?'

'How can you do this?' Aurelia asked. 'I saved your life at Palazzo Bon!'

'I'll give you that,' he said slowly. 'I'm not taking your life. Just your fingertips.' But he did not tell the surgeon to begin.

He looks different, thought Aurelia. *He's suffered. He's having doubts.*

'Please listen!' she said, desperately. 'Do you know how I got here? Magic! What else could it be? Magic that came from a cat Djinniya on a pirate ship! Yes, a pirate ship in the Venetian lagoon. We're surrounded. There are thousands of Barbary pirates here to harvest slaves. First, they're taking the women. Then they'll come back for the men and boys.'

Simoneto Ghezzo struggled to keep the alarm from his voice. 'Your picturesque tales don't work any magic on *me*. I work with real history, hard facts.'

'Then here's some hard reality for you. *I Fedeli* have betrayed us to the pirates.'

'You felt this in a wall?'

'No, I saw it *with my eyes*. Not in history, but *today*. When they have taken everything of value out of Venice – and that does *not* include the historians – the pirates plan to burn this city down. Up in smoke – all the palaces you've ever researched, all the libraries and all the bookshops containing all the history books you ever wrote.'

'You talk of my books? *You?*'

'Without real history books, my history fingers would be just entertainment. Shows for children, and grown-up children. Shallow. Empty.'

'From her own lips?' Simoneto Ghezzo marvelled. Then his face creased with suspicion. 'Are these just weasel words to save your life? Or your fingers.'

Aurelia said, 'It's to save *all* our lives. I'm not the girl you think I am, sir.'

I was that girl, thought Aurelia. *But I'm not going to be her any more.*

'I'm sorry,' she added. 'I dealt you a thoughtless blow. I did it too many times. I was so excited about myself that I didn't even notice—'

'I'm easy not to notice,' said Ghezzo quietly, 'apparently.'

'You have a brilliant mind. It's gone dark . . . because I robbed it of the light. It doesn't have to stay that way.' Aurelia continued, 'Now is *this* the history of Venice we want to write, as witnesses? Everything we care about is in danger! Look outside! You'll see I'm right.'

It seemed strange to say 'we' when talking to Simoneto Ghezzo. But Aurelia did so now, without hesitation.

Ghezzo moved over to the grimy attic window that looked down on to a shabby square far below. A posse of Corsair cats ran across it, followed by a dozen pirates, dragging girls in nets. The girls tumbled on the paving stones, crying out in pain and fear.

'My wife! My daughters!' whispered the surgeon.

'The girl speaks the truth. It's like 943 AD!' said Ghezzo. 'That's the last time the pirates came to Venice. They carried off the women of San Pietro di Castello. That day, however, Venetian men took to their boats, chased the pirates and got them back—'

Aurelia interrupted, 'Every single Venetian boat's been seized by the pirates. And Daniele Spatafora sold the Corsairs all our gunpowder.'

Ghezzo said slowly, 'I always had my doubts about *I Fedeli*. Spatafora – a classic upstart, desperate to put layers of money between himself and the truly old families of Venice. As for you, girl, you clearly did not mean to be here. This is some sort of mistake. Before this minute, you had an actual plan?'

'Not as such, but I think I might have the start of one now. But to understand it, you're going to need to believe some things that are not in history books – only in story books. First of all, mermaids. Good mermaids, living in a cavern under the city. They're on our side. Secondly, a Djinniya from Nizwa in Arabia, whose mistaken spell put the Castle of Jabrin inside the Palazzo Bon. Her name is Ghazalah, and she has a pet leopardess. Thirdly, there's an *Irish* Pirate Duchess. And Signor Rioba *really* talks. Oh and there are prophecies about me and Valerio, the Water's Daughter and the Landsman Prince – we're supposed to help save the city. Are you with me so far?'

Throughout this speech, Aurelia kept her eyes fixed on the historian's, watching his expression transform second by second from cynical to surprised to eager. His mouth relaxed into something that looked almost like a smile. His eyes opened wide.

When the surgeon whimpered, 'The girl's gone mad!', Simoneto Ghezzo said, 'Far from it! I believe it's *myself* who's been in the grip of some kind of insanity. Shocking as it is, there's *sense* in her story, and more than sense! In fact, sightings of mermaids are recorded in many respectable history books, including my own, which she'd know if she'd ever bothered to read them. A watery city *should* have aquatic protectresses. As for Djinnkind, there's a whole chapter about them in the *Qur'an*. Why should not a woman be a pirate? Or a leader of men? In history, we find Amazons and queens. Prophecy is often based on deep insights – so-called 'folk' wisdom is often extraordinarily wise. Moreover, I've personally never seen any reason why history and magic should be mutually exclusive – neither in Arabia nor in Venice.'

'Neither have I – I guess because of my fingers.' Aurelia's face burned. *I dismissed him without ever bothering to read him. Just as I misjudged Catarina, because I never really talked to her.*

Ghezzo asked, 'But how can your mermaids and a Djinniya help us against real pirates?'

'You probably know from your research,' Aurelia said respectfully, 'that the way a Djinniya works is to get inside someone and make them carry out her will. I'm thinking – if we could somehow persuade the Djinniya to jump inside the Pirate Duchess, we could change her plans. And if not, we can fight the pirates bridge to bridge.'

Aurelia locked her eyes on Simoneto Ghezzo's. They met hers, steady and resolute.

'So?' she urged. 'Would you rather mutilate me or save this city? What do you say?'

'I say, "Save this city".'

Ghezzo was already unshackling the surgeon. 'You are needed elsewhere, Dottore,' he said. 'This is war, and there will be wounded.'

41

Black Sails Massing

Carefully avoiding streets where screams announced the presence of pirates, Aurelia, the surgeon and the historian hurried to the Riva degli Schiavoni to see what could be seen. It was not a comforting sight. Black-sailed pirate boats were massing in the lagoon. The darkness on the horizon grew denser as more ships arrived to swell the throng.

The water below the *riva* began to froth. A beautiful head rose out of the waves, followed by a dozen more. Lussa gestured a greeting and then pointed in horror at the pirate-black horizon. Chissa and her colleagues opened their mouths but no sound came out. Then they turned to the historian, mouthing silent disgust.

'See!' said Aurelia, turning to Ghezzo. 'Mermaids! I'm afraid they cannot talk at the moment.'

The historian looked blankly. 'There's nothing but pirate ships as far as the eye can see.'

The surgeon nodded. 'Nothing.'

'Why can't they see you?' Aurelia asked Lussa, who mimed a bent back, pretending to be a human hobbling with a walking stick.

'They're too old? Oh wait, there's Valerio!'

A green-faced Valerio hung over the side of a little *sandolo* pulled by a team of mermaids. It approached the shore and Aurelia helped him climb on to the embankment. He had a Djinn jar tucked under each arm and one in his hand.

Only three, thought Aurelia. *What's happened to the rest?*

He told Aurelia, 'The pirates arrived back at the ship just minutes after you disappeared. So I wished myself in the mermaids' cavern. Somehow, that worked. But I only had time to grab three jars before I made the wish. What—?' He'd just caught sight of Ghezzo.

The mermaids lashed their tails in the water.

'Don't worry,' said Aurelia. 'He wants to help. He's been telling me about the last time pirates came. He says the Venetian men chased them away—'

'This time the pirates have all the boats,' said Valerio, 'unlike in 943 AD.'

Ghezzo bowed and nodded, giving Valerio a look of respect, researcher to researcher.

Aurelia said, 'If only we'd thought of cutting a few boats loose when we were out at the Pirate Duchess's ship.'

'Then they would have floated out to sea and been lost.'

'We could have wished them back to shore . . .'

'If we'd been clever enough. But we were not. We are not.'

Valerio held up a Djinn jar. 'Unfortunately I wasted one whole wish on the mean little scorpion in here, trying to help the mermaids to get their voices back. I learnt the hard way that this kind of binding spell can be unbound only by the person who cast it.'

Aurelia said, 'So we need Ghazalah and whatever concoction Musipul was helping her to work on at the Palazzo Bon. Let's summon them here. With a wish.'

Aurelia opened the lid of the jar and a small, semi-transparent camel calf hopped out, saying, 'At your service,' with a low bow of its head.

'Looks innocent, doesn't it?' said Valerio. 'But let's not trust it.'

'Why don't we just *walk* to the Palazzo Bon and fetch Ghazalah? The mermaids can meet us in the canal beside it,' said Aurelia. 'Why waste a wish on something we can do ourselves? I wish you weren't so profligate with the wishes!'

'And there goes another one,' remarked the camel calf.

'Wishing,' said Simoneto Ghezzo, 'is clearly not an exact science. Young people, I suggest you tell your mermaid friends to meet us presently at the Palazzo Bon?'

Musipul was standing moodily by the canal when they arrived. 'Someone's been in here scattering oily rags! Don't they realise date honey's highly combustible?'

'They absolutely do,' said Aurelia. 'But that's not why we're here.'

'What the frankincense – Fishwomen!' said Musipul, as Lussa's head suddenly rose from the canal, closely followed by Chissa's. Respect to you ladies. Respect! Why do they not return my greeting?'

'*Mouthless mermaids*?' Musipul said, when Aurelia had explained the situation. 'Oh, is there no end to the damage

Ghazalah does? Fortunately, I forced her to make ample quantities of the antidote in case there was the usual collateral damage. Speak of Satan, there she is!'

Ghazalah's face appeared at a first floor window. Ghezzo and the surgeon stared at her in frank admiration. Valerio gazed up, pale and angry. Aurelia thought, *No wonder! This is his first look at the creature who got inside him.*

Musipul told Ghazalah, 'Look what you've done to the lovely Fishwomen! What did they ever do to *you*?'

'I once knew a mean one-eyed shark Afreet,' said Ghazalah. 'You're that mean.'

'Use the antidote! Unbind them now!' Musipul ordered.

Sulkily, Ghazalah held up a bottle of black liquid, intoning, 'I hereby unbind the mouths of *all* warm-blooded magical, female creatures . . . with lustrous hairs and luxuriant lashes. May they all speak again.' She emptied the bottle into the canal.

'Yoiks!' cried Chissa, coughing. 'Ye did this to us, ye bungling, man guzzling Djinniya? Sink me! Ye be seventeen kind of stupid wiv a bad attitude for each o' them!'

The other mermaids joined in with gusto:

'Such a dolt she couldn't find a cup of coffee in Turkey!'

'A bog for a brain, is wot she's got!'

'And look at da gut-bucket on her! Who ate all the *baklava*?'

'Yea! Watch dat scurvy spirit sizzle to a little whiff of nastiness!'

'Wiv all da delicate charm of a brimming chamber pot!'

'We should bind *her* buttocks, belly and big toes! And dip her in da drink!'

Valerio piped up: 'Altogether now: HYENA-HEARTED HARRIDAN IN FANCY PANTS!'

Aurelia stared at him. 'Is that the Djinniya-possession talking, or you?'

Valerio said, 'No. That's just me giving her what she deserves.'

Throughout the gruesome onslaught, Ghazalah hung her head and stared at the ground. You'd have needed to stand very close to hear her whisper, 'If humans are made of dirt, what are Venetian Fishwomen fashioned out of? Slime and rudeness, that's what!'

Eventually the mermaids ran out of breath. Musipul said, 'I hope you have cursed her to your full satisfaction, ladies. Personally, I've enjoyed it very much. And now I think that, according to Djinn law of crime and retribution, you'll find that Ghazalah owes you a service or favour.'

Ghazalah shot her a venomous look. 'You could have kept that to yourself.'

'Why'd we want to get mixed up in any murksome Djinnery?' asked Chissa. 'Even 'twere it *competent*.'

Ghazalah flinched.

Simoneto Ghezzo said, 'We mortals are hearing but part of this fascinating exchange. But in the meantime, this young girl, Aurelia Bon, has an outstanding idea. My dear, tell the Djinniya.'

Aurelia said, 'The Irish Duchess must be back at her ship now. Ghazalah, you could . . . get inside her. And force her to sail away with all the pirates, never to come back.'

Musipul said to her mistress. 'This is your one chance to redeem yourself. Don't waste it. Off you float!'

'But before that,' insisted Aurelia, 'Ghazalah must free the lamp-boy, Momo.'

'No, you don't get it all your own way, Bon-Bon!' snapped Ghazalah. 'One favour at a time. Yes, I'll deal with the Duchess. But while I'm doing that you'll need to come up with a really good reason why I should do one more thing for you or this miserable city. No, don't look at Musipul. She can paint but she can't unlock a door.'

Ghazalah pulled a key out of her jewelled bodice. She waved it before plunging it back inside.

'So you'd all better hope,' she said, 'that I succeed and come back safely.'

Ghazalah grabbed the last Djinn jar from Valerio's hand, and suddenly she wasn't there any more.

42

A Legend Waiting for Me

Under her dirty face and lurid rags, the Pirate Duchess turns out to be a tall, blue-eyed bint, a bare few years older than Aurelia Bon. My first thought's to possess the creature in a second. But when I try to slip into her body, she surprises me. Suddenly six men are holding me upside down over a barrel of water.

The bint says, 'Look at the face on ye! One word from me and they'll drop ye in the wet. No word of a lie. Then I'll watch ye sizzle till all that's left is yer hooves and gaudy belt buckle, ye bold article! Being as how I'm in no great perplexity as to what ye are!' she hisses, speaking my own language perfectly yet with a certain lilt to it. 'Will ye come on now? You're not the first Djinni who's tried this slimy trick on me. And what have ye done with my hostages? I came back to my boat to find it empty of girls! I'm even down one boy slave so!'

'Nothing to do with me. Moreover, I am no Djinni,' I say haughtily as I can under my humiliating circumstances. 'You'll note that I am that superior article, a Djinniya.'

'A Djinniya! Even worse! The come-hithering carry-on of your kind! More pretty banter than Imru' al-Qais.'

I gasp. This bint knows not only our nature but our saying about an Arabic poet who wrote the tender poems I'd deployed in vain on young Aurelio Bon, may desert jackals tear his dark curls in Hell.

'So,' the Irish bint says, 'I'll absolutely not be letting ye inside to drive me astray in the head. Don't even be trying it. Meanwhile, sure I know your kind are nifty with the tongues. So we'll be speaking in my native English from now on, which'll also give us a little useful privacy from my men.'

She stands facing me squarely, utterly unafraid, which does discompose me a little, I must admit. I almost drop the terracotta jar I'm holding, with a bossy spotty little bint of a Djinniya serval cat inside it. Just what I needed! More felines in my life and in my jars. I wager Musipul had something to do with it. However, this one has at least agreed to work with me when I need my magic strengthened. So long as I don't try the tongue-binding shenanigans on her. As if I would! But everyone treats me like an ignorant spoilt child – even serval cat Djinn barely out of the egg.

Then the Irish Duchess surprises me again. 'So what say ye to a little sisterly solidarity?' the bint asks. Her tone's lamentably impudent and close up her hair smells brackish. This is one dirt-person who really earns her title! Do I really want to be inside that? No, I do not.

She orders her men to put me down on the deck and stand aside.

'My bit of a question is,' she asks me, 'why ye'd be *wanting* to get inside me at all? Ye must be working for the Venetians. Sure that cannot be a natural state of affairs for one such as ye. We should be working together to take 'em down. Pirate Duchess and Djinniya – who could survive us? We may be but a couple of females, yet, as they say in yer own country, "A mosquito can make the lion's eye bleed."'

'Anyone can quote a proverb. But you are no born Barbary pirate,' I tell her. 'You're a tall Irish bint with hardly any hips to speak of and inelegant personal hygiene. Why should anyone be afraid of you?'

This takes her aback. Yet even on the back foot, she positively swaggers. 'Sure I'm a Barbary pirate through and through. I'm sworn to kidnap, killing and booty. Ye have to hand it to me when it comes to ransoms, battles, whippings. I'm an awful girl for men overboard without mercy. I'm a fine one for the bloodthirsties . . .'

I yawn. Really, the skinny bint's trying too hard now.

'And you such a good Christian girl,' I say sarcastically, 'doing all these dirty deeds.'

'Sure now, ye're gettin' mighty particular! Don't ye come the crotchety colleen with me. For who are *you* to criticise –' she shoots a look down to my translucent pantaloons – 'Ye with the bad ways and the quite extraordinarily hairy legs? Let's cut to the onions. All those years I was a prisoner in Algiers, I heard a rake of stories of Djinnkind. How ye take over innocent humans and turn 'em into yer helpless slaves. The mischief ye do. Do ye know what my blathering parrot is called, by the way? Suleyman! Presently missing, and I've my suspicions . . .'

At the bird's name, I reel a little. Suleyman was the dirt-person king who enslaved all the Djinn with his magic. Hundreds of years on, that name still tolls hard in the ears of Djinnkind.

She says, 'Ye should hear the bold mouth on that bird!'

'Pets!' I agree. 'They give themselves such airs.'

'As if ye owed 'em something. Speaking of which, I'm here because of what *I'm* owed. Specifically, I've things to avenge so I do. Specific things. Specific city.'

'Venice, you mean?' I'm interested now. Perhaps this bint and I have things in common. I too have a reason – namely Aurelio Bon – to hate Venice and to bring her down. Shouldn't she and I be friends?

An image of Musipul's familiar sneer comes unbidden and unwelcome into my mind. I can hear her saying, 'For once in your life, do something right, Ghazalah.'

'Sure ye'll be wanting to know how the Barbary pirates got their clutches on me?' the Irish Duchess asks. 'I never talk of it, but for some reason I've a grand desire to tell ye about it now. I was just a girleen when it happened, a little nobody of a country brat with a big name: Emer Fionnuala O'Dowdy. No word of a lie. I was growing up in Youghal with my two young sisters, Nancy and Bridget. On the day that it happened, we were digging potatoes in a field above the sea. A most unreliable vegetable, the potato, liable to blight as soon as look at a hungry person. All our little lives, we'd been slaves of the potato – of its seeds, its shoots, its roots, its digging, its boiling, its roasting.

'As usual, while we worked, I spun stories to while away the time. Here's a fact to make ye laugh – I used to tell the little sisters so many pretty tales about the famous town of Venice. I promised that I'd take 'em there one day to sail gondolas down streets of gilded green water lined with floating palaces spun of lacy stone. I told 'em they'd be proper young ladies about the town, drinking thick and foamy hot chocolate with Venetian girls our own ages, who'd think us O'Dowdys the very berries and be naught but overjoyed to make our acquaintances. Lovely altogether! Whenever we dug potatoes together, Nancy and Bridget were after me for more elaborations of our fanciness in Venice, where there was nary a clod of earth nor a potato to dig. I was always happy to oblige, so I was.

''Twas a Venice tale I was a-telling when my mouth dried up at the horrible sight of a pack of Barbary pirates in tenders down in the bay below. And on the shore, a hundred Irish men stood in irons. Next we saw the pirates picking off the children harvesting seaweed on the beach. Those children were our friends. It put the heart crossways in me to see the poor young'uns chained and dragged away. Another rabble of pirates legged it for our granary. Others disappeared from sight. We thought they'd gone. Didn't we hope and pray they'd gone? But hadn't they been scaling the scooped-out cliff beneath us?

'Suddenly the pirates surged up over the edge right in front of our eyes. First thing they did was stuff our mouths with cork so we couldn't warn anyone else with our screams. Then they netted us. My sisters, ye'd think too tiny to be of use. Yet they took us all, even though I fought hard. We were separated at the shore. The dirt ingrained in our hands told our class, but they roughly checked our ears for signs of earrings that would show we were quality folk just pretending we weren't worth a ransom. I'm tall, as ye see, so the pirates took me for a grown woman, which is why they separated me from my wee sisters. I was forced to watch the little girls dragged off to another vessel, while I was put aboard this very ship, which was then called *The Wrath of Qat*.

'On the ship, I looked desperately for my parents. Were they dead? Then who would look after the little sisters? Who'd soothe 'em in their fright? Hold 'em tight and answer their questions? I asked all those things, when I dared. I got my answers in blows.

'It was only after the first night that I began to think of myself. I knew about the Barbary pirates and their ways. This was not their first raid on Youghal. My parents, if they had survived the raid, were poor. And so I was not destined for ransom and redemption to my home. My future was hard labour, or worse so. And the little sisters would be sold as household slaves.'

At this, the Pirate Duchess falls suddenly silent, pretending there's something in her blue eye.

Now I have to admit this is as gloomy a story as I've ever heard. I imagine the tears of the little sisters and the shrieks and flailing knuckles of young Emer Fionnuala O'Dowdy, bravely fighting the huge men, against whom she had not a puny chance.

She composes herself and continues. 'The pirates filled their ships with slaves till we were dangerously low in the water. Their rapaciousness was such that they'd rather sink than let go of a morsel of their booty. So it was with the second vessel, the one that held the little sisters. Its captain lost his wager with his greed. I myself saw the ship go down, so swiftly that there was no one left to save, even if our own captain had shown the mercy of slowing our progress for five tiny minutes. That he did not, though I screamed like a banshee over the edge of our boat until they cut me down with a whip. And so the little sisters died without ever having committed a sin, without ever having known a full belly or having heard a loving farewell from their sister.

'With my sisters drowned before my eyes, I grew very quiet in myself. I thought of the tales I'd told them of Venice, and how we'd be ladies drinking hot chocolate in Saint Mark's Square. I swore on their souls that I'd get free of those who'd snatched my little sisters from their dreams of gondolas and gilded canals.

'By then I also knew that if anyone begged for water or bandages for their wounds, the slavers thought nothing of beating them senseless as a lesson to the others. So I kept my flap shut. I asked for nothing. Slowly, slowly, we made our way south to Algiers, fed only a cat's lick of food all the way. The day the ship emptied us on to the dock, I realised that there were thousands of us captives – Irish, French, Italian, Spanish. We were hustled into a marketplace and hoops of iron were beaten round our ankles. Then we were lined up for inspection and sale. At the slave market, they ripped open my rag of a dress at the neck and wrote my asking price on my shoulder. I was cheap, but not quite worthless.'

I put in, 'There's a saying that in the *badestan* at Algiers you can swap a Christian for an onion.'

'No word of a lie. Haven't I seen it done? We were paraded around before the bidding began. I saw Algerian men and women wiping their beautiful eyes with sheerest pity for us. They doubtless knew what we didn't yet: that most of us were destined to be "public slaves", good for digging in quarries and dragging stone to build endless palaces for the Barbary royalty.

'My entire village was sold off that day. Over the next two years I heard of my fellow Irish villagers all a-perishing of overwork, the plague and homesickness. I might have died myself – something inside me had already gone dead with the drowning of the little sisters. There were kind masters, but my first purchaser was not one 'em. I was kicked, called a dog, not allowed to wash. As for food, my first master seemed to think I was born without a mouth. In the heat of Algiers, as I toiled on his crop, he'd have let me and my fellow slaves shrivel with thirst. And we would have, if kind local people hadn't secretly left bottles for us in hiding places all the slaves learnt to know. But the master – he even made us carry water, so we could hear it gurgle in our bronze jars. Yet it was death to help yourself to a drop.

'Of my ma there was no news, so I still nursed a biteen of hope. But my father . . . A brave, big boy from my village appeared one day at the *bagno*, scarred and with his back bowed. He looked twenty years older instead of the twelve months that had passed since the raid on Youghal. He told me that my father, like himself, had been sold at the *badestan* as a *galleotto* and sent to row the Levant coast. My pa was worked to death in two months. "Then his body was simply thrown in the water," said the villager. "All the masters cared about was lightening the payload so we could make faster progress. I said a wee prayer for yer pa as he sank." '

The Pirate Duchess looks at me accusingly. I point out, 'It's not only the Muslim people who take slaves. Venetians have always enslaved Moors and Turks whenever they could.'

'Sure I know,' the Irish bint continues. 'Slavery ye want to talk about, is it? Will ye come on now? Everyone's been hard at it, century by century, Christian and Muslim alike. From the Romans to the Ottomans! Sure it's all about greed and taking what's not yours, yet worse for it's about stealing bodies, using 'em and throwing 'em away *as if they had no souls in 'em at all*.'

Her voice clots and she cannot go on. So I help her out, saying, 'And then there's the so-called Christians harvesting Africans in their millions to slave on their plantations in the New World.'

The expression on her face reminds me that I'm speaking to a girl with the shadows of two drowned sisters behind her eyes. It's clear she wants to get on with her own tale. 'You were saying?' I ask.

'I didn't let my father's death break me. I decided to be strong. I decided to live.'

Her voice trembles then. It's a true five-hanky fable, but is she just trying to soften me up with heart-aching hokum, the clever little bint?

'My first master,' she continues, 'set me to work I knew – farming, in a *fah,* one of the kitchen gardens of Algiers. I planted, tended and picked grain to make my master fat. For two years I worked dawn until dark, and at night was shut up in the vast Beyliç *bagno* with the other Christian slaves. Like them, I got to learn that there's great eating on a chicken coop rat. I learnt to suck soil to assuage the pangs of hunger. I learnt to live in peace with the smell of my own sweat. But now,' and her tone grows dark and bitter, 'I never ever want to feel dirt under my fingers or feet again.'

There's something about that sentence that piques my interest: *I never ever want to feel dirt under my fingers or feet again*.

She doesn't notice me leaning forward. She's lost in her story.

'Meanwhile, I was clever. I'm an awful girl for the long-term plotting. I've the Irish gift for tongues, so I learnt Italian and Venetian from a fellow slave – a Signor Tosi who went to sea as a sailor but was carried off as a slave by the Barbaries. How the poor man pined for his wife and son, a fine boy called Momo, who was, he said, around my own age, which partly accounted for the fellow's grand kindness towards me. I, in turn, was grateful in my grief for a man who longed to be a father so. Signor Tosi fretted that his wife and son would starve themselves to raise a ransom for him. He also confirmed everything I'd ever told the little sisters about the glories of Venice – the gilded green water, the palaces, the foamy hot chocolate too.

'"And nary a potato?" I asked him.

'"Only for a rarity," Signor Tosi told me. "Polenta and rice."'

'*Then that's most definitely the place for me*, I thought.

'Of course there were no Muslim slaves in the *bagno*, but a young guard taught me to read and write in Arabic in exchange for English lessons. His wife sent me little parcels of food. I learnt how to recite from the Qur'an. Soon I was making myself useful as a translator to the *scrivan*, who accounted for all comings and goings at the *bagno*. Another kind man, didn't he make sure not to close the doors before I got safely home at night? Once I had the language, I charmed the children of my master with the kind of storytelling that had got the little sisters through hard seasons pulling potatoes back in Youghal. The little sisters would tell ye, if they still lived, that no one can touch me for the tales.

'I mixed stories of Djinn with legends of old Ireland. A banshee here. An Afreet there. A leprechaun or two. My reputation grew. Children sought me out – even the children of the richest and most powerful masters. I also made toys for them, using bits of wood and scraps of fabric I thieved wherever I could find 'em. The worst masters in Algiers make their slaves pay for their own keep, because they expect to turn a profit on us even before they sell us on to the next master or we die of overwork. With my toys and with coins that the *scrivan* slipped me, I paid for my wretched black bread and my fleabiting hammock in the Beyliç *bagno*. And didn't I also start to save?

'The children of more and more masters kept coming for the toys. And for the stories I told. Those children were as sweet in their wee natures as my own master was ruthless. I grew fond of their company, for some were the same ages as the little sisters and, well, children are children whether in Ireland or Algeria. For the pleasure of those young'uns, I invented a marvellous character: a perfect terror of a female Irish Pirate. She was fearless, special, a Duchess of blue blood and devilry galore. The more mad yarns I spun about her, the more the children adored me. Didn't my Duchess become their favourite monster? They loved to talk of her, trembling the while. My first master had a hate on the attention I was getting. So he sold me to a second one, fortunately a gentler class of gentleman altogether. At his *fah*, I acquired a whole new audience for my tales. Meanwhile, somehow the stories spread from the mouths of the masters' children and out into the streets of Algiers. It's a great city for the stories. Ye don't have to be a child, in Algiers, to believe in marvels, so ye don't, such a wondrous city it is, all set about with minarets and libraries and its great citadel glittering high above the turquoise sea!

'What started as stories to please children turned into rumours of a real Irish Duchess who sailed the seas, enslaving the slavers themselves! People wanted to believe in such a being, so they did. I began to overhear other people talking about the merciless Irish Duchess, who made all the other Barbary pirates look like blathering milksops so she did.

'While the Irish Duchess was doing the rounds of the taverns without me, busy at her great work of legend-making, ye need not doubt I myself kept a-grafting and a-saving. On Friday, our so-called day of rest, I worked harder than any other day of the week. I borrowed a bronze jug and carried water from the public wells to the homes of people who lived far from them. I would cry, "*Ab el ma!*" in an accent that had the locals thinking I was one of 'em.'

'Who wants some water?' I laugh. Her Arabic accent is indeed flawless. She dips her head just like a humble slave. 'Yes,' I tell her. 'Looking at that picture of innocence, I too would believe you someone who'd *never* spit in the water of her captors!'

She winks. 'Isn't that what I'm saying! What am I *like*? My pure accent, my clean hands and my downcast eyes got me regular customers.

'But our masters had predators of their own. One day, a Tuareg slave raiding party came to the *fah*. For a second time in my short life, I was snatched. My heart dropped as low as a cockroach's kidney for I'd heard terrible stories of my latest masters. Before we got too far into the desert, however, I escaped through a hole in a tent – for once it served me to be thin as a stick. Cart by cart and on foot, I relied on the kindness of Algerians, Tunisians and then Libyans who cut the iron hoop from my ankles, hid me from my pursuers and shared their dates and bread with me. So I kept myself safe – with their help – all the way to Tripoli. Truly, the people of the Maghreb are the most caring I've come across in all my many travels; it's a sore thing that the slave traders disgrace their countries so thoroughly that no one hears the truth of these things.

'In Tripoli, I stowed away on the first merchant ship I could find that was bound for Venice. Yes, that very same Venice that I craved to believe was the heart of the civilised world, a place of mercy and charity, her beauty but an outward sign of her grandness.'

Her tone is bitter now, I notice.

'When I was discovered we were already halfway to Sicily. But the Algerian captain was another charitable soul. He allowed me a precious bucket of water and a slice of soap to wash and later set me at his own table to eat. I trusted him with my story and he repaid my trust. He said he'd send a representation about my case to the British Consul in Venice. For my own safety, he advised me in the meantime to tie my hair in a sailor's queue and to swap my ragged dress for a pair of trousers, a shirt and a fustian jacket that he supplied himself. To keep my cover, I worked my passage to Venice, the captain's kind eye on me all the way, bless him for a good old soul.

'Only as we approached Venice did I don my girl's rags once more. While we waited in quarantine on the Lazzaretto island, I practiced my Venetian and Italian, all the pretty words I'd need to beg those grand folk to take me in. In my dreams, I had the Venetians returning me under their protection to Ireland, where I'd find my ma. She was the only member of my family who was not certainly dead.'

The bint's face darkens. 'Yet it turned out I was not considered good enough for Venetian charity. The senator who boarded my boat to interview me had neither decency nor compassion, for all he acted the Holy Joe, pretending to be saving Venice from the likes of a wee girl like me. It was a bitter day for me when I first met Daniele Spatafora. Sure it'll be a bitter year for him now that *he*'s about to meet *me* again.

'But back then, what recourse did I have? The captain, mortified, agreed to give me a place on his crew returning to Algiers. "Get back into your boy's clothes," he said, "and keep them on when ye get there. Your slave master will be looking for a girl. You've grown taller on this journey. We'll feed ye up on the way back and I'll find ye portering work at the harbour." In the mouth of this generosity, I didn't have the teeth to tell him no. A kind man, always. Yet—'

I grin like a saltwater crocodile, but more prettily, saying, 'I don't believe that a porter's job is what you did next.'

The Irish bint smiles. 'It was not, me old flower. I left Venice with impotent hatred burning in my heart. Then, on the long journey back to Algiers, I remembered that there was a legend waiting for me.'

43

Like Scything a Pond to Kill Dragonflies

By now it's as if we're old friends – me, a Djinniya, and she, an Irish Pirate Duchess. 'Will ye have a morsel to eat?' she asks. She orders a tray of rose Turkish delight and *halva* brought to the table on the deck where we parley. Soon after, to my delight, another tray arrives, piled with crunchy *luqaimat* dumplings glistening with sweet syrup. We're like two ladies at a genteel tea party. The bint has her men serve me as if I were a queen, saying 'Come now, ye mullackers! This luverly Djinniya's not going to jump into the disgraceful likes of ye! She's far too choosy.'

I like her style.

Less so, when she turns to me saying, 'Help yourself. Don't pretend you're not famished for a cake. From the look of the breadbasket on ye, you're one who'd eat a baby through the rungs of a cot if the infant were dusted with sugar.'

When the men are gone, I let her know what I've worked out. 'So back in Algiers you promptly *became* the Pirate Duchess you'd invented.'

'I did. All I had to do was claim the role. Whose was it if not mine, after all? And who knew it better than me? As for my real origins, that's my business. Didn't the slavers steal both my past and my identity? Didn't Daniele Spatafora *laugh* when I told him who I really was? When he disrespected the deaths of the little sisters I went wild in my thoughts, so I did. Ye could say it was his cruelty that set me free from my old self.'

'You decided to raise yourself to the nobility then?'

'Wasn't it time for a new name? There's a rake of pretty letters in the alphabet, and I chose the ones that made up the word 'Duchess'. I had only to dress myself like this –' she gestures to her tattered finery and scimitar – 'and swagger into a tavern, where I growled, "Raw steak and ale for the Pirate Duchess!" – and I was away. Men went down on their knees, swore themselves to my service. The worst and most dangerous men. No word of a lie.'

'Went on their knees to a slave girl?' I try hard not to sound impressed, though I slightly quite am. To cover my amazement, I cram my mouth with more cardamom-scented cream.

'Bockety, ain't it? And me hardly the size of a thrush's ankle. Those gowls never saw the terrified wee girlie snatched from a cliff in Youghal. They were dazzled by the bold reputation spun by my stories over weeks and months in the taverns of Algiers. I made sure they *stayed* dazzled.

'I've increased my grandeur at every point. I fire our guns in triumph every time we approach our home port of Algiers, so everyone in town knows a heroine's returning. I hunted down the vessel that captured me in Youghal . . . the hoary old *Wrath of Qat*. I bought her, renamed her the *Nancy Bridget* after the little sisters and made her the most feared ship on the sea. Every time I come home with booty, I hire men with bells and short horns to hullabaloo my arrival and give out cakes to children. To the Corsairs of Algiers, I'm *a Djinniya* of a duchess – magical, invincible, ruthless. I might as well be made of smokeless fire like yerself so! In fact, I've a notion that being a Pirate Duchess is rather like being a Djinniya. Don't we both adore to hear helpless humans pleading "Please don't enslave me! Please don't kill me!"'

I think, *I'm a mere amateur as a drama queen.* This *is a professional*.

'But let's get this clear,' I say. 'Have you ever actually killed anyone?'

She grins. 'Are ye astray in the head? In my mouth, of course, I've murdered millions. With these hands – barely a lamb-chop so. Yet these creatures –' she gestures around the deck – 'are my men to their very toenails and would do anything for me. I've personally earned my Duchess-ship with my brains. I command my own fleet. To Algiers, I've brought in English brigs, Portuguese caravels, Venetian cogs, hundreds of slaves, always men over twenty-five – the age at which Venetian noblemen become senators. Yet I never captured families on the shore. And I always drew the line at children, until now. As far as I'm concerned, all Venetians are fit for my revenge apart from Signor Tosi's son Momo and his mother, whom I intend to find and deal with kindly. Haven't I spent two years a-negotiating Signor Tosi's ransom? With the utmost secrecy, of course, for my clemency, if known, would damage my reputation. I was on the point of success when *I Fedeli* set 'emselves up in the ransom business, stopping all Venetian releases so that every penny collected was instead funnelled into their own bottomless pockets.'

As she says this, I recall with some prickling discomfort that my latest conquest goes by the name of Momo. And that he cries for his mother. But revealing my mistake now – that would be a mistake. This is something I can deal with quietly in the privacy of my own castle, later, away from accusing eyes.

The Duchess continues to rant. 'The rest of the Venetians, down with 'em! After all, Senator Spatafora had no care for me when I was hardly more than a child. I'll make smathers of him now. Perhaps the Spatafora monster has children of his own. If he does, I'd like to see *them* sleeping with two thousand other lice-eaten slaves in the Beyliç *bagno* and rising before dawn to work till the feet on 'em bleed.

'And then when I discovered the Djinn in jars at the apothecary, well, I thought, there's a little private booty just for me – wishes when I want 'em. So long as I deliver Venetian humiliation and Venetian gold, my men shall lionise me for it. Venice – the jewel of the Adriatic! At their disposal because I, Emer Fionnuala O'Dowdy, dared it, so I did.'

Of course there's no way I'm about to reveal to her the subtle, difficult truth about Djinn-wishes at this particular moment. I need something up my sleeve. So instead, I ask, 'Is this plan not lamentably *wasteful*?'

Look at me, protecting Venetians!

I say, 'It's like scything a pond to kill dragonflies – you only rust your blade. Is this revenge in proportion? Is it not *dangerous* for the pirate cause? For if you commit an outrage against Venice, then the civilised nations of the world will unite to defeat the Barbary pirates once and for all. And you'll be done for. As we say in my country, "An army of sheep led by a lion would defeat an army of lions led by a sheep." Your grudge against Daniele Spatafora is turning you into a sheep. Why not just take *him,* and make an example of him?'

Her eyes are hot now. 'Away with yer tired old sayings! Who are ye to cut tripes out of me? I'm no sheep! I want the Venetians to know that Daniele Spatafora's the *true* source of the misfortunes I rain down on 'em. I want 'em to turn on him *themselves*, in full knowledge of what he is.'

It's then that I remember her phrase, *I never ever want to feel dirt under my fingers or feet again.* And I suddenly know how to make use of it.

She doesn't want dirt under her feet? Only water? Well, we'll see about that.

While the Irish bint's completely lost in the glory of revenge, I jump inside the Pirate Duchess. Her teeth rattle as she screams, 'Will ye come on now, ye bold article? That's so *mank!* Do ye think I want those hooves and hairy legs slipping down my throat? What are you *like*? That's *never* fair at all!'

She tries to fight me off, but this time it's me with the advantage of surprise. Her blue eyes turn to mercury.

At the same time, I throw my all into a draining spell. I order the serval cat Djinniya to help intensify it: 'Drain! Drain! Drain!' The rush of water in my ears lets me know that for once I've got it right and that the mutinous little beast is helping me. I feel the boat descending in a rush of air. I feel it tilt.

Beneath us is now the shallowest trickle of water jumping with beached fish in the middle of a road of quicksand. And in the sun, that too is drying rapidly. For a moment, homesickness for the glittering dunes of Arabia swarms into my fiery heart. But this mud is black – not golden like the sublime sands of Nizwa.

For absolute safety, I make the Pirate Duchess use her hands – now glowing with ghostlight – steer her vessel straight into a fast emerging sandbank. The vessel totters for a dirt-person heartbeat and then it's down. All other boats follow and fall – with a grand shivering of timbers – on their sides and are shipwrecked. The Irish bint can't utter a word, but from the innards of her ship I hear what is indubitably a parrot, screaming in an Irish accent, 'Bucket of snots!'

As for the tiny Venetian boats that clustered around each pirate vessel like flies on an old *merguez* sausage – well, yes, I admit that a few of them are crushed to matchwood. But not all! With the serval cat's help, I execute a nearly perfect Disentanglement Enchantment followed by a Directed Float. The rope binding of each of the little Venetian boats unties itself. The boats rise neatly out of the mud and hover in the air like bats. I tell them to return to their original moorings. I notice a little waver in my magic then. Yet I'm quite sure that I get it right when I make them tie themselves up securely and neatly. The air is filled with the sound of old Venetian boats settling into their wooden bones.

At the last moment I leap out of the Pirate Duchess, Emer Fionnuala O'Dowdy. While she's still dazed, I find her chamber and what I need inside it. I tuck the two remaining Djinn jars under my arms, and then, smoother than a breeze and faster than fate (as we say in my country), I triumphantly depart what is literally a sinking ship.

As we also say in my country, 'Some people eat chicken, others fall off the cliff while chasing chickens.' I intend to celebrate my great success with chicken pudding, fully irrigated with the best cream, followed by a double helping of my favourite *halawet ahmad*. In my mind, my tongue already twirls around those nests of sweet vermicelli with pistachio. My servants make them superbly.

Now I'll go back and get the praise and petting I deserve. Given that I've saved their whole city with my *perfect* magic, the Venetians surely won't care too much about a handful of long-gone boys at the Palazzo Bon. Will they? Meanwhile I really must remember to do something about the son of the slave friend of the Irish Duchess. Alone of all the slaves, that Signor Toto? Soso? may have a hope. I'm becoming quite attached to this doing good thing, I find. I long for a mirror suddenly, in which to behold how doing good will have plumped up my lips and given a sparkle to my eye.

The only thing that leaves a faintly bitter taste in my watering mouth is this: I wish Musipul had been here to witness my absolute triumph.

44

Stalemate, with the Emphasis on Stale

At first, everyone was delighted with Ghazalah – at least those few who knew what had really happened out there in the lagoon. Most people thought that the pirates had beached their own boats accidentally, for after all no one knew the secret safe channels of the lagoon apart from the Venetians themselves. As for the draining of the water, that just seemed like a natural rebalancing of the elements after the outrageous amounts of rain that had fallen without apparent rhyme or reason for far too long.

Pious Venetians had even more reasons to be pleased because, with the help of her serval cat Djinniya, Ghazalah also cast a most excellent spell that extracted all the pirate arrows from all the saints in all the churches. She even healed their wounds, so the holy figures were good as new.

The lamp-boy, Momo, had been found wandering in the alley near the graveyard. He was thinner than before but none the worse for his adventure. However, he'd not a single memory of what had befallen him from the moment he set foot in the graveyard by 'The Palace that Eats Boys'. The city rejoiced in the return of her lost son with street parties and homemade flags. They were also preparing to welcome Momo's father, whose ransom had been paid by a mysterious donor. Freed from the *bagno* at Algiers, Signor Tosi was on his way home.

And yet . . . not everything was as it should be. No one knew where *I Fedeli* had gone at the hour of Venice's greatest need, and there was no sign of them since.

And the black Corsair cats were still on the prowl. There was not a rat left in Venice for the aggrieved Syrian cats. And now the bold pirate felines were climbing in windows, helping themselves to ragout, bread and cutlets. All the night, the air was seared with the yowls of Corsair cats at war with Venetian ones over wives and rooftop territories.

But the worst problem of all was turning out to be the very thing that Ghazalah had done to save the city: emptying it of water. Without the tide to scour it out, Venice had started to swelter and stink. Where the air once sang with cascading water, there was now just choking dust. Even the Grand Canal was reduced to a narrow channel of sludge that gurgled and slurped evilly. Some of the back canals were quickly becoming unbearable in the steamy heat that had followed all those months of rain.

Venice's deep wells were holding out, just. But if there was no rain, it was only a question of time before they too ran dry. And the sun blazed as relentlessly as the rain had once fallen. The parish priests urged people to be careful with water: 'Treat it as precious, like your children. It's our lifeblood.'

Water was already too scarce for washing, and no one could spare a drop to clean the streets. The stench of the canals – and indeed of hot unwashed people – was such that many Venetians walked around wearing the long-snouted masks that doctors used to protect themselves from the plague. This was a frightening sight, even by daylight.

The serene floating city was no more. Aurelia, like everyone else, felt the loss deep in her heart. She missed the sinuous liquid streets. Without water, there were no reflections, no flirting light, no sweet sounds of the waves caressing stone.

Venice is shamed. I feel her shame. I pity her, Aurelia thought.

She also missed the bells punctuating all the hours of the day.

Without them, all our hours are the same.

As for the pirate ships, weighed down with huge bronze bells, they were sinking ever more deeply into the reeking mud. Some of the boats had been holed in the sudden descent of the waters. Mud-thickened seawater was oozing through the cracks. In the heat, the liquid was fast disappearing from the water casks the pirates had filled easily when Venice was afflicted with the rain. Now, the sun was evaporating the water inside the casks. Washing was out of the question. So the smell of hot, bored angry pirates swam out across the mud. The drained *bacino* served as a terrible opera house: its dry air transmitted every swear word and curse efficiently straight into the ears of the Venetians.

Even inside the mermaids' cavern, the water was low. The mermaids, half-beached, flopped disconsolately in mud that was far from fragrant. 'Lackaday! Tell dat noggin' Man-Guzzler to fix wot she wrought!' Chissa urged Aurelia and Valerio, when they came to seek advice.

But when they went to consult Ghazalah, her laugh tinkled through the palace. 'That stubborn girl, the Pirate Duchess! May her tendons snap like sheets drying in a sharp desert wind! I bet she's thinking, "*Ab el ma?*" Ghazalah purred. 'Which means "Who wants some water?" Meanwhile, I'm *adoring* this heat.'

'This isn't funny,' said Aurelia. 'Not having water in Venice is a problem.'

'Who stopped the rain, bint? I seem to remember that it was *you*. It's not all my fault.'

'So you won't help us?'

Ghazalah opened her mouth with a certain look on her face that they'd come to know too well.

'Please!' groaned Aurelia. 'Not another proverb!'

'How can you deny me when there's one that's perfect? "When what you want doesn't happen, learn to love what does." Look! The roses are blooming early! Rose petal rice pudding tonight.'

'Maybe you can't learn empathy if you've never had it,' said Valerio.

Ghazalah muttered something about centuries in an amethyst flask and looked sorry for herself. Aurelia, shaking her head with disgust, told Valerio, 'It's hopeless. Let's go.'

It was a stalemate, with the emphasis on stale.

A light playful breeze continued to waft the fug of trapped pirates right through the city's already reeking streets. In the evenings, an almost edibly thick heat mist rolled around the city, well perfumed with drains and the sweat of hundreds of pirates and thousands of Venetians.

Then the first child coughed.

In their brief invasion of the town, the pirates had deposited fire starters in the form of kindling and oily rags. Those rags were invisibly dotted with the pirates' body lice. The apprentices who'd set themselves to hunting down and removing all the rags had no idea they were taking visitors on board – at least, not until they began to scratch. The lice carried typhus fever. That was no longer a problem for the pirates who either died or survived the sickness. If they lived, they were for ever after immune to it. But the Venetian apprentices had no such protection.

First, the victims felt feverish. Soon a rash reddened their bellies. It spread over most of their bodies, except for the face, palms and soles of the feet. By that time, those afflicted could not bear the light and began to rave. Some fell into comas. Soon a full-blown epidemic raged around the city. Thousands were abed with fever. Within two days, people had started to die.

At first, the Venetians tried to pretend that the foul air had brought a new kind of influenza to the city. The '*influenza puzzolente*', they called it, the 'stinking flu'. But the city's doctors knew typhus when they saw it.

It was all the worse because the Venetians could not take the sick to the special quarantine islands that were always deployed in the case of epidemics. Instead, Venice's narrow streets were perfectly designed to spread disease from house to house and person to person. The typhus took its toll on young and old.

The heat continued to beat down. Spring had transformed into a sweltering midsummer in just a few days. The levels of the wells were now far below safe. Venetians with relatives on the orchard island of Giudecca looked longingly across the vast field of mud, not knowing if their cousins and uncles and aunts were sick or starving. The mud was like quicksand – no one could walk over it. 'The orchards will feed them,' the Venetians tried to reassure themselves. There was no way, however, of knowing if that was true.

Nor were there any means of rescuing the girls who'd taken refuge on the island of Poveglia, now also stranded in the mud. Aurelia was acutely aware that, as each day passed, the supplies there must be dwindling. There *was* fresh water on Poveglia, and she trusted Catarina to keep the girls' spirits up. *She probably even knows how to catch fish*, thought Aurelia proudly. But what if the freshwater stream dried up in this sunshine? And what if they'd taken the typhus with them?

The doge was confined to his bed with fever, as was every single member of the Council of Ten. But in the mermaids' cavern, a different kind of council assembled: Aurelia, Valerio, Simoneto Ghezzo, Angelo Emo, the surgeon. These few humans, who knew the whole truth, had somehow stayed free of the typhus, except for poor Aldo, who'd cleared up more oily rags than anyone. He now lay abed with a burning temperature and a dark red rash, according to his anxious employer, the apothecary of the Redeemer.

Ghazalah and Musipul were also in attendance at the cavern, both unwillingly. Ghazalah would of course not soon forget the insults that the mermaids had heaped on her head when their voices were restored. She was also still preening herself on her success, refusing to see any darkness in the consequences. And Musipul had discovered that the mermaids were behind the Leopard's Bane that had cost her so much dignity. By way of a greeting, the Djinniya and the leopardess exchanged only curt nods with the mermaids.

Aurelia said, 'If we ask for a spell to let the water back in, then the pirates will attack. *I Fedeli* have sold all the arms so we'd be helpless. The Pirate Duchess would rather die of thirst than give up her vendetta – unless perhaps we pay some kind of ransom? In a way, Venice *does* owe her something.'

'We're thinking crooked,' said Angelo Emo. 'Ransoming will just feed the Duchess's greed and make her believe she can raise the price. She'll hold out for the musical girls too.'

Musipul said, 'My mistress is the one who must atone for her latest mistake.'

'I'm not going out there to abase myself to that moody Irish girl again,' said Ghazalah. 'May her tongue be cut in two by lightning. Yet I *suppose* I can give this surgeon some herbs from our courtyard that will help with the typhus,' she said grudgingly.

Dottor Fantin bowed. 'Your help is gratefully accepted. Our medicine is often sadly backward in comparison with that of your nation.'

Valerio said, 'I doubt if another meeting between Ghazalah and the Irish Duchess would work well. The two of them are . . . incompatible.'

'True dat,' said Chissa. 'Too much alike, perhaps. I reckon dat dis Man-Guzzler would make a rib-stickin' pirate. She loves to take wot ain't hers.'

'*I'll* go and talk to the Duchess,' said Aurelia. 'The prophecy says the Water's Daughter's *supposed* to parley with the "blue-eyed marauder" and "mend the past that stains these waters". So it's my personal duty to apologise to the Duchess for the evil treatment Daniele Spatafora meted out to her. I can explain how the same monster was to have power over my life too, if I became his daughter-in-law. But I must also have something to offer her.'

Musipul asked Ghazalah, 'Are you even *capable* of bringing the water back if the Duchess agrees to give up her plans?'

Quite humbly, the Djinniya replied, 'I think I am. I've been practising.'

Everyone looked at her with surprise. 'I've been making taps in stoups flow on and off. I've been filling puddles with clear water. I wanted to be sure. At first, it's true, I was ridiculously poor at it. And I fear I accidentally sent a small plague of locusts to the island of Giudecca so the orchards there are . . . gone. Irregardless, I've learnt the skills now. I can bring the water back, with maybe one Djinni to help me.'

'So I need to tell the Pirate Duchess that we can refill the *bacino* if she will go away and promise never to come back,' said Aurelia. 'But will that be enough?'

'I? *We* need to get there,' said Valerio. 'But unlike Ghazalah, we can't float.'

Musipul said, 'However – given that you eat less *baklava* than *she* does – the pair of you could ride on the back of a flying beast. Like myself.'

After a little rustling, two sumptuous furred wings rose up on the leopardess's back. A look of intense discomfort crossed Valerio's face as he said, 'So kind of you! It would be an honour.'

'Well then,' Musipul suggested, 'it would perhaps be prudent to quickly paint white flags with olive branches so the pirates don't aim cannon balls at us before we get a chance to deliver our message. I understand you have talent that way, boy?'

45

Negotiations

It was an awkward thing to be facing a girl to whom your city has done a grievous wrong. It was *particularly* awkward when that girl was furious as ten devils and surrounded by several dozen pirates whose fury was also written on their faces. And in Valerio's case, it was even more awkward as he struggled to wipe the vomit off his shirt. The short trip on Musipul's back proved that he suffered not just from sea-sickness but air-sickness too.

Aurelia and Valerio were greeted on deck by a dozen pirates, scimitars drawn. Each looked perfectly capable of running through a pair of twelve-year-olds on the command of the Pirate Duchess, who stood glowering at the poop deck, her arms crossed. She wrinkled her nose as Valerio approached.

'Here's me thinking that pirates were the famousest of stinkers,' said the Duchess by way of introduction. 'Venetian boys are worse, for all they act as if they smell of myrrh and frankincense. Did ye ever think of rinsing that shirt in water, boy?'

Aurelia said, 'There *is* no water. That's why we're here to negotiate.'

'Will ye come on now?' said the Pirate Duchess. 'Venice still hasn't learnt to respect me? Sending me whey-faced *children* with the gawks on 'em! Negotiate with that? I will *in my ear*! Now be off with ye back to your nurseries, or it'll be the worse for ye.'

Musipul rose up to her full height, snarling. The Duchess faced her down with absolute coolness. 'Do ye think I'll be fearing a spotty feline when I've lived among black-biled Corsair cats all these years past?' Then her tone softened to admiration as she said, 'I do love me a cat though. I can't help myself when it comes to 'em. I'm missing my Corsair cats more than I can say. Venice is treating 'em well?' She chuckled. 'Well, knowing my fine beasts, they're probably rather insisting on that. Meanwhile, I allow I'm surprised to see ye somewhat supernatural in the limb department. A flying leopardess? Grand, that is!'

She ordered her men to bring a large, fringed velvet cushion for Musipul. 'For obvious reasons, I'll not offer ye refreshments, for which I apologise,' she said. 'For a creature of *your* magnificence, I'd put a decent appearance on hospitality if I could at all. No word of a lie.'

No such courtesies were offered to Aurelia and Valerio. Instead, the Pirate Duchess asked abruptly, 'Where's that rascally Djinniya with the impressively hairy legs? Sure I'd pull my own eyes out any day in the week for a sight of that lovely face again, if only to punch it in the nose. My men are dying of thirst, while she's no doubt off romancing her phizzog in the mirror with seventeen different compliments and a curlicue for each of 'em. I hold her accountable for *everything* that's gone awry here.'

'Which is why we thought you might not be in the mood to negotiate with her,' said Aurelia. 'Also, I know *why* you wish to harm this city. I . . . understand it.'

'Ye're a witch with the second sight then?' The Pirate Duchess crossed her arms. 'And ye so scrawny and undersized with it. Don't be pleading the poor, famished fairy-tale orphan with me now.'

'Not a witch, but I . . . I saw what Daniele Spatafora did to you.'

The face of the Pirate Duchess flamed, then paled. 'How could ye see that? Ye must have been a puling infant when that happened.'

'I never puled,' said Aurelia. 'It's just that I have . . . some ways of seeing . . . that other people do not. And I'm sorry for the way Daniele Spatafora treated you. For greed and callousness, Daniele Spatafora was no better than . . . the pirates who took your little sisters.'

The colour drained from the face of the Duchess. 'The Djinniya told ye?'

'Yes. Everything. We also know *I Fedeli* are far from faithful. They've taxed the city to a state of poverty to make themselves rich. They've lied to us about where the money went. And we know they have sold secrets to you . . . as well as ships and arms.'

'Is there no end to what ye know, girl? Are ye some kind of child savant? But if – by whatever means – ye know all that,' the Duchess said, 'then ye know I'm nothing to your native vultures when it comes to bamboozling your citizens and feasting on their purses. Your *Fedeli* are worse than pirates – they've betrayed their own. I've bought only what *I Fedeli* had already stolen.'

'Yet you were taking it, knowing it was stolen,' said Valerio.

'Aren't ye the charmer? Stop your impudence or it will be the worse for ye! And didn't ye steal back the girls and women I had taken?'

'One of them was my sister!' blurted Aurelia.

'So ye have a sister,' said the Duchess quietly. 'Make sure ye treasure her well. Life is perilous. Sisters may be lost at any moment and they can never be replaced.'

Aurelia's chest tightened. She'd nearly lost Catarina. And it was only in the nearly-losing that she'd come to realise the true value of her.

Valerio bowed. 'You speak of the past. We've come with a proposition for the future. If you agree to leave Venice, then our Djinniya will make the tide return.'

'Stand downwind of me, sicky boy! *Our* Djinniya? She's more of a Pirate Duchess than I am! Ye have tamed her? Only a holy and learned sheik can do that, and ye Christians don't have one at your disposal, do ye? I'd like to—'

'Do we have an agreement?' Valerio's tone was stern.

'Well, boy, I'll admit ye seem to have come out from under thumb! But there's more to negotiate than ye children can know. The thing is, I came here to get my shiploads of Venetian slaves. Your notion of a bargain would mean me returning empty-handed to Algiers. Now that's a dangerous city to be disgraced in. Ye want me to chance my arm and dim the lustre of my reputation for absolute mercilessness? I'd rather rest becalmed here another season so.'

Aurelia thought, *Not so long ago, I was holding out for the grandeur of my history fingers, just like that, no matter what it cost.*

She said, 'It seems to me that as long as you're trying to best him in savagery then you're still in Daniele Spatafora's power. A man who is cruel to a child – you take him as your model, wanting only to outdo him. The thing is, I think you're better than that.'

'The thing is, me old flower,' said the Duchess, 'I'm probably not.'

'So you don't agree our terms,' said Valerio, despairing.

'Not yer exact terms. My counter offer is this, and pure decent it is, so mind it: I'll take *I Fedeli*. My colleagues in Algeria were expecting ordinary men, women and children. Instead, I'll help myself to a hundred greedy noblemen, and the prospect of fine fat ransoms.'

'You know where *I Fedeli* are hiding?' asked Valerio.

'How would I not? Those gowls fell for everything my ambassadors told 'em. They believe the mysterious Pirate Duchess their ally. Blinded by greed, that's how little they know! Once we've water under our bows again, we'll surprise the soft-skinned cowards. In fact, wasn't it *always* my plan to give *I Fedeli* a taste of the horrors they planned to inflict on their fellow Venetians? It's the galleys for them! Double-crossing those double-crossers! Lovely altogether.'

Valerio put his hand on Aurelia's arm. 'Can we accept the Duchess's terms? On behalf of Venice? To send a hundred noblemen into slavery?'

'How noble are they, really? How about temporary slavery, for one year? Time to think about the preposterous trick they played on this city. Signor Rioba shall tell the Venetians exactly why this was necessary. The Seldom Seen Press can print a *blistering* explanation.' Aurelia turned to the Pirate Duchess. 'I think we can agree to a year.'

The Duchess countered, 'But after that, their families must ransom 'em back – if they still want 'em at all.'

Aurelia thought of thin, nervous Contessa Spatafora. Daniele Spatafora had always terrorised his wife, but the poor woman would probably pay for his return, if only for the status of having a husband on her arm; even one who'd spent a year rowing the galleys; even one who'd come home with the calloused hands and sunburned complexion that would be social death in Venice. As for their son Marco, well his prospects would be dimmed by the disgrace too. He'd not be so welcome in the fashionable salons and the tailors would not be rushing to serve him.

And then, Aurelia realised with joy, *Mamma won't want me or Catarina betrothed to him! We'll be free!*

'Yes,' she told the Duchess, 'we agree your terms.'

'Excellent. First, we'll shave their heads and fancy beards . . . I shall personally shave the long, black beard of Daniele Spatafora, the one he stroked with actual smugness, so he did, as he threw me back on the mercy of the sea. I've a craving to see the shock on his face as he recognises me. I want him to see what he turned me into. I want him watching me approach with the razor while my men surround me, humble and respectful to my every whim. I want Daniele Spatafora pure gibbering with fear. I want to take his beard in my hand and say, "A courtesy, I'm doing yer city here. Removing a parasite, ye might say. Of course I'm doing it on behalf of the little sisters, that same Nancy, that same Bridget that ye, like some kind of frightful God, decided had no existence."

'Then I'll let him down so very slowly and so very gently, that it's not his head I'm taking off. It's his liberty I'm selling to galley owners.'

'Can anyone survive that?' asked Valerio.

'My instinct's that Daniele Spatafora is too mean to die. He'll be back. Speaking of which, I've not yet finished my demands. I want all my darling Corsair cats returned to me. Not a whisker nor the friend of a whisker must be harmed. Anyone who hurts my precious fur princes and princesses – I'll wrap their hurting hands in pitch and set fire to 'em.'

'You're heartily welcome to your fur royalty,' said Aurelia. 'However, that shall be in exchange for *all your* remaining parrots and our one remaining Djinn jar.'

'Ye drive a hard bargain, girl. Even my Suleyman? How can ye ask it? I've taught him to blather from a wee chick. No word of a lie.'

'Yes,' said Aurelia, 'I could have guessed as much from the style of his conversation. Suleyman and all the birds shall be treated like princes. I vouch for it personally.'

'How high-handed ye are, miss! I like it. I think ye are a biteen like myself.'

'Is your stomach fully emptied, boy?' asked Musipul pointedly as Valerio climbed on her back.

He nodded.

As Musipul flexed her wings, Aurelia asked, 'Have you thought how we're going to get – how many? a thousand? – Corsair cats back to these ships? You heard what the Duchess said – she won't leave without them, and she won't hand over the Djinn jars or the parrots until every last black-biled Corsair cat is back on its ship.'

Musipul plumed her whiskers. 'I've recently painted supremely flattering portraits of several domesticated Syrian cats who therefore owe me a favour. Some of their number hide wings in their flanks. Several might team up to carry a carpet that could carry away a dozen Corsair cats together.'

'They'd probably be happy to do so; there's no love lost between our Syrian cats and those Corsairs,' said Valerio.

'If you two can negotiate with an Irish Pirate Duchess, and leave with your lives, I think you can also handle a few Syrian cats,' said Musipul with something that sounded almost like admiration in her voice.

'How do you negotiate with a Syrian cat?' asked Aurelia. 'It's not as if you can *talk* with them.'

'That's where you're wrong,' said Musipul, landing lightly on the Riva degli Schiavoni, where Ghezzo, Ghazalah, the surgeon and the mermaids were waiting. 'Venetian cats can talk as well as I can. It's just that they usually can't be bothered to do so with foolish humans.'

46

Conclusions

The end of this story was once supposed to be Aurelia Bon's betrothal to Marco Spatafora. Obviously, that was never going to happen, was it? Perhaps it seemed more obvious that this book would conclude in the betrothal of Catarina and Marco Spatafora, with Aurelia shut away in the silent convent of San Zaccaria and Ghazalah bound back in a flask, lonely and trapped as any Venetian nun.

That would have made sense, no?

Neither of those things happened. No one was marrying into the Spatafora family any more. The whole clan languished in deepest disgrace. Marco's father, as the highest ranking officer of *I Fedeli*, had been convicted of embezzling Venice's slave-ransom money, draining funds away from the great sea wall project and selling off the city's arms and ships to the Barbary pirates. In fact, the Venetian public judged *I Fedeli* worse than pirates – because, unlike the pirates, they had no code of honour and had betrayed their own people. As you will have guessed, however, Daniele Spatafora was not there to hear the judgement. Like all the senior officers in *I Fedeli*, he was now serving his year as a galley slave.

The Venetians who'd survived the fever were hard at work re-equipping the empty boatyards of the Arsenale. What was left of the fleet was now under the command of young Angelo Emo, the officer who'd pleaded for mercy, all those years before, for a young Irish girl seeking refuge in Venice. That fact was still a secret, but now everyone knew that this same Angelo Emo had agreed with Signor Rioba, and had tried to warn Venice of the danger from the Barbary pirates – and of the corruption of *I Fedeli*. Now, Venice's most beloved naval fellow, Angelo Emo, was also growing more handsome by the minute, a fact that had not gone unnoticed in the Castle of Jabrin.

The orchards at Giudecca, stripped by Ghazalah's accidental plague of locusts, were back in blossom, with a good crop of fruit expected – thanks to a miracle, the Venetians thought, but actually thanks to a clever spell of Ghazalah's. There were so many things – including mermaids, Guls, Afreets and indeed one troublesome Djinniya and her artistic leopardess – that the Venetians did not know about. Nor would they soon be finding out that their beloved, lazy house cats had wings. They were probably still wondering, with relief, what had happened to the plague of noxious black cats. But you'll probably agree that this was for the best. For a few weeks, however, the *Poupée de France* wore a swashbuckling confection of silken rags in a style known as '*à la duchesse pirate*'.

As for Aurelia Bon, she'd not given up on her nine remaining history fingers. Yet she was no longer eager to deliver performances attended by hundreds of admirers. She could barely admit it even to herself, but the visions that her fingers delivered were increasingly less vivid than they'd once been. Aurelia was finding other ways to make history come alive – spending more time in various archives and libraries, reading faded documents that deepened the stories behind the glimpses her fingers still gave her. She found that she liked it in those peaceful places that smelt sweetly of paper-dust and ink. You may picture her lifting her head from intense study of a fascinating old letter, thinking, *When you're not the centre of attention, there's a chance to watch and learn, and it's actually more interesting.*

Catarina sometimes rowed Aurelia to her destinations. This was, of course, to their mother's horror: 'You were supposed to be the *promising* child! What if someone important *saw* you at this lowborn activity?'

However, Contessa Bon was now noticeably less tense with her more wayward daughter. There was no more talk of Padre Pino or the convent. Aurelia's father preferred not to speak of how nearly he'd betrothed his elder daughter to a *Fedeli* son. Instead, there were hints that Aurelia might one day be allowed to attend the renowned university in Padova. Aurelia still sent her daydreams down its learned corridors.

Meanwhile, Contessa Bon had stopped saying, 'Isn't it dreadful?' when it actually wasn't. She'd even shown an unexpected sense of humour, offering the *Fedeli* wives her antique glass tear-catchers to measure how much they were missing their husbands. (There were no takers.) She'd also come to be very fond of one Valerio Fialetti, as had Catarina and even Conte Bon himself. Valerio was now the manager of Remondini's printing works in Bassano del Grappa and could not come to Venice so often. However, every month he spent a few days working with Aurelia on her new book.

And then he'd dine with the Bons, their favourite guest at what was now a very cheerful family table. The Portuguese ambassador was also a regular visitor. Aurelia had come to think that – so long as the ambassador refrained from jokes – there was almost nothing nicer than a Venetian dinner party at home.

Valerio had learnt to be a little less earnest about research. Aurelia, transcribing a document in the archives under his supervision, was astonished to hear him say, 'You mustn't be afraid of making mistakes. Every good new idea came out of someone making a terrible mistake.'

'Like me. I made a terrible mistake,' she acknowledged. 'I was so caught up in my own legend that I distracted Venice from the peril of the Barbary pirates and *I Fedeli*. I was a sideshow, a dangerous one.'

So. Speaking of sideshows, Aurelia and Valerio celebrated their thirteenth birthdays (both in the same week) with a visit to the mermaids. They were surprised to find the mermaids semi-transparent – like aquatic Djinn.

'What's happened to you?' asked Aurelia.

'Nothing,' said Lussa. 'It be not ourselves but your eyes that be a-changing, becoming less open to magic. Most mortals over the age of thirteen cannot see us at all.'

'And that be how we likes it,' said Chissa, 'bein' as how we needs to remain a secret, niver to be disgorged. If grown-ups knew of us, they'd use us to drag in even more of the tourists dat already flood this town and might one day drown it.'

A familiar voice screeched down from a gold cage above. 'Here's me taking a slew o' tourists by surprise and making them scurvy dogs walk the plank, before this whole town turns into one great hotel! Cat o' nine tails if they refuse and bucket of baddamns all round!'

The former pirate parrots were settling in happily with the mermaids and teaching their mistresses many new and colourful phrases. The mermaids were delighted with their pets, fashioning intricate gold cages for them. Lussa had despatched scallop shells to the shores of the Nile, asking her mermaid cousins there to send hippopotamus, egret and crocodile dung. One of the mermaid cooks had invented a dung curry that kept Suleyman in paroxysms of greed.

Lussa wished Aurelia a fond happy birthday. She asked, 'Have ye not perhaps noticed, maid, that your own finger powers be also subtly lessening day by day? The visions be less?'

Aurelia flushed. *I didn't want to know that*, she thought. *But it's true*.

'But the studying is more,' said Valerio. 'So she discovers just as much. Aurelia, are you *crying*?'

A double skein of tears wound down Aurelia's cheeks. That was happening a great deal, lately. She'd taken Signor Rioba's advice to heart. She cried both for herself and for others, for she'd come to see in Ghazalah's self-absorption a mirror of her own. She'd learnt that history was made of real people, who could be hurt and even maddened into desperate acts. People like Simoneto Ghezzo. Now she was ashamed at how casually she'd destroyed the historian's living and his reputation.

It was sadly too late to show just how sorry she was.

Simoneto Ghezzo was dead, as had been predicted by his tombstone in 'The Palace that Eats Boys'. His many injuries never quite healed. His heart quietly gave out one night in his sleep. He'd been right about one thing. He was not a forgotten man. The surgeon had kept his own council about the real nature of his disappearance, claiming a concussion. The truth about his kidnap, and Aurelia's, would never be told.

In their general mood of shame and atonement after the *Fedeli* scandal, the Venetians made a great deal of their old historian. Simoneto Ghezzo's funeral was a fine occasion, with many eloquent orations, including one from Aurelia herself and another from Giovanni Remondini, who undertook to re-publish all of 'the great Ghezzo's fine and necessary books'. People nudged one another and nodded approvingly as Valerio took to the stage to make his own short but elegant speech. He was beginning to become known for his fine drawings and paintings. Aurelia watched her friend enjoying his moment of well-earned celebrity. His pleasure made her feel old and wise. She knew now that her fingers – like Ghazalah's beauty – had made things too easy for her. That ease had made her just a little bit rotten because people had admired her a little bit too much.

The surgeon was reunited with his family and was now famous not just for his disappearance, but as the doctor who'd saved more victims of the typhus than anyone. He'd even brought the apprentice Aldo back to perfect health from the very brink of death – in time for the latter to receive a silver medal for saving the musical orphans. He'd also taught Valerio an infallible secret cure for seasickness.

Signor Rioba had gone silent. There was nothing much to be angry about at present. Or if there was, it was still just brewing. What could it be? Well, as Signor Rioba would say, himself, 'Boof!

I'd rather fry up my own liver with pepper, salt and a smidge of coriander than tell ye before I'm good and ready.'

As for the Irish Duchess, the greatest mystery surrounded her. She'd set sail from Venice with her hundred *Fedeli* hostages. The last sighting of her was at a pirate outpost on the Dalmatian coast where she'd handed over the Venetian noblemen to a particularly ruthless broker of galley slaves. The bill of sale was the talk of the Mediterranean. For the *Fedeli* were not sold but leased for exactly one year of service. The lease also provided that if one Venetian died during that time, then the broker would need to replace him with twenty other slaves. Gossip was that the Venetians would therefore be treated to unusually humane shifts and decent food, though they'd be expected to work for it. At the end of their service, they were due to be handed back to the Pirate Duchess personally, and to none other.

But there was the strangest thing of all.

The Pirate Duchess never made it back to Algiers. Whether it was shipwreck or some foreign navy that had taken the *Nancy Bridget*, no one knew. No trace of Emer Fionnuala O'Dowdy had been seen again.

Over *baklava* and mint tea, Ghazalah told Aurelia, 'She was a bint with the shadows of two drowned little sisters in front of her eyes. You could touch her sadness with your hand, though you wouldn't want to.'

Aurelia said, 'Those little girls lost their childhoods as well as their lives.' Noting the sentimental look on Ghazalah's face, she dared to add, 'Isn't that rather like what happened to you, shut up in the flask when you were so young?'

The Djinniya said, 'And it's what would have happened to you, had you been sent to the convent, isn't it, bint? Your Padre Pino is a Barbary pirate if ever I heard of one. Is it true that he was found to be embezzling church funds?'

'Yes, he's in prison!'

'I hope they lose the key. As for our friend Emer Fionnuala O'Dowdy, well, I think she'd done everything she wanted to do. She'd turned from farm girl to slave to Duchess, all in the name of those little sisters.'

'Once she'd avenged them, and herself, she had nothing more to do.'

'Yes. But I believe we should be scanning the horizon for some surprise in the future. Because there's more to that Irish bint than there is to a hundred ordinary dirt-persons.'

Aurelia had only to raise her eyebrows for Ghazalah to dip her head apologetically.

'Pardon me, *humans*.'

47

Never Hunt Humans Again . . .

I suppose I've learnt something. A few somethings, to be honest. One is that I can't use my personal attractions for everything. Also – that my castle doesn't crumble if I don't flirt. The world does not stop giving me air, light and *baklava*. I get all these things for free even if I'm not all bedarlinged with sweethearts and always on the look-see for admiration. In fact, I understand now that my own craving for attention has trapped me more tightly than if I'd stayed confined inside that amethyst flask all these centuries.

Another thing I've learnt is to have a care for the risk of collateral damage when I exercise my magic – magic that is improving all the time, I might add. Strangely, the harder I work on it, the better it gets. Who'd have thought it?

In fact, my powers were never weak. I only thought they were. They were just slightly quite oopsical, because I was careless and listened to no one. I didn't need extra Djinn to help me. What I needed was *friends* both to applaud me when I did well and tell me kindly when I went wrong. Friends with tact, unlike Musipul. Afreets have all the tact of a shark.

Here's another true fact: to have friends, you have to be one. I also realise that I've only just escaped being an utter brute of an idiot, and that the danger isn't even quite over. I'm not yet perfect – for example, if I were living my best life, I wouldn't have eaten that last *baklava*. But I'm getting there.

For centuries, I mourned that I would die in Venice, so far from the magnificent date palms and undulating sands of Arabia, with only my exceptionally hairy legs to keep me warm. I would never again revel in the luxury of dry heat or the companionship of others of my kind – a Djinnderella who could never go again to a Djinn ball. (Do you see what I did there?)

But now I've made my act of atonement. I've apologised on my knees to all the young men I lured into my castle. Not before the need to do so was explained in no uncertain terms by Musipul. 'Do you understand at last? Human beings are not consumables! They have souls just like us.'

And then I remembered the moment I was a rat in Musipul's jaws, about to feel her teeth sever my spinal cord. I knew then what it was to be a hunted animal – like the humans I so easily slipped inside. My quarry. I shall never hunt humans again. Nor shall I call them 'dirt-persons', as that's not kind. I'm working on the kindness thing.

So, my apology to the young men was one I meant from the very core of my fiery heart, which is now scarred with sorry-ness. Those scars will pain me if I ever even think of doing such a terrible thing again. Being a spirit fashioned out of fire, I cannot cry – only make steam – but I felt a little prickle behind my eyes as I watched Momo rush into his mother's arms, followed by all the other young men who emerged blinking out of the 'The Palace that Eats Boys'. I eavesdropped on their reunions with their great-great-great-great-great nephews and nieces. They were told of their family histories in all the decades and centuries that they missed. In the course of a day, once out of the castle, they aged, withered and died, but at peace, surrounded by loving family.

Since I made my apology to the young men, Musipul has changed. The gnawing criticisms have lessened. She nuzzles me, plays my favourite Arabian music on her drums. She sometimes sits on my lap now, warbling her pleasure deep in her throat, an event that's as heartwarming as it's overwhelming. Yes, once again I have a young girl's heart, as I did before I first set eyes on young Aurelio Bon, may his spirit live in me like the scent of rose petals. I no longer crave to be revenged on him. I've turned Aurelio Bon into the most beautiful memory, like a perfume in a bottle. I can always turn to it. I can always remember that moment when he looked at me, when I was one of his choices, and he was just the first of mine. I may still be made of smokeless fire, but I've learnt not to burn down the world.

Even Uncle Nusrat says, begrudgingly, 'You are not who you were, Ghazalah.'

Unsaid is, *And that's a good thing for everyone.* But I notice he's untied the knots in his beard.

Look, I think, with Musipul in my arms, *I'm being loved without having to charm or flirt with anyone.* That makes me think of my friend the Pirate Duchess, Emer Fionnuala O'Dowdy. I'm glad that she's known the love of a good cat too. For surely among those brutal Corsair cats of hers, there's one who knows how to nuzzle.

Tonight, Musipul's touch on her drum is exquisite. Uncle Nusrat and I listen, entranced. Musipul strokes the drum's leather with the tips of her fearsome nails, making the instrument chuckle, sigh and throb. Her shoulders billow with emotion. Her nostrils flare as if the air were flooded with the scent of humid myrrh. It's the scent of home. It's the music of home. And we're all three of us going back there.

Now that my magic is healing, I've been experimenting. I've taken the Castle of Jabrin on successful excursions, first to Greece and then to Egypt. So I know I can get our home back to Arabia. Musipul has invited her friend the lion to visit us there soon. We're just waiting for Uncle Nusrat to finish his exquisite chart of the Venetian heavens so that he may leave it here for the benefit of Venice's people, who have so much to learn about astronomy. 'A gift for their hospitality,' Uncle Nusrat calls it, even though so few Venetians ever knew they were our hosts.

But there's just one thing. I'd rather like to take someone with me. There's a handsome Venetian naval officer who's caught my eye. Angelo Emo rather reminds me of Aurelio Bon, yet without the complications of a girl he already loves and is promised to. Plus, I haven't needed to jump inside him, because he shows every sign of wanting to gaze at my face and talk to me for hours, without any enchantment on my part at all.

Historical Notes

WHAT IS TRUE AND WHAT IS MADE UP
DJINN

The Djinn became known to Europeans in the early eighteenth century through the first translations of *One Thousand and One Nights* (also called *The Arabian Nights*) – a set of stories collected from various Middle Eastern sources over many years, starting in the eighth century. However, as this story shows, there is far more to the Djinn than *The Arabian Nights* can tell us.

Djinn are a part of the Muslim faith. Muslims believe in more than one world and more than one Heaven. The Muslim holy books, the Qur'an and the Hadith Qudsi, mention three kinds of spirit-beings who occupy different realms: Angels, Djinn and Demons. A whole chapter, or '*sura*', of the Qur'an is devoted to the Djinn (*sura 72, al-Jinn*).

As with any faith, in Islam there are differences between purely religious and scholarly thinking and the folk-wisdom and superstitions of ordinary people. Many colourful stories about the Djinn come from folk tales rather than from the scriptures. In writing this book, I've drawn on both scriptures and stories.

According to Islam, Djinn are spirit-beings who were created by God out of smokeless fire and wind. Angels, in contrast, were fashioned from light, and humans from earth.

There are at least thirty-one kinds of Djinn existing in their own parallel invisible worlds, though sometimes they join us in ours. They can see us, but we can see Djinn only when they choose to make themselves visible, often by shapeshifting into the form of an animal or even a human. Folklore says that, in human form, Djinn (particularly Gul) sometimes have donkey hooves, slanted eyes or hairy bodies.

There are many theories about the origin of Djinn. One is that, before Eve, Adam had a wicked wife called Lilith who was the mother of Djinnkind (the Devil being their father). Another is that all Djinn were created by God on just one day; some scholars say, two thousand years before mankind. Originally the Djinn enjoyed God's love but they lapsed into faithless ways. God sent an army of Angels against them. The Djinn repented but were driven away from Heaven by meteors.

Djinn can sleep, drink, eat. They're said to be particularly fond of bones and sweet foods. They can fall in love. They produce children. The Djinn are lively, sociable creatures. They tend to live in communities of their own kind, whether in tribes or nations, and have kings. They travel vast distances in an incredibly short time. They are much stronger than humans and can live up to a thousand years.

Being invisible, Djinn are great eavesdroppers. Before Islam, they were thought to steal news from Heaven and give it to human soothsayers. When Mohammed became the one true messenger of God, soothsayers were outlawed. The scriptures say Mohammed was sent as a Prophet to the Djinn, just as to humans.

Like humans, Djinn have free will, which means that they can choose to be good or evil. The ones who reject Islam are those who cause the most trouble. At the ends of their lives, Djinn, like humans, face divine judgement.

Djinn are to be feared by humans who are breaking the rules . . . being disrespectful or doing something that hurts other people. You must be kind to animals as they might be shapeshifted Djinn. Because Djinn are usually invisible, it's easy for a human to upset or hurt one by accident. To protect themselves from Djinn people pray, invoke the name of God or apologise to a Djinni they have offended.

Some believe women are more vulnerable to attack by Djinn than men. They must be very careful to be fully covered by clothing when outside as it's often in gardens or under trees that Djinn dwell – and also in places where people go to wash or relieve themselves. In folk tales, a Djinniya sometimes makes a mortal man fall in love with her. This is frowned on by Islam. Cross-species romances tend to end badly.

When a Djinni possesses a human being, it may be from the inside. The Djinni wears the outer body of the human, and the human behaves according to the will of the Djinni. That is why the phrase 'wear a Djinni' is used. If someone is possessed by a Djinni, they may behave badly or strangely – as Valerio does in this story. For this reason, the idea of Djinn possession has sometimes been used to explain mental health problems.

It's believed that a good and holy person can persuade a Djinni to leave the human body they're occupying. This can be done, as Ghazalah explains, by reciting the Ninety-Nine Most Beautiful Names of God or The Verse of the Throne from the Qur'an, persuading the spirit to behave as a good Muslim. If persuasion fails, the holy person may need to resort to a casting-out ceremony known as *ruqyah*. Folk-wisdom suggests many dramatic ways to exorcise Djinn or to keep them away. But sacrificing sheep or the use of amulets are against the teachings of the Prophet (as are binding spells using knots).

Most people in the West could tell you just one thing about the Djinn: that they must grant three wishes to whomever frees them from a lamp. As Ghazalah explains, this is a far too literal interpretation. First of all, not all Djinn live confined in lamps. They move freely in their worlds and in ours. Moreover, no one has a right to demand wishes from Djinn. In the Islamic faith, only bad humans would want to use supernatural powers to achieve their desires. If Djinn do appear to grant wishes, in fact they often just make it seem as if they did. In this way, they are like sorcerers and fortune-tellers – practitioners of fake magic.

As this novel is a historical fantasy, it contains elements of magic that are outside of the teachings of either the Christian or Muslim faiths: Ghazalah, Musipul and the little Djinn have some magical powers – as do Signor Rioba, the mermaids and Aurelia herself, with her fingers. I also invented the ghostlight and the mercury eyes as symptoms of Djinn possession.

From old French fairy tales to Disney, there have been many caricatures of Djinn as a kind of 'exotic', backward, ignorant yet dangerously cunning Islamic fairy – a sly, wild creature who *needs* to be forced to serve his or her human masters. Otherwise, he or she will misbehave horribly.

This patronising stereotype has little to do with the Djinn of the Muslim faith. And this way of writing about Eastern cultures is sometimes called 'orientalising'. It started centuries ago, back at the time when the Portuguese invaded Arabia, as this story recounts. Orientalism grew very popular in literature and art in the nineteenth century, when European nations were expanding their empires in Asia and Africa. The timing was no coincidence. Orientalist thinking was used to justify colonial conquests by the Western powers – who could pretend that their 'superior' and 'civilising' influence was needed to save the people of the 'inferior' and 'backward' Eastern and African cultures from themselves. Orientalist paintings frequently showed the colonised people being indolent: their great achievements in medicine, science and mathematics were underplayed. Women were often depicted as beautiful underdressed slaves in harems – to be pitied and stared at – or possibly stolen away to 'freedom', another way of justifying European intervention.

Ghazalah's life, in contrast, is limited by no one and nothing except her own flaws. She dresses the way she likes, enjoys dancing, eating sweets, making up terrible puns, playing tricks on people and having crushes. Ghazalah confidently sees the Venetians, Aurelio Bon and Angelo Emo, not as her masters or conquerors, but as her equals. In fact, according to Islam, all human beings are as equal as the teeth of a comb. That includes women. In the Qur'an, Eve is not blamed for tempting Adam to eat the forbidden apple in the Garden of Eden. Adam and Eve *together* choose to eat the fruit when tempted by Iblis or Satan.

Ghazalah, meanwhile, does not represent *all* Islamic females: there are as many ways to be a Djinniya as there are to be a Venetian or an Irish girl. Like those of Emer Fionnuala and Aurelia, Ghazalah's storyline is defined partly by her own character and partly by the way she reacts to events that befall her. All three girls learn the hard way to be better versions of themselves. The Christian children do not save Ghazalah from her bad ways. Several people are keen to teach the Djinniya a lesson, but in the end she teaches herself one (or two); just as Emer Fionnuala learns that not all Venetians are the same; just as Aurelia eventually comes to understand that – if you really love history – real research takes place in the archives and isn't just a glamorous sideshow performed with magic fingers.

The Portuguese conquered Ghazalah's part of Arabia and held it for a long period, but this book is written from the point of view of a meeting of *equal* cultures. Historically, the Mediterranean was dominated by a series of great empires. Two of them were the Venetians, who were Christian, and the Ottomans, who were Muslim. The splendours of the Doge's Palace in Venice are no more or less than those of Topkapi Palace in Constantinople (now Istanbul). The Venetians never conquered or dominated the Muslims or vice versa, except in individual battles. There were, sadly, atrocities on both sides, especially during the Crusades. Both sides turned prisoners into slaves. Yet for centuries, the Venetians and the Islamic world did not just fight. They also traded and learned from one another. The cultural exchange is visible in the architecture and art of both empires. Venice is sometimes described as an 'oriental' city, because of the strong influence of the East on the shapes of her windows, arches and even the layout of the Rialto Market, which is very like an Arabian souk.

VENICE IN 1763

Simoneto Ghezzo, Padre Pino and Daniele Spatafora are invented. So are *I Fedeli*, but in the early twentieth century a group called the 'Consorzio Venezia Nuova' raised millions of euros for a scheme to build a flood protection barrier called 'MOSE'. By 2014, a corruption scandal was revealed – and much of the money had disappeared.

This book is set towards the end of the Venetian Republic, which lasted nearly a thousand years. Francesco Loredan became doge in 1752, succeeded by Marco Foscari in 1762. Foscari served only ten months. Then came Alvise Mocenigo, who acted like *I Fedeli* in that he signed treaties with the pirates of Algiers, Tunis, Tripoli and Morocco, paying 60,000 ducats a year protection money so Venetian ships might sail the Mediterranean unharmed. But those same rulers who took the Venetian ducats turned a blind eye to the wildcat attacks by their Corsair subjects.

From 1768, a young admiral named Angelo Emo took charge of a Venetian campaign against the pirates. He brought the fight back to the pirates in their own lair, with raids on North African cities. From 1784 to 1786, Emo made the Mediterranean safer not just for Venetians but for everyone. He died in 1792, only a few years before Napoleon conquered Venice.

GRAVEYARDS IN VENICE

At the time this book is set, Venice was full of little cemeteries, or *campi dei morti*. It was Napoleon who decreed that the dead should be buried on the lagoon islands of San Michele and San Cristoforo and started works to join the two together. Since then all Venetians have been interred there and not in the historic centre of town.

LAMP-BOYS

By the eighteenth century, Venice was lighter by night than it had ever been before. In 1732, over eight hundred *ferai* lamps were placed around the city. But many places remained unlit, and, of course, the city was an impenetrable maze for foreigners. So those who could afford it hired *codega* boys who carried lamps (which burned on pork rinds) to lead them from place to place after dark.

THE BON FAMILY

An ancient family in Venice, first known in the island of Torcello in 407, the Bons moved into the historic centre of Venice in 806. They were not a particularly bad family. The Aurelio Bon of this story is entirely invented – as is Aurelia.

VENETIAN SEA WALLS

The sea walls of Venice were under construction from 1744 to 1782. Known as the *murazzi*, they were designed by Vicenzo Coronelli to protect the lagoon shoreline. They were the last great civil engineering work of the Venetian Republic.

REMONDINI

Venice was the centre for printing in Italy and the first place in Italy where a book was printed. Venetian printers produced books in many languages and published the works of Arab medical writers like Avicenna. The first printed text of the Qur'an appeared in Venice.

The Remondini were a family of famous publishers, papermakers and printers based in Bassano del Grappa on the Venetian mainland from the mid-seventeenth century until the nineteenth. They were creative, clever and successful.

The fashionable Giovanni Remondini of this book is an invention.

BARBARY PIRATES

The Barbary pirates terrorised the Mediterranean for more than 250 years. It has been estimated that, between 1530 and 1780, at least a million Christians were kidnapped from the seas and shorelines of Spain, Greece, Italy and beyond, and transported to the Maghreb on the northwest coast of Africa.

This compares with around ten million Africans enslaved by Europeans for work mostly in the New World. An anti-slavery movement began in the late eighteenth century, but it took many decades to outlaw a trade in which so many nations participated.

The Pirate Duchess is invented, as is the arrival of a pirate fleet in Venice in 1763. But Emer Fionnuala's adventures are based on the accounts of many true victims of the Barbary pirates, also known as the Corsairs. Barbary pirates did roam as far as Ireland and even Iceland.

When they arrived in Algiers, Tunis or Tripoli, male slaves were usually sent to do hard labour on building sites, cutting and carrying enormous pieces of stone. The palace of Dar Kbira at Meknes was a vast complex built almost entirely by Christian slaves. If they were lucky, slaves might work in the farms that fed the Barbary cities. At night they were herded into a large dormitory building known as the '*bagno*'. Harsh conditions there meant that the death rate was high. So for hundreds of years, the Barbary pirates put out to sea regularly in order to harvest more slaves.

Very few slaves escaped from the Maghreb. The great hope was to be ransomed. It was, of course, almost impossible for poor slaves to raise money for their own ransoms, especially as they had to somehow pay for their own food by working in their precious free time.

In Venice, the *Provveditori sopra ospedali e luoghi pii* (established 1561 to look after sacred spaces) were put in charge of ransoming slaves back from the Barbary pirates. And in each church, the *Provedditori* placed boxes for donations 'for the Recovery of the

Poor Slaves'. Sometimes rescued slaves (put in chains to make the point) would be paraded round the city to raise pity and funds. Often, charities provided just a proportion of the ransom. The family would need to raise the rest.

CORSAIR CATS

Even today, black cats are disliked by some people in southern Italy because of a folk myth that their ancestors belonged to raiding Barbary pirates, and were left behind by accident or deliberately – as spies.

THE CASTLE OF JABRIN

This magnificent building is near Nizwa, in what is modern day northeast Oman. The castle you can see today was built by Bil'arab bin Sultan, who ruled from 1679 to 1692. In recent years, the Castle of Jabrin was beautifully restored by the Ministry of Heritage and Culture and is now open to the public.

ACKNOWLEDGEMENTS

Any mistakes in this book are mine. I don't have much excuse for them as I've had so much kind help from my editor, Lena McCauley at Orion, my agent, Victoria Hobbs at A.M. Heath, my copy-editor, Amina Youssef and my proofreader, Ruth Girmatsion.

In Venice, thank you to Orietta Lavezzi, Elena Romano, Rosato Frassanito, Eugenio Rossaro.

In Oman, many thanks to all the staff at the Castle of Jabrin.

In London, thank you to Anna Ponticos, my very first and most discriminating reader, to Elias Avramides for the helpful descriptions of seasickness, to Mary Hoffman, Aisha Rahal, Amir Eden and the kind people at the Baitul Aziz Islamic Cultural Centre and Mosque.